Praise for

Splitting Harriet

"Tamara Leigh takes her experienced romance hand and delights readers with Chick Lit that sparkles and characters who come alive."

—KRISTIN BILLERBECK, author of *The Trophy Wives Club*

"Can a rebel ever truly be reformed? This story of a prodigal daughter returned home proves God doesn't want us to rehabilitate ourselves; he just wants us to let him change our hearts. A soul-satisfying read, Leigh's vibrant story of forgiveness and grace is peopled with characters as colorful as a club-sized container of Jelly Bellys."

—SIRI L. MITCHELL, author of *The Cubicle Next Door*

"Tamara Leigh delivers a thoroughly enjoyable story in *Splitting Harriet*. Harri dances off the pages and straight into our hearts with her hardheaded loyalty to the tradition-loving members of her church. Leigh digs deep as she delves into the inner workings of a church struggling with growth as seen through the eyes of its most compassionate and stubborn member. There's a Harri in each of us, which is why we love her so much."

—VIRGINIA SMITH, author of *Stuck in the Middle*

"Kudos to novelist Tamara Leigh. You'll fall in love with Harriet. She's quirky and slightly neurotic, a gal with a past who loves Jesus, snarfs jelly beans, and lives in a senior-citizen trailer park. *Splitting Harriet* raises the bar for Christian Chick Lit. This is a story with an edge, one that dares to go a bit deeper, yet entertains from beginning to end. Highly recommended!"

—ANNETTE SMITH, author of *A Bigger Life* and
   A Crooked Path

"*Splitting Harriet* is every bit as clever as its title. With a cast of characters sure to make you smile, this book will not disappoint. Harriet's bad-girl past and imperfect-but-trying present make her relatable to the average woman who cringes at the rebellions of her own youth. If you're anything like me, you'll become as addicted to Harriet as she is to candy!"

—TRACEY BATEMAN, author of *Catch a Rising Star* and
   Defiant Heart

"No split decision—*Splitting Harriet* is a fast, fun read. Harri is both as sweet as her Jelly Bellys and as forthright as a country waitress. Readers will cheer as Harri overcomes her fear of failure and of letting go to choose freedom, joy, and grace."

—SANDRA BYRD, author of *Let Them Eat Cake*

"I love Harriet—prickly yet caring, full of self-doubt but trying, loving God but struggling. In other words, Harriet is just like us. You will love her too as well as the others at First Grace. Guaranteed."

—GAYLE ROPER, award-winning author of *Fatal*
   Deduction and *Caught Redhanded*

Splitting Harriet

Tamara Leigh

Splitting Harriet

A Novel

MULTNOMAH
BOOKS

SPLITTING HARRIET
PUBLISHED BY MULTNOMAH BOOKS
12265 Oracle Boulevard, Suite 200
Colorado Springs, Colorado 80921
A division of Random House Inc.

ISBN: 978-1-59052-928-7

Published in association with the literary agency of Alive Communications Inc.,
7680 Goddard Street, Suite 200, Colorado Springs, CO 80920, www.alive
communications.com.

Library of Congress Cataloging-in-Publication Data
Leigh, Tamara.
    Splitting Harriet : a novel / Tamara Leigh. — 1st ed.
        p. cm.
    ISBN 978-1-59052-928-7
    1. Single women—Fiction. I. Title.
    PS3612.E3575S65 2007
    813'.6—dc22

                        2007029768

Printed in the United States of America
2007—First Edition

10 9 8 7 6 5 4 3 2 1

One more tale for my amazing son Skyler Hunt, who is not only responsible for my hero's totally cool name, but who brainstormed Harri and Maddox's story with me while practicing lay-ups at the basketball court. You are a blessing, a hero in the making for some young lady WAY down the line. I love you!

Acknowledgments

A heaping helping of thanks to my fabulous editor, Julee Schwarzburg, who once more helped me pull it all together with her insightful suggestions and gentle reminder to "show, don't tell." What a difference! I am so grateful that God chose for our paths to do more than simply cross.

Bunches of gratitude to my agent, Beth Jusino, who instantly "got" Harriet and whose personal experience with pink flamingos and Astroturf made me laugh and provided several "aha!" moments that found their way onto the printed page. You're the best!

Heartfelt appreciation to senior pastor Dr. Doug Varnado and administrative pastor Mr. Terry Owens of Community Church of Hendersonville for granting me permission to "fudge" on my fictional church's vision statement. I wasn't being lazy. Really. There was just no way I could write a statement as beautiful and God honoring as the one composed to capture the spirit of this incredible church, a statement that is more than mere words to its leaders and body of believers.

COMMUNITY CHURCH OF HENDERSONVILLE
VISION STATEMENT

We seek to know fully the Lord God Almighty, to experience His incredible goodness and grace and be totally amazed that He would choose to live within us. Our desire is to know Him so intimately and trust Him so completely that His will for us becomes the dominant desire of our lives. We seek to use the gifts that God has placed within us to serve others, seeking to meet every physical and spiritual need. Therefore, we welcome everyone so that we may point each to Him and to our Savior and Lord Jesus Christ who alone redeems and transforms us into His image.

on't want to think about anything. Which isn't all that hard to do when you've had one too many drinks. So I do what comes naturally under the circumstances—I feel. And who cares what happens, 'cause it's not likely I'll remember anything in the morning. And if I do, it'll all be fuzzy.

So feel away, Harri girl! Forget all your troubles. Forget Harley— the pig! Jason—the swine! Blade—the oinker! Oh, and don't forget to forget your family—church and otherwise. Just feel.

Closing my eyes, I command my body to *feel* the beat of the music that pounds from the speakers as I move with...

Um, let's call him Contestant Number One.

He pulls me closer than a good girl should allow. Fortunately for him, I don't fall into that category. At least, not anymore. This twenty-year-old preacher's kid—a.k.a. "PK"—is four years beyond that. And counting.

So tired of counting—

And I'm tired of this stupid little voice in my head that has been gathering volume ever since I was the recipient of a black eye and found myself homeless three months ago. Fortunately, a drinking buddy took me in. Unfortunately, she's more of a mess than I, which is how she ended up in an ambulance after I found her on the bathroom floor this morning. The good news is that she'll be all right—at least until she begs, borrows, or steals enough money to finance her habit. The bad news is that it shook me. Good thing I don't do drugs.

What do you call the alcohol swimming through your veins?

"It's legal," I slur, conveniently overlooking that I'm still considered a minor. "Yep, legal."

Contestant Number One pulls back. "What?"

I'd be embarrassed if I weren't so numb. I smile—at least, I think that's what I'm doing with my mouth—and drop my forehead to the shoulder of his sweat-soaked T-shirt. Ew! Wish my sense of smell were as numb as the rest of me.

He chuckles, slides a rough hand down my back, and presses me nearer, though I wouldn't have thought it possible. He thinks it's a done deal.

Doesn't have to be. You could slip out. Ditch him and his friends. Start fresh again tomorrow, good intentions and all.

Right. Like I did today, after the ambulance lights disappeared from view?

Fingers graze my wrist, trail upward, linger over the crown-of-thorns tattoo encircling my upper arm, slide around the back of my neck, then thrust up through my cropped, pink-tinted hair. Getting a grip on it, Contestant Number One pulls my head back, and our nicotine- and alcohol-scented breath mingle as I try to focus on his face.

What do they say about ugly girls getting progressively better looking with each drink a guy downs? Well, it goes both ways. Sometime during the two hours since I strutted into the biker bar, this guy has gone from one step above Gomer Pyle to only a dozen steps below Antonio Banderas. See, sometimes it's good to be numb. And I wish I were more so when his mouth descends.

Oh God, here I go again. And I do mean *God* as in "the Big Guy," even though it seems like years since I've spoken to or thought about Him without pairing His name with a curse. I don't want to be here. Don't want to do this. I want to…to…

"Oh, my girl! It *is* you!" squawks a voice whose distinctive Katharine Hepburn warble identifies her despite my smog-laden brain. "What are you doing?!"

Barely escaping a meeting of the mouths, I look over my shoulder into the wrinkled, dark-skinned face of my namesake, Harriet Evans. Though it has been two years since I've seen her, she appears the same. As does her companion standing shoulder to shoulder with her—Pam Worth, whose wigs are legendary at my father's church. Against the backdrop of bikers, beer bottles, and bars that run the length of two walls, the little old women are so out of place that there exists the possibility this is a dream. Meaning, I may not have to start fresh again tomorrow…

Harriet puts her fists on her hips. "You're drunk, Harriet Josephine Bisset!"

She sure seems real, especially those fiery eyes of hers. I shake my head. "What are you doing here?"

"Not what *you're* doing. My car died just down the road. And here I come in to use the phone, and what do I find? You! Actin' like and lookin' like"—she waves a hand down me—"a floozy."

"Hey! Who are these old biddies?" demands Contestant Number One.

Biddies? It might've been a while since I've seen Harriet or Pam, and my brain may be temporarily defunct, but they aren't going to take that sitting down…er, standing up.

"Biddies?" Harriet stamps her foot, and Pam follows suit. "You, Cro-Magnon, need a lesson in how to speak to your elders. Now take your filthy hands off that young lady."

"Young lady?!" He jerks me closer. "You had it right the first time—floozy." With that, he puts his mouth to the crook of my neck, and I think I'm going to be sick. Yep. I am. Right across the back of his sweaty T-shirt.

Though normally I'd be horrified—at least, as horrified as one can be in my state—when he lurches back and spits curses that ought to rain hellfire down on him, I laugh against the back of the hand I wipe across my mouth.

"Humph!" Harriet takes my arm. "Can't think of a more fitting punishment."

As Pam takes my other arm and they lead me across the bar, I become aware of the attention we've attracted. Everyone's watching—from the bartenders to the biker guys and gals to Contestant Number One's friends, whose faces no longer reflect drunken merriment.

This could be bad.

"Harriet. Pam." I swallow bile. "You should go."

"Not without you." Harriet tugs me toward the door. "Come on, Harri."

Outside, the chill night air hits like a bucket of ice water, and I gasp.

"Where's your car?" Harriet asks.

"I don't"—*burp*—"have a car. Friend dropped me off."

"A friend, hmm?" She shakes her head. "You got a cell phone?"

Stomach threatening to erupt again, I pry the phone from my back pocket and thrust it at her. No sooner do our hands clear than it happens again, and I'm on my knees in the dirt-paved parking lot.

While Pam pats my back, I hear Harriet's voice but have no idea who she's talking to. Not that I care.

Then we're waiting—for what, I don't know. And, again, I don't care. I just want my stomach to stop heaving and my throat to stop burning. I want to feel normal again.

When was the last time you experienced normal?

Behind us I hear the whine of rusted hinges as the door bursts open. Then men's voices, among them Contestant Number One's. Harriet's. Then Pam's. Not a nice exchange, and fear binds me as I focus past Pam to where little Harriet faces a bare-chested Contestant Number One and what would have been Contestant Number Two if not for the interruption on the dance floor.

"You get back in there!" Harriet jabs a finger toward the bar behind them. "Leave her alone, you hear?"

"I bought her three drinks." Contestant Number One snarls. "I deserve something for my money. And my ruined shirt."

"A paddlin's all you deserve."

"Oh yeah?" He takes a step toward her. "You wanna try, old biddy?"

I struggle to my feet. "Harriet! It's okay. You and Pam get out of here. I'll—"

"You'll do nothin'!" Harriet throws me a look.

Pam grips my arm and, with her other hand, starts fishing in her purse. "Don't you worry, Harri." She holds up a black object and presses a button that causes a bolt of blue to arc and crackle between two metal pins. "We old biddies can take care of ourselves."

No, they can't. They have no idea—

Tires squeal behind us as they churn up dirt and crunch to a halt. A car door opens and slams, then I hear a voice I haven't heard in years. "Back off!"

Heart struggling to find its beat, I peer over my shoulder, but Tyler doesn't look at me, his eyes on the two men who've pushed past Harriet to advance on him.

"You her boyfriend?" Contestant Number Two asks.

"Her brother," Tyler says. "Now if you don't want trouble, I suggest you go cuddle up with another beer."

"Beer ain't what I had in mind." Number One leers at me in passing and makes a rude gesture that no woman ought to be subjected to, especially in front of her brother.

As Pam screeches and swings her purse at his backside, a growl rips from Tyler. A moment later, his fist connects with Number

One's jaw and sends the man stumbling back. Number Two lunges forward, landing a blow to Tyler's gut as I cry out and strain to break Pam's hold.

"Stop it, Harri!" She jerks me back. "Tyler can take him."

And he does, though not without sustaining injuries of his own that make me turn my face away.

"There, now," Pam says. "It's over."

At least until Number One gets in on it again. And as the two men throw punches, Number Two struggles to his feet.

"Oh, no you don't!" Harriet looks to Pam. "Toss me that stun thing of yours."

She tosses it, Harriet jabs, and the man jerks and drops.

A moment later, Number One's on his back again, and Tyler's dragging me to his car, with Pam and Harriet following.

"She'll be back! You can take 'em outta the bar, but you can't take the bar outta them. It's in their blood."

As Tyler pushes me into the backseat, we come face to bloody face, and I see the question in his eyes. *Will* I come back? *Is* it in my blood?

I close my eyes, and when Harriet settles in beside me and presses my head into her lap, I begin to blubber. "I want to go home, Harriet."

A trembling hand smoothes back my hair. "Of course you do, my girl. 'Course you do."

One

Harri's Log: • Day of *The Coroner's* season finale
• 29 days until Jelly Belly replenishment
• 213 days until the completion of Bible #8

C hange is *not* good. In fact, it's bad. Especially where First Grace is concerned.

I stare at the skinny backside of the repairman who just informed me he's going to miss our church, which has become something of a second home to him. Though called out to repair whatever caused the organ to groan and grunt through last Sunday's service, he learned that Pastor Paul is forgoing further repairs and simply—simply!—removing it.

To add insult to injury, not only have drums been set up to the left of the pulpit, but there are ugly black amplifiers from which all manner of cords snake across the carpet—the lifeblood of electric guitars.

Forcing my clenched hands open, I attempt to gain control of my emotions. But a moment later, my fingernails are once more biting into my palms.

So Pastor Paul has done it again. In his determination to catapult First Grace into the twenty-first century, despite our being perfectly content to stroll our way into it, he's knocked out another wall in the house my father built.

I look back at the organ, beneath which the repairman hunkers, and slide my gaze over the beautiful instrument. For the past thirty years, it has provided all the instrumental accompaniment First Grace ever needed. Well, there is the piano, but prior to Pastor Paul's arrival, it merely supplemented the organ. Now it has come into its own as we transition to a more "contemporary" form of service.

The sharp crack of bone on wood returns my attention to the repairman. Clutching his head, he seats himself on his rear.

I rush forward. "Are you all right?"

He swears and rocks back and forth. "That hurt!"

I freeze. He took our Lord's name in vain. Right here. In the sanctuary. Unless he was actually crying out to the Lord for help—

Oh, Harri! Find out if he's all right, for goodness' sake! "You okay, Horace?"

"I'm gonna have a lump the size of a cheekful of chewin' tobacco."

Nice imagery. "Can I get you some ice?"

"I'll be all right." He lowers his hands. "Sorry about that 'Jesus' thing. It just sort of popped out."

Thing?

"Well, if I'm gonna have this thing out of here before Sunday, I'd better get back to work."

Thing again? First Jesus's name, now our beloved organ. Mere "things"? *Calm down. Remember whose daughter you are…in whose presence you stand.* I look up at the stained-glass window above the baptistery. Soaring to the ceiling, it depicts Jesus with wide open arms. *Remember what He would have you do.*

But surely He wouldn't want me to sit by as Pastor Paul shifts the focus from God to growing the size of the congregation. Yes, I know all about reaching the unsaved. But what about the saved—the older folks who have drifted away this past year? The ones who have yet to drift away but will likely do so once the organ pulls a no-show?

I pivot and march down the aisle between the rows of empty pews and, in the gathering area outside the sanctuary, nearly barrel into R.T., head of maintenance.

Screwdriver in hand, he jumps out of my way.

"Sorry, R.T."

"Uh-oh," he drawls.

I snap my head around.

His here-she-goes-again expression dissolves, and he shakes his head. "Not me." *Shake, shake, shake.* "I had *nothin'* to do with them drums and wires."

Perhaps not, but he has to be thrilled. The headphones around his neck often leak horrendous music. "Hmm." I resume my trek to the offices.

Harriet, my namesake and First Grace's secretary, looks up. "Uh-oh," the sixty-eight-year-old woman warbles.

That makes two "uh-ohs." I halt before her desk. "You know about the organ?"

"I do, my girl."

Softening at her affectionate use of "my girl," which always pulls me back to that night nearly eight years ago, it takes a moment to return to the matter at hand. "You know about the drums, Harriet?"

"I do."

"And the amplifiers and wires for the *electric* guitars?"

"I do."

I spread my hands out atop her desk. "How long have you known?"

She picks up a pen and rolls it between her fingers. "Since Monday when Horace told us what the repairs would cost." She raises an eyebrow. "*This* time."

"You've known since Monday? Four-days-ago Monday?"

"That would be the one."

"Why didn't you say something?"

She leans forward and, in a conspiratorial whisper, says, "Orders," then nods at the door at the end of the hall to her right. "From the top."

If it truly were from the top—as in God—I could accept it, but Pastor Paul is not God. I push off Harriet's desk. "He told you not to tell me?"

She shrugs. "Brother Paul—"

Brother! Why can't he simply be *Pastor* like my father before him?

"—thought it best that we not bother you." Harriet shoots me a knowing look. "For obvious reasons."

"You're saying I'm wrong to disagree with the direction he's taking our church? You, who have been here since the beginning and know what's at stake?" I draw a breath. "Despite his *vision,* First Grace will never be a fill-'er-up, one-stop shopping, all-you-can-eat church. This church has roots, is steeped in tradition—"

Harriet holds up a hand, the same which used to smack my little heinie when I got out of control in her preschool Sunday school class. "You know what happens to a tea bag that's steeped too long? Bitter. And so murky one can hardly see to the bottom of one's cup."

I scoff. "First Grace is not a cup of tea. It's—"

"Oh, grow down, Harri."

I've heard it before—"grow down" as opposed to "grow up"—and I don't like it any better than the other times she has pointed out that I need to lighten up, act more my twenty-seven years of age, and enjoy life. But I "enjoyed" it enough during my rebel years, as she well knows. "Why are you siding with Pastor Paul?"

"Done told you, it's not a matter of siding with anyone. It's a matter of doing what's right for the glory of God and this church. Were your mother and father here, I believe they'd concur."

But they're not here. Following Dad's retirement a year ago, he and Mom went on an extended mission trip to India. As for whether or not they'd concur, I don't know. Though that first year Dad worked alongside Pastor Paul to lay the groundwork for many of the changes undertaken these past twelve months, I can't believe my father would approve of chucking the organ. Yes, it was being phased out, but there's nothing "phased" about this. And what about the shift from weekly to monthly communion? And plans to install a projection screen at the feet of our stained-glass Jesus?

Harriet cups her leathery chin and taps the pen on her desk. "I don't suppose it would do any good to advise you to sleep on this?"

"None!"

Her tapping ceases and scrawny eyebrows arch.

R-E-S-P-E-C-T, Harri! With a sigh, I return my hands to the desktop and sink into my shoulders. "I don't mean to be disrespectful. It's just that…"

She covers my left hand with a brown, heavily veined one. "I know, but at times like these, remember that the choice of First Grace's new pastor wasn't a matter your father took lightly—that it was he who presented Brother Paul as his replacement."

I'm not likely to forget. I was as sold on him as my father and the committee that approved him, among its members the ever-popular Stephano Fox.

Stephano… Angst momentarily supplanted as the man's name bounces through my gray matter, I sigh. Though it has been three years since he took on the position of administrative pastor and our relationship is platonic, I can't help but moon over him. He is, after all, good looking, not to mention generous. In fact, the only reason First Grace can afford him is because he volunteers his time. Having sold off a business years earlier, the self-made Stephano is among the most eligible bachelors in Franklin, Tennessee.

"Harri?"

Yanked back from the edge of Stephano, I blink.

Harriet rolls her eyes. "I *said* we'd do well to honor your father's choice and let God work through Brother Paul."

A small voice tells me she's right, that while I may not agree with *Pastor* Paul's changes, I need to be careful not to become the stumbling block for others that I'm becoming for myself. But that other voice is louder—the one that fears change, the one that reminds me of where I went wrong all those years ago when it was *I* who determined First Grace was outdated, the one that conjures images of the path I fell hard upon when I walked away from my church, my family, and God.

"What about Stephano? What does he say about all this?"

"That we need to follow Brother Paul's lead."

I grind my teeth. As much as I respect Stephano for smoothly paving my father's last two years at First Grace with his boundless energy and organizational skills, I question him of late. Though he's an advocate of change, previously he always laid out his ideas for my father's and the board's approval before moving on them. Then Pastor Paul took over, and now the outspoken Stephano is suddenly content to let the other man do all the driving. Even when it looks as if the car's heading toward a barrier that's the only thing between the road and a sheer cliff....

I hear a whimper, and not until Harriet squeezes my hand do I realize it came from me.

"It'll work out. You'll see." She settles back in her chair. "This is, after all, the direction First Grace was heading."

I can't help myself. "*Heading?!* How did we go from heading to arriving? What happened to the *gradual* transition we were promised?"

Harriet narrows her gaze. "We've been in transition for over a year. And, yes, we were several months out from introducing drums and guitars, but First Grace can't keep throwing good money at that tired old organ. You know that."

I cross my arms over my chest. "So it's out with the organ and in with the drums and guitars."

She rocks her head back and forth. "And Brother Paul has been talking to one of our young ladies who plays one of those electric things."

Thing again, but this time it fits.

"Er, keyboard." She sighs. "That's it, keyboard."

I drop my arms to my sides. "What about Bea? Has she been told that her organ's being taken away?"

She glances at her watch. "Brother Paul is meeting with her this afternoon."

"So just like that? 'Thank you for your twenty-five years of service, but we don't need you anymore'?"

Harriet scoffs. "She's sixty-nine years old, a year older than me. Well past time she retired those arthritic joints of hers." She flexes her own.

"Bea's not going to like it."

"She'll adjust."

"Are we talking about the Beatrice Dawson who picketed the church six years ago when there was talk of replacing her organ with a piano?" Of course, under the direction of my father, a compromise was reached whereby the piano *supplemented* the organ. "Believe me, *that* Bea is not going to be happy. In fact, she might start circulating a petition—"

"If you rile her, she will." Harriet wags a finger. "As a staff member of First Grace, it's your duty to support the leadership."

How I long to remind her that not only am I part of that leadership—director of women's ministry—but I was left out of the decision to push up the timetable for the introduction of contemporary music. However, Harriet's right. She's *always* right. Even when she's wrong.

I heave a sigh. "I know. I just can't believe—"

The door opens, and Pastor Paul lurches at the sight of me. "Am I interrupting something?"

I turn to him. "Actually, I'm here to see you."

He gives Harriet a why-didn't-you-warn-me-so-I-could-slip-out-the-back-door look.

Not that I'm offended; he's as frustrated with me as I am with him. Though we got along well during his first year while my father acquainted him with the workings of the church, shortly before Dad handed over the reins, Brother Paul and I had a disagreement, the first of several.

I advance on him. "It won't take but a few minutes."

"Actually, I'm busy—"

"Five at the most."

He glances over his shoulder, and when he looks back, there's a determined glint in his eyes.

I halt before him. "It's about the drums. And guitars. And Bea's organ."

"Yes?"

"It was agreed that First Grace would *gradually* transition to contemporary worship."

"Yes."

"And now, suddenly, it's good-bye organ, hello rock and roll."

"Hmm."

"First Grace needs more time to adjust."

"Oh?"

"Granted, the growing number of young families are receptive to contemporary worship, but what about the older members who have been here since the beginning and stayed because they were fed God's Word in a way that spoke to their hearts?"

"Hmm."

Realizing that monosyllabic responses are all I've managed to pull from him, I narrow my lids. "Is that all you can say—'yes, hmm, oh'? Aren't you going to defend your decision to give tradition a kick in the pants?"

"Now's not the time. As I said, I'm busy."

"Uh-oh," Harriet once more mutters.

I draw myself up to my full five foot nine. "Until now I've kept my mouth shut." Well, not exactly, but it could have been worse. "But I can't continue to stand by while you dismantle everything my father worked hard to achieve at First Grace."

"I'm sorry to hear that."

"Furthermore—"

Movement at his back makes me peer past him.

Accommodatingly, Pastor Paul steps aside to allow an unobstructed view into his office. And there, standing before his desk, is a thirtyish man with curly, light brown hair and dark eyes that travel down me. Only to laugh at me on the return trip.

Oh no. Amazing how an unexpected audience opens one's eyes to one's behavior. The only good is that he's unrecognizable, so not one of our members.

In the next instant, my mortification yields to indignation. "You should have told me you had a visitor." I swing away.

As I make tracks past Harriet's desk, she gives a sorrowful shake of her head.

I know. I've blown it. Just had to let the rebel rear her head. And it hurts to acknowledge that despite the emergence of the new me, I'm not completely free of the old. Though my concerns are justified, I don't much like the me I let out of her cage.

"You can take 'em outta the bar," a voice from my past rasps between my ears, *"but you can't take the bar outta them. It's in their blood."*

I hate that voice. Grateful to reach the cover of the corridor, I turn down it; however, no sooner am I out of sight than I catch Pastor Paul's words.

"That, my friend, is Harri. And she's all yours."

Hold up! I nearly trip over my feet. I'm all *whose?* That man whose eyes laughed at me as if I were the silliest woman he's ever seen?

Then comes *his* response. "My father always said to beware of redheads."

Ah! I am not a redhead. My hair's auburn. *Not* red! I start to turn back.

No, Harri. If you haven't already lost your job, you will. And you need this job. Think: Gloria's Morning Café. Think: independence. Think: security. Just a bit longer, and you'll have enough money to realize your dream.

Forcing my feet forward, I put distance between myself and Pastor Paul and *that* man.

"You're fired."

Deep breath. "Oh yeah? That's what you think, Mr. High and Mighty."

Steely gaze. "You can go easy, or you can go hard. Regardless, you're gone."

Clenched hands. "This isn't over."

The camera pulls back to fit both characters into the scene, facing each other across a desk. Normally I'd side with Susan's boss, who's always overlooking his junior coroner's shortcomings. But considering my present circumstances, I feel sorry for Susan.

So she's hot tempered…

The poor woman's under a lot of pressure.

So she has difficulty dealing with authority figures…

She always bucks up in the end.

So she made a mistake that cost someone his life...

Come on, that was no corpse. It was an actor!

Kevin reaches a hand across the desk. "Good-bye, Susan."

My own hand hovers over a club-sized container of Jelly Bellys, and I mutter, "That's an olive branch." Not to mention one good-looking hand, attached to one good-looking bod, topped by one good-looking face. "Give it a shake."

She does shake—her head. "Like it or not, I'll be back."

"Ohhh," I groan. "Too late."

Susan walks out, and the camera returns to Kevin, who lowers to his chair and swivels around to stare at the overcast sky out his window. "So long, Susan."

And that's it for this season. Four months of reruns until I find out how this all pans out. Summer really isn't all it's cracked up to be.

I sink into my recliner and reflect on Susan's behavior and how disappointed I am with her. Of course, I mustn't forget she's hurting or that she feels betrayed. On top of it, she's dealing with guilt over the death of Kevin's best friend and the knowledge that had she kept her mouth shut, he'd still be alive. It has got to be tearing her apart. Well, not truly tearing her apart, since she *is* fictional. As opposed to Harriet "Harri" Bisset who is living, breathing, flesh and blood. And whose days at First Grace are surely numbered.

Pushing the remote's Off button, I close my eyes to savor the night breeze sifted by the screen door, but it's no use. My middle and index fingers start to twitch, my lips purse, and a vague memory of nicotine wafts across my senses.

Jelly Belly time. I reach into the container, scoop up a dozen beans, and pop them in my mouth. Though I'm usually more discerning about how I mix the flavors (there's an art to it), tonight I don't care. Tonight they're comfort food as opposed to pleasure food. Something to take my mind off the phone that has yet to sound its death knell.

I look at where it perches on a side table. I know it will eventually ring, and I'm not going to like what the person on the other end has to say, so I want it over with. No, my mistake isn't as serious as Susan's, but there will be consequences.

Once I returned home to First Grace's senior mobile home park—yeah, *senior*—and prayed through the encounter with Pastor Paul, I accepted I was wrong. I shouldn't have confronted him as I did.

I sigh. I believe a leopard *can* change its spots (in my case, tattoos), but it takes a miracle. Or expensive laser surgery. Unfortunately, God's making me take the long way around. No blinding light on the road to Damascus for Harriet Bisset. Just a battered conscience and a sense of impending doom.

After tossing back another dozen Jelly Bellys, my anxiety eases as I taste sizzling cinnamon…green apple…margarita (virgin, of course)…buttered popcorn…and is that tutti-fruitti? Too late. They're all jelling into one sweet-sour-spicy glob.

Then comes the death knell. I glance at the phone as it takes a breath between rings. Though I refuse to waste money on caller ID, I know it's him.

Get it over with.

The second death knell.

Pick it up!

I reach and, as I bolster myself with a deep breath, remember my mouthful.

The third death knell.

I look around, but the only thing at hand is…my hand. Spitting the glob into it, I grab the receiver. "Hello!"

"Harri, it's Harriet."

Harri/Harriet always glitches me, and tonight is no exception. Actually, it's worse, as I was expecting *him*. As the remains of Jelly Belly juice trickle down my throat, I turn my head aside to cough.

"You all right, Harri?"

"Yep. What's up?"

"Brother Paul."

Then he asked Harriet to—? No. As disillusioned as I am with him, canning me is not something he'd have our church secretary do. And certainly not over the phone. "What is it, Harriet?"

"He's been visiting some of us fogies this evening and asked me to tell you that he'll stop by to chat with you on his way out of the park."

Foul words slip to the edge of my tongue. Just the edge. *Sorry about that, Lord. And that. Oh, that was a really bad one. Sorry.*

"Harri?"

I gape at the mess in my hand. "It's nine p.m.!"

"Is it? Oh, you're right. Well, just a quick chat, and I'll be a couple minutes behind him. Thought I'd bring you a batch of my famous biscuits."

I jump out of my recliner. "Harriet, I'm wearing slippers, lounge pants, and a T-shirt." New, out-of-the-box house slippers with pink roses (last year's birthday present from Mom). Pilled flannel pants with a motorcycle insignia (a relic from my rebel days). A "Got Jesus?" T-shirt that hasn't been white in ages (the short sleeves of which barely conceal my armband tattoo).

"Well," Harriet says, "throw a robe over it."

"I have to change!"

"But, Harri, he and—"

"Stall him!" I drop the handset in its base and grab the Jelly Belly container. Four strides take me past the screen door to the kitchen and two more to the sink, where I drop the container on the counter and turn on the taps. One good shake and the sticky glob slops from my hand to the drain.

Can't believe I did that to Jelly Belly, which is as close to a friend as something edible can come, considering the little beans and lots of prayer helped me kick the nicotine habit years ago. Were there a Jelly Belly fan club, I'd ban me for life.

The stainless-steel soup pot in the drain rack catches my eye, and I lean forward and peer at my distorted reflection. Not only is my auburn hair wisping all over the place, but mascara is smudged beneath my eyes, and my smattering of freckles stand out more than usual against pale skin. Hoping Harriet can stall Pastor Paul, as her mobile home is a mere two-minute walk away, I soap and rinse.

Jeans and a light sweater, I determine as I tighten the taps, but then a knock sounds. I swing around, and as I light on Pastor Paul's mesh-shadowed face on the other side of the screen door, my arm connects with something.

Oh no! All the colors of the rainbow—and then some—soar past me. Little bean-shaped colors. Melt-in-your-mouth colors. Very expensive colors. And with a sound akin to hail, they hit the linoleum.

Reflexively, I step forward. And glimpse surprise on Pastor Paul's face as the beans beneath my slippers sweep me off my feet.

"Harri!"

I can't say what hurts more: the places where my body hit as I went down, the embarrassment, or that I'm lying among fourteen dollars' worth of Jelly Bellys that were supposed to last me all month.

Pastor Paul is suddenly stooping next to me, gripping my shoulder. "Are you all right?"

I squeeze my lids tighter. "No. Not all right."

"Is anything broken?"

Does my heart count? After all, it took a half hour to pick out the flavors that no amount of creative mixing can make palatable: licorice, mango, cappuccino—

"Would you like me to call an ambulance?"

"No, I—"

Hold up! That wasn't Pastor Paul. That voice came from some-where to my right and, instead of concern, reflected amusement.

Not *that* man! Not here. In my kitchen. With me flat on my back amid colorful little beans that surely confirm I'm the silliest woman he's ever met. As the heat in my face deepens, I decide embarrassment does hurt more than the loss of Jelly Bellys. Defi-nitely embarrassment.

Two

I open my eyes.

Above me, Pastor Paul smiles uncertainly. "Okay, Harri?"

I avoid looking to my right, where I glimpse khaki pants alongside the kitchen cabinets. "Tell me, are any Jelly Bellys left in the container?"

"Maybe a handful."

Might get me through the night. Of course, that depends on whether or not he's about to string me up and kick out from under me the high horse I've been riding. "Then I should be all right."

With a sigh, he straightens and reaches a hand to me.

I allow the hangman to pull me to sitting. It's then I'm socked with a visual reminder of my state of dress—house slippers, lounge pants, T-shirt. Lovely.

I pull my hand free and survey the disaster around me: dirt, dust, and Jelly Bellys. If only I hadn't neglected to mop the floor. Of course, it's not easy holding down two jobs, even though both are "officially" part time—mornings waitressing the breakfast crowd at Gloria's Morning Café and afternoons fulfilling the duties of the director of women's ministry at First Grace.

Still, it is a small kitchen, made smaller by the addition of two men, one of whom I'm going to pretend doesn't exist. Sweeping beans aside, I lever up. As I straighten, I press my shoulders back to the tune of *snap, crackle, pop.*

"Sure you don't want me to call an ambulance?" says the one who doesn't exist.

Can't take a hint, hmm? I turn. "I'm a lot tougher than I appear."

It's then I get my first real look at the man where he leans back against the counter. Not bad looking, but not great, and all because of a nose that's a little too narrow and a little too long. Speaking of long, that curly hair of his could use a cut. Not that it's long long, but the cleaner cut, the better. I do *not* like men with long hair. At least, not anymore. As for the eyes that travel down me, they're unremarkable. But, oh, those lashes!

"Actually"—he sweeps those lashes up—"you look pretty tough to me."

That was *not* a compliment, and I'm miffed, especially considering all I've given up to project my feminine side. I *am* the director of women's ministry, and though I hardly reflect it at the moment, he did see me in a skirt and blouse at church.

Pastor Paul draws alongside me. "This is Maddox McCray. Maddox, Harriet Bisset."

Six feet of lean, muscular man steps forward. "A pleasure to meet you, Harriet, or do you prefer Harri?" He extends a hand.

I slide my hand into his and am relieved when no current of attraction passes between us. While the absence of a wedding ring attests to his being single, I do not want to feel anything for this man whose eyes laugh at me. "Harri's best, as it avoids confusion with our church secretary, Harriet."

He gives my hand a squeeze. "I can't imagine anyone confusing you with that sweet little woman." Before I fully register that wasn't a compliment, he lowers his gaze. "Nice tattoo."

Suppressing the impulse to clap a hand over the crown of thorns revealed when my sleeve rode up, I mutter, "Leftovers," and pull my hand free.

"Leftovers?" His smile widens. "As in PK?"

He knows I'm a preacher's kid? I jerk my chin up, though not too far, as he's only a few inches taller than my five foot nine.

"Or, more accurately"—he hikes an eyebrow—"PKS?"

And he knows about preacher's kid syndrome. "Exactly who are you?"

"Maddox is a consultant." Pastor Paul steps forward with the air of someone about to referee a fight. "First Grace has hired him—"

"*First Grace* hired him?"

"Yes, Harri. The board recently approved and budgeted for a consultant."

The board, which didn't leak a word to me. Of course, it's no longer my father's board, as the faithful dozen have been replaced with younger members handpicked by Pastor Paul—and with the blessing of my father, who convinced several older members to step aside. Now only five of the faithful remain. A minority.

"And exactly what's this consultant supposed to do?" Yes, I'm revving up to be difficult, and I know I should back off, but the gears are engaged.

"Maddox will observe the workings of our church. Once he understands where we're at, he'll help us map where we need to go and how to get there."

I look at Maddox, one of those newfangled church-growth consultants who thinks that without a fasten-your-seat-belts gospel delivery system, we're a bunch of backward, puddle-jumping, tobacco-chewing—

Stop it, Harri! You are not Susan Braddock, EX-assistant coroner, and this is not a television show. You are at stake here, and so is God. Try not to disappoint Him any more than you already have.

Unfortunately, the best I can do is dumb it down. Wishing I could take an eraser to Maddox's self-assured mouth, not to mention those boyish curls, I say, "I suppose you had something to do with the decision to junk our organ."

"Actually, that was me," Pastor Paul says with…regret? "And according to Maddox, I went about it wrong."

He did? And it was this supposed church consultant who made him see the error of his ways? I narrow my gaze on Maddox. Something's not right. But before I can question it, the screen door squeaks.

"Oh, my girl!" A tin of biscuits in one hand, Harriet halts in the doorway. "What have you done now?"

As I look across the bean-spilled kitchen floor, regret returns in force. A whole month's supply… "I spilled my Jelly Bellys."

She turns to Pastor Paul, as if for confirmation that they weren't thrown.

I roll my eyes and on the unroll land in the middle of Maddox's gaze.

"I think I'll take a walk," he says.

I know what that's all about. He was here as a safeguard, but with Harriet's arrival, he can leave. Though I shouldn't begrudge Pastor Paul the precaution against false accusations that could bankrupt his family and career, my stomach churns. I may disagree with him, but I would *never* make false accusations.

"Brother Paul," Harriet says, "you two go in the living room, and I'll sweep up."

I step toward her. "No, I can—"

"Harri!" She gives me the "look."

I sigh. "All right, but let me get the broom." She may be a sprightly little old woman, but her bones are more brittle than mine.

A short while later, as I sit across from Pastor Paul hugging my Jelly Belly container and denying myself a single bean despite a terrible craving, I hear the click and rattle of tutti-fruitti, blueberry, very cherry, and forty-five other flavors (less the inedible ones) beneath Harriet's brisk strokes.

"Harri, I came to apologize."

I startle. Is this Jelly Belly withdrawal?

Pastor Paul nods. "I jumped the gun in introducing the new music."

"I don't understand."

"Maddox was scheduled to arrive last Friday. When he was delayed and it seemed like he might be delayed another week, Stephano and I went against his advice and decided to forgo this latest round of organ repairs."

Then Stephano was in on this? Or was he just going along with Pastor Paul—something he does more of lately and is infuriatingly out of character?

Pastor Paul clasps his hands between his knees. "Surely you noticed Bea couldn't get through a single verse this past Sunday without a stuck or missing note?"

*Every*one noticed.

"We had two options. More Band-Aids to limp it along, or re-leather the entire organ, rebuild the console, and replace the internal wiring." He shakes his head. "It didn't make sense to continue pouring money into it, considering it's being phased out. Thus, the board approved its removal."

I frown. "The board approved it?"

"The majority. It seemed the best thing, especially since, in the last six weeks, two of our young families have transferred their church membership. Despite our assurances that First Grace will continue to update its worship services and children and youth programs, they grew tired of waiting."

I knew about the families and felt bad about their leaving, but it was for the best. And it's not as if First Grace hasn't lost some of its older members as well.

Pastor Paul scoots to the edge of the sofa. "I believe I've been anointed to deliver God's Word in a dynamic, get-right-to-the-soul manner."

His *messages* I have no qualms with. He's good. Even as frustrated as I am, I have only to close my eyes and sink into his words to feel God. And word of mouth about his gift *has* drawn in younger families, among them the unchurched. But if that's not enough for them—

"Unfortunately, it's not enough, Harri. Call it shallow faith if you must, but today's Christians have needs that are different from past generations."

"Different needs? They don't need God like my parents did? And Harriet?"

"Leave me out of this," Harriet calls from the kitchen.

I knew she was listening. "What about the Feteralls? And Jack Butterby—"

"And you." *Aha!* say Pastor Paul's eyes.

Self-serving, says Harri's conscience.

"Look, Harri, after you left today, Maddox and I discussed the repair of the organ. In short, he feels we ought to give the older members time to adjust."

I nearly come up out of my seat. "Really?"

He holds up a hand. "Band-Aids. Full restoration is too cost prohibitive for something that will rarely be used once the switch to contemporary worship is complete. At that point, the organ will be removed."

My shoulders slump. "Oh."

"Bea knows all about it. Maddox and I met with her and several other residents at Harriet's home before coming here."

"And?" In anticipation of what Bea's reaction was, I flinch.

"She's not happy. In fact, she riled up several other residents."

That's probably putting it mildly.

"Problems are bound to occur, Harri, but I believe we'll get through them. What about you?"

"What about me?"

"I'm asking you to continue supporting me and the board. As the beloved old pastor's daughter, the reformed prodigal—"

Ouch.

"—you have the ability to influence older members who know you'll watch out for them. However, their best interests do not lie in a dying church."

I shake my head. "But it's not dying."

"Twelve years ago, membership exceeded six hundred. When I was hired, membership was below two hundred. That's a dying church."

And that hurts. "It wasn't my father's fault."

"I know."

Mine, then. That's what he's saying, and what I sometimes think in spite of my parents' assurance otherwise. After all, if a pastor can't control his own child, who is he to lead others?

Despite my body language that's surely throwing up Stop signs, Pastor Paul says, "While our numbers are on the rise—"

Since he took over from my father.

"—if First Grace is to thrive and continue to reach the unchurched, it's going to take its older members opening themselves to change. A willingness to mentor those with little or no spiritual depth. Sacrifice on all sides. Are you up to it?"

Nearly swamped by the old guilt that makes me cling to the status quo, I stare at all the pretty colors in the container I clutch to my chest.

"Harri?"

I look up at him and, out of the corner of my eye, catch Harriet peering at me from the kitchen. "Hmm?"

"We don't want a split."

A chill goes through me as I'm rushed with memories of the near split that bred rebellion in my sixteen-year-old heart when I learned that not everyone who professed to love my family did. I'd felt betrayed by members of the congregation who wanted a contemporary form of worship and threatened to start their own church if things didn't go *their* way.

"No." I rake my teeth over my bottom lip. "We don't want that." Not only for First Grace, but for Pastor Paul's eight-year-old son and thirteen-year-old daughter. Nor for his soft-spoken wife. Standing, I shift the container to my right arm. "I'll do what I can."

His relief—and is that a glimmer of triumph?—displaces the serious set of his face. Though I don't mean to be offended, I am. "However, don't expect me to go blindly along with everything. As you said, the older members are counting on me to watch out for their best interests."

He rises from the sofa. "Glad to have you on board. From here on out, you'll report not only to me but to Maddox."

Maddox who, according to him, I now belong to. *"She's all yours… "*

Pastor Paul looks toward the kitchen. "If you've got a minute, Harriet, I have a question about tomorrow's meeting."

She offers a smile that, despite advancing age having caused her teeth to shift out of alignment, is bright. "I can give you ten minutes. Gotta get my beauty sleep, you know."

I head for the door. "I think I'll catch some fresh air." However, I'm struck by an unanswered question. "Pastor Paul, you said you jumped the gun, so I'm assuming the drums and guitars will be removed before Sunday's service."

He shakes his head. "Maddox and I decided to go forward and present the new style of worship to see what kind of response we get."

"Oh." I *really* need some fresh air. I push open the screen door and descend the stairs to the little lawn I've been known to clip by hand when the push mower I share with my neighbors is unavailable. Planting my feet, I drop my head back to stare at the dark sky where God has hung a bazillion stars. So beautiful. So tranquil. So calming.

I groan. "I could really use a cigarette."

"Regular or menthol?"

I swing around. And there, leaning back on the fragile legs of my green resin chair, is Maddox McCray's head. Actually, all of him, but from the neck down he's in shadow. Was he there all this time, listening in on what became a personal exchange with Pastor Paul?

I take a step toward him. "Weren't you going for a walk?"

"I did. Saw all there was to see and came back." He reaches into his light jacket. "Regular or menthol?"

It's the second time he's asked, but this time comprehension kicks in. He's offering me a cigarette! Does he know how that sounds? Not that some Christians don't smoke, but in a position such as his, he has to know that such a vice can be a stumbling block for others.

"I don't smoke anymore." The chill in my voice could prove painful were it a metal pole he stuck his tongue against.

"Neither do I."

Frowning, I move closer and lean down to determine what the yellow and green packs are. Oh. Wrigley's Juicy Fruit and Double-mint gum—a.k.a. regular and menthol. I straighten. "I think I'll stick with Jelly Bellys." And if he thinks I'm going to share, he can think again. After all, it's something of his fault that I'm down to a handful. I turn and attempt to pick up where I left off with the night sky, but it's no good, not with my skinny rear in ratty lounge pants facing him.

"Oh brother!" I cross the lawn to the asphalt. As I start down Red Sea Lane, the little street that separates east side from west, I reach into the container beneath my arm and snag a bean. I know Jelly Bellys so well that at first chomp I identify it as orange sherbet. I chew slowly, savoring the resulting juice before swallowing.

Maybe one more—but just one, as it's bound to be a long night. This time I pick a caramel apple. Not my favorite, but not bad. It lasts to the corner of Calvary Court. One more? As I reach in, I catch the sound of footsteps, the stride of which is too far reaching and smooth to belong to Jack Butterby. It's *him.*

When Maddox draws alongside, I halt. "You're a risk taker, aren't you?"

The glow from the streetlight reveals a bewildered face.

I raise my eyebrows. "Aren't you afraid of false accusations?" Pastor Paul certainly was.

He glances around and grins. "With grandma and grandpa watching? No."

I glimpse the movement of Lum and Elva's bedroom curtains, and a smile tugs at my lips. "We watch each other's backs."

Maddox's gaze drops to my mouth. For a moment, his infuriating grin falters—only to return, broader than ever. "Must make you feel safe."

With a grunt, I resume my course. "If you don't mind, I'm going to finish my walk."

He falls into step again. "I don't mind at all."

Great! Of course, under the circumstances, who can fault me for one last indulgence, hmm? I reach into the container. And my elbow brushes his arm.

"That was you, not me." He gives me a sidelong glance. "Wouldn't want to be accused of impropriety."

"Then don't walk so close."

But he continues to do so. What could be his motive for strolling a mobile home park with a contentious woman—in slippers, lounge pants, and T-shirt, no less—at ten o'clock at night? I pop the bean in my mouth. Dr Pepper!

"Any licorice ones in there?"

So, he likes those nasty black pellets, does he? Figures. "Nope."

"Mango?"

Now that's creepy. He likes two of the three I can't stand. What are the chances of that? "Sorry, no mango."

"You sure?"

I shift the container to the opposite arm in case he gets any funny ideas. "Positive. Picked them out this morning in time for garbage pickup."

He stops. "You threw them out?"

"Nobody eats licorice or mango. That would be tantamount to eating brussels sprouts or rutabagas."

"Which I do."

Is he pulling my leg? Of course he is.

"Next time, set aside the licorice and mango for me."

I will not! And I almost say it. *What is wrong with me? Why such meanspirited thoughts?*

But I know the answer. Maddox represents change that threatens to rip out the stitches in the darned-and-patched fabric of Harriet Bisset, who launched into open rebellion with pumped-up music, shrunken hemlines, a get-with-the-times-or-be-left-behind attitude, and a loose interpretation of the Bible that was eventually abandoned altogether. Not only did I pay for abandoning my faith, but my family paid, including my brother, Tyler, who still isn't talking to me much beyond the obligatory "hey," despite having come to my rescue that night.

"Okay?" Maddox says.

"What?" I blink. "Yes. I'm fine."

"Glad to hear it, but I was asking for confirmation that you'll save the licorice and mango for me."

Figures. "If I remember. Of course, it could be a while. This was my allotment for the month."

"I can wait."

That could be a *very* long wait.

We walk in silence to the end of Red Sea, and as we turn onto Jericho Road, he says, "What's your favorite flavor?"

Thinks he's connected with me, does he? "Tossup between coconut and margarita."

"I like margarita, but you can keep the coconut—tastes like soap."

"It does not!"

He jerks his chin. "Does too."

"You—"

I can*not* believe we're arguing about this. Doing an about-face, I put over my shoulder, "This has to be the stupidest conversation I've ever had."

"I've had more intelligent ones myself." He pulls alongside. "But I believe this one has served its purpose."

"Purpose?"

"Broke the ice."

With rolling eyes, I turn back onto Red Sea. "Do you ice skate, Mr. McCray?"

"No."

"Then let me tell you what happens when pond ice breaks: what starts out as a good time becomes tragic as those near the break go down into the icy depths. *Not* a pretty sight. In fact, deadly."

He closes a hand over my arm, causing me to startle so hard I nearly drop my Jelly Bellys. "You're really set on disliking me."

I look into his features, framed by hair that the streetlight at his back casts a golden light around. "Where relationships are concerned, I've learned the hard way to be cautious. I don't take 'breaking the ice' lightly."

His semipermanent grin drops off the edge of his face, and he releases me. "You don't have many friends other than the older set, do you?"

I open my mouth to protest but close it at the realization that what nearly came out was "ouch." Not that I don't have friends my own age, but they're a select few, and I keep them at arm's length. I know it's wrong, but I put store in the advice of the infamous Diane de Poitiers, who said, "To have a good enemy, choose a friend. He knows where to strike." Something I learned the hard way as a disillusioned teenager.

"You're head of women's ministry." Maddox yanks me back to *this* year, *this* moment. "That's not just older ladies, but the younger ones whose needs are not being met. They require more than in-depth Old Testament studies, quilting circles, and oldies-but-goodies movie nights. They need programs that embrace old *and* young, programs tailored to *their* ages. And some just need a friend."

Though I'm trying not to flinch, inside I'm spasming. Not only because I've been tongue-whipped, but because he's right. I have put in place a couple of programs for the younger set, but it has been a halfhearted endeavor. And not very well received.

Oh Lord, I've become a stumbling block, haven't I?

"Now that the ice is broken," Maddox continues, "let me say this: by the time I leave First Grace, you and I will either know each other well or hardly at all."

In other words, *"So long, Susan."* Er…Harri.

Lord, please help me not to become my own worst enemy. Again.

"Do you understand the situation? That we're going to be working *together,* not *against* each other?"

Longing to immerse myself in one of my *God's Promises* books (and I own several *Scripture for Every Dilemma* offerings), I say, "As I told Pastor Paul, I'll do what I can to help First Grace accommodate its younger families and to help its older set to adjust—to the extent my conscience allows." *Oh, why did I have to toss in that last bit?*

He scrutinizes my face. "I assure you, neither I nor Brother Paul would ask you to compromise your God-given conscience."

God-given. Just to remind me of the difference between *my*

wants and desires and what he and Pastor Paul believe to be *God's*. "I'm glad to hear it."

"And I'm glad you're willing to work with me to equip First Grace to better reach its community."

I force a smile. "As Pastor Paul said, I'm all yours." *Why didn't I reword that?!*

His mouth softens. "That's right. You're all mine, Harri."

Something about the way he wraps his tongue around my name causes a shiver to flit across my skin. *Why* did I give him permission to call me Harri?

"At least the part of you that belongs to the women's ministry." He steps back. "I'll see you at tomorrow's meeting. Good night."

As he crosses to the other side of Red Sea, I frown. Where is he going?

He glances over his shoulder. "Thank you for walking me home."

Realization hits so hard that had the blow landed in the center of my face, it would have shoved my nose back into my brain. I look beyond him to the mobile home that is used to lodge First Grace's guest speakers.

No. Oh no!

Three

Harri's Log: • 1 day until the Invasion (drums and guitars)

• 6 days until the first rerun of *The Coroner*

• 28 days until Jelly Belly replenishment (must be strong)

• 212 days until the completion of Bible #8

It is not good for woman to sleep alone, especially after a day like yesterday. Thus, when I awaken, I am *not* alone. Sharing my full-size bed is the sweetest…cutest…tastiest…most satisfying—

As the clock radio belts out a Bill Haley and His Comets tune, I cuddle closer and give my overnight companion a little shake. But no rattle. No roll. Opening my eyes, I focus on the container clasped to my chest. Empty. Devoid of every last Jelly Belly. Of course, there is the bit stuck in my lower molar. Cotton candy?

I push onto an elbow and grimace at the sight of my bed that evidences my late-night search through God's Word: tissue box, crumpled tissues, highlighter, sticky-tab dispenser, God's Word translation, and four little *God's Promises* books that range in color from black to fluorescent orange.

I reach to the latter, only to jerk at the pain behind my eyes. Ugh. Hangover. But it has nothing to do with the empty half-liter bottle on the bedside table, the contents of which I downed before I started on the tissue box.

No, not alcohol—been there, done that. This was club soda. Big, nose-tripping bubbles that expensive sparkling water can't compare with. As for the hangover, while the Jelly Bellys probably contributed, the crying fits are the real culprit.

Grateful I don't have to be at the café until nine for Saturday's "sleep-in" crowd, I stand gingerly lest I jostle my brain. Halfway to the bathroom, I catch the sinfully deep rumble of a motorcycle and feel my hangover lighten. Jack Butterby's grandson must be visiting. Though the young man doesn't get out to Franklin often, his visits always lift up Jack. Doubtless, tomorrow will be a good Sunday for the elderly man, at least until the drums and guitars start up. Unfortunately, Jack isn't one of the lucky ones who wear a hearing aid that will enable him to dial down the volume.

I snort. Lucky. *Never* would have thought of hearing loss as something to be desired.

Hoping to catch a glimpse of Jack on the back of his grandson's motorcycle, I start for the window only to veer toward the bathroom when the club soda presses urgently on my bladder.

Moments later, the rumble of the motorcycle recedes. If they're heading for Gloria's Morning Café, they'll be gone by the time I get there. It's an hour before my shift—an hour I badly need, not only to allow aspirin and a hot shower to work out my kinks, but to spend time in God's Word, as I do every morning.

Forty-five minutes later, clad in a pink top and beige capris, shoulder-length hair pulled back in a ponytail, makeup camouflaging last night's wretchedness, my commitment to God's Word kept, I climb aboard my mountain bike.

Lum and Elva, whose mobile home is across the street, pause amid their weeding to call out a greeting. I raise a hand, then pedal down Red Sea Lane in the direction of First Grace's guest mobile home. As I near Maddox's new residence, I start to avert my gaze—nearly impossible owing to the pink flamingos that line the walk and the potted artificial shrubs that border the lawn—but Mrs. Feterall is out front walking her cat.

I brake alongside the sixty-five-year-old woman. "How are you feeling today, Mrs. Feterall?"

She fingers the blue silk scarf wound around her head, which conceals her chemo-induced hair loss. "It's been a good week, Harri."

Pucker, her earless cat—well, he has ears, but you can hardly see them—pads between her ankles, wiggles his rear, and settles to the grass.

I lay a hand on Mrs. Feterall's arm. "Anything I can do?"

"I was hoping you'd ask."

"Ah! More of my chicken and dumplings." Which is one of the foods she's able to keep down. Not because of any culinary talent I possess, but because it's bland. *All* my dishes are bland. Simply put, I'm a "no spice" girl, which keeps these taste buds in top form (the better to enjoy Jelly Bellys).

"Your chicken and dumplings would be nice, Harri, but—"

A friendly bark is followed by the appearance of a fox terrier from down the street. He passes between me and Mrs. Feterall and, a moment later, is doing his business on his favorite pink flamingo.

Mrs. Feterall nods at the mobile home behind. "What I'd really like is to know if we have a guest speaker this Sunday."

"Not exactly."

"Then *what* exactly, or should I say *who*?"

While I wasn't told to keep Maddox under wraps, and he did meet with Bea and other residents last night, I'm reluctant to talk about First Grace hiring a consultant. After all, it isn't my place. Or is it? Maybe Mrs. Feterall ought to be warned—at least about the drums and guitars, since she doesn't require hearing aids any more than Jack Butterby. *Stop it, you slippery little stumbling block!*

"Stop that!" Mrs. Feterall snaps, and I startle. But it's Pucker she's talking to. Pucker, who's gnawing on his lavender rhinestone leash.

Mrs. Feterall gives the leash a tug, and I look up. "What happened to his black spiked leash and collar?"

"Mr. Feterall says he misplaced them, but I think he tossed them out. He kept saying it didn't seem right walking a cat on a leash designed for a pit bull."

I'm with Mr. Feterall. Black leather and spikes, of which I saw my share during my rebellion, send the wrong message.

Another tug and the leash is freed from Pucker's teeth. Mrs. Feterall groans. "He nearly chewed it through." After a moment, she nods at the guest mobile home. "Come on, Harri, I know you know." She lifts her penciled-in eyebrows. "Mr. Feterall saw you two strolling down Red Sea last night."

Him too? Though it's only a matter of time before the grapevine about Pastor Paul and Maddox's visit with Bea makes it to this side of the park, I singsong, "Sorry, but a surprise is a surprise." *Progress, Harri!* I give Mrs. Feterall's arm a pat. "I'll bring chicken and dumplings for Sunday supper."

"All right, dear."

I push off and, as I pedal past the guest mobile home, glance right. But I catch no sight of a face in the window, no stirring of curtains, and no car in the carport. For all appearances, Maddox isn't "home." So maybe I could have told her—

Lord, help me!

I'm overworked, frazzled, and harried.

Oh, that's funny. *Harri*-ed. Not that I haven't heard it before, but it's a good sign that I'm able to laugh at myself.

"The Marigold table's yours." Gloria passes me on the way to the arbor beneath which her hostess stand is set.

I glance at the table draped with a marigold-splashed table-cloth and am relieved that the three elderly gentlemen aren't members of First Grace. Over the past two hours, Gloria's Morning Café has seen more than its share of residents from the mobile home park, and every single one wants my opinion on either the church consultant living among them or the state of the organ.

"Thanks, Gloria," I call. And I mean it. Harried or not, I need all the tips I can get in the event I'm fired from First Grace. After all, despite good intentions and time spent in God's Word, I know me. When it comes to Dad's church and the older members who stuck beside him—and me!—all these years, there's a good chance I'll stumble. Thus, if my savings account is to remain intact alongside the dream for which it's earmarked, I need to sock away more money.

Straightening from the Rose table I was helping clear, I look around the café. Another year and all this will be mine. Mentally hugging the promise Gloria made years ago when I gave my all to help turn around her declining business, I settle my gaze on the new busgirl, who stares at me from behind thick glasses.

"Think you can get the rest of it, Melody?"

"Uh…" She frowns at the bin into which I've stacked dishes. "Yeah, Har…ri."

Har…ri—that's how she says my name in her thick, Down syndrome speech.

My heart tugs. Though when Gloria hired Melody she said there was to be no coddling—that we shouldn't underestimate the young woman's abilities—two days ago she dropped a stack of dishes and was mortified to tears.

The Marigold table can wait. I scoop the last of the dishes into the bin. "I'll get this to the kitchen." I smile. "You wipe up, okay?"

She gives an answering smile shot through with sunshine. "Okay."

Halfway across the dining room, I'm overtaken by fellow wait-ress Lisa, who locks on me with bottomless blue eyes and mutters, "Coddler."

As we step into the kitchen, I narrow my lids at her. "So are you."

"Yeah, but I'm discreet. Speaking of which, how does your back feel?"

I startle. I didn't tell her about the Jelly Belly disaster. How did she find out about the fall I took? Or did she? I lower the bin to the counter alongside the commercial dishwasher. "What about my back?"

She gazes down at me from her two-inch advantage over my five-foot-nine figure. "Just curious as to how deep Gloria's poisonous looks sank."

Oh. So the boss caught me coddling Melody. "I guess we'll know soon enough." Pulling out my order pad, I sidestep the assistant cook as he lumbers past with a bag of cantaloupes.

"Harri?" Lisa calls. "What's going on at First Grace?"

Picked up on it, did she? Was it the mobile home park crowd or me? I'm tempted to confide, but I know better. After all, though Lisa and her family no longer attend First Grace, they were there when the trouble started that nearly led to a split. Not major players, but players. "When I figure it out, I'll let you know."

She catches her face before it falls—just as she does each time she offers the hand of friendship, and the best I can do is brush her fingertips. "All right, Harri, but if you want to talk, give me a call."

"You bet." I hustle out of the kitchen and into Gloria's path.

The robust, older woman halts before me and raises her eyebrows.

I sigh. "I know. No coddling."

"She can do it, Harri. If you want to help her—don't. Just show her you believe in her, and she'll start to believe in herself."

She's right. I made too big of a deal over the dropped-bin incident, bundling Melody off to the kitchen rather than assisting her with the cleanup. "Okay."

Gloria smoothes her sleek cap of silvered hair and glances around. "Marigold's waiting and now Daisy. So get out there and make us some money, hmm?"

Us. I like the sound of that.

As she turns toward her hostess stand, I look at the daisy-covered table, where sits the hip Chip Gairdt, the first hire Pastor Paul made when he took over First Grace. As usual, he seems out of place in a café frequented largely by senior citizens.

What is it with these youth pastors who believe they have to emulate their charges—spiked hair, the tips of which are bleached; loose-fitting, hip-skimming jeans; and sneakers with laces as loose as the jeans? Oh well. At least he's a nice guy—and his wife too.

The men at the Marigold table are ready to order when I appear, but they show no sign of impatience. This bodes well that I haven't forfeited a tip. However, to be on the safe side, I put their order in and bring their drinks before moving on to the Daisy table.

Chip glances up from his cell phone and smiles. He doesn't appear the least bit unnerved at being caught playing a game. "Hey, Harri!"

"Hey." What more is there to say? Unless he has some insight into this whole Maddox McCray fiasco… "So what do you think about the church hiring a consultant?"

His bent head bobs. "Cool. We're ripe for an overhaul."

Ripe? As in bad brown banana? "Really? I thought we were doing well. After all, our numbers are rising, and Stephano has done a wonderful job moving us toward change—and at no cost to First Grace."

"Yeah, but he's Corporate America." Once more, all he spares me is a glance. "This is *church*. Besides, Maddox comes highly recommended."

"Does he?"

"Oh yeah. He turned around a dying church in Knoxville— went from two hundred members to six hundred in two years. Pretty impressive for a beginner."

I startle. "Beginner?"

"Yeah. At least, in the area of church consultation."

And Chip has problems with Stephano and "Corporate America"?

"Oh no. No!" Chip jabs a right button repeatedly. "Gotcha, sucker!"

I look around at expressions that range from amused to annoyed. And Gloria is glaring. I lean down. "Watch it, or Gloria will send out the bouncer."

His head comes up, and with exaggerated trepidation, he says, "Ruby?"

Our cook, a large, intimidating woman whose genes are responsible for her son being among the top-ranked WWE wrestlers. "That's the one."

"Okay, okay." Chip returns his attention to the game.

Would my interest overstep the bounds of casual conversation if I asked him to elaborate on Maddox's experience—rather, *lack* of experience?

"Anyway, back to Maddox," he says.

That worked out nicely.

"Apparently, he got burned out or fired—"

Fired?

"—from some big marketing firm in Knoxville."

As in Corporate America?

"So this pastor hired him to help his church transition into the twenty-first century. And the rest is history."

I could use a little more data, but it's best to take what I've got and run. "Interesting."

Chip looks up. "Let me guess. You don't like him."

"It's too early to say." To *say*.

He smiles. "Give him a chance, Harri. After all, you didn't much like me when I started at First Grace."

That's not true! Well, maybe a little.

"Now, however, you've got a soft spot for me and Vi. Admit it."

Uncomfortable with my transparency, I latch on to his little wife. "Do you want to put your order in or wait on Violet?" I glance at the restrooms where she often retreats with their eight-month-old. Not that she's modest about breast-feeding. It's just that Gloria made it clear that breast-feeding without cover is not acceptable in an establishment whose patrons' aged sensibilities might be offended. Though I expected that first time would be the last time the Gairdts breakfasted at the café, they returned the next Saturday—and every Saturday thereafter.

"I'm on my own today." Chip returns to his game.

"Everything all right with Violet?"

He pushes the buttons a few more times. "New high score!"

"Is Violet okay, Chip?"

"Just a bit of morning sickness." He grins and holds up two fingers. "Baby number two on the way."

"She's pregnant?"

He rolls his eyes. "Uh, yeah." He thrusts a hand near my face and snaps his fingers. "Didn't get enough sleep last night, Harri?"

I *so* want to knock his hand aside. "Er…I'm good. And congratulations on baby number two. Violet's going to have her hands full."

He lowers his hand to his cell phone. "Me too. I'm an involved father, you know."

True, as I often see the little guy strapped to his chest, even when Chip's preaching to the youth. Okay, so in spite of his getup, maybe he isn't as immature—

"Hey, wanna see this new game I downloaded yesterday?" He starts pushing buttons again. "It's like Asteroids, but with ultra-tech fighters that blast the livin' snot out of all these freaky enemy droids."

Can't say I didn't give him the benefit of a doubt. I lift my order pad. "Maybe another time. I'm working, you know."

"Well, in that case, I'll have a spinach omelet, country ham, a side of grits, and a large chocolate milk."

"Anything else?"

"A few of those pastel mints would be nice."

I look at the hostess stand where Gloria keeps a dish of the melt-in-your-mouth sweets. Though they're meant to be a parting treat, Chip regularly raids the bowl. And right now Gloria's hovering over them, as if she knows exactly what we're talking about.

"I'll see if I can sneak you some." The *least* I can do considering the "insider" information he provided on Maddox.

"Actually, a handful would be better—you know, enough to get me through this afternoon's meeting."

He had to remind me. Not that I needed reminding. It's standard practice for the staff and lead volunteers to meet Saturday in preparation for Sunday. What isn't standard is that Maddox is bound to be in attendance.

I tell myself it's sneaky and disrespectful, but this little voice says it's not *that* bad. Besides, if I'm caught, it'll be by someone who's guilty of the same, meaning we're in cahoots. Sort of. And so, going into minute two of Pastor Paul's opening prayer, I give in to the impulse to gaze at those seated around the conference table—*not* something I normally do, but today's dynamics are different with the addition of Maddox, who walked in moments before Pastor Paul called the meeting to order.

Keeping my head bowed, I glance to my right where Joe, our aged treasurer, sits. In agreement with the pastor's prayer, he nods and makes little "um-hmm" sounds. Beyond him is Harriet, whose face is heavenward, lids lowered, mouth curved.

I turn my head a bit more to settle on our organist. Bea's eyes may be closed, head bowed, and arthritic hands clasped, but her flared nostrils and rapidly rising and falling chest are evidence it's not the prayer she's focused on.

Then there's Pastor Paul, whose brow is rumpled and jaw tense as he asks God to bless this meeting. Beside him sits Stephano Fox. Salon-blond head bent, hands clasped before his mouth, our administrative pastor seems unaware of the tear growing on the tip of his nose. Bigger and bigger—

Plop!

Not many men could show that much emotion and still look yum-yum good. In fact, I'm certain the eligible thirty-four-year-old is the reason our church has drawn in so many unmarried women. He's good looking, smart, and funny. Not that I have a crush on him, at least, not anymore.

On to Oona Baldwin, volunteer head of children's ministry. Cranking it up a notch, she nods and murmurs, "Yes, Father…oh, Father…yes…"

Oona is very spiritual. In fact, when she and her family joined First Grace following Pastor Paul's appointment, they were among the first to follow the new pastor's praise-God-with-hands-high example, and the movement has gained momentum, much to the eyebrow-raising dissension of the older set.

As for my relationship with Oona, we get along well enough. I just wish she wouldn't be so quick to offer suggestions on how to run the women's ministry. Having held the position at her previous church, she's full of ideas that wouldn't appeal to our older ladies—a rock-climbing retreat among them.

I shift to her husband, Blake, who volunteered for the position of pianist when our previous one retired and moved to Phoenix eight months ago. The man is one of the friendliest you'll meet—big teeth, expansive gums, and all. Hands clasped against his forehead, he chews a wad of gum with that strange, side-to-side jaw action of his. I nearly smile. However, Chip definitely makes me smile. One moment he appears intent on the prayer, the next he's scratching his head. A return to intensity. Then his right arm has an itch. Satisfied, he returns to his prayerful pose, only to bend and scratch his leg.

Mouth aching with the size of my grin, I sweep my gaze past an empty chair. And there's Maddox wearing a smile that reveals he has been watching me.

Oh. My. I'm in cahoots with Maddox McCray! I squeeze my eyes closed. Yes, he's as guilty as I, but this is different. Does watching me watch the others fall under his job description? Is he going to make recommendations about how I ought to conduct myself during prayer?

Lord, I hate being under the microscope! But I can't get away from it, especially now that Maddox has invaded not only my workplace but my neighborhood—

Back up! He hasn't been given the guest mobile home merely for lodging. I'll bet he was placed there to watch me and report on my interactions with the seniors whom Pastor Paul believes are under my sway. Clever. And sneaky.

Someone clears his throat, and I realize how quiet it has become. Opening my eyes, I peek at the others who are watching me as I was watching them earlier. "Sorry." I grimace-smile. "Had a lot to say." And I *was* talking to God, once or twice.

"Hear, hear!" Bea says. "I'm with you, Harri. *Lots* to say!"

I'm struck, as I often am when she's in a state, by how much she resembles the British actress Dame Judi Dench. And *nobody* crosses her, not even James Bond.

Pastor Paul rises. "For those of you who haven't met the consultant we've hired to help us during this time of transition, I'd like to introduce Maddox McCray."

Maddox stands. "It's a pleasure to be here. I look forward to working with you." A fleeting meeting with my gaze, and he returns to his seat.

Pastor Paul smiles. "Over the next few weeks, Maddox will be—"

"Is he a friend of yours?" Bea quips.

A slight hesitation. "He is."

Though I manage to keep the "aha!" from my face, Bea makes no such effort. "Really?"

"Maddox and I met at seminary."

Maddox attended seminary? And yet worked in Corporate America?

Bea turns to Maddox. "You're a pastor?"

He holds up thumb and forefinger an inch apart. "That close."

Bea has another "aha!" moment. "*That* close?"

He winks. "Kicked out of seminary in my third year."

She wasn't expecting that—nor were the rest of us, as evidenced by her stunned silence and Chip's dropped jaw, which reveals a mouthful of half-chewed pastel mints. As for Stephano, there's tension on his face one doesn't usually see; however, when he catches me watching him, he smiles.

Flutter, flutter, I melt like butter. Not that I have a crush on him.

I drag my attention back to Maddox, and when he raises his eyebrows, I realize I'm smiling all over the place. I narrow my gaze. Where were we? Oh! Right. Kicked out of seminary. Whatever he did, it had to have been bad.

Pastor Paul clears his throat. "Maddox decided to answer a different calling, one which not only took him to the top of his profession, but proved of great worth when a mutual friend enlisted him to turn around his dying church in Knoxville."

More good-ol'-boy stuff. Momentarily overcome with smugness that causes an image of Bea's face to rise, I wince. *Did you forget about your agreement to work with and not against Pastor Paul?*

"And what profession are we talking about?" Bea asks.

Pastor Paul hesitates, and I know the reason. "Maddox specializes in—"

"Marketing." All eyes swivel to Maddox. "That's my specialty."

Color spreads to Bea's ears. "Is that what we're doing now? *Marketing* God? Oh, I know it's the trend to turn houses of God into businesses—and don't you shake your head at me, Harriet

Evans—but I'll tell you right now that those who built this church won't stand for it!"

Harriet leans near and lays a frail, brown hand atop Bea's fair, liver-spotted one. "Now, Bea, let's not be hasty—"

"Hasty! Me?" She jabs an arthritic finger in the direction of Pastor Paul. "He's the one who wants to chuck my organ."

So Bea will be grateful to retire those arthritic joints, will she, Harriet?

I sigh. While it's widely known how much her hands pain her, playing the organ is too much a part of her life for her to quietly step down.

Bea whips around and gives me the finger jab. "Your father would roll over in his grave were he dead."

I jerk back.

"And your mother too, were she also dead."

Beside me, Joe shifts in his chair and frowns at the ceiling, as if trying to make sense of Bea's words.

Avoiding Maddox, though I'd bet my tattoos he's looking at me, I glance at Oona, who's as still as a sheet hung out on a windless day. Head angled, arms crossed over her chest, she stares at First Grace's organist with a minimally rumpled brow.

"Does he have any idea, young lady?" Bea demands.

I clear my throat. "Sorry?"

"Are you keeping your father apprised of these shenanigans?"

She knows I'm not. Of course, not for lack of her encouragement. I'm often tempted to run to my father, but communication is limited where he and my mother serve as missionaries. Thus, I'm given time to cool down, during which I conclude that not only is it wrong to worry him but he's no longer the pastor of First Grace. Too, since ending my rebellion nearly eight years ago, I've worked hard to prove I'm no longer a child who needs to cling to her daddy's leg. Fortunately, God's lap is big enough for me—when I avail myself of it.

"Well?" Bea prompts. "Does he know what's going on behind his back?"

All eyes are on me, everyone curious to know if the preacher's kid is tattling.

"He knows what's going on," Pastor Paul says in a calm voice, "because it's not going on behind his back."

Hoping my silence isn't misinterpreted as guilt, I watch as Bea snaps her head around. However, before she can challenge him further, he says, "I know I've pushed too hard in some areas, but when Ken Bisset presented me as his replacement, it was with a mind toward reviving First Grace, not maintaining the *shrinking* status quo."

Bea opens her mouth, but out of it comes Maddox's voice—at least, it momentarily appears that way. "Excuse me."

We look to where he clasps his hands atop the table.

"I understand there are issues that need to be addressed with regard to First Grace's future, but the purpose of today's meeting is to prepare for tomorrow's service."

"Maddox is right." Pastor Paul retrieves his copy of the agenda. "There will be time for discussion, but now let's focus on tomorrow's service."

"Which brings us back to my organ," Bea says.

A groan goes around the room.

I dream of that first tattoo and how I yelped and buried my head between my knees. I dream of that first cigarette and how I hacked and tried to clear the taste from my mouth. I dream of my first rock concert and how I spent two hours with my fingers jammed in my ears while moving my body in such a way as to convey I was "into" it. I dream of teeth-baring drums and electric guitars circling a trembling organ. I dream of curly hair. Light brown—

Which does *not* belong in my dreams!

I dream of our stained-glass Jesus that soars higher than the tallest building…that reaches arms wide…

But then I hear a deep-throated roar, and a motorcycle bursts through the stained glass, sending sharp pieces of Jesus flying toward me.

Someone cries out, and only when I awaken to find myself sitting up in bed do I realize it was me. And the shattered Jesus was a dream. A dream made terrible by the intrusion of the real world.

Beyond my window, a motorcycle rumbles down Red Sea Lane, and a glance at my digital clock shows it's pushing ten p.m. Bless Jack's grandson for visiting, but doesn't he know how important sleep is to senior adults? Not to mention me?

Fortunately, he's quick to cut the engine, returning Red Sea to its peaceful silence.

I drag the pillow from beneath my head, then over it, only to recoil at the hard bump into which I turn my face.

Oh Lord, not some vile insect.

I flick on the light and smile when a white Jelly Belly comes into focus—an unexpected treat. Popping it in my mouth, I snap off the light and lie back to savor the flavor of coconut. Fifteen minutes later, following a search through the bedcovers that turns up no more Jelly Bellys, I stare through the dark and try to comfort my sleeplessness with the promise that Jack's grandson is going to hear about this.

Four

Harri's Log:
- Day of Invasion (drums and guitars)
- 5 days until a rerun of *The Coroner*
- 27 days until Jelly Belly replenishment (holding up well—sort of)
- 211 days until the completion of Bible #8

It's the moment I've dreaded: congregation meets drums, guitars, and electric keyboard. Though years ago my father and the board resisted the pressure to move toward a contemporary form of worship, it has arrived. Now the question is, what will become of First Grace when it tosses out tradition with the dirty bath water? Might it cause a split? Or will the older set merely drift away as the younger set did all those years ago?

I watch the reaction of those entering the sanctuary—ranging from the older members who appear unsettled, to the younger ones who appear excited. This could be bad. After all, as a seminary professor once put it, the music ministry is the "war department of the church."

Oh Lord, deliver us from—

Okay, not *evil.* "Disaster," I whisper.

"You okay, Harri?"

I whip my head around and warm to Stephano's smile. "Yes! Just…watching."

Smile turning sympathetic, he lays a hand on my arm. "Don't worry. I'm watching out for First Grace's interests."

I know there's something I want to ask him, but his touch glitches the synapses in my brain. Not that I have a crush on him. "Thank you."

"My pleasure."

No sooner does he start down the aisle than I remember my question about his involvement in the decision to push up the timetable to transition to a contemporary form of worship. Oh well. He's probably just going along with Pastor Paul. Must pick and choose one's battles and all that.

A moment later, Bea enters through the side door. Speaking of battles…

She gives the pianist, Blake Baldwin, a nod, then crosses to her organ. Ignoring the four young musicians who are at their instruments, she settles onto her bench.

As the organ breathes its first breath straight out of the hymnal, the younger members' excitement fizzles. In contrast, the senior adults go from unsettled to calm.

I push off the back wall and join those filing down the far right aisle.

"Harri?"

I look around and see Pastor Paul's wife. "Leah."

"Could I speak with you a minute?"

As much as I hate being among the last to take a seat lest my tardiness reflect on my commitment to God, I reason that if the pastor's wife is willing to endure tut-tutting, the ex-pastor's daughter should be so brave. "All right." I follow her out into the gathering area, which is populated by the usual "lobby lizards" (those inclined to socialize and imbibe coffee while the rest of us imbibe God's Word).

Leah glances around to be certain we're out of earshot, then meets my gaze. "I want to thank you."

"For?"

"Agreeing to support Paul in making changes at First Grace."

"Oh." I cast back two nights to my exchange with her husband. I told him I'd do what I could, but I clarified that it was dependent on the best interests of the seniors. And I nearly restate this, but the light in Leah's eyes makes me pull back for fear of extinguishing it. She actually appears happy.

"Thank you," she says again.

"You're welcome. I'm sure he'll do what's best for everyone."

Her smile increases. "You have no idea how much First Grace means to our family."

I don't, but her sincerity allows a glimpse of something beyond the solemn face she usually presents. It's as if everything is riding on the transformation of First Grace. I suppose that means we have something in common.

She nods toward the sanctuary, the doors of which are now closed. "Should we see if we can slip in undetected?"

"We can try."

R.T., head of maintenance and self-appointed guardian of the sanctuary, grows visibly discomfited at our approach. Doubtless, he's weighing whether or not to suggest we use a side entrance.

Taking pity on him, I draw alongside Leah. "It'll be easier to slip in through a side door."

"Oh, certainly." She alters course, and shortly, we step into the sanctuary to the tune of "Amazing Grace." Though I rolled my eyes when I heard it as a teenager, it has been my favorite since my return to the fold—the words "saved a wretch like me" and "once was lost, but now am found" really get my emotions churning.

Leah steps past me. "Amazing Grace," she mutters on a sigh. She doesn't add, "again," but I know that's what she means.

Do not take it personally. After all, she probably hasn't been through anything like you've been through and wouldn't understand the significance of that ageless hymn. For her sake, I hope she never does.

She slips into a pew next to her thirteen-year-old daughter, Anna, who at times reminds me of a younger me. And this is one of those times. As Leah places a hand on her daughter's shoulder and leans in, Anna shrugs away. The point of contention becomes obvious when Anna flashes a resentful look and jerks earbuds from under her long, dark blond hair.

Leah's shoulders stiffen, and I feel her pain as if my own—rather, my mother's. Unfortunately, a better understanding of "Amazing Grace" may be in store for her after all. And for the merest moment, I long to reach out to Anna, to let her know someone understands what it's like being under the church's microscope. But I don't really know her, and besides, it's none of my business.

Spotting a seat four pews from the front, I walk past the older set who sing with reverent countenances and the younger ones whose hands are thrust heavenward, as if to snatch all of God's blessings for themselves. Just an observation…

I slide into the pew and nod at the young couple who shift in to allow me more space, then scan the Sunday bulletin. The page number for "Amazing Grace" is listed, and I quickly retrieve the hymnal from the seat pocket. Though I know the words by heart, there's something comforting about holding a hymnal—especially since it won't be long before they're removed in favor of words projected on a screen.

As the last verse passes my lips, I stare up at our stained-glass Jesus. Will he stay? Or will he be phased out like the organ? I know it's just glass and Jesus will be present regardless of whether or not this particular image of Him remains, but I ache at the thought of not seeing his arms stretched wide—as will the others who've spent years of Sundays gazing up at him.

Bea launches into another song, and I look left and right and pick out a dozen of my father's elderly flock. A moment later, I catch sight of the man in front of Mr. and Mrs. Feterall. Maddox has claimed the end seat of the right front pew. *My* pew—at least, according to the plaque screwed into the seat back.

I groan. Fortunately, the sound is lost amid the mournful tide of music piped out by Bea's organ. Dare I hope Pastor Paul's buddy won't notice the one-by-three-inch brass plaque engraved with my name and birth date? That its edges won't dig into his back? That its cool surface relative to the wood won't draw his attention? Of course, if he hangs around long enough, eventually he'll ask about it. Everyone does.

To my dismay, Bea plays through the hymn only to start back at the beginning. The pianist's mouth is ajar and his hands are frozen over the keys. As for the younger set, they exchange glances. Then there's Maddox. From his arms crossed over his chest to the tilt of his head, he's in observation mode. The congregation plods through the hymn, and as it once more nears its end, I sense a dark air of anticipation: will she or won't she?

She does, which is unheard of. Sure, occasionally she plays through a hymn again, but it's always at the end of a service to allow more time for those coming forward for prayer, salvation, or membership in the church.

Again, the hymn nears its end, and I look from the determined set of Bea's face to Blake Baldwin. Not only does he wear an equally determined look, but his fingers are poised above the keys, ready to pounce. And pounce they do. The moment the organ pipes out its last note, the piano looses its first, and with more gusto than most of us are accustomed to.

Though I don't doubt Bea is tempted to go head-to-head with the piano, she curls her fingers into her palms. Close call.

As Blake plays through *his* version of the classic hymn, more hands shoot up, and I'm certain the younger families are giving thanks for the cessation of Bea's organ. Judging by her flush of color, the message is received loud and clear.

I tense in anticipation of her storming off the platform, but she just sits there. Even when Blake finishes the hymn and reaches to a microphone atop the piano—the likes of which I've never seen— she doesn't move.

"Good morning, First Grace!" He greets the congregation with the air of someone who does this every Sunday, which he doesn't…or *didn't*. Why do I have this sneaking suspicion First Grace will soon be acquiring a music pastor?

"We're glad to have you join us in worshiping almighty God. Today we have a treat for you." He smiles over his shoulder at the band. "As you know, First Grace is in the process of revitalizing this God-fearing congregation in order to better reach the unchurched in our community as Christ would have us do."

He glances to the right, and I follow his gaze and catch Maddox's almost imperceptible nod. So that's how it is.

"One of the ways we hope to bring the gospel to those who are lost is through music. So in response to the needs of our community and our members' requests, we're pleased to provide a sample of the power of contemporary music to move the soul. But first, let's show our appreciation for our beloved organist, Beatrice Dawson."

She looks around as the congregation applauds, then rises and crosses to the side door.

"Please be seated," Blake says as the applause fades.

Overwhelmed by dread over the racket about to invade the sanctuary and sympathy for Bea who, doubtless, won't be joining us, I lower to the pew.

"Exciting times for First Grace," Blake says as the guitars, drums, electric keyboard, and his piano lay into it. And my response frightens me. Though I clasp my hands, the longing for unbridled rhythm that was born in the midst of my rebellion lifts its head to sniff the air. This is how it started—with Christian rock, then non-Christian rock, then punk, then heavy metal, then those I began to relate to and allow to influence me, then cigarettes and alcohol, belly piercing, tattoos, boyfriends...

Forcing a composed face, I rise and walk down the aisle toward the doors that seem a long way off. And longer yet when I become aware of the speculative gazes following me. At last, I step into the gathering area.

Lord, am I messed up or what?

Too late I remember the lobby lizards, but they're gone. On one hand I'm relieved, on the other resentful, as I'm certain it's the music that moved them from their coffeepots into the sanctuary. "Fine," I mutter and start toward my office, only to falter when I pass the glass doors that lead to the parking lot. As Bea heads for her car, I push through the doors and call to her.

She halts, and even from a distance, I can see her eyes are moist. "You okay, Bea?" I come around her car.

She clutches her purse to her chest. "It's over, Harri. The First Grace your father and his faithful built is gone, just as Edward's gone—"

She catches her breath at her husband's name. Widowhood has been painful for Bea, whose world was wrapped up in her childless marriage to a man who adored her, warts and all. She juts her chin toward the church. "God doesn't dwell here anymore."

"That's not true. First Grace is just...changing." How I wish I believed that. "God is still here."

"Where? In that...that..." She growls, causing her extra half chin to jiggle. "That *heathen* music? Which, I needn't remind you, put you on the road to ruin, not to mention your dear mother and father."

No, she needn't remind me. Nor that she's one of the few who hasn't forgiven me. "Please don't walk away."

"Why not? If my organ is to be taken from me, what's left?"

"God." My response surprises me, yet it shouldn't. Like me, she can't deny that Pastor Paul's sermons are moving. In fact, before he began implementing changes, I once saw her hand jerk up from her side. For a moment, it appeared it might go all the way.

"Bea, you know the organ needs to be fully restored. It was twenty years old when First Grace purchased it thirty years ago." *Wow. Keep going, girl. Maybe you'll convince yourself!* "It's too expensive, especially as the organ's being phased out and, six months from now, will only be used on special occasions."

"Precisely! If not for those electric monstrosities, there'd be no question about restoring it—no matter the cost! If you think I'm going to sit quietly by while the powers that be phase out my organ, you don't know me." She fumbles through her keys and starts jabbing at the lock with one. "Wrong key." She fumbles some more and returns to her jabbing.

She's in no state to accept help, just as she's in no state to drive the short distance to the mobile home park, and I lay a hand over hers. "Let me."

If looks could kill... But then her face crumples and eyes flood.

Risking rejection, I give her a hug. "I'll drive you home."

She nods.

Before she can come to her surly senses, I bundle her into the passenger side; however, as I slide into the driver's seat, she shakes her head. "I don't want to go home. Take me to my brother's house."

Which is a couple of miles up the road. No longer expecting her to settle into her favorite armchair with a glass of sweetened iced tea, I inwardly groan. Guess I won't be staffing the women's ministry table between services and Sunday school, or sitting in on the widows class. Of course, I'll hear about it, as well as my exit from worship, but right now Bea's in need.

Despite Bea's brother's urging that I call a cab after he and I spent an hour calming her, I declined. After all, it's a beautiful day and her brother's house is less than two miles from the mobile home park. An easy walk, except in heels and near-ninety-degree weather. At least I'm wearing slacks and a light blouse, and a mile back I abandoned the heels that now swing from one hand beside my purse.

When I pass by First Grace, I glance over my shoulder at the parking lot, which is beginning to stir with those leaving Sunday school classes. And once more, regret lodges in my emotions. I'm not sure I would have been able to return to the sanctuary had I not taken Bea to her brother's, but I would have liked to be around to gauge how well the new instruments were received. Of course, it's not as if I won't hear about it. In fact, I'm sure there will be messages on my answering machine. With that thought, I step up my pace.

A moment later, my right heel lands on a rock amid the scrubby grass bordering the road. Fortunately, I'm one of those "barefoot" women, yet not of the pregnant-in-the-kitchen variety. Thus, my feet are calloused and holding up fairly well.

Shortly, a car passes and honks, and I raise a hand. Turning onto the road that fronts the mobile home park, I set my sights on the entrance bordered by flowers planted by the residents. As always, I get a toasty feeling as I pass between the pillars. I love living here, as I've done since that night Harriet and Pam rescued me from myself. This is home—no loud parties beside, above, or below. No young, uninhibited neighbors. No loudmouthed music. Which reminds me, I will have to talk to Jack Butterby's grandson, since I'm sure I'm not the only one he awakened last night. Sweet of him to visit, but that motorcycle of his!

Speaking of which…I looked around as I neared Harriet's mobile home, and coming through the entrance on a chrome-y gunned-up machine is *not* Jack Butterby's grandson. Unless he's bought a new motorcycle and lost about fifty pounds.

I squint to see into the helmet, but the face shield is tinted.

The motorcycle slows as it nears, and it's then I notice the arm around the motorcyclist's waist and a head over his shoulder. The passenger is Jack, but that's not his grandson driving. I believe that's our new neighbor.

Flushed with awareness of my appearance—from my dusty feet and pant hems, to my light blouse that perspiration causes to cling to places best left unclung—I groan.

The motorcycle draws alongside, and as Jack calls out a greeting from the depths of his helmet, the motorcyclist lifts his face shield.

Nope, that wasn't Jack's grandson last night or yesterday morning. It had to have been Maddox.

"Hello, Harri."

"Hi."

He slides his gaze down me, which falters at about the level of my chest where my blouse clings, then jerks to my bare feet, which he stares at with an intensity unwarranted by dusty toes. "Had a nice walk?"

The strain in his voice sounds as if he barely made it to the other side of temptation and wants badly to look over his shoulder. Even if it means being turned into a pillar of salt. Though part of me recoils at arousing the man in him, another part is tempted to tempt him more, despite my absence of attraction for him. That would be the "bad" Harri who, I don't doubt, is lying in wait.

Dear God, You know I don't want to be that Harri again. Lead him—and me—not into temptation. Please!

I cross my arms over my chest. "I had a very nice walk."

"Done told you, Maddox. She went after poor Bea." Jack flashes his dentures at me. "I'm guessing she had you drive her to her brother's."

"Yes."

Maddox considers my toes a moment longer, then takes the long way around my chest—swinging right and looping up to look me in the eyes. "How is our organist?"

"As well as can be expected."

"Will she be back?"

"Of course. You thought otherwise?" Or should I say *hoped*?

"She's upset with the pending removal of the organ, and I worried that she might do something drastic."

Really? Or is he just saying what he thinks I—and Jack—want to hear? "She'll be back next Sunday." No need to tell him that getting the commitment out of her was roughly equivalent to getting her to surrender her Medicare card. But providing Pastor Paul doesn't further alienate her, First Grace still has an organist, like it or not. I only hope she doesn't pull the three-times-through-a-laborious-hymn thing again.

"Thank you for seeing her home and speaking with her," Maddox says. As if I did him a favor. As if my heart had nothing to do with it. I know I'm being overly sensitive, but I feel like a cat whose fur is being rubbed the wrong way.

"No problem." I shift my attention to Jack's long, wrinkled face beneath the helmet. "So what did you think of the new instruments?"

His motorcycle-induced enthusiasm falters. "Can't say I liked them."

Ha!

"But can't say I didn't like them either."

Oh.

"I suppose it's good for the young uns, though. They seemed to enjoy it."

I force a smile. "Sorry I missed it."

Maddox turns his helmeted head toward Jack. "We should get you home."

The older man beams. "Grandson's comin' to take me to lunch."

Wonderful. *Two* motorcycles in our *senior* community. I narrow my lids on Maddox's profile. "Tell him hi for me, will you, Jack?"

"Will do."

Maddox catches my gaze. "I'd offer you a ride, but two's the limit."

To my dismay, a thrill shoots through me. "And I'd accept, but…" I turn my attention to the muscular 1298 cc, liquid-cooled, 16-valve, in-line four-cylinder machine and convert my momentary breathlessness into a shudder of what I hope appears to be distaste. "I don't care for motorcycles."

I ignore Jack's rumble of dissension, knowing it's taking his all not to point out that once I cared very much for motorcycles.

Maddox arches an eyebrow. "That surprises me."

"Oh? I suppose the tattoos fooled you."

His mouth tugs. "Tattoos?" He draws out the plural *s,* and Jack chuckles.

Ugh. Did *not* mean to pluralize. However, rather than rise to his curiosity, I say, "I think Mr. Butterby's ready to go home now."

He nods and eases his motorcycle past me and down the street, observing the fifteen-mile-per-hour speed limit all the way out of sight. And I almost wish he wouldn't so I'd have one more reason to dislike him.

As I resume my trek down the street toward Red Sea Lane, I thank God that He set aside Sunday as a day of rest—rest I'll need if I'm to get through the week ahead. Thankfully, I'm Maddox-free for the remainder of the day.

Five

O h, good." Mrs. Feterall peers into the pot. "You brought enough chicken and dumplings for all four of us."

Always do, as they insist I join them when I cook.

She lowers the lid and motions for me to follow. However, at the entrance to the kitchen, I halt. "Did you say *four* of us?"

"Oh yes. After the service today, we invited our new neighbor to join us. You know, that nice young man you took a walk with the other night."

I'm being stalked!

"I was certain he was going to turn me down, but when I said you were joining us, he accepted."

So much for being Maddox-free. I prop up a smile. "Great."

"Mr. Feterall and Maddox are out back on the porch." She steps forward and, in a conspiratorial whisper, adds, "You do know he's a bachelor?"

That's what his ringless left hand says, but I am not interested. When I marry, it will be to a "courting" man who won't hinder my relationship with Jesus—meaning he won't be of the type who gets kicked out of seminary, gets fired from a job, or rides a 1298 cc, liquid-cooled, 16-valve, in-line four-cylinder motorcycle. "Yes, I did notice the absence of a ring."

"As did every one of our unattached ladies." She smoothes the scarf around her head. "Did you see the way they ogled him during service? Second only to that dear boy Stephano."

Stephano, who rebuffs their advances. Not that it stops us—er, *them* from hoping. "I'm afraid I missed out on the ogling, had to leave early."

"Oh me! That's right. How is Bea?"

"Fine, though I'm sure she'd appreciate a call."

"I'll call her after dinner." She gestures for me to precede her into the kitchen.

I start past her only to falter. "You didn't say what you thought of today's service. Was it good?"

"Oh, you know Brother Paul—always delivers an excellent message." She presses a hand to her heart. "Your father couldn't have chosen a better replacement."

Groan! "And the music? What did you think of it?"

"Outside of Bea's hissy fit? The new instruments are a bit harsh, but they weren't as bad as expected. And they did hold the young folks' attention."

Which is what I heard from several of those whose calls I returned this afternoon, as well as the park residents who showed up at my door. As for the ones who thought the music was odious—a surprising minority—I'd assured them it would get better with practice.

"Let's get the chicken and dumplings on the table, Harri."

I move ahead of Mrs. Feterall into the kitchen and only then notice the absence of her cat from between her feet. "Where's Pucker?"

She crosses to the screen door that lets onto the back porch, and my heart sinks at the prospect of eating outside. Despite the awning that offers some relief from the early June heat, it's going to be hot and humid. Especially eating chicken and dumplings!

"Strange thing, that." Mrs. Feterall shakes her head. "Though Pucker doesn't put much store in men, much like you, Harri—"

The rest of her words slip through my ears like water down a drain. "What do you mean I don't put much store in men?"

"When was the last time you had a date, young lady?"

I snort. "Just because there's a shortage of decent men—"

"There's Stephano."

Who, as evidenced by the past three years that have been dry with regard to sharing anything other than First Grace's workload, is out-of-bounds. Which is good. I'm not sure what I'd do if he were "in bounds." That could lead to things I do *not* want to be led to.

"Well, Harri?"

"As I was saying, just because I'm not dating doesn't mean I don't put much store in the opposite sex."

Mrs. Feterall gasps. "You know I don't like the *s* word, Harriet Bisset. Even if it *is* in the context of gender."

I do know, as she made radiantly clear to the teenage girls who attended her Sunday school class years ago. "Sorry."

She parts her deeply creased lips; however, it's her husband's voice that wends its way from the back porch. "Mmm-mmm! I can smell that chicken from here."

Oh no... If I can hear him, *they* heard us.

Mrs. Feterall holds the screen door wide for me as I step out onto the back porch.

Pushed back from the table, Maddox once more balances on the back legs of his chair—the juvenile! "Hey, Harri." There's a sparkle in his eyes that shows he enjoyed my exchange with Mrs. Feterall.

"Hey." As I carry the pot to the table, I catch sight of the creature sprawled across Maddox's slanted lap. Never has the nearly earless feline looked more content.

The emotion that springs on me—envy!—makes me startle so hard that I nearly drop the pot.

"Whoa!" Mr. Feterall says. "Nearly lost it there, Harri."

Avoiding Maddox's gaze as he lowers his chair to the porch, I mutter, "Must have miscalculated the distance." I sidle toward the chair beside Mr. Feterall, but his wife gets there first, and I'm forced to take the chair next to Maddox.

As I mull over the emotion that nearly saw chicken and dumplings splattered all over the porch, Pucker repositions himself on his new friend's lap.

That was not *envy! I mean, imagine envying a cat. And all because of his position on* that *man's lap. Now were it Stephano's lap— different story. But Maddox's—preposterous!*

"Oh me!" Mrs. Feterall rises. "I forgot to make a salad. I meant to, but…I don't know why I didn't."

Mr. Feterall lays a hand on her arm. "No need, dear. We'll get our greens from Harri's chicken and dumplings."

"Mr. Feterall's right." Maddox levers up to peer into the pot, much to Pucker's distress, which he makes known by sinking his claws into his host's pant leg.

That thing about a woman scorned? Regardless of gender, it's ten times worse when the species is feline, as evidenced by my mother's spoiled-rotten cats, Dumplin' (named after Mom's favorite dish) and Doo-Dah (named for an old song that was playing when she and Dad met). Thankfully, my brother took in both cats when my parents went on mission.

Maddox winces. "Though I'm sure you make a fine salad, Mrs. Feterall, Harri has plenty of greens in her dish." He sits back down, and Pucker resettles.

She looks at me. "Are you sure?"

I nod. "Oh yes. No need."

"All right."

Mr. Feterall's hand continues to rest on his wife's arm. "Would you say grace, Maddox?"

"Certainly."

I bow my head, but the only part of his prayer I hear past my self-talking attempt to explain away my misplaced envy is when he concludes with, "Harri putting chicken and dumplings on our table and not in our laps. Amen."

Mr. Feterall chuckles. "Thank you, Maddox."

"Okay," I say in a bright voice. "Dig in." I lift the lid and, out of habit, rise to ladle for Mr. and Mrs. Feterall. Thus, I'm compelled to ladle for Maddox.

"You'll be needing lots of this." Mr. Feterall pushes salt and pepper toward Maddox. "No one does bland as well as our Harri."

Were I trying to make a good impression on the man, I'd be mortified.

Mrs. Feterall turns her scarf-covered head toward her husband. "Now don't you give Harri a hard time. She makes it just the way I like it." She looks at her guest. "Can almost always keep her cookin' down."

A grin breaks out on Mr. Feterall's face. "Trust me, Harri's a good cook, but you'll still want some seasoning."

"Thank you, Mr. Feterall, but one of my shortcomings is assumptions." Maddox meets my gaze. "Unfortunately, it occasionally lands me in trouble." He scoops up a spoonful of chicken and dumplings, chews without change of expression—

That's good.

—and swallows. "I see what you mean." Maddox reaches for the shakers. To his credit, he only sprinkles a little of each before retrieving his spoon. To his discredit, he goes back for seconds. Then thirds.

"Not hungry, Harri?" He gives the salt another vigorous shake.

I look at my meal, which is too hot to eat in the stuffy, still air. "Uh…yeah."

The meal seems to last forever, not only because of the man beside me whose foot my own restless feet bump several times, but because of the warm air that moistens my brow and neck and chest. Fortunately, the bulk of the small talk is between Mr. and Mrs. Feterall and their new neighbor, with the highlight being Mrs. Feterall's news that she has only one more round of chemo. Praise the Lord! A few other interesting items emerge, among them that Maddox has never married, his father passed away two years ago, he's close with his mother, and he's the youngest of three siblings.

As Mrs. Feterall is more than willing to impart information about me, some of my past is also revealed. Maddox learns that, with the exception of a couple of bumpy preschool years, I was "the sweetest little girl" (he smiles), that I was clever and smart (he looks impressed), and that I went through a "rough time" when First Grace nearly split during my teen years (he studies me long and hard).

At last, an opening to conclude the meal presents itself when Maddox sits back and compliments me on my chicken and dumplings.

"Thank you." I scoot my chair out. "I'll clean up."

"Oh no, dear." Mrs. Feterall starts to rise. "I'll take care of it."

"No! I mean…my legs could use a stretch. You just sit there and relax."

"But you made the meal, and it hardly seems fair—"

"I'll help her."

Heart making a beeline for my throat, I jerk my gaze to Maddox as he deposits an indignant Pucker on the porch.

Mrs. Feterall beams. "Well, aren't you sweet!"

I shake my head. "That's not necessary. I'll clean up while the three of you visit."

Maddox winks at me—the good-for-nothing!—and lifts the pot. "I appreciate the offer, but my legs could use some stretching as well."

Lovely. As he carries the pot inside, I stack the dishes and silverware, putting my waitressing skills to good use to ensure that his further assistance won't be needed.

"Nice young man," Mrs. Feterall says.

Mr. Feterall nods. "Yes."

The creak of the screen door alerts me to Maddox's return. I heft the dishes, and he holds the door wide for me.

"Thank you." I step past him into the kitchen. To my dismay, he follows and reaches to assist in lowering my burden to the counter.

"I've got it." I turn so sharply that the pile teeters. Fortunately, my reflexes are in top form, and I set the dishes alongside the sink without so much as a nick.

"You're good," Maddox says as I turn on the taps.

"Better than good. You should see me balance six different orders while—" Eek! What possessed me to engage in banter?

"I look forward to it. Gloria's Morning Café, right?"

"Um-hmm." Wondering what else he knows about me, I grab the dishwashing liquid and, with more force than necessary, squeeze a stream into the water. Thus, I have no reason to be surprised when the cap bursts off and shoots a dollop in the water with the enthusiasm of a kid cannonballing into a swimming pool. And just like with the kid, the displaced water slops over the edge. I jump back, but not before the front of my jeans takes a hit.

"Whoa!" Maddox pulls the bottle from my hand.

I felt nothing—nothing at all!—when his fingers swept mine. That was surprise. Not attraction.

He looks down my damp clothes, then hands me a towel.

"Uh…thanks." I blot at the moisture.

"So you're one of those hand-wash people."

I glance over my shoulder at where he leans against the sink. "What?"

He gives the dishwasher a pointed look. "Prefer to wash dishes by hand rather than machine."

I make a face. "I'm a dishwasher junkie. Unfortunately, the Feteralls' machine has been out of commission for the last few months."

"In that case, why don't I wash and you dry?"

"That won't be necessary."

"I insist." He gazes out the window above the sink. "Especially as it appears the Feteralls are enjoying a private moment."

Sure enough, Mr. Feterall's chair is near Mrs. Feterall's, his arm draped around her and her head on his shoulder. "Oh."

Maddox turns off the taps and begins easing the dishes down through a foot of sizzling bubbles.

Wishing there were some way out of this Norman Rockwell-esque moment, I retrieve another hand towel.

"I apologize for waking you last night." He hands me a plate that nearly slips through my fingers.

"Sorry?"

"I saw your light come on and figured my return must have woken you."

What was he doing looking down the street at my mobile home? Staking it out? Keeping an eye on me?

Whoa! Am I overreacting? With a smile that feels puckered, I say, "You did wake me. And, I suspect, others, which means you might want to rethink the motorcycle. This is a senior community. In fact"—*Oh, Harriet, you're a genius!*—"you might want to consider an extended-stay suite. Not only are they comfortable, but you can come and go as you please."

He laughs. "Eventually, I'm going to win you over, Harri." Then he flicks suds at me, a glob of which lands on my nose.

As I stare cross-eyed at the bubbly stuff, a choked sound exits my mouth. And a moment later, something comes over me that shouldn't. I thrust a hand into the sink and splash sudsy water in his face. At once shocked and pleased with myself, I steel myself for anger…rebuke…anything but the grin that widens across his wet face as he does unto me as I did unto him—*after* he did unto me!

The slopping handful douses me head to shoulders, and with a yelp, I do unto him. As he does unto me. As I do—

At least, I try. But as I lunge toward the sink, I slip on the slick floor.

"Gotcha!" Maddox jerks me upright, causing me to stumble into him. And for a moment, we stand toe to toe, chest to chest, eye to eye.

He's the first to blink, and I'd be pleased if not for the unwelcome realization that I *am* attracted to him. That was no ordinary current. That was raw electricity.

Maddox releases me and pushes a hand through his wet curls. "Bad timing."

What does that mean? That he also felt something? That because of our positions at First Grace, now is not the time to feel things like that?

He grabs the towel I used to blot my clothes. "I'll clean up. You go back out and—"

The screen door creaks, and in walk Mr. and Mrs. Feterall, followed by Pucker. "Well, look at this, Mrs. Feterall. They done had a water fight."

Her smile is weak. "Looks like."

I step toward her. "Are you all right? The chicken and dump—"

She waves a hand. "Stayin' down fine. I'm just tired. Came on suddenlike. Think I'll lie down a spell."

"Would you like me to help you to bed?"

"That would be nice, Harri."

I put an arm around her and lead her from the kitchen. It takes a half hour to get her into her nightgown and settled in, but when I leave her bedroom, her breath has taken a turn toward deep and restful.

Mr. Feterall comes down the hall toward me. "How's she doing?"

"On her way to sweet dreams."

His sigh expresses the weariness that he hides from his wife. "Thank you, Harri."

I give him a hug. "My pleasure. Now I'll finish cleaning the dishes and get out of your hair."

"Maddox and I took care of them. You get on home and get some rest yourself."

Then Maddox left? Good. "I'll do that. 'Night." A few moments later, I walk into the warm night air.

"How is she?" Maddox stands at the base of the steps, my pot tucked beneath an arm, dusk forming a halo around him.

"Resting fine." I descend the few steps. "I thought you'd gone home."

He tilts his head to the side, and I notice that his formerly damp hair is mostly dry. "And leave you to walk these big bad streets by yourself?"

I reach for the pot. "Good night, Mr. McCray."

"Maddox," he corrects, ignoring the cue to relinquish my property.

Fine. I move past him. "Don't you have a motorcycle you ought to be revving up?"

I sense more than see his grin as he draws alongside. "I walked. Took me all of a minute. Speaking of motorcycles, I assure you that, in future, if I'm out later than nine, I'll cut the engine and walk it in."

"The residents will appreciate that."

"Another thing. I apologize for the water fight—not sure what came over me."

I glance at him and am struck that, once more, we're taking a night stroll.

"Still…" He shrugs. "You have to admit it was fun."

It was not! Well, maybe a little…

"And, since I'm in the apologizing mood, I'm sorry for taking your pew."

I jerk my chin around. He *did* notice the plaque.

He halts in front of my mobile home. "I've heard of church members staking out pews, but I've never seen one marked."

"It's not my pew. Anyone can sit there."

"Then?"

I hate explaining what I've had to explain over and over again. In fact, before I blew out of Dad's church at the age of eighteen, I was so fed up, I pried off the plaque, bent it back on itself, and tossed it. When the prodigal returned two years later, there it was. Mom and Harriet had rooted through the church trash until they found it. As a repentant twenty-year-old, I'd stared at the plaque with its kink, and my heart felt as if it might drown at further evidence of the pain my rebellion had caused. Though I still don't care for the plaque, I accept it for what it means to my parents and the older members of the congregation.

I meet Maddox's gaze. "The plaque is a commemoration."

"Of?"

"My birth."

"Why on a pew?"

"Because I was born on the floor in front of that pew." I cross my arms over my chest. "My mother never missed my father's sermons. When she arrived at church that day, she was in labor but kept it to herself as she was determined to make it through the service."

"You're telling me that no one noticed a woman in the front row huffing and puffing?"

"Apparently not. She was very discreet."

Through my open living room window comes the ring of the phone. Another senior concerned about today's music? Over the next two rings, I say, "Before the ambulance arrived, I was born with the aid of our secretary, Harriet Evans, after whom I'm named."

Maddox's mouth curves. "Astonishing."

"And now you know my deepest, darkest secret."

Up goes an eyebrow. "I doubt that."

As I struggle for a diversion, Maddox returns to the topic I caused to jump the tracks. "According to the date on the plaque, you're about to turn twenty-eight."

Another liability of Mom and Dad's attempt to publicly commemorate my birth. "That's right."

The phone starts up again, and I grimace.

"Ringing off the hook?"

Not as much as expected, but he doesn't need to know that. "And knocking at my door. The older folks are concerned about the music and the organ's demise."

He pushes his hands into his pockets. "It's perfectly normal. In fact, if no one complained, First Grace would likely have an even bigger problem on its hands."

"What do you mean?"

"A healthy church is diverse. The challenge is to strike a compromise between traditional and contemporary worship without dividing the body of believers."

"And you think such a compromise can be found?"

"That's what I've been hired to do—revive First Grace while keeping as many of its older members involved as possible."

"You're talking idealism, not realism."

He takes a step toward me. "Look, Harri, I'm not saying we won't lose members over the changes. We will, and most of those lost will likely be older members, but if we work together, First Grace will come out of this a better church."

As I stare at him, I'm shaken by an impulse to brush back the curl in the middle of his forehead. Not only does it make him seem exceedingly young, but vulnerable. And appealing. None of which fits the man who has come to shake up my father's church.

"Really bad timing," he murmurs, drawing my gaze to his mouth.

In the next instant I realize he knows exactly where I'm staring and that his self-confessed tendency to make assumptions is working overtime. I look up. "What do you mean 'bad timing'?"

"You know what I mean."

Do I? Well, if I do, I'm not admitting it, especially because I could be wrong. "Sorry, no."

He sighs. "I like you, Harri, and like it or not, you like me. And I don't think it's entirely because of my motorcycle."

I drop my jaw. "I do not like you. Or your stupid motorcycle."

"Then Stephano Fox is more your type?" He raises his eyebrows. "Eligible, prominent, rich—"

"Oh, grow up!" I snatch my pot from him and stomp up the steps to my front door. "And while you're at it"—I look at where he stands in the middle of my little lawn—"get a haircut."

Surprise crosses his face. "Haircut?"

"It's time someone told you that it's not appropriate for a man your age to appear so…" What? Appealing? Disarming? Cute? "…boyish."

His face splits with a grin, which gives way to laughter.

As I cast about for something to put him in his place, he strides to the stairs. "This is who I am, Harri. Though I'm conscious of my position and influence, and I adjust when necessary, I don't try to be someone I'm not. More important than my transportation, music, clothes, or the length of my hair, is what's inside."

I don't like where this is going, but as much as I long to retreat, I'm rooted.

"Like you, I was a rebel—and in some ways, still am—but just because I've gotten right with God doesn't mean I can no longer express myself and enjoy life." He peers closer at me across the darkening night. "Of course, you can't say the same, can you? For fear you'll go bad again, you hide among people two and three times your age and deny yourself what you want."

How does *he* know what I want? I do not want a motorcycle, or music that moves my body, or clothes that flatter—

"Truth is, you don't trust yourself. More, you don't trust God."

I draw a deep breath. "Truth is, Maddox McCray, you don't know me." I open the screen door. "Good night." Chin up, I retreat inside my mobile home and cross to my answering machine. Only two messages. Well, at least the return calls will keep my mind off that motorcycle-riding, *supposedly* reformed rebel.

Six

Harri's Log: • 1 day until *The Coroner* rerun
• 3 days until the next showdown between Bea and the invaders
• 23 days until Jelly Belly replenishment (missing them bad!)
• 207 days until the completion of Bible #8

ou're next." A voice tickles my eardrum.

What's *he* doing here? He never eats at the café. I look over my shoulder into one of the yummiest faces to be found in these parts. Kissable lips melt into a smile that grooves his mouth and displays beautifully-shaped teeth. Why is he still single?

"Hi, Harri."

He continues to invade my personal space. Not that I mind. "You surprised me, Stephano."

"Mission accomplished." He steps back.

How I'm tempted to tell him I'll share my personal space with him anytime. Lowering my order pad, I turn to him. He looks good—designer golf shirt, relaxed khaki shorts, and flip-floppish sandals without the $5.99 price tag I'm accustomed to (probably more like $59.99). "What are you doing here?"

He glances at the other diners, most of whom have at least a good thirty years on him. "The same as everyone else—having breakfast."

"Oh…well, of course." I push back the strands that have escaped my ponytail. And that's when I remember his peculiar opening line. "What do you mean I'm next?"

His teeth disappear from his smile. "The shadow—McCray."

Maddox, who has spent the past three days "observing" the staff of First Grace. To my relief, I've been spared, though not much longer, apparently. "When?"

Stephano rocks back on his heels, then forward, and that's when I catch a whiff of cologne. Undoubtedly it's expensive, but it makes my nose twitch.

"You're his tomorrow."

There's that *his* thing again.

"As for today…" Stephano's teeth flash again, but this time his smile looks smug. "He's spending the day with me on the golf course."

Hardly the place to observe Stephano in the role of administrative pastor. Ah. I narrow my lids. "Since when is Thursday a golf day?"

He winks and, to my surprise, taps my nose. "Since I got bored with Fridays. You see, Harri, there are certain benefits to not being on the payroll."

I wouldn't know.

"Ah!" He settles to his heels. "Look who's here."

I follow his gaze to Maddox, who's closing in on us. I have no reason to feel guilty over how near Stephano and I are standing; nevertheless, I take a step back.

Stephano thrusts a hand at Maddox. "Glad you could make it."

As they unclasp hands, Maddox looks at me. "Hello, Harri."

It's the most he has said to me since his lecture on Sunday. But that's probably because I've steered clear of him.

"Hello, Maddox." I look him over. He may not like the idea of observing First Grace's administrative pastor on the golf course, but he won't appear out of place dressed as he is in an outfit similar to Stephano's.

"So, do we seat ourselves?" Maddox asks.

"No. Gloria will." Of course, then she might seat them at one of my tables.

"Just make sure she seats us at one of your tables," Stephano says.

Groan. "Actually, all my tables are—"

"The Pansy table just opened up, Harri." Gloria appears over Maddox's shoulder.

Thank you. I look around. Melody, who has become increasingly efficient these past days in the absence of coddling, has finished clearing the table. I return to Gloria. "Yes, but—"

Gloria waves a hand. "Right this way, gentlemen."

So I'm to be stuck waiting on them. Not that I'm ashamed of waitressing. Though I earned a bachelor's degree in business administration while working part time at the café and previous to taking on the position of director of women's ministry, I love my job. It's just too early in the morning for a dose of Maddox.

"Good job on the Pansy table," I say as Melody cautiously carries a bin past.

She blinks behind her thick glasses, then bursts into a smile. "Thanks, Har…ri."

Resisting the temptation to relieve her of the dishes, I cross to the Dogwood table that's waiting on its check, then it's on to the Pansy table.

"What can I get you to drink?" I pull my pad from my apron.

Maddox looks up. "Coffee—full octane, black."

Goes with the hair and the motorcycle.

Stephano peers over the top of his menu. "I'll take a large glass of milk."

My kind of guy—clean-cut, wholesome, and drives a car. Well, on occasion a truck. And mustn't forget that souped-up Jeep he drove to the church picnic last year.

"I'm ready to order if you're ready, Stephano."

Stephano lowers the menu. "Three no-yolk scrambled eggs and buckwheat pancakes."

"A nice, healthy choice." I turn to Maddox. "For you?"

"I'll have the biscuits and gravy that Jack Butterby recommended." He hands me the menu. "I'd also like two eggs over easy."

"Not exactly a healthy choice."

"No, but I'm sure I'll enjoy every bite."

"They're your arteries."

Maddox just smiles.

Stephano shifts a frown from Maddox to me. Guess I shouldn't have said anything about Maddox's arteries. "I'll be back with your drinks."

Lisa corners me at the beverage station. "That's Stephano Fox, isn't it?"

"Yep." I lift the coffeepot.

"And the other one?"

"Maddox McCray."

"The consultant First Grace hired."

Word sure gets around. I pour Maddox's coffee. "That's him, all right."

She pushes a hand up through her short brown bob. "Lucky you. Two eligible men among a sea of seniors, and they're yours."

"Hardly." I sidestep, retrieve a glass, and dispense Stephano's milk.

"Well, let me know how it goes."

"Yup."

Fortunately, the next half hour proves tolerable, as I time my trips to the Pansy table to coincide with ongoing conversation. I slip in, slip out, and supply single-word responses to their requests for more coffee, milk, and condiments.

"Can I get you anything else?" I lift Stephano's plate, which is barely half cleared. Either he didn't like the buckwheat pancakes and no-yolk eggs, or he wasn't hungry.

He glances at his watch. "Just the check. Our tee time's in twenty minutes."

"One check or two?"

"One." He winks. "I'd say this qualifies as a business expense."

I turn to Maddox and lift his plate, which is just shy of licked clean. "Be right back." Sliding his plate beneath Stephano's, I turn to find Melody right in front of me. Lurching back to prevent a collision, I lose my balance, stumble sideways into Maddox, and seat myself hard on the table in front of him. The remains of Stephano's breakfast is tilting toward Maddox, but fortunately for him, I'm really good at what I do.

"Nice save," Maddox says as I right the dishes with minimal clatter. Not that the mishap doesn't draw the attention of the other diners.

I look down and meet his gaze. However, I'm allowed only a glimpse of his amusement before his outstretched arm draws my regard. I follow it to his hand to find it turned around my upper arm. Why didn't I feel its steadying influence?

Ha! No current. See, I'm *not* attracted to him! However, the moment he uncurls his fingers, I nearly go limp. Well, maybe there *was* a bit of electricity. Ever so slight.

I'm tempted to flick the grin off his lips, especially when something forbidden rises between us. A kind of breathlessness that transports me back ten years to a musclebound guy named Harley who drove a Harley and who took a rebellious, infatuated teenager for a ride down paths she *never* wants to travel again.

"Yeah, nice save," Stephano belatedly concurs, as if to remind us of his presence.

I whip my head around, and he raises his eyebrows, making me intensely aware that I'm sitting on a table between two men. Clutching the dishes, I stand. "I'll expect a very nice tip for saving your clothes from baptism by breakfast."

"Absolutely," Maddox says.

Melody has retreated several feet and is blinking behind her glasses.

"Sorry, Har…ri." Her voice is tearful. "I was coming to… help."

I hasten forward. "It's okay." I steal a peek past her to where Gloria watches the scene from behind her arbor, bottom lip caught between her teeth, as if for fear Melody might break down in the middle of the restaurant.

I smile at the young woman. "No harm, no foul."

"No harm, no…?"

"Foul." I give the dishes a nod. "Want to help me get these to the kitchen?"

"Okay."

As she looks around for a bin, I determine a bit of confidence building is in order. "Hold out your hands."

She frowns but reaches out, and I pass the dishes off with a silent prayer that "coddling" wouldn't have been a better idea.

I watch her head slowly toward the kitchen, then turn and, ignoring Maddox, clear the remainder of the table. "Be back with your check."

"What about my coffee?" creaks a little old lady when I near the Magnolia table.

"Right away, Miss Julia."

"Uh, Harri," says Lum, from the mobile home park, as I pass the Rose table where he and Elva are seated, "think our waffles are done yet?"

"I'll check on them."

I duck into the kitchen, and Lisa appears. "Close one. Thought for sure that Maddox guy was going to wear Stephano's breakfast."

"Me too." I unload next to the dishes Melody brought in ahead of me.

"I did it!" the young woman trills with a huge smile that contrasts sharply with her horror minutes earlier.

"Yes, you did." I pat her shoulder. "Thank you for helping."

"Wel...come."

"Now I need to prepare a check for the Pansy table, get coffee for the Magnolia table, and check on the Rose table's waffles. Oh! And the Daisy table hasn't ordered."

Does anyone other than a server have any idea of all the juggling involved in waiting tables?

"I'll get the coffee to the Magnolia table," Lisa offers, "and check on the waffles."

"Are your feet clean? 'Cause I'm about to kiss them."

She laughs. "Don't worry. I'll find a way for you to make it up to me."

Uh-oh. However, there isn't time to determine if it would be better to risk frustrating my customers.

Shortly, I place the Pansy table check in front of Stephano. "Thank you for coming." I sweep my smile to Maddox. "Pay at the door, and don't forget that nice tip."

"Taken care of," he says, and I'm just a little worried by the calculating look in his eyes.

Lord, please don't let it be one of those "wise guy" tips I occasionally receive from those who expect quality, made-to-order food in fast-food time. I grimace in remembrance of a guy who wrote in the tip blank, "Don't play in the streets at night." It ruined my day, especially after he monopolized my time with a leisurely stroll through the menu and a change of order minutes before his original order came up.

After Stephano and Maddox make their exit, Gloria motions me to the hostess stand. "I was asked to give you something."

Certain this has something to do with Maddox's tip, as he didn't leave one on the table, I steel myself for what's likely to disappoint. Thus, I'm rendered bug-eyed when she sets a little red and white packet in front of me.

"It's from the guy at the Pansy table. You know, the one whose lap you nearly landed in."

I lift the bag printed with two of my favorite words in the English language: *Jelly Belly*.

"He asked me to tell you to save some for him." Gloria leans forward. "Is there something I should know about?"

I drop the dreamy smile. "No! He was just being…nice." *Very* nice. Though the little bag holds only 1.7 ounces of Jelly Bellys, they aren't cheap. Even in bulk, they're expensive, but handful-sized…

Gloria narrows her all-seeing gaze. "And just how did he know Jelly Bellys are your favorite? And don't tell me it's coincidence, preacher's daughter."

There's that expectation again by which all PKs are manipulated. "Long story. Unfortunately, not one I have time to tell if I'm to keep our customers happy." I start to turn away.

"He also left you a five spot. It's in your drawer."

Wow, a twenty-five percent tip on top of the Jelly Bellys! A man after my own—

Oh, no he's not!

"What?" Gloria asks.

"Er…just imagining how I'm going to spend my windfall."

From the look on her face, Gloria doesn't believe me, and she shouldn't. As much as I dislike Maddox, I like him. But that doesn't mean I'm going to enjoy him shadowing me tomorrow.

Of all days to be late, this is not the one. Rather than walking, I should have toodled over in my VDub. Of course, it wouldn't have saved me more than five minutes.

As I hasten toward my office, a curse comes to mind, but I squelch it. I don't say words like that anymore. Unfortunately, they're still in my head, and to add to my dilemma, Maddox is in my office.

"Running late, hmm?" He glances at his watch as he straightens from where he's been leaning over my desk.

I halt inside the doorway and look to the framed pictures that held his attention—a five-year-old, pigtailed Harriet between Mom and Dad on her first day of kindergarten; a preteen Harriet with Mom, Dad, and Tyler; and Mom and Dad celebrating their thirty-fifth anniversary last year. I meet Maddox's gaze. "I overslept. Sorry."

"Overslept?"

"I had the six-to-eleven shift at the café." I shrug. "Only meant to grab a quick nap, but I guess I was more tired than I realized." And it's his fault. No, he didn't awaken me again last night with that obnoxious motorcycle. It was the Jelly Bellys. Having done without for six days, I'd watched my good intentions of portioning out the little red and white packet go south right before bed, when I succumbed to the remaining three quarters. The resulting sugar high saw me owl-eyed until midnight.

"Insomnia?" Maddox asks.

"Of sorts."

"Do you get it often?"

I am *not* discussing my sleep patterns with him! "So, how do we do this? Should I ignore you while you follow me around? Or do you prefer an ongoing narrative?"

He comes around my desk. "Generally, ignore me—if you can."

Well, doesn't he have a high opinion of himself?

He smiles, and that turning of his mouth, combined with the curls on his forehead make him look *so* cute in spite of his less-than-perfect nose.

"From personal experience, I know it's not always easy to do, but right now I'm just observing, so I'll stay in the background as much as possible."

I give the hem of my button-up blouse a tug and smooth my skirt. "Let's get started, then." I step around him.

"Did you enjoy the Jelly Bellys?"

Oops. Should have thanked him. "I did." I lower to my chair. "Thank you. It was sw—" No. *Sweet* is hardly appropriate. "It was nice of you."

"And?" He sticks out a hand.

I stare at it and note that his fingers aren't long, but not stubby either. Not too thick, nor too skinny. In fact, they're just right. Nicely formed digits.

He wiggles them, and I startle at the realization of where my thoughts have slipped off to.

"Licorice," he prompts. "Mango."

"Oh! The inedible ones."

"In your opinion."

I bite my lip. "Actually, there were only three licorice and one mango."

With a look of disappointment—maybe he really *does* like those flavors—he draws back his hand. "You didn't chuck them, did you?"

"No, I just forgot to bring them."

"You had me worried there." He sits down in the chair in front of my desk. "Maybe I can drop by your place later and pick them up."

He's got to be kidding! I may be *slightly* attracted to him, but that doesn't mean I want him interrupting *The Coroner*. Yeah, it's a rerun, but now that I know what the series was building toward, I can look for the clues I missed the first go-around. Plus, it would hardly be appropriate for him to "drop by" my place. "How about I bring the beans to tomorrow's meeting?"

He leans back in the chair. "I had my heart set on some JBs."

"Sorry." Deciding it's time to show him what's involved in the women's ministry, I pull phone messages from my inbox, all written in Harriet's slightly shaky hand. While Maddox watches, I return seven calls, which range from concerns about tonight's quilting circle to questions about this fall's retreat.

At length I hang up from the last call, having soothed one of our older ladies who has argued with her best friend and no longer wants to room with her at the retreat. I assure her I'll find them other roommates, though I'm certain that before the week is out, they'll want to room together again.

I glance at Maddox, who smiles but says nothing, just watches me with his hands clasped at his waist.

I'm struck by their emptiness. "Shouldn't you be taking notes?"

"Not necessary."

"Oh." Is this how Mona Lisa would feel were she more than paint and canvas on display before gawkers? I turn to my computer and pull up the flier I created to promote next Friday's women's event—an "Oldies but Goodies" showing of the 1954 classic *Sabrina*. As I check the copy, Maddox rises. Bored? Good. But rather than leave my office, he comes around my desk and leans in over my shoulder.

I glance up, but he's focused on my computer screen. "I've created a flier to promote next week's movie night." I position the pointer over the Print button. "Everything seems in order, so I'll just print it out—"

"*Sabrina,* starring Humphrey Bogart." The censure in his voice makes my teeth clench.

Lord, please help me not to say something I'll regret—even if Maddox offends me seventy times seven!

"That's right. The ladies love him and Audrey Hepburn."

"Then this women's event is for older women?"

"It's for all of our women—old *and* young."

He frowns, the vague reflection of which I catch in the computer screen. "How many women usually attend movie night?"

Why this feeling I've been handed a shovel to dig my own grave? "It varies, but usually between fifteen and twenty."

"And of those, how many are younger than…say…fifty?"

That's one shovelful of dirt. Dropping my gaze to the keyboard, I momentarily wonder why the letters aren't in alphabetical order. "It's not unusual for a couple of the younger women to attend."

"And those *couple* of women, do they stay through the movie?"

Another shovelful. "Sometimes. However, most have young children, so they have to get home to them."

"Then you don't offer child care for this event?"

Yet another shovelful of dirt. "There isn't enough need."

"Ah. And the ones who do show up, even if only for a portion of the movie, do they attend the next time you hold a movie night?"

This hole is getting awfully deep. "I believe—" No, I don't. And I am *not* going to lie! I lift my gaze to the onscreen flier. "I'm not sure any of them have returned."

"Why do you think that is?"

Once more catching his reflection, I nearly startle when he leans nearer. "How many of the younger women do you think have heard of Bogart or Hepburn?"

"*I've* heard of them, and I'm only twenty-seven."

"All right. Let me rephrase that. How many are familiar with them outside of their reputation as stars of the silver screen?"

"*I* know them. In fact, I've seen several of their movies." I raise my eyebrows and boldly stare at him—well, his reflection. An instant later, I'm struck by the tickling suspicion he's focused on *my* reflection.

"I see. Well, either you're a movie buff—"

"Nope."

"—or you, unlike most of your contemporaries, are surrounded by older folks."

I grit my teeth.

"You live in a senior community, Harri. For nearly eight years now, I believe. They're your core group for socializing. You regularly visit with them, eat with them, and in many cases, place yourself at their beck and call."

Who has he been talking to? And what business is it of his—?

"They're safe. Nothing and no one to tempt you. Just 'day in, day out.'"

I'd argue, but I'm not talking to him anymore, especially not with all the angst he's stirring up. Angst that might lead me to defend myself inappropriately.

He leans nearer. "Entirely predictable."

His breath in my hair sends a shock down my center, and I whip my head around. "Correct me if I'm wrong, but you said you were here to observe."

He looks at my mouth before straightening. "That's right. However, it would be remiss of me to overlook something as glaring as a women's event that should cater to old *and* young but leaves the latter out in the cold."

Now is not the time to get defensive. Cool it! I try. I really do. "Well, if you know so much about women's ministry, what would you suggest we do to attract a younger crowd?"

The smile that lifts his mouth evidences I've landed in his web. Which is sticky. And binding. And very dangerous. "Glad you asked. How about a movie marathon—the classic *Sabrina,* which your older ladies are familiar with, followed by the Harrison Ford remake, which ought to pull in younger women."

"But that would amount to four or more hours." *And on a Friday,* if my memory serves me quite correctly. Not good, even if *The Coroner* has entered rerun season.

"Actually, more than four hours, as you'll want to discuss and compare the movies and address themes relevant to the Christian life."

I shake my head. "You're crazy if you think old *or* young women are going to sit through two movies, which are basically the same, then hang around to discuss them."

"They will if you have a hook."

I drop back in my chair. "Okay, Mr. Marketer, tell me about this hook."

To my surprise, he walks away. To my greater surprise, he retrieves his chair and sets it next to mine. "First of all"—he pulls the keyboard toward him—"we're going to call it a 'miniretreat.'" With that, he takes off like a jet, and over the course of an hour transforms my cutesy flier into something approaching a work of art. Something far beyond the scope of the usual "Oldies but Goodies Movie Night."

He sits back. "What do you think?"

"Sounds great, but making it happen… That could be difficult, especially as we're only a week away."

"Then push it back a week."

I gasp. "No! The third Friday of the month is always movie night. For years that's how we've done it."

He frowns.

"And believe me, you don't want to mess with these ladies' calendars."

His frown reaches his eyes.

"Movie night is kind of like a woman's cycle, and since the majority of them are no longer menstru—" *Cannot believe I said that!* "It…uh…marks the passage of time."

After a long moment, during which I'm certain he's fighting laughter, he says, "So we stay with next Friday."

"Next Friday." Even if I don't get any sleep.

"All right, the first thing you want to do is coordinate child care with Chip."

Chip who, as youth pastor, should be able to supply names of teenage girls eager to earn spending money.

"Then you need to enlist Oona to oversee the teenagers and coordinate the children's activities. Lastly, you'll have to coordinate the funds with Stephano."

That I don't look forward to, as he can be tight-fisted. Refreshments? Fine. Door prizes? Possible, with the proper amount of groveling. But a drawing for a day at the spa for those who correctly answer all the questions about the movies? Not that it isn't a great marketing idea. Just that it *is* a marketing idea.

"It's sad that a day at the spa, rather than God, is going to make this event a success." I settle on Maddox's dark eyes, which are swept by those boyish, good-for-nothing curls.

There is nothing appealing about a man who still has the boy about him!

He cants his head to the side. "Think of it as a door into a room you've only glimpsed through the window, Harri."

And while you're at it, look at his nose. Nothing boyish or cute about that ski slope.

"You have to turn the knob and open the door before you can walk in."

I return to his eyes. At the moment, they reflect nothing of the boy about them either.

"However, once you enter, that's when you start appreciating all you glimpsed from the outside. That's what we're doing—opening the door for young and old so that each can appreciate what the other brings to the experience of God. So if it takes giving away a day at the spa to start bridging the gap, so be it. Yes, it's shallow, but on the other side of the pond lies deep water for those willing to wade out into it."

I'm drawn to a curl over one eye that seems to be the diameter of my pinkie.

"Are you listening, Harri?"

I jerk my gaze to the computer screen. "Sorry. I'm just a bit distracted."

"By what?"

"Uh…lots to do. I'm going to be busy."

"Provided you enlist Chip and Oona and tap into volunteers, it's doable. And, of course, I'll help however I can."

Score another point for a man I never intended to like. I look over at him, which proves to be another mistake, as not only do those curls give rise to a pinkie itch, but his smile gives rise to a lip itch. Which gives rise to something in the space between us. Which causes his smile to falter and his gaze to waver. Which gives rise—

—to a drawl that, in concert with the rap of knuckles, says, "Knock, knock."

I jerk my head around, and there stands Stephano in the doorway wearing a matched set of inquisitive eyebrows.

I go into full body flush. Not that I should feel guilty. Though Maddox and I are sitting side by side, we aren't even close to touching. In fact, I can't smell his cologne. Not that he's wearing any. He just smells like a man—you know, after the scent of a morning shower wears off and before the grind of the day leaves him all salty—

"Am I interrupting something?"

Thankfully!

Maddox rises. "Harri and I were putting the finishing touches to the flier she designed for next Friday's women's event."

The flier *I* designed?

Stephano looks between Maddox and me, a glimmer in his eyes. "Movie night again, hmm?"

I stand. "Yes, but we're doing it different this time to appeal to the younger women—a movie marathon contrasting a classic movie with its remake."

"Meaning we need to hit you up for funds." Maddox steps around the desk.

Stephano nods. "Usually around fifty dollars to cover movie rental and refreshments, isn't it, Harri? Well, just fill out the form, and I'll have Joe cut a check."

"Actually"—Maddox halts before him—"it will be closer to five hundred dollars."

Stephano's eyes widen. "Five hundred?"

"Make it six hundred. Not only do we expect a larger-than-usual crowd, but there's the added cost of child care, door prizes, and the day-at-the-spa giveaway."

"Child care? Door prizes? Day at the spa?"

Not my idea! I long to trumpet, but a glance at Maddox reveals nothing in his demeanor to suggest he's sidetracked by Stephano's censure. Of course, neither should I be. Pressing my shoulders back, I meet Stephano's gaze. "If we're going to get the younger women involved, we have to give them something more than an old movie, popcorn, and soda pop."

His mouth curls into something that *looks* like a smile but *feels* like something else. "Of course it sounds like a wonderful idea; it's just not what I expected from you, Harri."

Was that a dig? "How's that?"

He glances at Maddox. "It has marketing written all over it."

A four-letter word, even if only in spirit. One I can't stand in the context of church.

"We'll get the paperwork filled out and on your desk by the end of the day," Maddox says.

"All right." Stephano's gaze nails me. "I'll talk to you this afternoon."

I nod and stare at the doorway he vacates.

"Where do you think he'll take you to dinner?"

I look to where Maddox stands alongside my desk. "What?"

"You and Stephano." Though his mouth turns up, he doesn't show any teeth. "Dinner date."

I *did* hear right. And Maddox couldn't be more wrong. "For your information, Stephano and I are not dating."

"I believe that's about to change."

I roll my eyes. "And what makes you think Stephano is going to ask me—?"

Hold up! Maddox did spend a day with him on the golf course. Is it possible Stephano talked about me?

Flutter, flutter. Did he lead Maddox to believe that he was interested in me? *Ooh.* But what about the past three years? Why does he now—?

"You wouldn't be opposed if he asked you out, would you?" Maddox thumps me back to earth.

The automatic response of "What woman wouldn't accept a dinner invite from Stephano?" is flattened by the realization that our conversation has once more taken a turn toward the personal. "I don't believe that's any of your business."

His left eyebrow strolls up his forehead. "You're right."

Of course I am. It's only his business if he's the one asking me out. Which he's not. And I'm glad.

He hooks a thumb in a belt loop. "So where were we?"

"Uh…? Oh!" I bend near the computer and hit Print. When the flier pops out, I head for the door. "I'll just run off copies for insertion in Sunday's bulletin."

"I'll come too." He follows me down the hall.

As I near Harriet's desk, she raises her eyebrows. "Having a good day, Harri?"

"As good as can be expected." I give her a meaningful look.

"And you, Maddox?"

"Excellent. Harri promised to show me how the copier works."

Ha-ha. I step past Harriet's desk as she reaches to a stack of phone messages.

"You have three messages, Maddox. One sounded important."

And that's how I lose my shadow. When I emerge from the supply room fifteen minutes later, Maddox is nowhere to be seen.

"He headed outside to make his calls."

Hopefully, he'll stay there. I lower the fliers to Harriet's desk. "These are for the Sunday bulletin."

She scans the flier, then glances up and smiles. "Stretching you a bit, is he?"

"What do you mean?"

"This seems fun. In fact, I might have to free up Friday and join you ladies."

Which she rarely does outside of quilting circle. And I can't help but resent the implication that *my* programs aren't fun.

She settles back in her chair. "You and Maddox make a good team."

"No, we don't!" I stalk past her and, shortly, close my office door. "This seems fun," I mimic. "Fun! As if left in my hands, the women's ministry is boring!" I drop into my chair. "We do *not* make a good team."

An hour later, Maddox has yet to reappear, so I head for Stephano's office.

"Come in," he calls in answer to my knock on the door.

To my surprise, he's hunkered in front of his desk, poring over…paint chips. "Hey, Harri. Whatcha got for me?"

"The request for funds we discussed."

His smile fades. "Ah."

"What are you doing?"

"Deciding what color to paint my office."

That's odd. He's always up to his eyeballs in church business. I've *never* seen him show interest in anything related to interior decorating.

He motions me forward. "I'm leaning toward Cocoa Crème"—he taps a dark brown paint chip—"but I also like Tuscan Summer." He places a golden brown paint chip alongside the other. "What do you think?"

"They're both nice. Um, when did you decide to paint your office?"

"Yesterday. I was staring at the walls and they struck me as drab. As much time as I spend here, I really ought to have something more restful."

Staring at the walls…restful… Neither fits Stephano.

He raises his eyebrows. "So which one?"

"It's a matter of personal taste."

"But which would you choose?"

I scrunch up my nose. "The Tuscan."

"Nah. Definitely the Cocoa Crème."

I press my lips inward to hold back a sarcastic, *Glad I could be of help.*

Stephano pulls out a pen. "Let's see the damage."

I pass the form to him, and after perusing the six-hundred-dollar request, he signs his name. "I hope Maddox knows what he's doing."

"You don't think he does?"

"This whole church consultant thing… It doesn't feel right. Too calculated."

"Yeah." Of course, prior to Maddox's arrival, many of the things that Pastor Paul spearheaded and Stephano supported didn't feel right either.

He holds the form out to me. "There you go." No sooner do my fingers brush it than he pulls it back.

I frown. "What?"

"Just wondering when you're going to ask me to ask you out."

As I stare at him, working his words forward, then backward, I feel my eyes bug. He's asking me out. Stephano Fox is asking me out. Just as Maddox predicted. But wait! He's not exactly asking me out. He's wanting *me*…to ask *him*…to ask *me*…out. I think.

What kind of line is that? It's weird. And arrogant. As if *I* would be so desperate to ask a guy out. Though I've had my share of boyfriends in the past, I never asked the guy out. Call me old-fashioned, but no matter how good-looking Stephano is, I am not asking him out.

I shake my head. "I can't believe you—"

He throws a hand up. "It was a joke, Harri."

"Oh. Then you…don't want me…to ask you…to…"

"Of course not."

Then he doesn't want to go out with me. On one hand I'm disappointed, on the other relieved. That "line" of his was off-putting.

"Actually"—he turns up the volume on his puppy dog eyes— "I was wondering if you'd have dinner with me tonight."

A girl could fall for those eyes. If they weren't joking! I thrust my hand out for the form. "Give over."

"What about tonight?"

"Look, Stephano, I don't have time to stand here being the butt of your jokes."

"I'm not joking. I'd like you to have dinner with me."

Then he's actually asking me out without my having to ask him to ask me out?

"What do you say?"

I watch his mouth form the words and, in a moment of weakness, consider the thin upper lip relative to the lower lip. In another moment of weakness, I try to imagine what it would be like to be kissed by those lips. In yet another moment I'm tempted—

Oh no! Not that! "I can't. Um…the quilting circle. It's tonight."

"But aren't you usually done by seven thirty?"

Right before *The Coroner*—another reason to bow out. Actually, the main reason, because I'm no longer the needy, gullible teenager who was afraid to say no. If Stephano did kiss me after a romantic, candlelit dinner, that's as far as it would go. Maybe I should accept his invite.

"Harri?"

"Yeah, we're usually finished by seven thirty."

"Then I'll pick you up afterward."

"No! I mean…" I clear my throat. "I follow *The Coroner,* and tonight is a rerun of last season's first show."

His eyebrows leap. "You're turning me down to sit at home and watch a rerun?"

It does sound pathetic. "I'm…hooked."

He sighs. "Wouldn't want to come between you and your show. Have fun tonight."

"Thanks." I reach for the form he extends, only to have it flutter from my fingers. We both bend to retrieve it, our hands meet, and a spark jumps between us, not unlike what I felt when Maddox saved me from taking a fall in the Feteralls' kitchen.

So what do you think about that, Maddox? You're not the only one with electricity in your veins. In fact, I'm certain Stephano has more than you!

I pull my hand back and return his smile. I catch movement to my left, and my eyes meet Maddox's before he passes by. And I can just imagine how this might appear.

"Sure you don't want to take me up on my dinner offer?"

I pull the form from Stephano's hand. "Can't, but thanks." I jump up and head for the door, only to glance over my shoulder.

Shaking his head, handsome, utterly eligible Stephano returns his attention to the paint chips.

Harriet Bisset, the man just asked you out—twice! And after all these years of cozying up to the spine-tingling, albeit dubious, possibility of him showing an interest, you turned him down—twice! Are you nuts?!

Don't forget The Coroner. *Last season's first show.* But as I point myself in the direction of my office, the truth nips at my heels: temptation…temptation…

And more of the same is sitting in my office when I step inside.

Maddox looks up from the chair before my desk. "So where is he taking you?"

"He's not." I plop down in my chair and roll close to my desk.

He leans back. "Let's see… Since I'd be surprised if he didn't ask you out, that would mean—"

"That it's none of your business." Do *not* want him analyzing my reason for turning down an opportunity I should have jumped at. And why didn't I? What would it have hurt? Of course, Maddox would probably say I turned down the invite for fear I'll go bad again. And he'd be right.

"Right again," says the man I'm staring through.

"What?"

"It's none of my business."

Whew. "No, it isn't."

"So what's on the agenda for the rest of the day?"

I check my watch. "I need to make preparations for tonight's quilting circle."

Maddox clasps his hands between his knees. "While you're doing that, you can fill me in on all it entails."

So he can mess with another of my events? I angle nearer my computer screen, placing it between me and Maddox lest I bare my teeth. "What do you want to know?"

"How it's promoted, how many ladies attend, age range…"

This is going to be one long afternoon.

$\mathcal{S}$crapbooking? Phooey! I'll take needle and thread over glue sticks and polka-dot paper any day." Bea's lips purse so tightly they whiten. "If those missies want to learn a true art form, they're welcome to come watch me quilt, but I want no part of being told how to fancy up my pictures." She glares around the table at the nine of us who've gathered to piece a quilt that will be auctioned off to benefit our local domestic violence shelter. "Besides, I put my pictures in albums years ago."

I scan the others' faces for their reactions to Maddox's suggestion that we combine the quilting circle with scrapbooking, the latter holding a wider appeal for younger women.

Elva pauses in the midst of drawing her needle through a seam that binds her Hole in the Barn Door quilting block to the others. "It might be fun. Draw in a bigger crowd—"

"And what's wrong with our crowd?" Bea lowers her block to the table.

While several of the others hurriedly return to their needlework, Elva stares at the woman across the table. "Nothing's wrong with our crowd, Bea. I'm just saying it's not a bad idea to get together with younger ladies." Her eyes widen. "Why, now that my granddaughter's married, she's gotten into this scrapbooking craze herself. I'll bet she'd come."

All that's missing from Bea is smoke curling out of her ears.

Elva shifts her gaze farther down the table to her daughter. "What do you think, Maria? Would my granddaughter come?"

"Not for quilting, but scrapbooking…" The slightly less round version of Elva smiles. "Just think, Mom, three generations and it wouldn't even be Thanksgiving."

Mrs. Feterall clears her throat. "My niece doesn't attend First Grace—doesn't attend church at all—but she's hooked on this scrapbooking. Maybe she'd come." She touches her scarf-bound head. "She and I have gotten close this past year."

"And who knows, we might just convert some of those die-hard scrapbookers," pipes up Jack Butterby.

Yes, Jack, the lone male in our group. Before being widowed four years ago, he attended with his wife and sat outside the circle, reading a book. When her health deteriorated, he took to sitting beside her and guiding her hand as she made her stitches. Near the end, she could only lean against his shoulder and instruct him in the placement of those stitches. And Jack persisted despite thick, awkward fingers, the tips of which were so rough they often snagged the material. After his wife passed, he surprised us by continuing to attend, and now he's one of our better quilters. In fact, when he's not working on a "project" quilt, he's often constructing one for a grandchild.

Harriet looks up from the far end of the table. "Sounds like a fine idea. It would give us an opportunity to minister to one another." As Bea gasps, Harriet centers her attention on me. "That Maddox McCray is something else. Full of ideas—first the *Sabrina* movie marathon and now this Quilt Till You Wilt/Crop Till You Drop event." She nods. "A fine young man."

Bea stands. "Minister to one another—bah! As if we need young missies telling us our business." Her eyes roll past me, stop on Elva, then jump back. "As for Maddox McCray, you'd do well to keep your eyes to yourself, Harriet Bisset, or that *fine young man* will land you in the kind of trouble that made you go wrong when your poor daddy was struggling to hold this church together."

I catch my breath twice, the first in response to the pain caused by her words, the second in response to the pain caused by my needle. I whip my hand up to reveal the silver shaft embedded in my index finger.

"Blood!" Mrs. Feterall sounds the alert. Moving faster than I would have thought possible, she lurches out of her chair and pulls my wrist aside. And disaster is averted as the drop of red falls to the linoleum rather than my painstakingly pieced block.

A nearly unanimous sigh goes around the circle. Nearly, for at this moment, Bea couldn't care less about the quilt.

Mrs. Feterall removes the needle from my finger and presses a scrap of material to the welling prick—standard procedure. "You okay, Harri?"

"I'm fine."

An air of curiosity descends, and I know everyone's thoughts have returned to Maddox and me. Thankfully, they know better than to water the weeds Bea planted in my corner of the garden. Although Maria…

I glance at her where she leans forward, eyes locked on me as curiosity strains the seams of common sense. And I'm not the only one watching her. However, when Maria doesn't pull out the watering hose, Bea grunts. "Gotten too warm in here for me. Think I'll head home." Abandoning her quilting block, she gathers her sewing items.

Jack rises to just shy of his stooped six feet. "I'll walk with you, Bea."

Gratitude momentarily softening her face, she nods, and he follows her across the gymnasium.

"So, what's this about you and Maddox McCray?" Maria finally pops, but not before Bea turns the corner.

She whips around, nearly causing Jack to fall over her.

Oh no! "Uh, nothing."

"Nothing!" Bea shrills. "For the past three years, you and every other single woman have mooned over Stephano. Finally, he asks you out, and you turn him down."

How did she find out? Though Maddox was suspicious, I can't believe he'd say anything to Bea.

"Stephano asked you out?"

The Katharine Hepburn warble pulls my attention to Harriet, who stares at me over her glasses. "Yeah." Should I mention that it started with him asking *me* to ask *him* out?

"The poor thing is heartbroken," Bea accuses.

I turn in my chair to face her. "Stephano's heartbroken?"

"That's right. Kroger's frozen dinner aisle."

Stephano was at Kroger's? Yes, he needs to eat, but I'd never have placed him in a grocery store. Doesn't he have a housekeeper who does things like that for him?

"There he was. Staring at a box of meatloaf and peas." Bea gives a sorrowful shake of her head. "Three times I had to say his name before he heard me. Well, I can tell you that when I found out he'd been reduced to cardboard fare because you have eyes for this Maddox McCray, I couldn't have been more disappointed." She points an arthritic finger at me. "You're passing up an opportunity you'll regret."

Jack steps alongside her. "It's late, Bea. Let me walk you home now."

She squares her shoulders. "Mark my words, Harriet Bisset. Mark. My. Words."

As Jack leads her away, I brave the stares of those who remain around the table. Eyes bright with the caffeine of curiosity, they await all the stimulating details.

I make a face. "Stephano is *not* heartbroken, and I do not have eyes for Maddox."

None of them looks convinced, least of all Mrs. Feterall who was privy to the water fight between Maddox and me in her kitchen.

I pick up my needle. "Now where were we?"

"Your love life," Maria pipes up.

"I do not have a—" Determinedly, I focus on my quilting block.

Harriet clicks her tongue. "Ain't that the truth."

Amid the murmurs of assent, I jab my needle into the material, jerk it through, and jab again. Twenty minutes later, quilting block in place, I grab my sewing box. "Show's on in fifteen minutes. Gotta go."

"Have a nice evening." Mrs. Feterall gives me a smile that I do my best to return before looking at the others, who nod and murmur their own good-byes.

As I cross the gym, I feel them watching me. Wondering. Pronouncing judgment. And the moment I'm out the doors, the buzz will start.

I swing around. "Nothing is going on between me and Maddox, okay?"

They smile.

I turn on my heel and gain all of three feet before catching the sound of voices. No sooner do I identify them than Maddox and our youth pastor, Chip, appear in the corridor outside the gym. Oh no.

They draw up short and look from me to the ladies at my back. Ladies who have just been handed a golden ticket.

Chip slings his hands into pants pockets that extend the length of his thighs. "Done for the night, Harri?"

I trudge the last few steps to the doorway. "Yeah, I'm heading home."

Maddox tilts his head to the side. "On foot?"

"Yeah."

"I'll walk you."

Call me a doofus, but I didn't see that coming. "Oh, I don't want to put you out."

"I was just leaving. Since we're both going that way, we might as well go together."

Why does that have to make sense? I peer at the ladies who aren't making the slightest attempt to appear uninterested, least of all Harriet, whose eyes are twinkling over the tops of her glasses.

"It is starting to get da-ark," Maria singsongs.

"All right, you can walk me to my door." *As in D-O-O-R, ladies! And wipe that smirk off your face, Chip Gairdt!*

Maddox turns to the youth pastor. "Thank you for the run-through. We'll talk more about your ideas later."

They shake hands, then Chip gives a thumbs-up. "Have a nice evening." He wiggles his eyebrows at me. "You too, Harri."

As he swaggers down the corridor, I stare at his backside and fight the urge to chase after him and yank up his droopy waistband that's allowing his hems to drag.

"Shall we?" Maddox asks.

Over my shoulder, I say, "Good night, ladies."

"'Night, Harri, 'night, Maddox, 'night, Mr. McCray," they call.

Maddox pushes open the door that leads outside, then the murmuring and twittering start. Great!

I step past Maddox into the softly lit night to traverse the sidewalk that borders the courtyard.

He comes alongside. "Nice night."

Easy for him to say. *He's* not the one being talked about behind his back— Well, okay, he is, but it's different for a man.

"Smell the irises, Harri?"

There's something very wrong about that question. "Irises?"

He nods at the courtyard. "You don't smell them?"

"No." And he does? This former rebel who's more often surrounded by the smell of leather and motorcycle exhaust?

He grasps my forearm. "Stop and take a whiff."

Knowing the sooner I humor him, the sooner we can move on, I draw a breath.

"Smell them?"

"Yep. Smells good." I start to resume my course, but he holds me there.

"What do they smell like?"

"Flowers, okay?"

He imitates a game-show buzzer. "Wrong. They smell like grapes." His hand drops from me. "Don't you ever stop and smell the roses?"

"I thought I was supposed to be smelling irises." I start down the path toward the mobile home park.

Maddox follows but doesn't speak again until we enter the park. "You're upset."

So he can read body language.

"Is it something I did?"

And he's perceptive.

"Harri?"

I quicken my pace, but he lays a hand on my arm again. "What's wrong?"

I jerk around. "You're what's wrong. You and your lousy timing. Those ladies think I turned down a date with Stephano because of you. That I have eyes for—"

Lord, tell me I didn't say that.

Maddox's lids narrow. "So he did ask you out. And you did turn him down. Because you have eyes for me." Though darkness is falling, there's no mistaking the curve of his mouth.

I stamp my foot. "I do not!"

"Well, it's that or you're afraid of dating. Which is it?"

I pull free and continue down the street. "Good night, Mr. McCray."

"Of course, I'd prefer that you have eyes for me."

As I turn onto Red Sea Lane, he comes alongside again.

Spying the pink flamingos that line the walkway of the guest mobile home, I sigh. Twenty yards and I'll be able to shake him…eighteen…fourteen…

"It's not a sin to feel attraction, Harri."

I halt, and Maddox's momentum carries him beyond me. When he turns, I'm ready for him. "I know exactly where stuff like that leads. And so do you, Motorcycle Man!"

Surprise lowers his jaw. Then comes laughter.

I skirt past him. "Thank you for walking me home, but I can take it from here."

He lets me go, but not without a parting shot. "Let me know when you'd like to try out my motorcycle."

Ah! That…he…I…

I force one foot in front of the other and, all the way down the lane, feel his gaze. When I reach my mobile home, it's shrouded in shadow. I need to pick up a bulb to replace the one that burned out in the security light months ago. Not that I have anything to worry about; the park is safe. No burglars, no Peeping Toms, no—

A low, stuttering growl sounds as I start up the stairs.

—monsters?

I peer at the landing. Something's there. I take another step, and once more a growl issues from my uninvited guest. Placing it, I lurch back. "Oh no!" He wouldn't do this to me. He doesn't hate me that much.

"Harri?"

I jerk my head around to see Maddox speeding down the lane, as if to rescue me from some evil creature. I sure hope he's up to it.

In his haste to reach my side, he nearly collides with me. "Are you all right?"

I point to the landing. "There."

"A snake?"

"Worse."

He moves forward, only to halt when a porch light comes on across the street and illuminates the landing. "It's just a cat in a carrier."

I shudder. "That is not 'just a cat.' That's Dumplin', one of my mother's cats."

"Okay."

"You don't understand. That beast hates me. He—"

A screen door squeaks behind us. "Everything all right, Harri?"

I glance over my shoulder at where Lum and Elva have come out onto their porch and am horrified that they might think an unwelcome advance is responsible for the disturbance.

"Harri's fine," Maddox calls. "She just came home to an unexpected visitor that goes by the name of Dumplin'."

"Oh dear, that's right." Elva nods. "Your brother dropped him off a couple hours ago."

Thank you, Tyler. You could have warned me. Of course, then I would have had time to come up with an excuse. This way he could get in and out without being subjected to a stilted conversation with his prodigal sister. As always, I experience a pang over my inability to reconcile with him. I've tried to get back to a semblance of where we were before my rebellion—big brother/little sister— but he rebuffs my efforts. Not that I blame him. My parents weren't the only ones who suffered fallout from my rebellion.

I force a smile. "I'm sorry I disturbed you, Lum…Elva."

"No problem. We'll get back to our program."

I raise a hand. "Good night." In the next instant, I catch my breath. Program! *The Coroner* is about to come on. Must get rid of Maddox. But what about Dumplin'?

I meet the hostile yellow eyes that stare at me from the carrier. Is it possible to feed and water the beast through the bars? It could work. At least, until he needs to relieve himself.

Right. Litter box. Yuck.

Maddox sighs. "I should get home."

"No!"

By the glow of the porch light, I catch the rise of his left eyebrow.

"Uh…" I glance at Dumplin', who's watching me, plotting to pounce the moment he gets me alone. "Do you like cats?"

Maddox's right eyebrow joins the left.

"I mean, I'm sure it's lonely being away from home without family or—"

"Not at all." He looks at the carrier. "So you're scared of a cat named Dumplin'."

"Hey, don't let the name fool you. That is one mean cat."

"Doesn't seem mean to me."

"Trust me, he's mean. And he growls."

Maddox starts to smile. "Can't say I've had much experience with cats, but I've never heard one growl."

"This one does. And he bites. And scratches."

He strides to the porch. Dare I hope he's going to come to my rescue? Be my knight in shining armor—uh, *leather*—and spirit Dumplin' away to his castle—er, pink-flamingoed mobile home?

He ascends the steps and hunkers down. "Hey, Dumplin'. How you doing?"

You know what that scheming, no-good cat does? Rubs against the bars!

"Hear that? He's purring."

I hear, all right. Sounds like a big, fat bumblebee with a stutter. But he's not fooling me. I know all about that stinger of his.

As Dumplin' butts against the bars, Maddox pushes a finger through and rubs his head. "Nice kitty."

I put my hands on my hips. "So you'll take him home with you?"

"Sorry, Harri, but cats aren't my thing."

So much for my knight...

"There's a note for you." He loosens a piece of paper from the carrier.

"Gee, thanks." I move forward and narrowly avoid contact with his fingers.

"And he left you a litter box." Maddox nods toward the corner of the porch. "Complete with a fresh supply of litter."

No doubt of the ultraclumping variety. I unfold the note.

Harri,

Two cats are one too many. Too much litter, too much shedding, too much scratching at my new furniture. Time for you to step up to the plate. Take good care of Dumplin'. Mom will appreciate it.

Tyler

Just...Tyler. Not that I have the right to expect anything more, but would it hurt to add *Sincerely*? Not *Fondly*, not *Warmly*, just *Sincerely*? "He could have at least left me Doo-Dah."

"What?"

"My mother's other cat."

Maddox rests his forearms on his thighs. "I gather you and Doo-Dah get along?"

I ascend the steps and drop down beside Maddox. *Harriet Bisset, what do you think you're doing?* I have no idea. It just seemed the natural thing to do. *Natural?! You. Maddox. Alone. At night. In the dark.* Well, there is the light from Lum and Elva's porch… *Yeah, and in case you haven't noticed, that's your leg brushing his.*

I lurch to the right.

"I don't bite, Harri."

I jerk my chin around, only to have my gaze land on Maddox's mouth. "It's not biting I'm worried about."

I gasp at the words that could only have come from me. Again a movement across Red Sea Lane draws my attention. Though Lum and Elva's living room curtains appear still, I'm certain they are checking on us.

"Bad timing all around," he murmurs.

I'm unnerved by his smile. "Yeah."

"So what have you got against Dumplin'? Or should I say, what has he got against you?"

Much safer topic. I lower my sewing box to the porch. "A series of unfortunate events that started with neutering."

Maddox's eyebrows rise. "You're not going to win my sympathy with that one."

"It wasn't my doing. At the last minute, something came up and my mom couldn't take Dumplin' to get him fixed, so I took him."

"And he hasn't forgiven you."

"Nope. Then there was the shower incident."

"Cats and water don't go well together, Harri."

"No kidding. Dumplin' got skunked, and I was enlisted to do the tomato juice thing." I shudder. "Never again. But what sealed the deal was when I was taking out my parents' garbage and didn't see him sunning on the steps. I tripped on him. He went flying, I went flying, and I landed on him."

He pushes his fingers through the bars again. "Poor guy."

I scoff. "I'm the one who ended up with a limp."

"Still, I'm sure it was traumatic for him, especially considering your history."

Great. Sympathize with the cat.

Maddox lowers his gaze to Tyler's note. "So now you're stuck with Dumplin'."

I hand him the note. "What do you think?"

He reads it. "Obviously, he's not happy with the situation."

"Nah." I force a smile. "He just doesn't like me much."

"Your brother doesn't like you?"

Oh dear. I'm responsible for this turn of conversation, aren't I? "Though Tyler tolerates me, he hasn't forgiven me for playing the prodigal so well."

"Because you haven't forgiven yourself?"

My forced smile dissolves. "What?"

"It's hard to forgive a person who hasn't forgiven herself. Hard to trust someone who doesn't trust herself. Maybe that's how it is with Tyler. He sees the goody two-shoes existence you live and knows it's not you. He wants his sister back, but not a sister who hardly resembles the one he remembers."

I asked for that—opened the door and ushered him into my

personal life—fangs, warts, and all. I really need to watch myself around this man. I push to my feet and reach for the carrier. "I should get Dumplin' inside."

As I curl my fingers around the handle, Maddox settles a hand on mine. "I'm trying to help."

"Well, you're not." With a huff, I lift the cage, and he has no choice but to release my hand. "Good night, Maddox." I drag the screen door open, turn the knob, and struggle to fit myself and the carrier through the doorway—at which Dumplin' takes offense and lets out a rumbling growl.

Ha! I jerk my chin around. "Tell me that wasn't a growl."

Maddox nods. "That was a growl, and one to which I can certainly relate."

Ah!

The last thing I want is Maddox's assistance, but he rises and pulls the screen door wide. A moment later, I step into my mobile home and close the door—not in his face, but close. Breathing harder than the exercise warrants, I cross the living room and lower the carrier beside the sofa table.

Dumplin' looses another growl, this one punctuated by a hiss.

I prop my hands on my hips. "Well, isn't this cozy?"

A knock sounds, and I stomp to the door and throw it open.

Maddox holds up my sewing box. "Trade you for the Jelly Bellys you owe me."

I reach for the box.

"Uh-uh. First the Jelly Bellys, then the box."

"Fine."

Shortly, carrying the Ziploc bag I retrieved from my kitchen counter, I push through the screen door and find Maddox with his back to me.

"Have you ever tried counting the stars, Harri?"

"No." I hold out the Ziploc.

He continues to stare at the night sky. "It puts things into perspective. How small we are…how mighty God is…how alone we are without Him…"

I glance at the pinpricks of light starting to show and am swept by a memory of lying on my back in the grass, staring at the dark sky, holding hands with a hairy-knuckled guy by the name of Harley, sighing out a breath of pungent smoke—

Ugh! "Sorry, but you're too deep for me, Maddox." I give the baggie a shake. "By special request."

"Thanks." As he takes it, his gaze finds mine and I'm jolted, not only by how different this night feels from that other night, but how different this man is from that boy-trying-to-be-a-man. No props. No rebellion-fueled emotions. Only Maddox and me and stars too numerous to be numbered. And somewhere in there a kiss waiting to happen. *Which leads to you know what!*

I step back and look at the little porch between us while the imaginary kiss fades until it disappears altogether.

"A series on dating," Maddox says, as if coming to a decision.

"What?"

"For single women—a series on dating. Perhaps a Wednesday night offering to balance the Old Testament Bible study the older women attend."

I scoff. "You honestly think there's a need for a series on *dating*?"

"I *know* there's a need."

"And how do you—?" He's talking about me.

"Good night, Harri." As he walks away, he slips the bag in his back pocket.

"Hold up!"

He turns. "Yes?"

"I want to see you eat the Jelly Bellys."

There's no mistaking his upwardly mobile mouth. "Do you have a fetish I ought to know about?"

That *did* sound wacky. "I just don't think anybody eats those flavors."

"Why else would I ask you to save them for me?"

"To mess with me."

He considers me, then pulls the baggie from his pocket, picks out a bean, and pops it in his mouth. "Mmm. Licorice."

No grimace, no hard swallow, just an expression of enjoyment that bothers me straight down to my toes.

"Satisfied?"

Fine, so he likes licorice, but that's not the worst of it. I cross my arms over my chest. "Keep going."

He pops another, only to go suddenly still and spit it out.

"So you like mango, do you?"

"That was no mango. That was cappuccino."

Oh. Forgot I tossed that one in as well. "Sorry, I figured that if you like licorice and mango, you'd like the other one I can't stand."

"Hardly." His grimace is replaced with a grin. "Though I suppose that means we're compatible, hmm?"

I narrow my lids at him. "What about that timing problem, hmm?" Oh. My. Word. I just let him know that at another time, another place— I swing away and yank at the screen door.

"Harri?"

I look over my shoulder.

He holds up something. "Mango." Then he's chewing the bean for all it's worth.

I blow a breath up my face. "Good night, Maddox." I close the door and, at long last, am wonderfully, blessedly alone.

Wrong, as evidenced by a bloodcurdling growl.

"Great. I suppose you need to use the litter box, hmm?"

Rather than rub against the bars as he did for Maddox, Dumplin' arches his back and hisses.

I heave a sigh. "Okay, I'll grab your litter box, then let you out. But no funny stuff, or you're back in there."

A half hour later, I stare at my darkened bedroom ceiling, awash in loss at having missed the first rerun of *The Coroner.* And it's Maddox's fault. *Everything,* including Dumplin's rejection of the litter box in favor of my kitchen floor, is his fault.

Nine

Harri's Log:
- 1 day until the next showdown between Bea and the invaders
- 6 days until the "Oldies but Goodies" miniretreat
- 6 days until the next rerun of *The Coroner* (must learn how to program the VCR due to the miniretreat)
- 21 days until Jelly Belly replenishment (save licorice and mango)
- 205 days until the completion of Bible #8

e has not treated us as we deserve for our sins or paid us back for our wrongs. As high as the heavens are above the earth—that is how vast his mercy is toward those who fear him. As far as the east is from the west—that is how far he has removed our <u>rebellious acts</u> from himself."

It's not the first time I've highlighted Psalm 103:10–12, nor the first time I've double underlined *rebellious acts*. Each time I do so, I feel a strong kinship with the psalmist, David of Goliath fame—the same David of Bathsheba shame. A forgiven man.

Just as you're forgiven, Harri.

Right. I close Bible #8, a pink, bonded-leather copy, then rise from the kitchen table and cross into the living room. At the corner bookcase, I slide my gaze over Bibles #1 through #7, each read front to back and gussied up with alternating highlighter colors. With a satisfied sigh, I slide Bible #8 alongside #7.

Showered, dressed, fed, and my daily reading of God's Word under my belt, I'm ready for the day. What could go wrong? Well, there is Dumplin'. I eye the hallway. No sign of him, and I'd be worried if sometime between my shower and Bible study he hadn't christened the litter box. *Never* thought I'd be excited by a clump of waste.

Five minutes later, I step out into a gently warmed morning and pause to draw a breath of air and survey the day. Maddox would be so proud of me—

What is the matter with you, caring about what Maddox thinks? I hasten down the stairs and walk my bike to the lane. However, as I start peddling down Red Sea, I'm once more struck by wistfulness. It's a beautiful day—looks good, smells good, feels good. The way God intended.

Just past Maddox's mobile home, I brake so hard that the back end of my bicycle skids. The pink flamingos are gone, as are the plastic evergreen shrubs. All that remains are rings of dead grass where each had stood.

Maddox. He did this! Probably thought the flamingos and plastic shrubs clashed with his "he-man" motorcycle. Wait until I get my hands on him! Wondering if it's possible to do so before today's staff meeting, I pedal hard out of the park, harder past the church, and squeal to a stop at the rear of the café.

Calm down, Harri. Gloria's counting on you to make the customers' visits pleasant, especially the park crowd, who are likely more upset than you. I push my bike into the rack alongside the door and enter the kitchen.

Ruby, the cook, looks up. "Mornin', Harri."

That's it? Nothing about the flamingos? Glancing at the others whose hustle attests to the large Saturday crowd, I retrieve an apron. "So…a typical Saturday morning?"

Ruby flips an omelet. "Not happy about the flamingos, hmm?"

I do a double take. "You heard?"

"'Course I heard."

"The older folks are real upset, hmm?"

"Only Bea Dawson, far as I know."

Only Bea?

"She lit outta here a half hour ago, so I haven't heard much since." She turns to her waffle batter. "You'd best get out there and pick up the slack."

In something of a daze, I step into the dining room. I half expect to find myself in a foreign land, but the usual crowd occupies the tables—half of whom are from the park, none of whom are trying to catch my eye and wave me toward their tables.

"Rose, Dogwood, and Tulip." Gloria appears at my side. "And Pansy—he specifically requested you."

I follow her nod to a man who appears more at home than he has the right to.

Same table, same chair as when he joined Stephano for breakfast.

"He's been waiting ten minutes," Gloria says.

As I stare daggers at him, he glances up from his newspaper. And smiles.

I press my shoulders back. "Then I'll start with Mr. McCray."

Gloria leans in. "They *were* tacky."

Though I'm to believe that no one but me and Bea are upset over the desecration of our flamingos, everyone seems to know about it. "Tackiness is not the issue."

She sighs. "Just don't forget that the man tips well."

I head for the Pansy table.

"Harri," Jack says as I pass.

I back up. "Good morning, Jack." I turn my regard to his grandson, whose mouth is full of raisin french toast—no doubt about that. "Hey, Bill."

"Hiya, Harri."

Jack touches my arm. "My guess is you had a bit of a surprise this morning."

"Didn't we all?"

He shrugs. "Threw me for a moment, but it does look nicer."

A conspiracy. I lift my pad. "I'd better get to my tables."

Mr. and Mrs. Feterall and Lum and Elva catch my eye as I near Maddox, but there's no urgency in their expressions. Can*not* believe they're okay with this.

I halt alongside the Pansy table's single occupant, press my palms to the table, and lean in. "Okay, what have you done with our flamingos and shrubs?"

Maddox considers me. "*Your* flamingos and shrubs? How's that?"

If I had feathers, they'd be ruffled, but in that moment I realize how ridiculous my argument is going to sound. "It's…tradition.

The guest mobile home is where all the flamingos go when the residents remove them from their yards."

"Is that right? A kind of retirement community within a retirement community. For plastic pink flamingos."

Heat rising in my face, I straighten. "Something like that."

"And what about the plastic shrubs?"

I glance at where Harriet's neighbor, Ross, sits. It was he who donated the plastic shrubs when he removed his Astroturf and sod and installed real shrubs five years ago. "They're a nice touch."

Maddox leans back. "No, they're not. They're dog magnets, the same as the flamingos. Surely you noticed the dead grass around every one of them?"

He has a point.

"They're in the storage space under the mobile home. When my work is done at First Grace, I'll put them back if that's what the residents want."

I blink. "Oh."

He smiles. "So, how's Dumplin'?"

My scowl returns in force. "He gave me a present last night."

"Cats can sense when they're not welcome."

He's saying it's my fault?

He reaches for his menu. "If you're ready, I'll place my order now."

Shortly, I hurry away from Maddox's table—correction!—the *Pansy* table.

"He's baaaack," Lisa intones as I enter the kitchen, and she heads out carrying plates loaded with omelets and hash browns.

She smacks her lips. "Nice catch. Let me know if you decide to throw him back."

I stalk over to Ruby and stick Maddox's ticket under her nose. "Can you put a rush on this?"

"That church consultant, hmm?" Her eyes twinkle. "The one who asked to be seated at one of your tables."

Lovely. Thanks to Maddox and his special request, Lisa isn't the only one who thinks I've reeled in a prize fish.

"He's n-nice," Melody says behind me.

I whip around.

She retreats a step. "You mad, Har…ri?"

Why am I letting that man get under my skin? "No." With an apologetic smile, I give her arm a squeeze. "Just a little frustrated—and not with you."

Her shoulders ease. "I get frust…ed too." From her pocket, she produces something small and red and white. "This make you feel not so frust…ed."

I swallow hard to keep from drooling at the sight of Jelly Bellys.

"Mad…ox gave it to me."

Mad ox. As an image of a raging ox with steam billowing from its nostrils rises, I press my lips to hold back laughter for fear Melody will believe it's directed at her.

She shakes the packet inches from my nose, and I declare I can smell those delectable little beans right through the cellophane. "Want some, Har…ri?"

"You bet, but let's wait until the morning crowd thins."

"Okay." She drops the packet in her apron pocket and, with a bounce, heads out.

"About Mad ox's order…," Ruby says.

With a hopeful smile, I turn. "Help me out?"

She catches the assistant cook's eye. "Two eggs over easy, and make it snappy."

"Thanks, Ruby."

She comes closer. "About the time you take over this place is about the time I'll be due for a raise. Don't forget that, hear?"

I meet the gaze of one of the few who knows of my arrangement with Gloria. "Gotcha."

Ruby resumes her place at the counter. "By the time you bring me more orders, Mad ox's breakfast will be up."

Twenty minutes later, Maddox is chatting with Gloria as he pays his bill. And now the question in everyone's mind is: did he or didn't he?

I watch for him to make the drop, but when he walks out the door, there's no evidence that Gloria has another packet of Jelly Bellys waiting for me.

"Har…ri! Look!"

I turn to where Melody stands next to the Pansy table.

She waves a red and white packet. "He gave you one too!"

I'd be thrilled if not for the entire café watching.

"Well, look at that," Harriet says as I stand frozen alongside her table. "Your favorite! Mm, mm, mm. A man who takes the time to find out what a woman likes."

I am *so* embarrassed.

I try to look away, but what's happening on the other side of the conference table is fascinating. Hardly appropriate for a pre-Sunday meeting, but fascinating. And I'm not the only one who should be giving First Grace's treasurer my undivided attention but instead am watching Chip smoosh a purple ball with jiggly spines. Harriet's also watching, as is Stephano, whose dismay turns pained when Chip compresses the ball so hard that it births a translucent purple bubble out the side—right on top of the table.

Mouth forming an *O,* Chip leans around the little guy in his lap. Eight-month-old Radnor tears his eyes from the deformed purple ball to take in his daddy's face, then beams and rubs his chubby hands together.

Sooo cute! Certain I'm not the only one who thinks so, I glance around. Stephano still looks pained. Okay. Harriet gives me a toothsome smile and winks. See!

I start to sweep past Bea only to back up. Her pinched mouth of minutes earlier is relaxed and the corners slightly tilted. Unfortunately, once she becomes aware of my attention, her lips compress and lids narrow.

You're not fooling me, Beatrice Dawson! I move on to the man who occupies the chair beside the vacant one between him and our organist.

Maddox is also watching Chip, Radnor, and the spiny purple ball. But like Bea, he becomes aware of my regard, and for an unguarded moment, we smile at each other.

Pink flamingos, Harri!

Radnor shrieks, causing our aged treasurer to fall silent.

At the cessation of Joe's droning—something about a new procedure for counting the Sunday offering—all eyes that weren't already on Chip and son turn to them to find that the purple ball has birthed a bubble out the other side.

Our youth pastor grimaces. "Sorry." He picks it up. "Isn't this the coolest thing you've ever seen?"

Bea harrumphs, but Joe nods. "Never seen anything like it."

Chip smiles all around, then pushes his chair back and, gripping Radnor, rises. "We'll just…" He juts his chin at the back wall. "…stand over there."

Ten minutes later, whether or not any of us are involved in the handling of the Sunday offering, we're clear on the new procedure. Then Oona's running us through a set of glossy children's Sunday school materials under consideration to replace our outdated ones. As always, she's articulate, organized, and maddeningly suited for church leadership. Unlike some of us. But, God willing, this time next year someone more qualified will step into my shoes and I'll be running the café.

"You're up, Harri."

I gaze at Pastor Paul. "Uh…right."

Lord, please help me to speak clearly and present the movie night event with enthusiasm and confidence. And if they hate it, help me not to take offense. It is, after all, Maddox's idea.

I snatch up the bulletin inserts for Friday's miniretreat and hand them off to my right. As I do so, Stephano catches my eye and smiles, something he's done a lot lately, and it's getting to me. He has such a nice smile.

Once everyone has a flier, I explain how this movie night will differ from others and what they can do to help promote the event. With the exception of Bea, whose low grunts let it be known that she couldn't care less, the event is received with interest. To top it off, Oona and Chip commit to coordinating the child care.

Maddox smiles encouragingly, and I stand taller. "So let's get the word out, hmm?"

All rise, bringing an end to the meeting.

I bend to retrieve my purse and catch sight of the red and white bag in the front pocket. Time to celebrate. As the conference room empties, I pull out the packet and carefully open the seal to prevent a spill that would leave me Jelly Belly-less. The little yellow one nestled atop the others calls to me. Lemon. Always a winner.

"Harri?"

I return the packet to my purse, then look to where Stephano leans a shoulder against the door frame. "Yes?"

"What are you doing tonight?"

Once again, I war with myself—wanting to bite but afraid of the sharp hook that could prove difficult to remove.

"Um…"

Maddox appears in the doorway. "Excuse me, Stephano." He meets my gaze. "Just wanted to say good job, Harri."

I glance from Maddox, who's smiling, to Stephano, who has lost his smile. "Thanks."

Stephano straightens. "Have a nice evening, Harri."

I'm half relieved, half annoyed. "You too."

As he turns away, Maddox steps farther into the room.

Why do I have this feeling that his return was calculated? Narrowing my lids at him, I pop lovely lemon in my mouth and crush it between my teeth. Then I'm gasping. That was no lemon. That was mango. In disguise!

I practically leap the table to reach the wastebasket next to the door. *Spit. Spit. Hack. Hack.*

"Are you sick?"

I shake my head, scrape my tongue with my teeth, and spit some more.

Maddox's shoes come alongside me. "Something you ate?"

I jerk my head up. "A mango Jelly Belly." I bend forward again.

"You ate a mango? I thought you didn't like them."

"I don't! The little bugger was impersonating a lemon. Not a green fleck in sight. It happens, you know." I shudder in remembrance of the few times I've been tricked.

He chuckles. "I'll get you some water."

Why didn't I think of that? I watch him cross to the side table where a water pitcher sits. Feeling just this side of stupid, I spit some more.

"Here you go." Maddox thrusts a cup beneath my nose.

I gulp down the water, but despite my efforts, the mango taste lingers. "I don't suppose you have any gum—of the mint variety?"

"Always." He pulls a pack from his pocket. "Doublemint."

Recalling the night outside my mobile home when he offered me a choice between Juicy Fruit and Doublemint in lieu of a cigarette, I accept the piece he hands me and chew it for all it's worth.

"Better?"

"Yes, thanks."

"I guess this means you owe me one."

"What?"

He nods at the packet that peeks from my purse. "A Jelly Belly, one of my choosing."

"You're kidding."

"Remember our deal? That mango you ate was mine, so you owe me one." He sticks out a hand.

"Fine." I drop my precious supply of Jelly Bellys into his palm. *Please don't pick an orange sherbet, or chocolate, or strawberry cheesecake—*

"Root beer," he says.

Or root beer.

He picks out a brown bean and hands me the packet.

"If you want, I'll sort out the beans you like, and you can take them with you."

"Nah, I'll get them later."

I return the packet to my purse. "Well, thank you for the tip this morning—Jelly Belly *and* monetary—and for giving Melody her own stash of beans."

"I'm glad it made her happy." Maddox leans back on his heels. "I was impressed with your presentation."

"Thank you. And thanks for the idea…and the flier…" I frown. "You should have been the one to present it. I was just along for the ride."

He shrugs. "It was a team effort, but speaking of rides, once my work at First Grace is done, I'd like to take you out on my motorcycle."

I gape at him. "I told you, I'm not into motorcycles. They're dangerous."

"Look, Harri, it's only an 800 cc—"

"No, it's a 1298 cc…"

I've seen Maddox grin before, but the light in his eyes has never been so bright. "Just checking to make sure you knew it as well."

I put my hands on my hips. "All right, so at one time I *was* into motorcycles, but that part of my life is in the past, and that's where it's going to stay."

"Chicken."

I will *not* succumb to peer pressure. Even though it would be a good excuse to feel the wind in my face again—

Oh, no you don't!

Maddox pushes his hands into his pockets. "So about your pink-plastic-feathered friends… Forgive me?"

I make a face, then turn and, over my shoulder, say, "Maybe."

He follows me into the corridor. To my relief, he heads in the opposite direction, but not before tossing at my back, "*Maybe's* halfway to *yes*. I can live with that."

Ten

Harri's Log:

- Day of the showdown between Bea and the invaders
- 5 days until the "Oldies but Goodies" miniretreat
- 5 days until the next rerun of *The Coroner* (must locate VCR manual)
- 20 days until Jelly Belly replenishment (Thank goodness for Maddox's "tips")
- 204 days until the completion of Bible #8

he removal of the pink flamingos is a blip in the lives of most park residents. Sure there were a few calls on my answering machine following yesterday's meeting, but no one's up in arms. Except Bea…

I look up from my hymnal to where she holds court at the front of the church, and I offer up a silent prayer that last week's showdown won't repeat itself.

"Taken?" asks a voice to my right. And there in the aisle stands Maddox eyeing the empty space beside me.

Why didn't I set my Bible there? I shake my head and duck behind the hymnal. A moment later, we stand shoulder to shoulder.

"Share?" He leans toward me.

"Uh…" Unfortunately, there's no other hymnal in the seat pocket. Grudgingly, I shift mine toward him and am grateful when he doesn't attempt to assist in holding it.

As the stragglers root out seats, Bea starts in on the next hymn—a very old one I haven't heard in forever. And I'm not the only one, as evidenced by the predominantly aged voices and the rustle of hymnals being searched for the page listed in the bulletin. I find it quickly and add my voice to the others.

With a sigh, Maddox taps the page where the date of the hymn is listed—1726—then nods to a group of visibly bored youth. One is even blowing bubbles!

"You have to engage them," Maddox breathes in my ear. "Engage, engage, engage."

Tempted to pinch him for causing a shiver to run down my spine, I sing louder.

To the relief of all—honestly, the ripple could be felt!—Bea rises at the conclusion of the hymn and makes her way to her front row seat. To my surprise, Jack, who prefers to sit at the back, is there.

As with last week's service, Blake greets everyone and thanks Bea. "Now, if you'll open your bulletins, you'll find an insert." Paper rustles around the sanctuary. "Our women's ministry director has an awesome evening planned for the ladies, complete with child care for those with young children. So after the service, please sign up to attend."

A murmur of interest goes around the sanctuary.

Down, pride! Down! It wasn't you. It was Maddox. And God!

"Now if you'll pull out the second insert, you'll find the words for the songs we're going to lift up to the Lord. God willing, next Sunday the words will be projected on a screen behind me."

A moment later, the guitars, drums, electric keyboard, and piano are off and running, and I'm as tense as a rat backed into a corner.

"Thinking about taking off again?"

Maddox has got to stop breathing in my ear! I jerk my head around. "Is that what you're doing here? Blocking my escape?"

"No, that's just a bonus."

I clench my hands, causing the bulletin to crumple.

"Come on, Harri—"

He's breathing in my ear again!

"—give it a chance."

I will *not*. Not when that so-called music makes me want to cut loose, toss my hands high, and move! I know where that leads—to no good.

"Close your eyes and listen. If you don't want to sing the words, pray them."

Oh! I just tapped my foot. Or maybe that was a cramp.

"You know you want to."

"I do *not*."

Lord, my old self is lifting its head and sniffing the air. You don't want that. You like the new Harri, not that wild thing who turned from You and partied, partied, partied!

"David danced in the streets." Maddox raises his eyebrows.

"That was different."

He sighs and returns his attention to the band. When the timbre of his voice wends toward my ears, I cross my arms over my chest.

Yes, David praised the Lord in a mighty way, but he didn't then go and smoke a pack of cigarettes, drink too much, and awaken in a very bad place the morning after. Well, there was that indiscretion with Bathsheba...

Sorry, Lord. I'd like to raise my hands and voice, but who knows where that might lead. Well, You know, but I don't trust myself. I was bad. And what if, deep down, I'm still bad?

You've been forgiven, Harri, a little voice squeezes in. *When are you going to accept it and trust God to be sufficient?*

"Don't even think about it, mister!"

Dumplin' pauses midreach.

I shake my head. "Don't you dare."

He looks back at the object of his desire, then squats and begins to lick the very paw with which he nearly sank his claws into my sofa.

Did I win the battle, or will those claws be out again the moment I turn away?

"I'm keeping an eye on you." I back into the kitchen where my avocado and tomato sandwich awaits a slice of swiss and a smear of mayo to serve as my dinner.

I plop the swiss on and crane my neck to check on Dumplin'. Still licking.

Spread the mayo. Licking the other paw.

Crown the whole thing with another piece of bread. Licking his neck. (How *do* they do that?)

Slice the sandwich and set it on a plate. Working on his lower chest.

Carry my sandwich into the living room. Plops down and starts in on his belly.

Take a bite as I lower to a chair. Lifts his head and looks toward the screen door.

A moment later, I also hear the voices and, as they draw near, identify one as belonging to Maddox. I make it to my feet just as he and Mrs. Feterall arrive on my porch.

"Oh, Harri, listen to this," Mrs. Feterall says when she spots me heading toward them. "Maddox here fixed my dishwasher."

Bracing a smile, I open the screen door. "That's great."

Maddox, wearing a white T-shirt and faded jeans, catches my eye, momentarily fixes on my mouth, and winks. Winks!

Mrs. Feterall walks past me. "So I told him about your leaky plumbing, and he said he could fix it. Go on, Maddox." She shoos him toward the kitchen. "Have a look."

I ease the screen door closed. "Actually, it's a small leak— nothing I lose sleep over." That old soup pot works just fine, and I only have to empty it twice a week.

"I'll take a look." As Maddox crosses into the kitchen, my gaze is drawn to the back pocket of his jeans that holds a screwdriver and a wrench. Manly. No little toolbox for Maddox McCray.

"Oh me! Isn't this your mother's cat, Harri?"

I shift my regard to that good-for-nothing lump who has resumed his bathing—below his belly! "That's Dumplin', all right. Tyler needed a break, so he dropped him here."

"He must have been desperate."

Who *hasn't* my mother told about the rift between me and that cat?

Mrs. Feterall crosses to the sofa. "Here, kitty, kitty."

Good luck. Dumplin' is not a "Here, kitty, kitty" kitty. He's a—

Dumplin' steps lightly to her and rubs against her calves.

He's just trying to make me look bad. I turn and head into the kitchen. As Maddox reaches into the cabinet beneath the sink, his short sleeve rides up and I catch sight of the jawbone of a skull. "Nice tattoo," pops out of my mouth, the same thing he said to me the night he glimpsed the crown of thorns circling my upper arm.

He pokes his head out and grins. "Leftovers."

That's how *I* responded! Except I was self-conscious, whereas he doesn't seem the least concerned about revealing his wild side. And to prove it, he pushes up the sleeve to reveal the tattoo in its hideous entirety. "A little much, hmm?"

I transfer my gaze from the hollow-eyed skull to Maddox's darkly deep eyes. "Considering your line of work, you ought to have that thing removed."

He lets the sleeve fall. "It goes with the motorcycle."

Ah! I start to retreat, but he pulls me back with "How many signed up for Friday's event?"

My indignation wanes as I'm shot through with the excitement I felt while staffing the booth. "It was the most amazing thing." I advance toward him. "In all, thirty-two ladies signed up—young and old. And we'll probably hear from more this week. Why, it's possible we could have as many as fifty."

"Great."

I draw a breath. "Thank you for your help."

"You owe me one."

I freeze. Owe him? What?

He ducks back beneath the cabinet. "Just don't let me leave here without my Jelly Bellys and we'll call it even."

Whew! "Sure." I turn away.

When Maddox enters the living room five minutes later, I'm glowering at Dumplin' from my recliner. The sycophant is purring loudly where he stretches alongside Mrs. Feterall's thigh. Just to spite me.

"All fixed." Maddox halts beside me. "It just needed a good turn of the wrench."

I push up out of the chair. "Thanks."

"Look, Maddox, isn't he wonderful?" Mrs. Feterall rubs Dumplin' beneath the chin. "I love cats." She gasps. "Harri, maybe we could arrange a play date for Pucker and Dumplin'."

A play date? They are *not* children. They're cats. Finicky little—

Oh dear, she seems so hopeful. "I…guess we could." A light comes on in my head. "Or maybe Dumplin' could come to your place for a sleepover."

She frowns. "First we need to make certain they play well together."

Feeling Maddox's gaze, I look at the bookcase where he slipped off to. He raises his eyebrows, then returns to my shelves. "Quite a collection of Bibles."

I have no reason to feel as if I've been caught with a controlled substance, but I'm flushed with guilt. "Would you like a glass of iced tea?"

"Thank you, but Mrs. Feterall filled me up." He runs a finger across the spines. "King James, New King James, Holman Christian Standard, the Living Bible, New American Standard, New International Version, the Message, God's Word Translation." His attention drops to the shelf below. "And a multitude of *God's Promises* books."

He doesn't know the half of it. Well, maybe half, since that shelf holds about half of those I've purchased over the years. The other half are on my bedroom nightstand.

Maddox turns. "Are you considering becoming a minister like your father?"

"Oh no," Mrs. Feterall says. "Harri's just well read. Reads a Bible a year, don't you, dear?"

"Something like that."

Once more, Maddox shows my mouth more attention than is warranted. "Interesting."

No, it's not! Determined to prove that I have a life, I step forward and grab a book from the shelf that holds my "keeper" fiction. "Have you read *Escape from Fred*?" I turn the cover toward him. "It's about a preacher's son. Funny."

His mouth twitches. "I've read it, as well as the first two in the series."

I return the book to its slot. "Then there's Linda Windsor, Tracey Bateman, Rachel Hauck, Allison Pittman—"

"Do you read anything besides Christian fiction?"

"From time to time." No need to clarify that the last time I shopped in a bookstore other than my friendly Christian one was years ago.

"I should get back to Mr. Feterall." Mrs. Feterall gives Dumplin' a parting rub.

"I'll walk you home." Maddox sounds all gallant, but I know about the skull tattoo.

I hurry into the kitchen and retrieve the Ziploc that contains four Jelly Bellys. "Here you are." I thrust the bag at Maddox as he holds the screen door for Mrs. Feterall.

"Thanks." He focuses on my mouth again, then touches his own. "Uh, Harri…"

Surely he doesn't think he's owed a kiss for fixing my leak? I cross my arms over my chest and shake my head.

He starts to say something, then leans in and swipes the corner of my mouth with an index finger.

I stumble back. "What do you think you're doing?"

He turns his finger out to reveal a smear of mayo.

That's why he kept staring at my mouth. I smile sheepishly. "Thanks."

"Anytime."

And he means it. Despite his insistence that the timing is wrong, Maddox doesn't seem able to help himself.

Lord, why did You throw him in my path? And Stephano! You know I'm not ready for this. Ah! You're testing me. Well, I intend to pass with flying colors. Then, when You're good and ready, You'll give me someone to settle down with.

"Good night, Harri."

I jerk my chin. "Good night."

Maddox takes Mrs. Feterall's arm and guides her down the stairs.

I watch them until my tummy sends up an SOS, then turn back to my avocado and tomato—

There's Dumplin'. On the table. Crouched by my plate. Licking the mayo oozing out the side of my sandwich.

Harri's Log:
- Day of Sabrina—"Oldies but Goodies" miniretreat
- 7 days until the next rerun of *The Coroner* (VCR ready for tonight's episode!)
- 15 days until Jelly Belly replenishment (halfway mark!)
- 199 days until the completion of Bible #8

Eleven

*G*reat event, Harri."

That's the consensus, but it's nice to hear from Pastor Paul's wife. Remembering the lively discussion that followed the double feature, I smile. "I gather you're a Harrison Ford fan."

Leah glances around to be certain we aren't overheard by the ladies cleaning up. "That Bogart *has* to be an acquired taste. Honestly, I just don't see it. As for Audrey Hepburn, she was perfect!"

Which is where many of the younger women crossed over. They *loved* Audrey. As for the older women, several were impressed with Harrison and admitted he was every bit as good-looking as Humphrey. But the discussion got good when we turned to themes relevant to the Christian life, and Leah showed a side of herself I'd only ever glimpsed. The woman really knows her Bible.

She sighs. "I wish I could have convinced Anna to come, but she's distant lately. That teenage thing, you know."

"Is everything all right?"

"No." Leah's shoulders dip. "As a matter of fact, I've been wanting to talk to you, as you understand better than anyone what Anna's going through."

Oh dear.

"Everyone expects so much from her, including her father and me. There isn't room for mistakes, especially with everyone watching her every move. Her skirt's too short. Is that mascara she's wearing? Why is she talking to that boy?" Leah's voice rises. "Shouldn't she be more involved in the youth group? Surely the preacher's daughter should set a better example—"

"Leah." I nod at the other ladies who are attempting to appear uninterested.

"I…I'm sorry. I shouldn't be burdening you."

"You're not. Why don't we talk outside?"

Shortly, we sit on a bench beneath moonlit clouds.

"So how is Anna dealing with the pressure of being under the microscope?" I ask.

"How did you deal with it?"

The muscles in my face tighten, but it's a reasonable question. "Not well, as you've probably heard."

She nods. "I'm starting to fear that Anna might react the same, especially because this has been a long time in coming."

"Oh?"

"She went through a difficult time at the last church Paul pastored when—" Leah shakes her head. "The thing is that these hormones of hers are all over the place, and with all the changes at First Grace, she's growing away from us."

Just as I did with my family.

"I don't know what to do." Her voice catches. "When you were in Anna's place, what did you need?"

I turn my face up to the sky that offers not the slightest breeze to clear the warm, humid air wafting across my skin. What *did* I need? "I don't know, though I do remember being lonely. That it felt as if there wasn't anyone I could talk to or trust."

"Because you felt betrayed."

I smile wryly. "You've heard it all."

"I'm sorry, but people talk."

Of course they do. "Yes, because I felt betrayed, but also because of the pedestal I was trying to keep my balance on. As you know, preacher's kids aren't supposed to make mistakes, question their faith, or have lives outside their parents' ministry. They're supposed to be perfect."

She closes a hand over mine. "Harri, would you talk to Anna?"

Panic flutters up my throat. "But I don't know her. Beyond a 'hi' here and there, we've done little more than make eye contact."

"I know, which is why I thought I'd bring her to next month's event. Perhaps you could strike up a conversation."

With a brooding teenager? Oh dear. "Um, that might be difficult."

Her hand squeezes mine. "You'll try, won't you?"

Double dear. Of course, what's the likelihood Anna will show up for Quilt Till You Wilt/Crop Till You Drop? "I'll try, but don't expect a miracle."

Are those tears in her eyes?

"Thank you. And thank you for putting together tonight's event. I enjoyed it, especially seeing the older ladies chumming with the younger ones."

They *were* chumming. I had smiled at aged voices mixing with youthful chatty ones. Warmed to hear Lorraine Ibbley sharing a recipe with two young ladies and the three giggling when Lorraine advised the use of puréed prunes as a sugar substitute. Been touched when I overheard Mrs. Feterall using Scripture to console a young woman.

"Harri?"

I startle to find Leah's face near mine, her hand on my shoulder. "Are you all right?"

"I was just…somewhere else." I push up off the bench. "I'm glad you enjoyed tonight. Hopefully, the quilting and scrapbooking event will be as successful."

She stands. "I'm sure it will."

"Even without a day spa giveaway?"

"That was definitely a draw. I have *never* seen Emily so animated."

None of us have. The thirty-five-year-old woman, who still wears her Mennonite head covering despite having attended First Grace for five years, went from shoulders hunched and nose stuck in a Styrofoam cup to shoulders thrown back and nose in the air as she rushed forward to claim her prize. "Yes, that was a side to her I haven't seen."

Leah gives me a hug. "Good night, Harri."

We pull apart, and I feel off balance, as if I've had something to drink that I shouldn't. And yet, it's not an unpleasant feeling. "Good night, Leah."

She turns, and as I start to follow, I'm struck by a scent. Maddox is right. Irises do smell like grapes. But why am I only now noticing it when I've been sitting among them for the past quarter hour? I look up, but the stars Maddox encouraged me to take in are hidden by clouds. And, suddenly, I want to see them.

A half hour later, having assisted with the remaining cleanup, I replay my conversation with Leah as I traverse Red Sea Lane. I'm surprised that I opened up to her—not in any detail, but more than I usually allow. As for Anna…

I let myself into my mobile home, put the talk I agreed to out of my mind, and focus on *The Coroner* rerun that awaits me. But before I switch on the light, I sense—rather, *see*—trouble. The VCR lights should be lit.

I flip on a lamp, which sends Dumplin' running. *And well he should,* I fume as I catch sight of the chewed cord that's been pulled from the socket. *Well he should!*

"No, Harri."

"But you don't even know why I'm calling—"

"You want me to take Dumplin'. Well, I'm not going to. Two cats are too many for a bachelor—the smell, the litter they track everywhere, and the fights those two get into. No. Dumplin' is all yours."

I grit my teeth. "All right, but we could trade. Dumplin' for Doo-Dah."

"No."

I sag against the headboard. "Why?"

"It's called responsibility."

Something he doesn't think I'm capable of, though surely I've proven myself time and again.

"Look, Harri, for the past nine months I've had both cats—"

"But you're a cat person!"

"The point is that the burden has been on me. You didn't even offer—"

"You were the natural choice, especially since you'd just lost George…" *Oh, why did you bring that up? You know he's sensitive about that mangy cat.* "Sorry." Of course, is it my fault that his gallivanting feline ignored the advice not to play in the streets at night? He was worse than Dumplin', always getting into scraps—

That's why Tyler dumped Dumplin' on me rather than Doo-Dah. Because of the scrap Dumplin' and George got into years ago that left the latter minus a piece of ear. Tyler was *not* happy. In fact, it's amazing that he didn't unload Dumplin' on me sooner. I ought to be grateful.

Yes, you should. If he'd turned down Mom, all of it would have been in your lap, which was the original plan per her suggestion that you move home while she and Dad were on mission.

I sigh. "No problem, Ty. I've got Dumplin' covered. In fact…" *Do I have to?* "…if you need a break, I'll take Doo-Dah off your hands."

Silence.

"Hello?" Did he hang up on me? "Hello?"

He did, and though I accept that things aren't well between us, I'm hurt. It has been years since he hung up on me.

Sinking farther down the headboard, I push the handset's Off button, only to yelp when the phone rings. Since it's approaching ten, I consider not answering, but when one lives among senior citizens, late-night calls are not to be taken lightly.

"Hello?"

"You hung up on me."

What's he doing on the other end? "No, Ty. *You* hung up on *me.*"

"No, I didn't. I was just in shock."

Replaying the conversation that ended with my offer to take Doo-Dah off his hands, I roll my eyes. "Hardy-har-har."

"Seriously, that was a nice offer. Thank you."

He's acknowledging that I did something right? I start to go all warm and fuzzy, which is a state usually reserved for the restocking of Jelly Bellys, but then he speaks again.

"I may be going out of town next month, so I'll keep your offer in mind."

Good-bye, warm and fuzzy.

"It was a sincere offer, wasn't it, Harri?"

"Yes. I'd love to do it." So I'm exaggerating, especially tossing out *love* in reference to Dumplin' *and* Doo-Dah, but Tyler rarely responds to a peace offering—so rarely that it has been a while since I made an effort.

"Great. So how's the job going?"

This can*not* be my brother. "Which one?"

"At the church. I understand lots of changes are happening over there."

Which he must have heard of through friends, as he now attends a megachurch—the better to blend into the background, I heard him tell Mom.

"Yes, First Grace is going through changes. You'd hardly recognize it."

"And you're okay with that?"

"Not really, but some of the changes are for the better, I suppose."

"You're not causing trouble, are you?"

The hair on my neck rises. "As little as possible."

His silence has teeth. "You do realize that the reason Mom and Dad undertook this mission was to give the new pastor room to make First Grace his own?"

"The thought occurred to me." I wince at my sarcasm. *Great! The longest conversation you've had with Ty in years and you're about to blow it!* I draw a deep breath. "You know, you might like the new First Grace. You ought to drop by."

"No, thanks. I'm good where I'm at."

His tone warns of what's coming, and I flounder for a way to keep him on the line, at least until we get back to the semblance of civility I enjoyed after my offer to keep Doo-Dah. "How about you, Tyler? How's the world of accounting?"

"Not too bad now that April 15 is behind me. Look, Harri, I've got to go."

"Oh. Good night."

Hearing the click, I'm swamped by a feeling of loss. Though I regret the mess my rebellion made of my relationships, the one with Tyler carries the deepest wounds outside of those inflicted on my parents. I miss my big brother, and if I could restore what he lost years ago, I would. But she's long gone. And I'm to blame.

Twelve

- 4 days until the next rerun of *The Coroner* (must duct tape VCR cord)
- 12 days until Jelly Belly replenishment
- 196 days until the completion of Bible #8

I had a blessedly uneventful weekend. On Saturday, I fobbed off Maddox's table on Lisa (probably should have thought that through, as it cost me a Jelly Belly tip and I've been "clean" two days too many). The meeting at church went well, except for the amount of attention Stephano paid me, Bea's bitter comments about the projection screen, and Maddox's announcing the formation of a "vision" committee to be comprised of a diverse group of church members. On Sunday, Maddox sat elsewhere when I squeezed a place for myself between two hefty ladies, Bea behaved, and the introduction of the projection screen suffered a setback when the bulb didn't light and the replacement bulbs couldn't be found.

Okay, so not exactly uneventful, especially in light of the mutterings when the band started up and the contemporary music selections weren't to be found in our hymnals. I really didn't care for the looks some of the younger folks slid Bea's way, as if she was responsible for the AWOL bulbs. Of course, her smug expression didn't help.

Today at the café, she sits alone at one of four tables that have been pushed together for the Red Hat Society meeting held the third Monday of each month. Elegantly decked out in a flowered hat and purple gloves, she wears a wistful expression.

No, she wouldn't sabotage the projection screen. As I start to turn away, a slow smile spreads across her face. Though I'd bet a handful of Jelly Bellys (had I a club-sized container) that she isn't smiling at anyone in particular, I follow her gaze.

That would have cost me a lot of Jelly Bellys. I glance from a smiling Jack, who must have slipped in while I was in the kitchen, back to Bea, who gives him a wave. Dare I hope romance is in the air for these two who've lost their spouses?

"Oh, look! Bea's already here."

I turn and meet Harriet's twinkling eyes beneath the brim of a red pillbox hat edged with purple feathers.

"Of course she's here." Pam, whose arm is linked with Harriet's, pushes back her red cowgirl hat to better display a flamboyant blond wig. "Bea's always early."

Harriet halts before me, and I curtsy to the founder of First Grace's chapter of Red Hatters. "Greetings, Queen Harriet."

As I straighten, she gives me a nod and smoothes her purple drop-waist dress. "Everything in order?"

I size up the early lunch crowd that occupies a fourth of the available tables. An hour from now, it will be a different matter. "Yes, Your Majesty. Allow me to show you to your seat." Hostess is a role I play every month, and one I never miss, though I have to swap my usual morning shift at the café with my afternoon shift at church.

As Harriet and Pam take their seats, Harriet scans the tables. "I understand we're expecting a larger-than-usual turnout."

I unfold her napkin and hand it to her. "Mrs. Feterall invited a potential member to join you, Lorraine's bringing one herself, and Elva's daughter, Maria, is coming."

"Maria!" Bea pins Harriet with her gaze. "She's not fifty."

Harriet inclines her head. "Next year, I believe."

"But we're a Red Hatter group, not a Pink Hatter."

Pam turns to Bea. "That's because no one under fifty has been interested in joining. Of course, if they'd like to join, they're welcome to."

Color blooms on Bea's cheeks. "Says who?"

"Says the Red Hat Society," Harriet intercedes. "And I wouldn't be opposed to having younger ladies join us. It would liven things up a bit."

Bea scowls. "We don't need livening."

Pam rolls her eyes heavenward. "Lord, would You give our friend Bea something to smile about? She's ruining a perfectly good day."

Bea smacks the table with a gloved palm. "Don't you be praying for me, Miss Hoity-Toity."

I brandish my order pad. "Ladies, can I get you something to drink while you wait for the rest of your party?"

Bea glances toward Jack, then lowers her hands to her lap.

"What do you think about younger ladies joining our group, Harri?"

I blink at Harriet. "I think it would be great if Maria became a Pink Hatter. She'd fit right in." A sidelong peek at Bea reveals narrowed lids and tightly pressed lips. If not for Jack's presence, she'd have a lot to say to me.

Shortly, I scurry off with their drink order, and when I return, they've been joined by Elva, Maria, and Lorraine Ibbley. But that's not all. I falter at the sight of the lady on Lorraine's right, who wears a pink hat rather than red and a lavender outfit rather than purple. As if joining the Red Hatters is a done deal. Why, she can't be much older than me! What's Lorraine thinking? Yes, Pink Hatters are welcome, but this woman is a bit young—by at least a decade! And just where did Lorraine find her?

Ah! Church. She's one of the two with whom Lorraine was sharing her pruney recipe this past Friday. So much for all that chumming.

"Coming through!" Mrs. Feterall sings out. "We're late!"

I sidestep, and she pats my arm in passing. Her red pirate's hat with its purple plume buoys my mood, and I smile. However, as she hastens toward her fellow Red Hatters with a guest in tow, my buoy deflates. Another Pink Hatter. Hopefully, not of the twenty-something/almost-thirty variety—

The twenty-something glances over her shoulder. "Hiya, Harri."

Vi is Mrs. Feterall's guest? She's nowhere near thirty! In fact, she's barely out of her coming-home-from-the-hospital pink stocking cap!

I stare at the group as they greet one another—except Bea, who looks like I feel. This will *never* work! The age gap is too wide.

"Who would have thought?" Gloria draws alongside me, her smile rubbing against the grain of my emotions. "Makes me want to take red spray paint to one of my old straw hats."

"But you've never expressed an interest in becoming a Red Hatter."

She winks. "Perhaps once I retire, which is in the near future, I believe."

Warmed by the dream that momentarily displaces the chilly threat under which my emotions labor, I nod. "Yes, the near future."

She lays an arm across my shoulder. "I'm looking forward to it, though I have no idea what I'll do with all that time I'll have on my hands."

I smile. "Enjoy life."

"Doing what? Twiddling my thumbs?"

"Well, for starters, you'll be able to sleep in, spend more time with friends, travel, maybe take up gardening—"

"Grow old." Her voice catches, lids flicker, mouth compresses, causing alarms to go off in the middle of my dream.

I don't want to ask the question that settles like dead weight around me, but I have to. "Gloria, are you sure you want to sell the café?"

"I'm sure, Harri." She sighs. "It's just that I've begun to wonder how I'm going to fill my days. Oh, on the surface, retirement sounds wonderful, but it's bound to get old. And drag me down with it. Maybe what I really need is a change."

I'm relieved that my dream is intact, but I'm worried for her. "Like what?"

"I wish I knew." She throws a hand up. "But now is not the time to explore options. We've got work to do." She starts to turn away but comes back around. "Will you have time this week to sit down with me and Ruby to discuss the fall menu?"

One of my contributions—a menu that changes with the seasons. "Sure, but with all that's going on with the women's ministry, it will have to be in the evening."

"That's fine."

She heads back to her hostess stand with her usual bustle and sense of purpose. What *will* Gloria do when she passes the café into my hands?

"Oh, Harri!" Harriet beckons. And once more I'm faced with a table full of Red Hatters and the Pink Hatters who have launched an invasion.

Over the next half hour, I try not to be offended when the Pink Hatters agonize over the lunch selections they deem to be too high in carbs—Maria excluded (she fits, as I knew she would). I try to hide my frustration when the side salads are left untouched ("light" dressing isn't light enough). I try to hide the roll of my eyes when a chicken tortilla soup is sent back to the kitchen for another *without* the swirl of sour cream. I try not to snort when the Pink Hatters order peach cobbler and chess pie and all but lick their plates clean. Moreover, I try to stamp out my jealousy when I observe the three generations enjoying one another's company…and my smugness when Bea refuses to be drawn into a conversation with the Pink Hatters…and my disappointment when Lorraine's guest makes Bea crack a smile.

As the group draws out their visit over refills of coffee and tea, the lunch crowd picks up and Gloria asks me to take two more tables.

"I hear your movie night was a success," Lisa says as I enter the beverage station.

My hackles rise, not because the event was a success, but because of what that success appears to have bred. "We had a great turnout." I set out three glasses.

"Seems like there's some bonding going on with your ladies. Must make you feel good to know you're part of the positive changes happening at First Grace."

"Yeah."

"Still, it's hard, isn't it?"

Just as I'm about to pour, I leave the pitcher of fruit tea hanging over the first glass. I meet Lisa's gaze, and though denial reaches my tongue first, honesty rolls over it. "It is hard. It's happening so fast. Everything familiar is…disappearing."

Ack! What's that in my throat? And creeping up my nose? And stinging my eyes? And making my hand tremble?

Lisa takes the pitcher from me and gives me a side hug. It's over before I can protest, yet I'm not sure I would have.

"Listen, Harri—"

"Hello, Harri…Lisa."

I swing around, and there's Maddox with one foot in the beverage station—a big no-no, especially as there's all this wet stuff in my eyes.

He frowns. "Is everything all right?"

"Yes." I clench my hands to keep from wiping my eyes. "What are you doing here?" Hardly friendly, but it has the desired effect of distracting him from my emotional state.

He shrugs. "Having lunch."

"But you're a Saturday regular, and it's Monday."

"Is there a rule against frequenting the café on Monday?"

"Of course not. It's just…you surprised me." *At an awkward time, I might add.*

"That's a relief. For a moment, I thought you were unhappy to see me." He glances at Lisa. "So are you going to shove me off on Lisa again?"

I certainly am. Oh! But mustn't be hasty—it's been days since I had a Jelly Belly fix. "I'd be happy to wait on you."

"Then I'll ask Gloria to seat me at one of your tables." He strides away.

"Thanks for throwing me a bone," Lisa says.

"What?"

She rolls her eyes. "Don't worry. I know it's you he's interested in. Still, it was nice waiting on him Saturday."

"But he's not interested—"

"Get real. The man knows what he wants. And I think you do too."

I gasp. "Lisa Beauregard, you have no idea what you're talking about."

"Prove it." She taps my shoulder. "You." She taps her chest. "Me. Dinner at my place. Friday night."

Another Friday night without *The Coroner*? Of course, I could record it, but then I'd have to resolve the issue of the chewed VCR cord (must buy duct tape). And even if it were a night other than Friday, I'm not good at the "girlfriend" thing—all that nonsense like painting each other's toenails and sharing secrets. Not my thing. "I'd like to, but—"

"You're turning me down? And after you were ready to kiss my feet the day you nearly ended up on Maddox's lap?"

She's calling in a debt. And one I owe her for always picking up my slack when I overreach. "All right. What time?"

"Six thirty." She steps from the beverage station. "I'll do din-din. You bring dessert."

Shortly, I halt beside Maddox's table where Gloria sits leaning toward him. "Oh, Harri!" She lays a hand on my arm. "Maddox has the most interesting idea."

Oh no.

He settles back in his chair. "A monthly jamboree at the café."

"Excuse me?"

"A night out for the senior citizens." Gloria is nearly bursting with enthusiasm. "And we could offer dance lessons."

I'm stunned. And not a little annoyed. What about "old" does this man not understand? A moment later, I'm forced to eat the thought as Elva jumps out of her chair. Wielding her feather boa, she prances around the table.

All right, so they do have a bit of life left in them, but that doesn't mean they're up to dancing lessons. I force a smile. "But this is a breakfast and lunch café."

"Just once a month." Gloria nods. "And we could offer a limited menu—soups and salads and such. Maybe buffet style."

"Um…sounds like something we should discuss."

She rises. "When you and I meet with Ruby to go over the fall menu, hmm?"

"Sure." Hopefully, by then she'll have forgotten the cockamamie idea.

Gloria pats Maddox's shoulder. "Enjoy your meal."

Once she's out of earshot, he says, "I never cease to annoy you, do I?"

"I'd prefer it if you never ceased to amaze me."

"Really? I'll work on that."

I scowl. "You, Maddox McCray, are a menace. Now may I take your order?"

"After you tell me about movie night."

I almost groan at the realization that I haven't discussed it with him—unforgivable, considering he's largely responsible for its success. I clear my throat. "You didn't hear?"

"I heard the buzz on Sunday, but I'd like to know what you thought about it."

"It went over well. As a matter of fact"—I nod at the Hatters—"it's the reason we have Pink Hatters here today."

He looks at their table and raises a hand in acknowledgment.

Following his gaze, I'm jolted to discover that all the ladies are staring at us. Why? And what's with the wiggly eyebrows? I catch my breath. They think Maddox and I…

I fumble in my apron pocket. "They're wanting their checks. I'll be back."

As I hasten across the dining room, the kazoos come out—the official instrument of the Red Hat Society. Even Bea is putting one to her lips. Someone's birthday? Must be. But then, why are they still looking at me? It's not—

Oh no. It *is* nearly my birthday, and as this is as close as the ladies will get before their next meeting, this could be for me. *Could,* but there's no precedent for it. Though I've waited on them for years, they've never kazooed me.

When I'm six feet from the table, it happens. The ladies rise, and the kazoos let loose a nasal version of the birthday song, accompanied by the Pink Hatters who insert my name in the blank as they lustily sing it through.

My dismay spills over as I feel all eyes on me, especially Maddox's.

Harriet steps forward. "Happy birthday, Harri!" She hugs my stiff form and whispers, "At least pretend you enjoyed it."

As she draws back, I ease my upwardly mobile shoulders and force a smile.

"Did we surprise you?" Pam asks.

I nod. "Didn't see it coming."

Mrs. Feterall beams. "You have Maria to thank. She suggested it."

Elva's daughter winks. I *knew* she didn't fit into this group!

Vi comes around the table toting a large gift bag. "Happy birthday, Harri."

My heart leaps. Maybe it's a club-sized container of Jelly Bellys. Meaning my long wait is over. Meaning I can mark off the next twelve days on my calendar. Oh joy! As I reach for the bag, I can taste them. A whole mouthful. Mixed at random. I don't care. Even if a licorice slips in, or a cappuccino, or a mango—

Not a mango. I curl my fingers around the cord handles, but the bag gives only a slight, downward lurch as I take its full weight—its lighter-than-should-be weight. Definitely not a club-sized container of Jelly Bellys. A box, then? In that case, a random mouthful is out of the question, but if I'm careful, I could make it last twelve days.

"Go on, open it," Lorraine prompts.

My embarrassment over the kazoo serenade forgotten, I set the bag with its profusion of pink tissue on the table.

Pam stamps her foot. "Tear into it!"

They're all watching with expectant smiles, except Bea, whose mouth is pinched. Okay. Here goes. Come on, Jelly Belly! I pull the tissue out and reach in. The box is square. And black. With gold writing that spells out a brand name and description that demolishes my Jelly Belly fantasy. Unless it's a joke.

I set the box on the table, pry open the flap, and bend it back to reveal something round and glossy and pink. Not a joke. In a manner of speaking.

"Well?" Harriet says as the others twitter with excitement.

Hide your disappointment. Hide your horror. It wasn't meant to be meanspirited. But what were they thinking?! They know I don't do this anymore.

I peer at Bea from beneath my lashes. Her mouth remains puckered, but there's an I-told-you-so glint in her eyes as she regards the others.

"Take it out," Maria says.

Bea snorts. "I told you it was inappropriate."

Silence falls, then spreads to the other diners who are probably guessing the contents of the box to be along the lines of something lacy and racy.

Bea crosses her arms over her chest. "Didn't I tell you?"

"No!" I pull the pink helmet out and hold it up for all to see. "It's great."

I feel the relief that goes around the table. That wasn't so hard. But why is Pam coming at me like that?

She snatches the helmet and shoves it on my head. "You're a Pink Hatter now—a junior one of us." She lets out a cowgirl whoop and slaps me on the back.

I recover from my stagger, and Harriet gives me an encouraging smile as I stand there wearing a *pink* motorcycle helmet. Of course, it does fit pretty well. On the light side, comfortably padded, and with a good visual field. Perfect for a long ride down a country road with the wind buffeting my face. And the light color would keep my head relatively cool, unlike black that gets so hot.

"Now all she needs is a motorcycle," *that* voice says.

I whirl around.

Maddox looks me down and up. "And maybe some leather riding pants."

In that moment, I know. "It was you," I say between clenched teeth.

"Well, of course it was, dear." Mrs. Feterall plods to my side. "Maddox came for supper on Saturday, and when I mentioned that the Red Hatters couldn't decide what sort of hat to get you, he suggested a helmet. We hunted through the shops but couldn't find a pink one, so we bought a white one and Maddox painted it." She taps the glossy surface. "A nice shade, don't you think?"

"*You* were behind this?" Bea shrills.

Maddox nods.

"Why, of all the—"

"Bea?"

She jerks around, and the anger she was about to unload falters at Jack's approach.

"Can I take you home?"

She stares at him, then sweeps her gaze around the Hatters. "Yes, thank you."

He offers his arm, and I release my breath. *Thank You, God. And Jack!*

"What about my check?" Bea asks.

I pull the sheaf from my apron pocket, locate hers, and hold it out.

Jack pinches it. "My treat." He smiles into her startled face.

"Thank you, Jack. And…" Her eyes swivel to me, land on the pink helmet, and avert. "Happy birthday, Harri."

Whew! "Thank you, Bea."

Once they're out of earshot, Pam mutters, "Close call."

Lorraine shakes her head. "Poor Bea. She's really had it hard lately."

A gurgle erupts from Pam. "She's the one with a beau—and Jack at that. Do you know how long I've been making eyes at that man? *Humph!* 'Poor Bea' indeed."

"Now, Pam…" Lorraine eyes the wigged woman. "Bea needs our prayers, and we shouldn't begrudge her just because Jack is paying her attention. She's been real lonely since Edward's passing."

Vi sighs. "They say young love is cute, but I think old love is *much* cuter."

All those who fall within the parameters of "old love" give her their undivided attention.

Though Vi's comment is clear evidence that nothing good can come of admitting baby Pink Hatters to the Red Hat Society, I feel her discomfort and a sympathetic pang.

"Yes." I nod, the movement making me uncomfortably aware that I'm still wearing a pink helmet. "It is cute. We could learn a lot from…" Old lovers? Our elders? "…uh, those with more experience."

"I agree," Maddox says.

Gratitude transforms Vi's face. "I hope I didn't offend anyone."

Pam gives a hearty laugh. "You are precious, Violet Gairdt. Just precious!"

Some chuckle, some laugh, but they're all in agreement.

"Well, that wraps it up." Harriet adjourns the meeting of the Red Hat Society.

Everyone starts gathering their purses and wishing me a happy birthday as I hand them their checks. And I'm left wearing a pink helmet with Maddox at my side.

"So about that motorcycle ride."

I drag off the helmet. "I am *not* getting on a motorcycle with you."

"You don't like the helmet?"

It *is* a pretty shade of pink. And glossy. And comfortable. But I will *never* wear it as it was intended. I tuck it under an arm. "It was sweet of them, and nice of you to paint it, but it doesn't fit my lifestyle."

Annoyance flickers in his eyes. "Better a club-sized container of Jelly Bellys?"

"Exactly."

He takes a step nearer. "You know something, Harri? You need to get a life."

I stare into dark eyes that are darker than I remember and feel my defenses rise. "Look, Maddox, you can't force a person to like something she doesn't care for."

"No, but when it's fear disguised as dislike, there's plenty of wiggle room."

I gasp. "You think I'm afraid?"

"Absolutely."

"Well, you're wrong."

He juts his chin toward the front of the building, causing a curl to bounce on his brow. "My motorcycle's outside. Put that helmet on, and prove you're not afraid."

What is with everyone wanting me to prove something? First Lisa challenges me to prove I'm not interested in this man; now he's challenging me to prove I'm not afraid of a little motorcycle ride.

I huff. "Not only am I working right now, but it would be inappropriate for an employee of First Grace to be seen on a motorcycle with the hired hand."

His eyes flash, but before he can counter, a voice calls, "Harri!"

I look at Mrs. Feterall, who's waving her hat to catch my attention. "Yes?"

"Don't forget that we need to set a play date for Pucker and Dumplin'."

Great. I give her a thumbs-up, and she scoots after her fellow Hatters.

"A play date," Maddox murmurs. "*That* I'd like to see."

I'd bet he would.

"Have a good day, Harri." He stalks away.

Lowering my gaze to the pink helmet that feels more comfortable tucked beneath my arm than it should, I sigh. "What am I going to do with you?"

I thought I could be out from under the obligation of dinner with Lisa in an hour and a half and be home again before *The Coroner* came on, but it's seven fifteen and we're only now sitting down to dinner. And yet the past hour hasn't been tedious. Though I've had to steer Lisa clear of discussing my personal life, especially with regard to Maddox, the conversation has been lively. I'd forgotten how much fun she is and what a good time we had hanging together as teens before... Well, before everything that went down at church, which her family became involved in.

The reminder drops like a weight through me, and I stare at the lemon caper chicken she sets before me.

"No. Really. It was nothing." She gestures at my plate. "Just a little something I whipped up."

Her teasing jolts me. "Um...looks great."

"Oh, stop! You're making my head swell."

I chuckle. "Sorry. My mind was somewhere else. But if this tastes as good as it looks, I'll lick my plate."

"It tastes better than it looks. I studied with the best, you know."

"Sure."

She settles in the chair opposite mine and gives a toss of her head, which ten years ago would have sent a curtain of brown whipping over one shoulder, but now barely serves to shift the short brown strands on her brow. "I'm serious, Harri."

"You studied to become a chef?"

"In New York."

"But I didn't—"

"Let's say grace. It's best eaten while hot."

I bow my head, and Lisa begins. "Heavenly Father, we thank You for this meal and the company of friends."

Does she really consider me a friend?

"We thank You for the past, the present, and the future, and the certainty that all three make up Your plan for our lives."

Where is she going with this?

"Lord, as Harri and I fellowship, let us put our mistakes behind us—"

Ah.

"—enjoy the present to its fullest—"

Optimistic.

"—and be confident in knowing that when we follow You, our plans will succeed. Amen."

I lower my clasped hands. "Thank you, Lis." I haven't called her that since we were teens.

"You're welcome." She lifts her fork. "Now get ready to lick that plate clean."

It looks and smells good, but I really am surprised at how good it tastes. The chicken breast is done all the way through, and yet it's as juicy as dark meat. "Wow. You really are a chef."

"Nope."

"But you said—"

"I didn't complete my training."

"Why?" *Sheesh, Harriet! It's none of your beeswax!*

She shrugs. "I fell in love."

I stop midchew and, around the piece of chicken, say, "You did?"

"His name was Pierce, he was a fellow student, and prior to our last semester at culinary school, he decided to return to the commune where he grew up."

I can't believe she's sharing this with me.

She cuts into the baby asparagus. "Being in love, I went against my family's wishes, my conscience, and my religion, and joined him. It took me two years to realize my mistake and another year to extricate myself."

Sounds somewhat familiar.

Her gaze drops to my plate. "It's getting cold."

"Oh." Though the chicken has passed from hot to warm, it's still delicious.

"So you see, Harri, like you, I went astray. Unlike you, my family didn't welcome me back." Her smile is sad. "Well, my sister did—to a point—but my parents… They don't have much to do with me."

Just the opposite of what I've had to deal with. "I'm sorry. I didn't know." Because I wasn't interested in knowing what led her to apply for a job at the café a year ago. Because I slighted her attempts to renew our friendship. Feeling hollow at the realization that, past her smiles and banter, the heart of the one sitting across from me is heavy, I lower my fork.

"Oh no, you don't." She jabs a finger at my plate. "Lick it clean."

I said I would, didn't I? When all that remains are rivulets of lemon caper sauce, I lift the plate and stick out my tongue.

She laughs. "*That* I won't hold you to."

Still, I lick away.

"Now that's the Harri I remember."

I almost take offense, but in spite of the promises I've made myself not to allow people near enough to hurt me again, there's a fullness in my heart that's warm and comfortable and pleasantly different.

Lisa pushes back. "Time for dessert!"

My contribution, and I'm more than a little sheepish considering the time and effort she put into dinner. All I did was buy a pint of Ben & Jerry's Chunky Monkey.

I help her clear the table, and soon we carry our bowls of ice cream into the living room and settle on the couch. A clock on the entertainment center catches my eye. It's a quarter till eight.

Nothing to worry about. The VCR's programmed, and Dumplin' can't cause any mischief locked in your bedroom. The show will be waiting for you, and you won't have to sit through commercials—a bonus!

"This is good." Lisa dives into the bowl. "I love bananas."

"That's why I got it—banana ice cream with fudge and walnuts. Couldn't go wrong." I falter at the expression on her face. "What?"

"You remember that I like bananas?"

"Of course. You always had one in your lunch, and when we had sleepovers, you sliced one on your morning cereal. What's the big deal?"

"I'm just surprised that you remember."

Come to think of it, so am I.

"Thanks for remembering, Harri."

I meet her big blue gaze across the three feet between us. "It was nothing."

She considers me. "You know, it's okay to talk about the past. In fact, it's a good way to learn from it."

This is the reason I didn't want to get together. I do not need to rehash things that no longer affect me.

"When I share my story with youths at my church," she continues, "you wouldn't believe how it unburdens me to know that my bad choices can help others. Sure, it doesn't mean they won't make the same mistakes, but it gives them something to think about. And someone to talk to if they feel like it."

I start to shrug off what's heading toward a lecture, but those last words are a reminder of the favor Leah Pinscher asked. A daunting favor should her daughter, Anna, cooperate. "If a teen decides to confide in you, how do you respond?"

Interest flashes in Lisa's eyes.

Did I just open a door better left bolted, barred, and banded?

"Mostly, I listen. That's what they want—someone to sit down with them and hear what they have to say."

"That's all?"

"Usually, though, if you gain their confidence, they often start to ask questions and seek advice. And so you tell them what you learned from your mistakes, support the changes you made with Scripture, then let them decide whether or not to use what they've been given."

"Okay, but *do* they use it?" Not sure *I* would have.

"A lot of times you're just tilling the soil for someone who's better at planting a seed and growing it, but it has to start somewhere."

"I guess." I slide my spoon through a pool of melted banana ice cream and snag a chunk of fudge. As I aim it at my mouth, I glance at Lisa.

An encouraging smile awaits me. "I've told you a bit about my past. Do you want to talk about yours?"

The spoon jerks in my hand. Fortunately, the chunk plops back into the pool of banana ice cream. I shake my head. "I prefer to focus my energy on the present and the future."

"Okay, then tell me what you're going to do about Maddox."

"*Do?* There's nothing I need to do about him." Other than wait him out. And just how long does it take a church consultant to do his thing and move on?

"Well, I can tell you what I'd do if I were the one he was interested in."

"Really, Lisa—"

"I'd put that pink helmet on and ask him to take me for a ride."

I narrow my lids. "And you'd be comfortable jumping on the back of a motorcycle and letting some guy take you to only God knows where?"

She rolls her eyes. "I wouldn't 'jump on,' Maddox isn't just 'some guy,' and a ride is all it would be. Not to 'only God knows where.' A little fun. That's all."

That's what I once thought, but I know better. I set my bowl on the sofa table. "I should probably get going."

Silence is all the answer I receive, broken by a click and whir that comes from the vicinity of Lisa's modest entertainment center.

"It's just my VCR," she says dully like someone who has had the joy let out of her.

Ouch. I didn't mean to hurt her feelings. I'm simply not comfortable discussing my personal life, especially when it borders on my past.

She lowers her bowl beside mine. "Can't stand to miss one of my favorite shows, even if it is a rerun."

Speaking of which, my own VCR should be kicking on about now. If I hurry, I should be able to catch the last forty-five minutes.

"Have you ever watched *The Coroner*?"

My rear barely off the sofa, I whip my head around. "You like *The Coroner* too?"

Her eyes widen. "You like it?"

"It's my favorite show."

Her face brightens. "Well, then, why are we sitting here talking about things you don't want to talk about when we could be watching our show?" She snatches up the remote, points, and clicks.

"I should—"

"Sit down." She waves a hand. "At the first commercial I'll nuke some popcorn, and we'll have it made."

Hard to resist, especially when the familiar theme music sounds and a montage of scenes flicks across the screen.

I drop back. "Sounds good to me."

And it is good, even if strange, to sit beside her over the next hour, stuffing my face with popcorn as she stuffs hers, grumbling over my breath at the commercials as she grumbles under hers, and jointly aha-ing over the unfolding story line with which we're both familiar. Just like old times.

I'm glowing. A nice feeling, even if off-putting. Though a voice in my head warned time and again about letting my guard down, I enjoyed Lisa's company—so much that after *The Coroner* ended, I lingered and we talked. Of course, it helped that she didn't probe further. It was nice. Just two friends—

I open my eyes where I press my forehead against the steering wheel and stare into the dimness. Friends. Did I really think that? Me. Lisa. Friends? That's moving fast. We're two women with something in common, namely *The Coroner,* and that's all. Forget that we're the same age, grew up together, were once great friends, both fell away from our beliefs, and now waitress at the same café. *The Coroner* is all we have in common.

And I'm lying through my teeth—er, thoughts. As much as I don't want a friend my own age, the feeling of fullness in my heart is nice.

A tap on my window makes me jump, and I snap my chin up to meet Maddox's gaze on the other side.

Heart whacking against my ribs, I press the button in the door and lower the window. "What are you doing here?"

He folds his arms on the opening. "I was on my porch when you drove by five minutes ago. When you didn't get out, I thought there might be something wrong."

I stare into his night-darkened face. "Nothing's wrong. I was just…"

What's that smell? Cologne? No. More pleasant. Sharp. Crisp. Clean.

I peer nearer, and light from the porches up and down the street catches in his hair. It's damp, meaning he must have recently climbed out of a shower, and the scent is some brand of manly soap. Very nice. Uh…just an observation.

"You were just what?"

"Thinking."

He lights the face of his watch. "Out later than usual. It's past eleven."

"I was out with—" I scowl. "How do you know I was out later than usual? Are you spying on me?"

"Just observant." His eyes scan our sleepy little neighborhood. "Around here, it's an event to see or hear anything after nine. So where did Stephano take you?"

"Stephano?" I blurt out.

He smiles. "Never mind. Just checking."

That was a tricky way to discover if I was out with Stephano. And he does have reason to think it possible, as Stephano continues to pay me more attention than our working relationship warrants. I glower. "That wasn't very nice."

"You're right. Sorry." His face is too shadowed for me to tell if it reflects remorse, but I'll bet it doesn't.

I grab my purse, but as I reach for the door handle, he pulls it open. I swing my legs out, and he closes the door behind me.

He looks up. "Nice night."

"Yeah." I step past him and cross to my porch, only to halt when I catch sight of what sits beside the door. I'd know that shape anywhere. And the colors inside, dimmed though they are by the night. In fact, were I a dog, I could probably smell them through the container.

"Happy birthday, Harri."

I turn slowly around. "You gave me Jelly Bellys. A club-sized container."

"The little packets were getting expensive."

His smile hits me in the solar plexus, and for a moment I'm tempted to launch myself at him. Bad idea. "Thank you." I scoop up the container of forty-nine flavors. Love the clicking and clacking of all those little beans!

"Well, I'll let you get to bed."

I whip around. "Want some?"

"What?"

I thrust the container forward. "Jelly Bellys. Want a handful?" Oh my! Did I offer a handful? As this supply is eight days ahead of schedule, I'll have to portion it out through this last week of June, then through the entire month of July. I can't afford to be throwing Jelly Bellys his way.

"Sure." A moment later, Maddox settles onto the porch.

Well, I wouldn't eat licorice and mango anyway, so I'll just pick those out for him. I drop down beside him, unscrew the lid, and freeze at the absence of the plastic seal. "Oh no. It's been opened."

"Yes. I picked out the licorice and mango—didn't want you to suffer any more mango-in-lemon's-clothing mishaps."

Considerate. Unfortunately, this means I'll have to fork over the good stuff. *Selfish, Harri. Very selfish.*

I start to pass the container, only to realize how much larger his hands are than mine. Maybe I should scoop some out for him. *Stop it!* I hold it out to him.

He shakes his head. "Birthday girl goes first."

Don't mind if I do. I lower the container between us and scoop up a handful. As I withdraw my hand, Maddox reaches in and his fingertips brush mine. *Sizzle, sizzle.*

Did he feel that?

Our eyes lock.

He did.

Lowering my chin, I try to pick out the colors in my hand. Is that cotton candy? Oh, why do I have to feel what I do every time I get near this supposedly reformed rebel? Or is it toasted marshmallow? And why are my fingers still tingling? Might it be a cream soda? And does Maddox really believe I'd just up and climb on the back of his motorcycle?

"My first was a peach."

While only a foot separates us, I have an overwhelming urge to bridge the space.

He points to his mouth. "A peach."

Sure is. A very nice mouth.

"Aren't you going to eat any?"

I follow his gaze to my hand. "Oh. Of course." A moment later, I swallow and have no idea what flavor just swept a path through my taste buds.

Lord, this isn't good. Maybe Stephano, but not Maddox.

"Something wrong, Harri?"

"Nothing." I pop a Dr Pepper and chew, chew, chew. "I'm just wondering how long you expect this consult thing to take."

"Can't wait to get rid of me, hmm?" Though his mouth is on the upside of a smile, the space between us tenses. "Every church is different. Fortunately, First Grace is receptive to change, its pastor easy to work with, and there are adequate funds to transition the body into the twenty-first century." He tosses a bean into his mouth. "Once the vision statement is agreed upon and the committees in place to oversee the plans—I'm projecting four months from now—the bulk of my job here will be done. After that, I'll check in from time to time and make recommendations and adjustments where necessary."

"Then you expect to be gone before Thanksgiving."

He pauses with a bean in front of his mouth. "Afraid I'll interfere with your holiday plans? That you might be tempted to spend them with me rather than the octogenarian set, a bunch of faded, pink flamingos, and a tub of Jelly Bellys?"

I wouldn't have put it in so many words, but he sums it up so well that I'm forced to acknowledge that it is what I'm afraid of. That what I feel for him will get out of control and I'll do something that will set me back years. That I'll stumble. So hard I might not get up again. It frightens me. Pushes me toward denial—actually, a lie. And one, I realize, he's expecting.

I nod. "As I don't deal well with temptation, it's best to stay away from it."

I feel more than see his surprise and, in the silence, struggle for something to turn the conversation. "So do you like consulting?" Lame.

Maddox's gaze ranges over my face. "I do. In fact, I believe it's what God intended for me all along."

I poke through the beans. "Then you don't regret leaving the marketing firm?"

"No. However, you should know that I didn't leave. I was fired."

It's true, then. Not only kicked out of seminary, but fired from his job. How reformed can he be?

"But before your imagination gets carried away, I'll tell you what happened."

He's going to confide in me?

Maddox pours his Jelly Bellys into his shirt pocket and clasps his hands. "I worked at the marketing firm six years and made my way up through the ranks. During my last year, I began dating the daughter of one of our senior partners. Six months later, I asked her to marry me, and she accepted. Over the next four months, she tried to erase all traces of the rebel with whom I'd come to terms, elevate me to her social standing, and convert me to her faith." He smiles wryly. "Which I was too head over heels to look into before then. We'd talked about God and Jesus, and I assumed we were on the same page, but her Jesus was different from mine."

"How so?"

"Her faith taught that salvation is gained only by works—an individual's efforts rather than God's grace."

Meaning she discounted the cross—didn't believe a person could be saved simply by accepting Christ. "You're right. Her Jesus is different from ours."

Maddox nods. "Grateful we hadn't married in haste, I broke off the engagement. Two months later, I was fired."

"What reason did they give?"

"They said I wasn't doing my job, that I was unreliable and they'd received complaints from clients."

"*Did* they complain?"

"The only thing I gave them cause to complain about was my refusal to drink while entertaining them, and it had never bothered them before. In fact, it was something of a joke that they could count on me to get them home safe."

I lean back on my hands.

"But I believe it was part of God's plans, and I did learn some valuable lessons." He looks across his shoulder at me. "Of course, there is one lesson that I thought I had down but find I'm once more struggling with."

"And that is?"

He lowers his gaze to my mouth. "The one about keeping my business and personal life separate."

I push up off my hands, but that only brings us closer. And a moment later, he leans in and slides a hand around the back of my neck.

"I've wanted to do this forever," he says against my lips, then his mouth closes over mine, and I don't say no…don't pull back even though a kiss has become as foreign to me as cigarettes and alcohol. I do nothing to discourage him. Which is encouraging him, isn't it? As is my hand that slides up over his shoulder, fingers that grip the material of his shirt, lips that give as they're being given to…

Maddox draws back. "Now tell me you didn't want that too." He smiles.

What did I do? Rather, what did he do? I gasp. "You kissed me!"

He glances at my hand that, for some reason, is still gripping his shirt.

I snatch it back. "You kissed me."

He consults his watch. "Think of it as a gift—when you give someone something she really wants. In this case, for her birthday." He rises and reaches a hand to me. "It's now Saturday, give or take a minute. Happy birthday, Harri."

Ah! "Next time I'd appreciate it if you limit your gift to Jelly Bellys." I thrust my hand out only to frown over the single bean stuck to the center of my palm. What happened to the others? I *know* I didn't eat them.

"You dropped them about midway," Maddox says.

I look down, and sure enough there are little beans scattered across the steps. But they had to have made some noise, and I didn't hear—

Which is the point, isn't it? I grab the Jelly Belly container and slam on the lid. "Thank you for the Jelly Bellys. And that's all." I stand. "Good night."

"'Night, Harri."

I let myself into my mobile home and groan as Dumplin' cries mournfully from my bedroom. Happy birthday to me…

Fourteen

Harri's Log:
- Day of Dumplin'/Pucker play date (must think positive)
- 5 days until *The Coroner* rerun (tempted to have Lisa over)
- 31 days until Jelly Belly replenishment (Maddox is good for some things)
- 190 days until the completion of Bible #8

irst Grace will never be the same. Not that I thought it would after everything that's happened, but it was still recognizable—at least, on some levels. Now this...

As the other churchgoers file out of the sanctuary, I stare at the projection screen mounted over the baptistery and beneath our stained-glass Jesus. In huge letters, it thanks us for coming. And just about everyone is going on about how convenient it was to have the worship songs up in front of them...the scriptures Pastor Paul referenced...the talking points...

I drop my chin and wish it were yesterday again. Yesterday when Gloria forced me to take a day off in honor of my birthday and I slept in. If not for the phone call, I'm certain I would have slept past ten. It was my parents, and it lifted my spirits to hear their voices and excitement over their mission work. I'd savored the fifteen minutes I'd been gifted and refused to waste a single one on voicing concerns about the direction First Grace is headed. Of course they asked, but I made light of it. And when the conversation ended with more "Happy birthdays" and "Love yous," I felt as if I'd been given a hug.

In an effort to recapture the feeling, I close my eyes and hear their voices—Dad's all deep and rumbly, Mom's warm and cheery.

"Harri?"

Ohhh. *So* close.

Mrs. Feterall is headed down the aisle toward me, followed by Mr. Feterall, who's followed by Maddox. Why do I have this feeling I'm about to be deeply annoyed?

Mrs. Feterall halts before me. "We are still on for this afternoon, aren't we?"

I nod. "Early dinner and play date at my place."

"Wonderful! Do you mind if we bring Maddox along?"

I slam my gaze to his. I certainly do mind! After all, he kissed me! As for it being a gift, despite his conceited claim that I wanted it, I did not. And I do *not* like the look in his eyes that's full of remembrance of Friday night, nor the smile on the lips that touched mine.

Mrs. Feterall pats his shoulder. "You could use a good meal, couldn't you?"

"I could. If it's anything like Harri's chicken and dumplings, I'm in for a treat."

That's what he thinks. I'll teach him to go and kiss me without my permission! "Then it's settled. I'll see you at my home around five o'clock." And sometime between now and then I'll whip up something that will discourage him from ever again accepting an invite to my home. The…lip kisser!

I give the Feteralls a wave and hurry down the aisle. Hmm. Wonder what would sit well with Mrs. Feterall's stomach and, at the same time, offend Maddox's taste buds.

Stephano falls into step with me as I pass into the gathering area. "You don't seem happy, Harri. It's the projection screen, isn't it?"

I falter. Forgot about that, but it definitely has a lot to do with my turmoil. What in the world am I supposed to do with my hands during worship?

"A bit much, hmm?" he presses.

"You don't care for it?"

"I supported the idea when it was proposed months ago, but now I'm thinking we've gotten ahead of ourselves."

I halt. "Why are you backing off? You used to be all for these changes, and now you seem…reluctant."

He shoves his hands into his pockets. "I don't like the way things are happening. For three years I've given my time to First Grace, and at no charge because I believed it was what I was called to do. I felt I was part of this body—that I was making a difference. Now, since Paul decided to bring his friend on board, I'm being squeezed out. It's as if all my hard work has been swept under the rug." His voice catches.

I reach to him and squeeze his shoulder. "You're important to First Grace. No one discounts that."

"You really believe that?"

"I do." Movement off to the side catches my eye, and I meet Maddox's gaze where he stands in the middle of the gathering area with a young couple. And here I stand with my hand on Stephano's shoulder. I drop it.

"Seems like Maddox McCray is intent on taking everything from me," Stephano mutters.

Everything? Meaning his influence at First Grace? Meaning me? Though he has been trying to get together with me, Stephano can't be serious. And yet it sounds as if he is. If so, what should I do? As evidenced by the past few years of fantasizing over being on his arm, I am drawn to him. Maybe I should explore this a bit further. After all, if I am ready to date, Stephano would be a better choice than a rebel like Maddox.

I lift my chin. "Are you still interested in taking me out for dinner?"

His eyes widen. "Are you, Harriet Bisset, asking *me* to ask *you* out?"

That is *so* not right. "I…"

"Yes, I'm interested." A smile wipes away all evidence of distress. "How about tonight?"

"That would be great—" *Have you forgotten some little something?* "Sorry, but I have other plans."

His brow darkens. "With Maddox?"

"Actually, with the Feteralls, but they did invite Maddox along. They're coming to my place for dinner and…," I clear my throat, "…a play date."

"Did you say *play* date?"

"I'm taking care of my mother's cat, and Mrs. Feterall thought it would be fun to get Dumplin' together with her cat. Sounds crazy, but I agreed."

He crosses his arms over his chest. "And Maddox thinks it would be fun to attend your kitty play date?"

I give an "I'm with you" roll of the eyes. "I'm sure dinner is all he's interested in."

"And I'm sure you're wrong."

He's talking about me, and considering Friday's kiss, he's right. In the next instant, I have an idea—not a good one, but it comes out before I can think it through. "Why don't you join us? I'm just going to whip up something for dinner, and the cats are going to play."

He peers at Maddox. When his attention returns to me, there's a determined glint in his eyes. "What time?"

"Five." But even as I say it, I know it's in bad taste. Of course, I *was* looking for something to offend Maddox's taste buds...

"What's that smell?"

Lowering my chin behind the auburn hair that falls over my face, I give the contents of the pan a stir. "Brussels sprouts." I smile. "Or maybe it's the rutabagas."

"I thought so." Maddox's enthusiastic response causes me to drop my smile like a hot potato. That night when he and Pastor Paul came to my mobile home, I had pronounced that a taste for licorice and mango Jelly Bellys was as unheard of as a taste for brussels sprouts and rutabagas, but I was certain Maddox was pulling my leg when he claimed to like them. Wasn't he? Of course, he does like licorice and mango…

He steps alongside me, followed by Pucker, who is once more wearing a spiked, black leather collar. Doing the "bump and rub" against Maddox's leg, Pucker issues a throaty "meow," which would normally bring Dumplin' skidding across the linoleum if I hadn't closed him in my bedroom until my hands are free to introduce the felines. As it is, from the depths of my mobile home comes the sound of claws on wood.

If I didn't love my mom so much, I'd—

"I'm flattered that you remember what I like." Maddox reaches to take the wooden spoon from me.

I don't mean to jerk back, but my reaction to the brush of our fingers is a little much. *Oh maaaan! This is bad.*

I take another step back—the better to look up at him—however, my gaze snags on his white polo, the short sleeves of which allow a glimpse of his tattoo, the unbuttoned collar of which allows an eyeful of tanned chest.

He's a motorcycle man in gentlemen's clothing, and don't you forget it! I gesture toward the pan of brussels sprouts and saucepan of cubed rutabagas. "You think I made these just for you?"

His head lists left. "I was under the impression you didn't care for them."

"I don't, but I'm sure Mr. and Mrs. Feterall will enjoy them."

"Brussels sprouts and rutabagas?" Mrs. Feterall intercepts our conversation.

Maddox and I turn to where she and her husband sit at my little kitchen table.

"You…like them, don't you?" I ask with an undertone of pleading.

Mrs. Feterall appears pained. "I like rutabagas, but brussels sprouts give me gas."

"Me too." Mr. Feterall pats his belly. "And rutabagas…" A look passes between him and his wife. "But I'll give them a try, Harri."

I turn back to the counter where my salad awaits a good tossing. "Well, maybe Stephano likes them."

Beside me, Maddox tenses. "Stephano?"

"Stephano's coming, dear?" Mrs. Feterall says, almost warily.

"Yes, I invited him." I pick up the tongs and toss, toss, toss. "He called to say he's running late but should be along any minute."

All is quiet, and I wonder if Mr. and Mrs. Feterall are as put out as Maddox.

Mrs. Feterall clears her throat. "So, Harri, when are you going to put that helmet to good use?"

My little adventure with the salad tongs ends as I follow her gaze to my refrigerator. On top, next to the Jelly Belly container, sits the pink helmet that I have every intention of packing away.

"I understand Maddox has offered to take you on his motorcycle," Mr. Feterall says.

"He has." Toss, toss, toss. "There!" I carry the salad bowl to the table. Though I pretend not to see Maddox or feel his look, it's impossible to ignore Pucker, whose front paws are on the stove door and whose nose is pressed against the window.

"He's hungry," Mrs. Feterall croons.

Maddox scoops up Pucker. "Come on, big guy. You can sit on my lap."

Pucker meows, and I hear what sounds like Dumplin' flinging himself against my bedroom door.

Mrs. Feterall looks over her shoulder. "What is that?"

I set the chicken on the table. "Dumplin'. He's…uh…eager to meet Pucker."

"Why don't you let him out?"

She sees no evil in cats, does she? "Let's wait until after dinner when we can give them our full attention, hmm?" I return to the counter, dish up the rutabagas and brussels sprouts, and set them on the table.

"Knock, knock!" Stephano calls through the screen door.

Avoiding Maddox's gaze where he sits beside Mrs. Feterall, I wave Stephano in.

The screen door swings closed, and he surveys the room. "Nice mobile home."

It is nice. Old and outdated, but nice. "Thanks." I give the table a nod. "Join us."

As my rear settles in the chair beside Maddox, it hits me that I should have taken the chair beside Mr. Feterall. A moment later, Stephano sits down in it, and I'm sandwiched between the two men.

"I'd be honored if you'd allow me to say grace." Stephano reaches left and right. "Let's join hands."

At my hesitation, he retrieves my right hand from my lap, and I feel…yes, electricity. I expect Maddox to take the same liberty, but he smiles and holds out his hand.

I slide mine into his and bow my head. *Groan!* I'm lopsided. Despite my certainty that the man who holds my right hand is the better choice, my left hand is responding more enthusiastically to Maddox. Determinedly, I turn my attention to Stephano's prayer—a nice prayer that blesses the meal and those gathered around. As he winds down, his voice catches, and I steal a peek. Sure enough, there's moisture on his lashes.

"And, Lord, we ask that You be with First Grace and its members as the body transitions to dual services—"

What?

"—and begins implementation of a building campaign."

My chin comes up while my left hand goes numb in Maddox's tightening grip.

"Amen." Stephano smiles, as if unaware of the bomb he just dropped.

As I attempt to wrap my tongue around coherent words, I give my right hand a tug and my left hand a jerk, thereby reclaiming both.

"Dual services?" Mr. Feterall glances from Stephano to Maddox.

"Building campaign?" Mrs. Feterall shakes her head.

Maddox's eyes are on Stephano. "At the moment, it's just talk." His voice is tight with reproof. "Talk that was to have stayed between those privy to it."

"Sorry." Stephano grimaces. "Guess I missed the part about keeping it hush-hush."

My tongue kicks in. "Then it's true? First Grace is moving to two morning services *and* launching a building campaign?"

Maddox lowers Pucker to the floor. "Both are under consideration." He gestures toward the pan of roasted chicken. "May I?"

How can he think of eating at a time like this?! "What do you mean *under* consideration?"

He spears a thigh. "Among other things, the vision committee is looking at First Grace's growth and how best to handle the projected increase in numbers. Eventually there won't be enough space to accommodate those moving into the area and looking for a church home. We're considering two phases. Phase one is to move to dual services to spread out the congregation and make room for visitors. Phase two is to raise money to enlarge the sanctuary." He frowns. "Am I eating alone?"

Stephano and the Feteralls begin passing the food around. Not until Stephano thrusts the brussels sprouts in front of me do I break eye contact with Maddox.

I scoop up what looks like a miniature head of cabbage and pass the sprouts to Maddox, who plops two big spoonfuls alongside his chicken.

Ugh! He's actually letting those things touch his chicken.

"What's this?"

I turn to Stephano, who's peering into a bowl with distaste, and am flushed with embarrassment. "Rutabagas."

"Never heard of them. A favorite of yours?"

"Actually," Maddox says, "they're a favorite of mine, and Harri was kind enough to cook them up for me—and brussels sprouts."

My relief at having the blame shifted off my shoulders is momentary, as in the next second I realize how it must sound that I cooked for Maddox.

"Is that so?" Stephano's knowing tone makes me bristle.

"Sweet of her, isn't it?" Mrs. Feterall says.

Stephano hands the bowl to me. "Think I'll pass."

If only I could too, but I place a spoonful opposite the brussels sprouts, leaving a wide berth for the chicken to come.

Maddox accepts the bowl. "Thank you."

You are not welcome!

My conscience gives me a hard pinch that nearly unseats me. *This is your doing. It wasn't enough that Stephano's presence would offend Maddox. You had to go and serve stinky vegetables in hopes of offending his taste buds as well.*

I stare at my plate.

Lord, I need a spiritual checkup. I'm trying to be open to change for the good of First Grace, but this talk of dual services and a building campaign makes me sick. Is this what You want—to uproot my father's—er, Your church and replace it with something that has the potential to grow like a weed? Note: weed.

"Is it the rutabagas, Harri?"

"What?"

Mrs. Feterall offers a sympathetic smile. "They do smell powerful."

"I'm sorry?"

"You look a little green." She reaches a drumstick across the table and places it on my plate. "Try the chicken, Harri. It smells wonderful."

"Might neutralize the rutabagas." Mr. Feterall is trying to be helpful.

I pick up my knife and fork. "Thanks."

Mr. Feterall clears his throat. "Tell us more about the dual services and building campaign, Maddox."

"Though nothing is decided yet, moving to dual services is the least expensive way to accommodate the growing numbers until enough money can be raised for the enlargement of the sanctuary—if enlargement fits the vision being developed."

What does he mean *if*? Is he saying dual services might be all that's needed? That it might not be necessary to enlarge the sanctuary?

"So two services?" Mr. Feterall's brow rumples. "I heard that when First Baptist went to dual services, they kept the early morning service traditional and introduced a contemporary service during the late morning hour. Is that what you're talking about?"

Hold up! That doesn't sound so bad. Traditional for the older folks, contemporary for the younger ones. Might work.

Maddox lowers his knife and fork. "The last thing we want is to separate the young from the old, which could happen should a traditional *and* contemporary service be offered. A healthy church is a diverse church where young and old form one body. The challenge is to find the place where all can feel their needs are being met."

Mrs. Feterall holds up a finger. "But you can't please everyone."

"Regardless of how we handle the transition, we'll lose members, but if we do it right, we should be able to preserve the core while drawing in other seekers."

Mr. Feterall wags a slice of french bread. "But the question is, *do* we want to draw in others?"

Maddox pauses in the middle of cutting a brussels sprout. "That is why the church is here—to give the saved a place to worship and to bring the unsaved to Christ."

Mrs. Feterall nods. "Amen."

Her husband pats her hand. "That's all fine, dear, but what about them kids who wear black clothes and chains? Why, we've already had several show up, haven't we, Stephano?"

"Yes. Can you pass the salt and pepper, Maddox? This is really bland."

"I should have warned you." Maddox hands the shakers to him. "Harri isn't into spice. Bland is more her style."

Spoken like a true authority on Harriet Bisset, which doesn't slip past Stephano, who stiffens beside me.

"Let me tell you," Mr. Feterall continues, "I thanked God when those kids didn't sit near me."

Maddox lowers his fork. "Are you saying they shouldn't be in church?"

"Not if they're gonna cause trouble."

"*Did* they cause trouble?"

"Not really, but they caused a stir."

"Distraction," Stephano says without looking up from his vigorous salting. "They were a distraction."

Maddox's lids narrow on Stephano, who's now having a go at the pepper. "Did they return the following Sunday?"

Stephano scoffs. "Thankfully not."

"Why?"

As if to explain something very simple to someone very stupid, Stephano draws a deep breath. "They didn't fit in."

"Because no one made them feel welcome?"

"Oh no!" Mrs. Feterall shakes her head. "Brother Paul spoke with them. They shook hands, and I heard him invite them to come again."

"Which they didn't." Stephano's jaw shifts. "You see, you don't dress like that, walk like that, or talk like that if you're seriously seeking God."

My thoughts exactly, at least until I'm whacked upside my conscience by Scripture about judging others, intolerance, and hypocrisy. That last one takes me to the book of Matthew, when Jesus called the Pharisees hypocrites for shutting the kingdom of heaven to those who were trying to enter. That's exactly what we were doing by keeping a wide berth between ourselves and the teenagers. Shunning them, just as I was shunned when I needed someone to reach out to me.

I look at my plate and the wide berth between rutabagas, brussels sprouts, and chicken. Perhaps if I allowed them to touch, one would complement the other and taste all the better for it. I start to nudge the sprouts toward the chicken but pull my fork back. No. Food's a different matter.

Wondering what's taking Maddox so long to respond to Stephano's pronouncement, I slide my gaze to him.

He's staring at Stephano, jaw clenched, as if it's taking his all not to blast him out of the water. Finally, Maddox says, "You're saying they weren't seeking God?"

Stephano shrugs. "At best, they were curious. *That's* not seriously seeking God."

"It's a start."

"Then why didn't they return the following Sunday?"

"Perhaps if others had welcomed them as Brother Paul did, they would have."

"I doubt it. Besides, can you imagine the number of families we'd lose if we started attracting kids like that?"

"True," Mr. Feterall murmurs.

Maddox continues to regard Stephano. "If Jesus, who showed us how to treat others, didn't care what His followers wore or how they looked, why should we?"

"He's right." Mrs. Feterall nods.

Oh dear. The line is being drawn. Maddox and Mrs. Feterall on one side, Stephano and Mr. Feterall on the other. So where does that leave me?

As if wondering the same thing, Maddox glances at me. "First Grace is not a country club, Stephano. It's a church and is called to welcome the least among us."

With a clatter of utensils, Stephano sits back. "What do you think, Harri? Did those kids belong at First Grace?"

Lord, all I wanted was to serve a nice dinner and sit back and enjoy our play date—well, not exactly.

"Yes, dear, what do you think?"

I look at Mrs. Feterall. Sticky situation. Must find a way out. "Well, as rebel in residence—"

Rebel in residence? Where did *that* come from?

"—I can honestly say that just because someone dresses and behaves in a rebellious manner does not mean they're not open to the pursuit of God."

Did that really come out of me? Was that You, Holy Spirit? 'Cause I know I didn't mean to say that. Shallow and light was the intent, not playfully deep. And revealing…

"See!" With a flourish, Mrs. Feterall slides a spoonful of rutabagas into her mouth.

"I don't know," Mr. Feterall mutters.

I lift my fork. "Now, since we aren't here to debate church politics, I'm going to concentrate on this gourmet meal I've prepared for your enjoyment."

To my relief, the matter of who is welcome at First Grace is dropped, and the rest of the meal is eaten in relative silence—relative because Dumplin' has begun yowling in between assaults on the door, and Pucker is growling as he paces the hallway.

"I'll help," Maddox says as I rise to clear the table.

"Oh no, I'm good at this." I wave him down, but he lifts his plate—picked clean of rutabagas and brussels sprouts—and reaches for the salad bowl.

Fine. "Stephano, Mr. and Mrs. Feterall, if you'd like to go into the living room, I'll get the coffee brewing and serve up the pie."

They push back their chairs.

"Is that a pink motorcycle helmet?" Stephano's voice is a mix of incredulity and censure.

Why didn't I pack that thing away? "It sure is."

"I didn't know you were a motorcycle enthusiast." *Anymore,* his eyes add.

"I'm not." I reach for Mrs. Feterall's plate. "It was a birthday gift from the ladies in our Red Hat Society."

"Then it's for show."

"Actually," Mrs. Feterall crosses into the living room, "Maddox wants to take her for a ride."

Her unintentional double entendre doesn't escape Stephano. "Sounds dangerous," he murmurs.

Shortly, it's just Maddox and me, and once the table is cleared and the dishes loaded in the dishwasher, it's still just the two of us. And he's still tight-lipped.

I spoon grounds into the coffee maker and nod over my shoulder. "You're welcome to join the others. I can handle it from here."

"I'll cut the pie." He steps to the counter. "I could use a few more minutes to cool down." As I turn to him, he peers over his shoulder. "That'll teach me to accept an invite when I'm clearly not wanted, hmm?"

No, it will teach *me* not to behave in an un-Christlike manner. "I'm sorry. I was just…you know…" I sweep a hand toward my mouth.

His brooding self retreats. "The kiss?"

I whip my head around to confirm we're still alone. We are, and the voices beyond don't miss a beat. "You shouldn't have done that."

He slides a knife into the pie. "No, but I did, and there's no going back."

I start to demand an explanation, but he puts a finger to his lips. "This isn't a conversation we should be having now."

I lean nearer him. "It's not a conversation we should have at all!"

He stares into my upturned face, looking at my eyes, then at my nose, then my lips…

A loud thud resounds from the depths of my mobile home, followed by a high-pitched cry that causes goose bumps to spring to my flesh.

Grateful for Dumplin's fury, I back away from Maddox, then wrench open a cabinet door and pull out cups and saucers.

"You know," Maddox drawls, "you might want to rethink this play date."

And just who asked him?

Fifteen

I'm up a tree without a ladder. And it's Maddox's fault. When the fur went flying after the introduction of Dumplin' and Pucker (who might now be truly earless), it was Maddox who threw open the screen door to separate them. Unfortunately, it was my mother's cat that went through the door. And down Red Sea Lane. And up a tree.

I clutch a panting Dumplin' to my chest, thumb throbbing from the teeth he sank into it when I pulled his mewling carcass from the branches. I wince as he once more curls his claws into me—a reminder of what I can expect should I persist in my efforts to bring him down. So here I sit, out on a limb, while I wait for Maddox to return with a pillowcase.

"Doing okay, Harri?"

I glance down at Stephano, whose eyes are squinted against the setting sun. "Yeah." I sigh, and in response, some of the tension leaves Dumplin'. He buries his head in the crook of my arm, and grudging sympathy creeps over me. I draw my hand from his chest to scratch his neck. Lo and behold, he relaxes further and…

He's purring! In *my* arms. Running that little motor of his—

Ow! He clawed me again.

No, wait. He's kneading dough—that happy little paw-and-claw thing model cats do when they're content. Makes no sense, and yet he purrs and rocks his body gently as he sinks and retracts his claws. Dumplin' *is* kneading dough! On me!

I draw my fingers higher, and he raises his chin to grant me better access. As I scratch away, our eyes meet, and nowhere in his unblinking orbs is there anything that resembles hatred. In fact, that little glimmer might be sorrow. Or pain.

"Poor baby."

He bumps his head against my arm in such a way I could almost believe he likes me.

Passing my hand over his neck, I falter at the stickiness beneath his fur and the red smudges on my fingertips. "Did that mean old Pucker hurt you?" Scratch, scratch. "You were just defending your territory, weren't you?" Scratch, scratch.

Purr, purr, purr.

"Got it!" Maddox is advancing, pillowcase in hand.

Suddenly, I can't stand the thought of sticking Dumplin' in a bag. Whatever trust he has placed in me will be destroyed. "Thanks, but we don't need it after all."

Disbelief radiates from Maddox's face. "What?"

I lift Dumplin' to my shoulder. "We can do it, can't we, baby?"

Maddox is at the base of the tree now. "Harri, he'll go nuts, and you'll fall." He reaches for an overhead branch.

"We can do it."

But he's already on his way up. A moment later, he's in front of me, bracing against a branch with the orange-tinted sky at his back brightening his curls. If I didn't know better, I'd say that's a halo he's wearing. "Okay, rebel in residence, hand over the cat."

I'd be offended if I hadn't earlier labeled myself as such. Eyeing the pillowcase in the waistband of his jeans, I shake my head. "It'll scare him more."

"Sorry, Harri, but though you and Dumplin' have decided to bond at this inopportune time, I'm not letting you break your neck."

"Listen to him," Stephano calls.

Before I can react, Maddox slides a hand between my shoulder—*zip-zap-zzzzzt!*—and Dumplin'. "I gotcha, big guy." Keeping Dumplin's legs facing outward, he tugs the pillowcase from his jeans and hands it to me. "It'll go easier if you help."

Surprised by regret that my newly formed bond with Dumplin' may be severed, I open the case.

"He gotcha, hmm?"

I follow Maddox's gaze to my swollen thumb. "Among other places."

"Make sure you put some antibiotic cream on it as soon as you get home." He rubs the cat's head. "Sixty seconds and it'll be over, Dumplin'."

Dumplin's eyes bulge as he goes down into the pillowcase, then there's a deep-throated meow and flailing.

Maddox snatches the mouth of the pillowcase closed. "Fifty seconds, Dumplin'." He gives me a wink and, ten seconds later, is on the ground.

"Now what are you going to do?" Stephano eyes the thrashing linen Maddox dangles away from his body.

Maddox glances at me as I jump down beside him. "I still have thirty seconds." He starts back toward my mobile home.

On the opposite side of the street, Mr. and Mrs. Feterall walk side by side, the latter soothing the distraught Pucker cradled in her arms.

"Is he all right?" I call.

Mr. Feterall nods. "Missing a piece of ear, but otherwise fine."

Mrs. Feterall doesn't seem so certain. "Er…Harri, maybe this wasn't a good idea."

Ignoring Stephano's snort, I smile apologetically. "Can't say we didn't try."

Mr. Feterall raises a hand. "Thank you for dinner, Harri."

When Stephano and I reach my home, Maddox is easing the screen door closed. He descends the stairs. "Dumplin's under your bed."

Does this mean we're enemies again? "Thank you for your help."

"Sure." He looks at Stephano.

Silence rolls in, the kind that speaks volumes—as in who'll be the first to leave?

I step forward. "Thank you both for coming to dinner. I'll see you at work."

Maddox nods. "Thank you for the rutabagas and brussels sprouts."

"Anytime." Oops. Didn't mean that.

Maddox gives me a sly smile and walks past. "Coming, Stephano?"

"Actually, I'd like to speak with Harri a moment."

Maddox inclines his head. "Good night, then."

As he starts down Red Sea Lane, Stephano smiles lazily. "Crazy way to end the day, huh?"

"Yeah." Though what I really want is to get inside and end the day properly with a handful of Jelly Bellys, I turn to him. "What did you want to speak to me about?"

"I have tickets to the symphony this Friday. I was hoping you might like to join me."

"Um…"

He makes a face. "Don't tell me. That show of yours again."

I splay my hands. "Sorry, I'm hooked. Were it any other night—"

"Saturday, then."

Did I just open that door? *Yes, you did. And you should have known he was on the other side.* "Saturday would be great."

His smile is triumphant. "Dinner. Seven o'clock."

"All right." Shortly, I close the door. I'm breathing heavily, and it all has to do with the feeling of being hunted. How have I gone from being an aspiring spinster to a "most wanted" something or other? What's with Maddox and Stephano? And why me? It's all fine and dandy to fantasize that either one might show an interest in me, but I know where dating leads—to kisses like Maddox's. And beyond.

God, I know You know what kind of trouble I'm capable of. Ten Commandments kind of stuff. And I know You don't want me getting near that stuff again, so won't You help me? You know, point me in the right direction. Directly, if possible, because You know me and the Holy Spirit—not always in sync.

A knock makes me jump. What now? I jerk open the door, and there's Maddox, the sky at his back having lost most of its glow on its journey toward night.

His smile dims to a frown. "You all right?"

"Yes! What do you want?" I'm too wound up to cringe at my obnoxious response.

"I brought antibiotic cream."

"Oh. I probably have some somewhere, so thank you and good-bye."

"Harri?" He pulls open the screen door and steps in. "What's wrong?"

"Nothing. I'm fine."

"You're not. Did Stephano say something to upset you?"

"Of course not!"

"He didn't get you all riled up again with talk of dual services and a building campaign?"

"No. He asked me out on a da—"

Oops.

Maddox's brow gathers. "And?"

"And what?" Of course, I know what "what" is.

"Your answer?"

"Not that it's any of your business, but I said yes."

I should be pleased by the disappointment he doesn't hide, as Stephano could be the means by which I dissuade Maddox from pursuing me, but I'm not.

His jaw shifts. "Don't you find it peculiar that, after all the opportunities Stephano must have had to pursue you, he chooses now to do so?"

I do, but I'm not going to admit it. "I don't know what you mean."

"Yes, you do, but let's get it out in the open." He takes a step nearer. "Stephano views me as a rival, someone who has usurped his authority at First Grace. It makes him feel powerless. Resentful. So much so that when I show an interest in a woman he has overlooked, suddenly he wants to make up for lost opportunities." His lids narrow. "Do you understand, Harri?"

Don't take offense. Don't—

"I understand that no woman wants to be told that the only attraction she holds for a man is a means to best another man. Just as I understand that all the opportunities Stephano missed may simply have been a result of…" I draw a deep breath. "…bad timing."

Maddox holds me in the grip of his gaze. Then, suddenly, his tension drains, and though he doesn't move, it feels as if he's taken a giant step back from me. "I think you know that my interest in you had nothing to do with Stephano."

Had? Meaning he's no longer interested?

"Regardless, I apologize if I offended you." He sets the antibiotic cream on the desk by the door, then turns, pushes the screen door open, and walks away.

Good. But then, why do I feel this terrible regret?

Sixteen

Harri's Log: • Day of dinner with Stephano (WILL have a good time!)

• 6 days until *The Coroner* rerun (Hosting Lisa—pizza maybe?)

• 31 days until Jelly Belly replenishment (Do NOT miss Maddox's Jelly Belly tips! Wonder if I'm the reason he didn't breakfast at the café today.)

• 184 days until the completion of Bible #8

So what do you want to do with your life, Harri?"

I look up from where I've been contemplating the depths of my coffee for—

How long *have* I spent at the bottom of this cup? Couldn't say. Only that the last of the three calls Stephano has taken since we arrived at the restaurant was when I zoned. "What do you mean?"

He throws a hand out. "You have a degree in business administration, and what are you doing with it? You're a waitress."

Should I be offended? Let me think about that…

"Yes, you're also director of women's ministry, but we both know how that came about."

Must I think about it? Not that he's off the mark. The women's ministry job *was* a favor to help me transition from waitressing to finding a job where I could use my degree, but I couldn't bring myself to give up the café. It was there I felt the first twinges of healing when Gloria agreed with Harriet that the word of a scrawny, pierced, tattooed prodigal could be trusted—within reason. There that I was spoon-fed the love of the residents of the senior mobile home park who showed their forgiveness and support by showing up day after day. There that I allowed God back in. And then, Gloria offered to sell me the café…

"Eventually, Harri, you'll have to strike out on your own, especially now that your father's out of the picture."

Yep, I'm offended. Mentally, I rifle through Scripture as I promised myself I'd do in situations like this. Maddox, of course, is behind the promise made following last Sunday's encounter. I hadn't behaved well toward him, and it has been nagging me—and getting worse with each passing day that builds the wall thicker between us. Which is good, or so I tell myself. I should be relieved that he hasn't continued to pursue me, and I've only caught glimpses of him over the past six days, yet I miss him. But I don't want to think about him. Scripture is what I should be thinking about. Something that deals with offenses…

Ah! Proverbs 17. Or is it 19? Both? Regardless, overlooking an offense is a virtue. And I can use all the virtues I can get.

"What I'm trying to say," Stephano continues, "is that surely you want more for yourself."

Do not take offense! Okay, but enlightenment is definitely in order. "I do use my degree. Not only has it benefited the women's ministry, but it has proven its worth in helping Gloria turn around her café."

"How so?"

Uh-oh. Went too far. My role in revitalizing Gloria's business is *not* public knowledge and isn't supposed to be until I sign my name on the dotted line. After all, though I'm on my way to realizing the dream, the possibility lurks that I'll mess up, and the last thing I need is to do it in front of everyone.

I shrug. "So maybe I'm exaggerating, but from time to time I advise Gloria, and what she's followed through on seems to have helped."

He's not satisfied. I can tell from the pinching of his brow. The shifting of his eyes. The opening of his mouth.

"You may be surprised," I rush on, "but I'm content with where I'm at." Sort of.

Now it's Stephano's turn to consider the depths of his coffee. "Then you're okay with the direction First Grace is headed?"

I knew he would return to the topic of dual services and a building campaign, and I should be grateful that he dropped the matter of my involvement with Gloria. "I'm uneasy, especially with how quickly everything's happening, but I'm doing my best to support the changes. The same as I did when *you* were behind those changes while my father was still pastor."

"That's just it, Harri. Since Maddox showed up, I've been hung out to dry. After your father retired and it was Brother Paul and me, everything started coming together. He respected my opinions and pushed through most of what I advised."

That's how it was? But I thought Brother—er, *Pastor* Paul—was the one calling the shots, and Stephano was merely supporting him.

The man before me sits heavily back in his chair. "But then he started questioning the direction First Grace was heading and suggested we bring in someone to help us keep our perspective." He sweeps a hand before him. "Enter McCray."

I don't know what to say. But I know how to feel: ashamed. My angst toward Pastor Paul has been misplaced. It's true that he went along with Stephano's plans, but he recognized that a change needed to be made.

"Sure, I was invited to be a part of the vision team," Stephano continues, "but it's impossible to push through my ideas without them being debated and revised so much that they're barely recognizable." His shoulders sink. "It's all about making everyone happy. And you can't make everyone happy."

I feel sympathy for him, even though he's the one who was pushing First Grace so hard. "I know, but I'm sure Pastor Paul and the team are trying to get as close as possible without straying from biblical principles."

Wow. That sounded deep. And wise. Was that really me? I squelch the impulse to pat myself down to root out whoever has hitched a ride inside my clothes.

Stephano shrugs. "Hard to say." He glances at his watch. "I'd better get you home—church tomorrow, you know."

Ten minutes later, as he merges onto I-40 to leave Nashville behind, I lay my head back against the seat and look past him at the sparkling skyline. The BellSouth Building, more affectionately known as the Batman building due to its opposing spires that resemble that Caped Crusader's ears, stands above the rest. And draped in the sky, just to the right of the spires, is an enormous, haloed moon.

I love the Nashville night skyline almost as much as I once loved the Nashville nightlife. It's compact, a wonderful mix of old and new architecture. Of course, as evidenced by huge construction cranes and skeletal structures poking into the skyline, Nashville is on the grow. Suddenly—or so it seems—everyone wants to live here. Unfortunately, many of the transplants are bringing with them their appetite for all things "cosmopolitan." Which is what they were fleeing when they uprooted from places like Los Angeles, Chicago, and New York City, isn't it? And it's not just Nashville that's dealing with the influx, but outlying areas like historic Franklin, where affordable housing has been replaced by million-dollar mansions. Yes, I'm selfish. But I miss what was.

The drive to Franklin takes twenty-five minutes, during which Stephano answers one call and makes another—the former something to do with a golf date, the latter about changing the shape of the in-ground pool he's having installed.

He bangs a "U-y" on Red Sea Lane and halts his sports car in front of my mobile home. "It was nice, Harri."

I reach for the door handle. "Thank you for dinner."

"Harri?"

I look around, and his face is before mine. Then there's his mouth. And it's swooping in.

An *oomph* jumps from my lips as his mouth locks on. For the first few seconds, I'm too stunned to react; however, over the next two or three, curiosity kicks in. So this is how Stephano kisses.

Unfortunately, he's one of those "wet" kissers, as opposed to Maddox who's…not wet…not dry…somewhere in between…somewhere just right.

Stephano draws back. "Nice, huh?"

Don't wipe your mouth. "I…didn't expect you to do that." Did anyone see? His windows *are* tinted…

"It *was* a date, Harri."

"Of course it was. You surprised me, is all." I curl my fingers into my palms, even though I'm certain that if I don't do something about my mouth soon, I'll chap. "Well, good night, and thank you for dinner."

"You're welcome."

In hopes of exiting the car without his aid, which could easily lead to him walking me to my door, then another kiss in full view of those whose curtains are shifting, I pat the door in search of the handle.

"Oh!" Stephano springs from the car, bounds to my side, pulls open the passenger door, and helps me out. "How's the cat?" he asks as he walks me across the lawn. "Did he recover from the pillowcase?"

"Seems to have. I haven't found any cat hair on my pillows recently. And, to my surprise, he actually seems to be warming toward me."

Stephano halts before the steps. "Smart cat," he murmurs, then leans in.

"Uh…" I give a nod left and right. "Neighbors, you know."

He straightens. "Right. Well, good night."

I pull my keys from my purse and let myself in. As I close the door and flick on the light, I sigh. Provided no one saw the kiss in the car, I'm scot-free. Of course, sometimes imagination is more lethal than reality. Who knows what my fellow mobile home residents might think happened in the car?

Before I can worry about it further, Dumplin' slinks out of my bedroom.

I eye him. He eyes me. Are we good? His tail is gently swaying—a promising sign, as opposed to the jerk and twitch he often displays when I return. "Hey, Dumplin'."

He winds around my leg.

I blink. Not a hallucination. Dumplin' *is* rubbing against me. As if he likes me. As if he missed me. "Oh, kitty!" I scoop him up.

Maybe I moved too fast, or maybe I just read him wrong, but he's not going for it. With a hiss, he launches out of my hands and, with a whip of his tail, darts down the hallway.

"Fine! No Jelly Bellys for you, mister."

Not that I feed him many. My stash is too precious to waste on that ungrateful beast. However, I did toss him one last night, and the night before. Just one each time, but he seemed to enjoy the treats. Well, tonight is his loss. My gain.

I walk into the kitchen and go straight for the Jelly Bellys. Of course, the pink helmet is still on the refrigerator. I grab the candy and stalk into the living room. The bedroom is my destination, but a glance at my answering machine makes me alter my course.

I press the Play button and unscrew the lid as the machine informs me I have one message recorded an hour ago.

"Harri, this is Leah Pinscher. Anna's gotten herself into trouble. She won't talk to us, and I don't know if she'll talk to you, but could you try?" A strident breath. "Call us when you get in, no matter the hour."

Time doesn't stand still. It keeps ticking, counting off life second by second. Seconds that add up to minutes…hours…days… months…years. Seconds that can only be retrieved through memories.

As I stare at the machine, memories pile on me. Memories of the first time I got into trouble, when the police caught me and my friends smoking in the park. Memories of how frightened I was despite the defiant face I presented to my parents. Memories of the next time I got into trouble, when a friend coaxed me into joining her for a joyride in her father's new sports car. Memories of the sense of empowerment at the lessening of my fear and remorse. Then there was the time after that, and each time I cared less about repercussions and the people I hurt. In fact, it became a game to see how far I could push my parents. I shudder, remembering the satisfaction I felt at knowing my actions were causing them anguish, just as their decision to remain at First Grace despite the attacks on our family caused me anguish.

Lord, I was so far from You. And proud of it. With eyes wide open and heart tightly shut, I hurt not only my family, but my father's flock. I don't like the Harri I became, and I know You don't either. I set my life right so I could leave all that bad stuff in the past, and that's where I want it to stay. I do not want to revisit the me I was. Use someone else. PLEASE.

No.

"No?" I press my forehead to the Jelly Belly container. "Lord, I don't want to do this."

"Freely you have received, freely give."

Instant Scripture—a side effect of spending too much time in those little *God's Promises* books. "Do you mind? I'm trying to talk to the Lord here."

"Why do you call me, 'Lord, Lord,' and do not do what I say?"

More Scripture. "Okay, so it is You, but I can't do this."

"Do good and share with others, for with such sacrifices God is pleased."

Hey! I tithe. On that matter, no Scripture comes to mind, and I'm tempted to shove Jelly Bellys in my mouth. I draw a deep breath. "Lord, I'm the wrong person to talk to Anna. I'll only mess her up, not to mention me."

"He who refreshes others will himself be refreshed."

I drop to the sofa. "But what about 'Each man should give what he has decided in his heart to give, not reluctantly or under compulsion, for God loves a cheerful giver'?" I tap my chest. "Reluctant. That's me. Nowhere near cheerful. Couldn't You send someone like Lisa, who's open to sharing—"

Lisa! I reach for the phone, only to draw back. I'm certain Leah's call was meant to be kept in confidence, so I can't enlist Lisa's help. Or can I?

Shortly, a sleepy-voiced Lisa answers my call.

"It's me, Harri."

"Is everything all right?"

"No." I spill my dilemma, leaving out the identity of the one I've been asked to help. "And…"

"You don't want to do it."

"No."

"Have you prayed about it?"

"A lot."

"And what does the Lord want you to do?"

"Talk to her. But I can't help her. All I'll do is sit there, and she'll hate me for being there."

"You don't know that."

"It's what I would have done."

"Maybe, but you have to remember that she's… How old did you say?"

"Thirteen."

"Well, you were sixteen. Believe me, she has to be more scared and confused than you were. Also, she's probably more reachable."

"I doubt that."

"Listen, Harri, I know you're uncomfortable with this, but God stretches us when we're outside our comfort zones. This isn't just for this girl. It's for you. In fact, maybe it's more for you than for her."

Not what I want to hear.

She yawns. "Do what God's asking, and let me get back to sleep."

"But what do I do?"

"Just listen. If she wants to know something, don't lecture. Short and sweet work best and might prompt more questions."

"Okay."

It takes five minutes for me to get up the nerve to return Leah's call. As I dial the number, I assure myself that if she really wants me to talk with Anna, the earliest it might happen is tomorrow. Wrong. She asks me to come over now. Only after I change into jeans and a long-sleeved T-shirt do I realize something is missing—my keychain that holds a key to my mobile home and car. It's not in my purse, on the desk by the door, or beside the answering machine.

As much as I'd like to take it as a sign that the Lord has changed His mind about my speaking with Anna, I know it isn't. So what to do? It's too dark to pedal a bike, and the Pinschers' home is five miles away. As for hitching a ride from a fellow resident, not only are the seniors tucked in for the night, but whoever I ask would want to know why I've been called to our pastor's home. So I'll have to phone a cab and hope its arrival doesn't awaken anyone.

I lift the handset from its base and, having lost interest in Jelly Bellys (almost unheard of), tote the container into the kitchen. I set it on the refrigerator, and the pink helmet catches my eye—a reminder that there is one resident who's not likely tucked into bed. And who's also discreet. But that would mean getting on the back of his motorcycle and wrapping my arms around him.

Do I look stupid? I whip up the handset and punch 411. Soon I'm connected to a cab company. When the man on the other end tells me he can have a cab out in thirty to forty minutes and I protest, he gruffly reminds me it's Saturday night.

"I'll pass, but thanks." Not allowing myself time to consider what I'm about to do, I grab the helmet.

On the second rap, Maddox answers the door, and the light from his living room is so bright at his back that it makes me squint. "Harri?"

His hair is wilder than ever, sticking out all over the place, as if he's been raking his hands through it.

He frowns at the helmet beneath my arm. "What's going on?"

"I'm ready to prove that I'm not afraid." I head for his motorcycle.

"Do you know what time it is?"

I look around. "I do, and I'm sorry. If I hadn't lost my keys, I wouldn't bother you. Now I really need to get over to Pastor Paul's, so if you could step it up—"

"Paul's?"

"I'll explain later. Can we go?"

"All right, but I'll meet you at the park entrance."

Good idea. It's not likely many of the residents are up, but it wouldn't do for us to be seen—or heard—together on Maddox's motorcycle in the middle of the night.

Five minutes later, Maddox appears out of the dark walking his motorcycle.

I fall into step beside him, and not until we reach the road does he mount up. "Let's do it." He puts his helmet on and swings a leg over.

Okay, Harri, put your leg over and arm around him. No big deal. It's not a thrill ride. Nothing waiting at the end of it. Nothing to be ashamed of. Just point A to point B. But, oh, those memories! They're back, replaying the bad choices I made…my lack of discretion…one reckless day and night after another…

"Harri?"

I blink Maddox's face into focus. "What?"

"Are we going to do this or not?"

Not. Though I told Leah I was on my way, she'll have to wait until I can get a cab out to her place. "Maybe this isn't a good idea."

"And maybe you should have asked Stephano to take you." His voice is gruff, and I know he's referring to my date…that he likely saw our return…is probably wondering what went on behind tinted windows. "I'm sure you'd feel safer with him."

I catch my breath. "Is that what you think? That I'm afraid of you? I'm not."

"Then get on."

"Fine." I shove the helmet on, secure the strap beneath my chin, and put a leg over. No sooner do I settle behind Maddox than the current leaps from him to me. I've made a mistake. I *am* afraid of him. Afraid of what I feel when we touch. Afraid of how much more I'll feel when I loop an arm around his waist. Afraid bad Harri will not only take advantage of me, but of him.

The engine rumbles to life, causing my blood to thrum. Wow.

Maddox says something, but I close my eyes and feel what I haven't felt in a long time.

"Harri!"

I look at his profile over his shoulder. "Sorry?"

"Put your arms around me."

Scooting closer, I lay a hand on either side of his waist.

A sound erupts from him, and he grips my wrists and pulls me tighter against him.

Overwhelmed by the thrill of being on a motorcycle again and an awareness of the man in front of me, I stiffly hold myself as far apart from him as possible. A moment later, we're on the road, and the warm night air turns cool as the motorcycle stirs it to life. I draw a breath and am struck by the scents of grass, pine, dust, pavement, and Maddox.

I search beyond the scent of the man before me. Unimpeded by the hustle and bustle of day, the night smells of hundreds of things unseen—some identifiable, most not. Regardless, the bouquet is made sharper by the speed at which we travel through it. It's wonderful, but frighteningly seductive.

Over Maddox's shoulder, I focus on the painted yellow lines that blip past at ever-increasing speed. But still I breathe in the night. More, I feel it. Almost as strongly as I feel the man whose waist I clutch. This was a very bad idea.

I lower my helmeted head to his shoulder. Another bad idea, as it increases my awareness of him. Fortunately, he eases the motorcycle into a turn, and as I lift my head, he halts alongside Pastor Paul's driveway.

I scramble off.

"Now that wasn't so bad." Maddox's wry voice hits me between the shoulder blades.

I remove the helmet before turning to him. "Not my cup of tea, I'm afraid."

In the light from the porch, I see him raise an eyebrow. "If you keep telling yourself that, maybe you'll start to believe it."

I narrow my gaze on him. "Thank you for the ride."

"Anytime." I start to turn away, but he adds, "You know, you're going to miss me when I'm gone."

I'm only slightly surprised to feel a pang caused by his pending departure from First Grace. Of course, it's months away, and by the time he leaves, I'll be beyond eager to see his backside…er, the last of him. I shrug, and though I have every intention of denying I'll miss him, I say, "Maybe."

I catch his smile as I turn away.

"How are you getting home, Harri?"

I hadn't thought about that. Of course, if I phone a cab the moment I walk into the Pinschers' home, the timing could be perfect. I start to turn back, but the front door opens, and Pastor Paul appears.

He advances on me, and I can see the weariness that etches his face. "Thank you for coming, Harri." He looks past me to Maddox. "I don't know that it will help, but Leah seems to think so."

"Are she and Anna inside?"

"Yes, go in." He pats my shoulder and moves aside. "I wasn't expecting to see you, Maddox."

"Harri needed a ride."

As I near the door, Pastor Paul's next words, spoken at a volume surely meant to escape me, whisper across the night. "I appreciate you bringing her, but it isn't the best idea you've had."

I turn. "It was my idea."

He swings around.

"And no, it wasn't a good idea, but I lost my keys and couldn't get a cab for at least half an hour."

"Of course. Well, when you're ready to leave, I'll have Leah drive you home so Maddox can get back." Thereby avoiding the possibility of questions over what First Grace's consultant and women's ministry director are doing out so late—on a motorcycle, no less.

When I enter the house, Leah pulls the door of her husband's small office closed and walks toward me. "I appreciate your coming, Harri."

I manage a smile. "Where is she?"

She glances over her shoulder at the door. "In there."

I can do this. *Lord, please help me do this.* "What kind of trouble did she get into?"

Pain flickers in her eyes. "She took something from a store."

Déjà vu. Fortunately—or not so fortunately—it was one of the few things my parents never caught me doing. If they had, perhaps my rebellion would have ended there, but I was emboldened by my success, and more so when the crowd I was mixed up with extolled my "sleight of hand" (a.k.a. thievery).

"Was she arrested?"

Leah presses a hand to her heart. "Thank God, no. We were shopping, and she asked if she could go to the teen section while I picked out some shirts for her father. That's where it happened.

Elva's daughter, Maria, works there and saw her take a bracelet. She recognized Anna and immediately paged me."

"What did Anna say about what happened?"

"She didn't respond, not even when I found the bracelet in her pocket. She ignored me as if I wasn't even there. And neither has Paul been able to reach her. The moment we got home, she went into his office and hasn't moved from the chair since." Leah touches my arm. "Please try. I don't know what to do."

And *I* do? "All right. Do you want to go in with me?"

"I don't think you'll get anything out of her with me there."

"Okay." *Lord, this is* not *okay! Though I could have played the starring role in* I Was a Teenage Preacher's Kid, *I don't know how to deal with teenagers in crisis. Nothing worked for me except getting kicked in the teeth over and over until there was nothing for me but to crawl back to You and my family. Practical experience. Practical pain. Practical redemption.*

"You're scared, aren't you?"

I nearly take offense at the compassion in Leah's eyes, but I know that she feels for me and the position she's placed me in. "I've never done this, and I don't know what to say."

"Neither do we, but if there's anyone who can relate to Anna, it's you." She smiles softly. "Just let God work through you."

And if I make things worse? Shoulders back, I step past her and grip the doorknob.

Anna sits in a large chair opposite, her petite figure overwhelmed by its depths. Guessing it was strategically chosen over the sofa, I return to a time when I isolated myself from anyone who might try to sit beside me and smother me with her presence. Score one for Anna.

I ease the door closed. "Hi, Anna."

From behind a curtain of long, dark blond hair, she looks me up and down before returning her gaze to the bookcase behind her father's desk.

I move farther into the room. "Though I often see you around church, and I know you've seen me, you probably don't—"

"I know who you are and what you're doing here." Once more, her resentful green eyes turn on me. "I don't want to talk to you or anyone."

"I know, but considering what it took me to get here, I'm going to sit down."

A glimmer of interest enters her eyes.

I sink to the sofa and ease back, only to realize how tired I am. But then somewhere a clock is chiming the eleventh hour. Ten minutes later, the only thing that has changed is that I've burrowed deeper. Hmm. I do have to get up early for church. Maybe I should try another tack.

I reposition one of the cushions in a corner of the sofa and turn so that I'm more lying than sitting. Apparently that arouses Anna's interest enough for her to flick her gaze over me.

I clear my throat. "It was a motorcycle."

Life in Anna, as evidenced by a flutter of lashes.

I clasp my hands behind my head and lower my lids.

The girl's stubborn streak persists to the edge of sleep. "What do you mean it was a motorcycle?"

I lift my lids. "That's how I got here—on a motorcycle."

"So?"

"I haven't been on one for more than eight years. It scared me a little—actually, a lot." Feeling my mouth curve, I let the smile come. "It also excited me."

Her mouth tightens. "I've heard about you, and your motorcycles, and your guys, and…"

Regret pierces me. "I'm sure you have." I straighten and push up my sleeve to reveal the crown of thorns. "Just so you know that everything you've heard about me—all the rumors of how I rebelled against my family, church, and God—are true."

Her eyes widen on either side of a nose that, for the first time, strikes me as being a little large for her pixieish face.

"Like it or not, I understand what you're going through, Anna—at least, some of it. And if you ever want to talk, I'll sit down with you."

She crosses her arms over her chest. "I don't want anything from you or anyone."

"I know the feeling." I rise. "I guess that concludes our talk. Good night."

I feel her stunned silence as I cross to the door but don't look back. I've done what God asked of me, and now it's up to her.

As I step into the hall and close the door, Leah and Paul appear. Their worried faces catch at my heart, but it's their joined hands that give it a hard squeeze. How many times did I see my own parents' fingers tightly intertwined, as if each was a life preserver for the other? Too many.

Lord, please spare these two the anguish I caused my parents. And if You can use me to make a difference, do. I'll try, even if it hurts to go there again.

Pastor Paul leads me toward the front door.

"Did she say anything?" Leah asks.

"A little. Unfortunately, she's not ready to talk, but when she is, I've told her I'll be there."

Pastor Paul summons a smile somewhere between gratitude and sorrow. "Thank you. I know we've had our differences, but I appreciate your coming out tonight."

"Yes." Leah nods.

I smile. "I'd better get home."

Leah turns to a table and scoops up her keys. "I'll drive you."

Ten minutes later, I swing my legs out of the car. As I close the door, I'm broadsided by impulse and tap on the window. She lowers it, and I meet her gaze. "I'll be praying for your family."

Moisture rims her eyes. "Thank you."

I cross my lawn, bound up the steps, and throw open the screen door—only to falter at the sight of what protrudes from the knob.

Mystery of the missing keys solved.

Seventeen

Harri's Log:
- ? days until Maddox returns from Knoxville, where he's been for twelve days and counting (Why am I counting? And when is he coming back?)
- Day of *The Coroner* rerun (Lisa's taping for us to watch tomorrow night.)
- Day of Quilt Till You Wilt/Crop Till You Drop event (forty-seven signed up—oh my!)
- 18 days until Jelly Belly replenishment (holding up well, though wouldn't mind a Jelly Belly tip—exactly when is Maddox returning?)
- 171 days until the completion of Bible #8

"Did you miss me?"

His voice carries across the gymnasium and loops the loop in the vicinity of my heart. He's back. And how I wish his return didn't affect me. How I wish I were oblivious to the passing of days since he told me I'd miss him and I assumed he was referring to the completion of his consulting job at First Grace.

"Did you?"

At the sound of his shoes advancing over the wood floor, I call over my shoulder, "Oh? Were you gone?" I resume the task of arranging the centerpiece around which finger foods will be placed for those attending Quilt Till You Wilt/Crop Till You Drop.

"What about my motorcycle?" He goes around the table, places his palms on it, and leans into my peripheral vision. "I'll bet you missed that."

I meet his dark eyes fringed by long, long lashes. *You did miss him. Even those curls that could use a haircut and that imperfect nose.*

He grins. "Admit it, Harri. You liked sitting on the back of my big, bad motorcycle."

Why are we having this conversation? After all, considering the words we exchanged about Stephano's pursuit of me, Maddox should have closed up shop on any feelings he had for me. Did he?

I step back to clear his soaped scent from my senses. "I assure you, riding on your motorcycle is not an experience I intend to repeat. So how was Knoxville?"

"Ah. You were asking after me."

"Actually, Pastor Paul made the announcement that you were called back to the church there."

He gives a crooked smile that makes me want to press it straight. *Not* a good idea. "You're a tough one, Harriet Bisset."

"I'll take that as a compliment." I return to where I earlier set out paper plates, utensils, and napkins. "Were you able to work out the kinks in the Knoxville church?"

To my dismay, Maddox follows and hovers as I straighten the utensils. "I wouldn't call them kinks. The church's vision needed to be revised to accommodate a greater increase in numbers than originally projected."

As I fan the pretty pink napkins, I draw a breath that makes my nose tingle with awareness of the scent of him. Buying time to allow the heat in my face to recede, I reposition the plates. "Then the church is continuing to grow."

"Very much."

I smile. "Thanks to the marketing genius of Maddox McCray."

The turned-up corners of his mouth ease. "I'm good at what I do, Harri, but the thanks goes to God. He's the one moving through that body of believers. I'm just allowing Him to use me to His end."

Noble comes to mind, but I nip the sarcasm. "Sorry. I didn't mean that the way it sounded. Or if I did, I shouldn't have. I'm just still not sure about all these changes."

"I know." His smile puts in another appearance, and he sweeps his gaze around the gymnasium. "It looks like you have another successful event on your hands. Close to fifty participants, Harriet told me."

A thrill goes through me. "That's right, and the majority are under fifty years of age. Amazing, hmm?"

His regard falls to my bowed mouth. "You're heading in the right direction, Harri, not only for the ladies of First Grace, but for yourself."

I start to thank him but am stopped by that last bit he just had to tag on. Meaning what? That *I* was heading in the wrong direction previous to his arrival at First Grace? That without him, I—

"What's happening with that series on dating we talked about?"

Had Maddox popped me between the eyes, I can't imagine being more startled. I didn't take him seriously that night on my porch when he talked about the stars and the enormity of God. "You were serious about that? I thought you were baiting me."

He frowns. "I *was* baiting you, but I was still serious about reaching out to First Grace's single young women."

I shrug apologetically. "I haven't put anything together. Of course, even if I'd taken you seriously, I doubt I would have had time for it. I've been busy." Not only organizing tonight's event but putting together the café's fall menu and helping plan the jamboree that Maddox so helpfully suggested. Then I was asked to speak to Anna again, but with the same result. Lastly, there's my social calendar, which, though previously nonexistent, now includes Lisa, Stephano—

"How's Stephano?"

Is he just guessing that Stephano is one of my reasons for being busy? "Um…fine." Actually, more than fine. With Maddox's departure came renewed enthusiasm that shifted him nearer his usual high-gear self.

"Are the two of you starting to see each other regularly?"

Awkward with a capital A. "We've gone out a few times." In addition to the night Stephano took me to dinner, which ended with Maddox delivering me to Pastor Paul's home à la that big, bad motorcycle, there was the symphony in the park last Saturday and lunch this past Wednesday. But getting serious? Stephano kissed me again both times, but it didn't compare to Maddox's kiss, or the night I wrapped my arms around him as he sped me through the dark.

"Anytime you'd like me to take you for another ride…" Maddox says as if reading my thoughts.

He *is* still interested. I look down and give my jacket a tug.

"I'll let you get back to work." He steps past, leaving the lingering scent of soap on the air. And a knot in my throat.

Lord, is it really the bad Harri who's attracted to Maddox? Or is it the good Harri who's simply too afraid to trust You and Your will for her life? I really do like his motorcycle…

"I've never done this before. Is this your first time too?"

I nod.

Leah studies my attempt to create a lasting memory with fancy scraps of paper, adhesive, stamps, stickers, decorative scissors, and—oh yeah—photos. "Nice choice of papers, Harri. And the speech bubbles are cute. You don't like it?"

What is there to like? Though I followed the demonstration given by Elva's granddaughter, my scrapbook page resembles something I would have toted home from kindergarten. "I probably should stick with quilting."

"Nah, you just need more practice," Lisa says at my elbow—Lisa who surprised me when she showed up for tonight's event, entering First Grace's doors for the first time in a dozen years. "I'll bet you didn't catch on to quilting immediately."

I look longingly at the quilting table. Only three of the older ladies are there, among them Bea, who I expect to appear as scandalized as her tight-lipped expression presented at the start of the event. Surprisingly, she seems to be engaged, even if grudgingly, as two young ladies bend over her quilting block and point and murmur and nod. Harriet and Elva are similarly engaged, yet unlike Bea, they make no attempt to suppress their smiles and laughter.

As for the others in our quilting circle, with the exception of Jack, who bowed out of tonight's event, they've joined me for this demonstration of the supposedly addictive piecing together of photographic memories.

I scan the others' first attempts—some good, some not so good. Turning back to my sorry attempt, I grimace. Whatever happened to six orderly photos to a cellophaned page? What about all this space wasted on decorative borders and doodads? In the time it's taken to compose a rather ugly collection of three pictures, I could have filled half an album.

I shake my head. "Way too much work."

"A labor of love." Leah smoothes a hand across her page that features four cropped photos of Anna. "I just wish she knew how deep our love is. And God's."

Weaving my gaze among the participants who have left their scrapbooking to enjoy the finger foods and each other's company, I settle on the far wall, where Anna has been camped out for the duration. But she's no longer there.

When three sweeps of the gymnasium bring no Anna to light, foreboding creeps over me. As she has been grounded since the shoplifting incident, might she have slipped away to make up for lost time?

"Oh!" Lisa bemoans. "I got glue up your nose." She holds up a cropped photo of the two of us at her fifteenth birthday party. Far more than the glue up my nose that she's dabbing at, I'm struck by the existence of the photo she kept despite the distance that tore between us years ago. And by the smiles on our faces…both of us oblivious to what a difference a year could make.

"Hey!" Maria calls from the other side of the table. "Squeeze together." She brandishes a camera and gestures for Leah and Lisa to move in on either side of me.

"One…two…three!"

An uncertain smile makes it to my lips before the flash goes off.

"Moving on!" She hurries to a table brimming with experienced scrapbookers.

"Do you remember this?" Lisa taps the photo.

"I do. Those were…good times."

She grins. "Nice that they're back, hmm?"

Are they? I *have* enjoyed spending time with her over reruns of *The Coroner,* and the banter at the café has been uplifting. "Very nice."

Lisa scans a page of speech bubbles. "So what should I have come out of your mouth? Maybe, 'I'm a party animal!'?"

No, that came later.

"How about 'This girl just wants to have fun'?"

That came later too.

"Or 'I am so outta here!'?"

Later yet. As soon as my eighteenth birthday hit, I was out the door—

Remembering the missing Anna, I glance at Leah, who's humming as she searches for the right spot to place a miniature bow. Not wanting to alarm her, I say, "I'll be back."

Five minutes later, bathrooms, hallways, and deserted classrooms yielding no sign of Pastor Paul's daughter, panic begins to unfold.

Lord, please don't let her be doing anything foolish.

Knowing I'll have to tell Leah her daughter is missing, my feet drag as I head back to the gymnasium, but then I catch sight of the doors that lead to the parking lot. It's half an hour before the event concludes, so Jack might be out there, since I slyly suggested that Bea would appreciate someone to walk her home. If Anna left the building, he might have seen her.

I have my answer when I step out into a black- and gray-smudged night set with sporadic clouds under a bright moon.

"Hello, Harri." Jack raises a hand. "This young lady and I have been having a chat."

Farther along the bench sits Anna, looking even more petite compared to Jack, whose bulk is hardly diminished by sitting.

"Oh?" I cross to them and glance from one to the other.

Jack nods. "We were talking about the dangers of smoking."

A subject with which he's painfully intimate, having lost his wife to throat cancer.

His brow grooves. "Seems Anna here doesn't care what happens to her lungs."

Oh dear. "I'm afraid to ask how you got on to that subject."

Jack rises. "Best let her tell you." He pats me on the shoulder as he walks past. "Think I'll see if Bea's ready to head home. 'Night, Anna."

She turns her head away.

When it's just Anna and me, I lower to the left corner of the bench and clasp my hands to wait her out. I don't have long to wait.

"Old people think they know it all."

"Some of them *do* know it all."

She makes a sound of disgust. "I knew you'd defend them."

"What I mean is that, relative to you and me who have years ahead of us before we experience enough to advise anyone on certain aspects of life, the older folks have a lot to teach us."

She peers at me through the silken hair falling across her brow. "And yet you want to advise me on being a preacher's kid."

I want to advise her? As much as I long to deny it, I decide to shoulder the blame. "That's different. Being a preacher's kid is one of the few things I have a great deal of experience with—good and bad."

"Good!" She snorts. "What's so good about being a PK?"

"Well, I got to grow up in a godly home where I never had to question whether I was loved. Of course, I did question it— loudly—but it was mostly to lay a guilt trip on my parents." Regret washes over me. "And it worked. I hurt them."

Anna stares at me.

Oh, I hope I didn't just plant a seed. "But back to the good things. Outside of my parents and my brother, I had a huge family—my church family—who covered me with prayer. Of course, they did stick their noses in my business, but I now realize it was because I was precious to them."

"Not all of them."

Then she's heard about the split First Grace barely sidestepped. I tumble back twelve years to the discord, gossip, and hurtful words hurled at my father that, ultimately, splattered his wife and children. "Things happen, Anna. Things change. God made us individuals with different wants and needs, and sometimes we have to move apart before we can stand together." *Wow! Don't I sound philosophical?* I roll my eyes. "If that makes sense."

"Not really."

I feel a flush of embarrassment, which reverses itself when I'm struck by the humor of it—humor I'll take any day over painful memories. I chuckle.

Anna regards me as if I'm an alien life form, then starts to grin. Unfortunately, her face turns serious again. "Miss Harri?"

"Yes?"

She drags her teeth across her bottom lip. "The old people. Some are all right, but others aren't happy with the changes my father's making. Like...Bea Dawson."

I draw a deep breath. "Change is never easy, and not just for the older folks. It's been hard for me too."

She shifts around to face me. "Yeah, but you didn't send a nasty letter to my father…"

Oh no. "Was it Bea who sent the letter?"

Her mouth turns down. "Yeah. She accused him of driving out the old people and said he's not half the pastor your father was. That he's only in it for the money."

The *money*? "How did you get ahold of the letter?" No way her father would have shown it to her.

Guilt flushes her cheeks. "I found it in his desk. And, no, I shouldn't have been going through it, but when I overheard him and Mom talking about it, I had to see it."

I sigh. "You're more like me than you know, Anna Pinscher."

"You did it too?"

"Yes, except Bea's letter to *my* father was one of support when he stood his ground despite the pressure for a contemporary form of worship. Unfortunately, there were some hurt and angry members. So I guess that's what I meant when I said that sometimes we have to move apart in order to stand together—find other churches that better meet our needs if we're to remain united in our belief that Jesus is our Savior."

Anna considers me with such intensity that I feel like an algebra problem infested with negative exponents. Her mouth curves slightly. "That's kind of deep."

Another chuckle escapes me. "And that's my cue that I'm out of my league. So tell me how you and Mr. Butterby ended up talking about smoking."

She drops her chin, losing the smile that was so close to appearing.

"Did he catch you doing something you shouldn't, Anna?"

When she pries a pack of cigarettes from the pocket of her light jacket, my heart sinks.

Lord, she's only thirteen. At least I was sixteen.

She turns the pack in her hands. "When he showed up, I was sitting here wondering what would happen if Mom walked out and found me smoking." She glances at me. "What would she do?"

"Love you."

"What?!"

I'm almost as surprised by the words that glided over my tongue. "Not that there wouldn't be consequences, but she'd love you. Just like God loves you."

Anna returns her gaze to the cigarettes. "She definitely would have been angry."

"I'm guessing you wanted her to find you smoking."

She flips her hair back. "What makes you say that?"

"Well, if you wanted to get away with it, I doubt you'd do it where you're bound to be caught, whether by your mom or a church member. Then there's the matter of the bracelet you took from the store."

She glowers. "What about it?"

"I think you took it with the intention of being caught—that you recognized Miss Maria and knew she would page your mom rather than call security. That way, you could get your mom's attention without long-reaching consequences."

Anna's defiance falters and shoulders slump. "How'd you know?"

"Did something similar a few times myself."

"Really?"

"I thought that my initial attempts at rebellion would show my father how deeply I was affected by the actions of those I believed had betrayed us. That he would leave First Grace." I sigh. "But he listened to God in spite of the pain his immature daughter caused him and the rest of his family."

She hooks the hair out of her eyes and behind an ear. "You think I'm being immature?"

You don't want to lose her now, Harri. "Thirteen. Hmm. No, I think you're hurt and confused and need someone to understand."

"You."

"Not necessarily, but I am a PK who has been where you are and done worse, so I suppose I qualify. It's up to you whether you make use of my so-called expertise."

"Then you're okay with talking to me?"

I smile. "I'm here, aren't I?"

"I know my mom asked you to talk to me that night you came to our house."

"She did, and I admit that it wasn't something I wanted to do, but that was because I was afraid of dredging up old memories—living them again through you."

"You're not afraid anymore?"

I draw a breath of the balmy night air. "Actually, I am afraid, but I believe this is God's will. Besides, I think it's also helping me."

Anna considers me, then rises. "Can I come visit you in the park?"

Wow. "Anytime."

She extends the pack of cigarettes. "I opened it but didn't smoke any. Would you get rid of them for me?"

I reach forward, only to falter at the possibility that once more holding a pack will lead me into temptation…that my nicotine craving will return…that I'll light up just one… And here I sit without any Jelly Bellys to avert disaster.

"Miss Harri?"

"Uh…yeah." I curl my fingers around the pack but feel nothing. It's just a small box, the contents of which don't affect me beyond the paranoid workings of my mind.

"I'd better get back before Mom comes looking for me." Anna walks away but turns at the double doors. "Thank you."

"You're welcome."

She steps inside, and as she heads toward the gymnasium, her mother appears.

I jerk my hand behind me, flip up my top, and shove the cigarettes in my back pocket. Thus, when Leah peers past her daughter through the doors, all evidence of Anna's attempt to let her mother know how unhappy she is, is gone.

Leah gives a wave, and I wave back. She and Anna walk away, and I lean back against the bench. *You did it, Harri. You got to her. And maybe made a difference.*

I feel as if a rope I didn't know was around my chest has loos-ened. I look to where the endless night sky moves me in a way I imagine it moved Maddox that night on my porch when he talked about how big God is. "Happy, Lord?"

When I return to the gym, Jack is helping Bea into her sweater, and on her cheeks is a becoming flush of color. The others from our quilting circle gather their supplies as they throw knowing looks Jack and Bea's way. Though some of the younger ladies have also begun to collect their supplies, quite a few are still jabbering and crop, crop, cropping. Among them moves Leah, who thanks them for attending the event. Behind her trails Anna—an improvement over the length of the gymnasium she kept earlier between her and her mother.

With a flush of well-being, I smile. Maybe this PK did make a difference.

"Bad habit."

I focus on the man who crosses to where I sit in my resin chair in the glow of my porch light. "What?"

A smile beneath that long nose of his, Maddox halts and looks at my hands.

I follow his gaze, and a noise escapes me when I see the cigarettes.

"So was it me who drove you to smoke again?"

"No! I wasn't smoking."

He leans to within inches of my face and sniffs. "Hmm. You don't smell of smoke. In fact, you smell pretty good."

So does he— I strain back. "Do you mind?!"

He straightens and his eyes settle on my mouth. "It's a good thing I showed up."

"Why?"

"To keep you from lighting up and ruining that nice mouth of yours—wrinkles, you know."

I wish he wouldn't stare at me like that. It makes me buzz. And we're not even touching.

"And, of course, to keep you from falling back into those old ways."

"For your information, the cigarettes aren't mine. They're…" I avert my eyes. "They belong to a friend."

"Really?"

"Yes, she asked me to toss them out, and I forgot."

"Then this friend was using the cigarettes as a prop?"

"Something like that."

He nods. "As for why I'm out so late, I was doing the same as you—looking at the stars. At least, until you strolled past."

Then he was sitting outside when I walked down Red Sea Lane fifteen minutes ago. Nervousness flies all over me at the possibility I might have done something unladylike. The miniquesadillas we served at the event *were* pretty spicy, and they have been troubling my stomach—enough that I decided not to go in for Jelly Bellys and risk losing them with the quesadillas.

"How did the event go?" Maddox leans back against my little porch.

"Very well." *So* relieved at the change of topic. "All the ladies seemed to enjoy themselves. Of course, a lot of that's owing to Oona Baldwin." Hey! I didn't say that with grudging. Though Oona's past attempts to make herself useful have been more an annoyance than a help, this time I was grateful. And surprised at how easily she moved between coordinating child care and assisting with the event.

"I understand she has previous experience in women's ministry."

I nod. "When I leave First Grace, she'd be the perfect—" *Oops.*

"When you leave?" He straightens.

"Well, I don't plan on working there forever, you know."

"I suppose not." He frowns. "What *do* you plan on, Harri?"

Buying Gloria's Morning Café and living happily ever after among the regulars—feeling safe, accepted, my future assured. Not that I'm ready to share that with him. After all, I may be *this* close and getting closer with every paycheck, but it's only a dream until I have the deed in hand. "One never knows where the path may lead. Take, for instance, your path to First Grace." That ought to get him off the topic of my future. "Did you ever see yourself earning a living as a church consultant?"

"Actually, it crossed my mind, but this isn't about me." He comes near and gazes down on me with an intensity that makes me want to melt into my resin chair. "It's about you and your plans."

Why this feeling we're once more on the topic of Stephano? Why this need to set Maddox straight? And why does he have to look so "mmm mmm good" in the moonlight?

"If you're asking if I have plans to marry and have children, the answer is yes."

When his intense look falters, I stand. Fortunately, he takes a step back. Not so fortunately, the two feet separating us is more than capable of conducting electricity.

"But they're not immediate plans," I clarify. "And they're dependent on who God sends my way."

"And how will you know the man God sends your way?"

With the attraction between us on the verge of blowing a fuse, I back up. No sooner does my calf hit the resin chair than my rear heads south. If Maddox hadn't grabbed my arm, I would have landed hard on my chair, which would have been far better than where I do end up—mere inches between us rather than feet.

His head descends, and he asks in a rumbly voice, "What if *I'm* that man?"

Oh…my… What if he *is*?

His mouth on mine is light, something more than a caress, something less than a lip lock. Just right. As is the hand that leaves my shoulder and brushes the lobe of my ear as it slides into my hair. It's been a long time since—

Actually, I don't remember anything quite like this. This is more. Waaaay more.

In case you didn't notice, Harri, that's a red flag! You are kissing Motorcycle Man. In the dark. Fifty feet from your bedroom.

Before I can disengage, Maddox pulls back and drops his hands from me. "Still bad timing," he mutters on a breath that makes him sound winded.

"Yeah." Was that my voice—all weak and shaky? Of course, my mouth doesn't quite feel my own. I trace the top lip, then the bottom. Kind of thick. And tingly.

Maddox retreats farther and grips the back of his neck. "But at least we've established that you're wasting your time with Stephano."

My hand freezes at my mouth. "Is that what you were trying to do?"

He lowers his hand. "Just an observation."

"Well, I don't agree with it." Actually, I do. The reality is that this tattooed former rebel is more up my alley than Stephano. I like the way Maddox carries himself, how comfortable he is with his past, the ease with which he speaks of his relationship with the Lord, his penchant for the stars, the way he talks to me (when he isn't antagonizing me), and the way he kisses. But that doesn't give him the right to make up my mind about him!

I move forward. "In future, keep your observations to yourself." I skirt past him, bound up the stairs, and let myself into my mobile home.

The instant before I flip the light switch, I catch the glow of Dumplin's eyes in the far corner. Sure enough, my mother's cat is resting on the bookshelf beside my collection of Bibles, plump paws tucked in.

Feeling a need to cuddle something warm and soft and loving (I fantasize), I eye him. Will he allow it? I cross the room. "Hey, Dumplin'."

He blinks.

"How about some company?"

He yawns.

As I reach for him, I realize I'm still holding the cigarettes, and that they in no way resemble the ones Anna handed over. I toss the pulverized pack to the table and pull Dumplin' into my arms, only to be surprised by the sound of his little motor.

"Ah," I croon. "Maybe you should hang out with the Word more often."

He purrs louder.

I sigh. "Me too." I grab my pink Bible, and the three of us—me, Dumplin', and God—spend an hour together.

Eighteen

- Day of Doo-Dah (Why did I agree to keep him for Tyler?)
- 6 days until the next *The Coroner* rerun (Lisa hosting)
- 10 days until Jelly Belly replenishment (getting low; must ration)
- 163 days until the completion of Bible #8

He kissed you again?"

I make a sweep of the restaurant to be certain no one is listening. It's that dead time between ten and eleven, only three of the tables are occupied, and the customers are either engaged in conversation or have their noses in newspapers.

I meet Lisa's gaze. "Yes."

"When?"

"Last Friday night."

"*Last* Friday? As in last night's Friday, or eight days ago Friday?"

"Eight days ago Friday."

"And you didn't mention it when we got together Saturday?"

Hence, the problem with friends. "I wasn't comfortable talking about it then. It's unnerving—you know, having both Maddox and Stephano pursue me. I don't like it."

She feigns a faint against the drink station's counter. "Let me get this straight. Unlike *some* of us, you have two eligible bachelors hot on your trail. And you have a problem with that?"

"I'm not ready for this."

She blows a raspberry. "Excuse me! How old are you?"

"You know how old I am."

"Yes, but do you?"

I give her "the eye."

She sighs. "Okay, repeat after me: 'I am twenty-eight years old.'"

Why did I confide in her? Everything was going fine—talk of last night's rerun and chitchat. Chitchat that got out of hand when Lisa mused over Maddox's continuing absence from the café and Stephano's establishment of a favorite table. When she concluded that it must mean things are getting serious between Stephano and me, I set her straight. Unfortunately, I didn't choose my words wisely.

"Say it, Harri: 'I am twenty-eight years old.'"

I grit my teeth. "Twenty-eight years old."

"I am an adult."

"Adult."

"I am allowed to have fun."

I narrow my lids at her.

Her shoulders drop. "Within reason."

"Fun within reason."

"I'm allowed to enjoy the company of men."

"Yeah, yeah."

"Say it!"

"I'm allowed to enjoy the company of men—within reason."

"Har…ri?"

Lisa's lashes flutter at the sound of Melody's voice, but before I can turn to the young woman, she says, "Mad ox is back."

He sure is, and he's standing behind Melody with a smile that disturbs me to my toes. Not that I haven't seen him in the week since we kissed, but I've avoided anything more than eye contact—nothing at all below the nose.

I prop up the corners of my mouth. "Maddox. Wanting a late breakfast?"

"Actually, just coffee."

I peer past him to the hostess stand, but Gloria's nowhere in sight. That leaves me the task of seating him, which is good, because I can fob him off on Lisa. But no sooner do I step forward than she bustles past.

"I'd be happy to seat you. Is the Dogwood table all right?"

I feel my eyes pop wide. "Uh, maybe the Honeysuckle—"

Lisa waves away my protest. "Two tables for me, two for you."

Another problem with having friends. They think they know what's best for you.

"This way." She gestures to Maddox. "The table has a nice view of the church."

He holds my gaze a moment longer, then follows Lisa across the café.

The sound of cellophane and little beans tumbling against one another returns me to Melody.

"More Jelly Bellys." With a gap-toothed smile, she gives the bag another shake. "Isn't Mad ox nice? He all ways a-member me."

I glance at his retreating back. "Yes, Melody, Maddox is nice."

She turns away. "I take my break now."

Five minutes later, I set a mug of steaming coffee before Maddox. "Can I get you a pastry with that?"

He looks up. "No, but I will need another coffee."

"Someone's joining you?"

"Yes."

Who? "Just coffee as well?"

"And cream, I believe."

"I'll be right back."

Thirty seconds later, I set the second cup of coffee and a pitcher of cream to his left. "Let me know if you need anything else."

"Sit down, Harri."

I freeze. "What?"

"The coffee's for you. We need to talk."

"Why?"

"There's something you should know before today's meeting."

I'm being fired. This close to owning the café, and I'm being fired!

"Your job is safe, Harri."

I catch my breath. "It is? Because it's really important if I'm going to…"

He raises an eyebrow. "To…?"

"It's just that I take my job seriously."

The flicker of suspicion recedes, but not entirely. "Join me."

I slide into the chair beside him. "Is something wrong at First Grace?"

"Nothing that can't be alleviated by what I'm about to tell you." He lifts the pitcher of cream. "Say when."

I let him pour to the rim. After a good stir, I lift my cup. "So what did you want to talk to me about?"

"You recall when Stephano talked about the dual services under consideration?"

I return my cup to its saucer with a loud clink. "Not under consideration anymore?"

"No. Next month when the kids return to school, First Grace will offer dual services—eight and eleven with Sunday school in between."

I lower my gaze to my coffee. "Oh."

"It's not just to accommodate the numbers, though that's a priority. It's to provide options to those in our community who are searching for a church home."

Our community? Since when did *he* become part of *our* community? After all, when he's done with First Grace, he's out of here. But I don't say it, especially as I know my angst is rooted in fear of change. I curl my hand tighter around the cup. "Okay."

Maddox's shadow falls over me, and I catch the scent of coffee on his breath. "It's a good thing, Harri. You have to believe it."

No, I don't. "Both services will be identical?"

"As discussed over your cat's play date—"

I resent the smile in his voice.

"—both services will be fairly interchangeable. We are not going the traditional versus contemporary route." He slides a hand around mine on the cup. "If you're not careful, you'll break it."

The cup is the least of my concerns.

"Trust me." He squeezes my hand. "Going to dual services is for the best."

I long to tell him that one service is plenty, that there are other churches better equipped to reach the unchurched, but I don't need to spend any more time in my Bible to know that such thinking is far from God honoring.

Lightly, Maddox drags his fingertips across the tops of my fingers, causing my breath to stick. "Say something, Harri."

"Do you feel it too?" I practically burst.

"What?"

"The…" Why did I say that?! What was I thinking? I'm not thinking. I'm feeling. And shouldn't be. Especially at a time like this.

"Ah, that." He smiles and once more draws his fingers across mine. "I feel it. Have dinner with me tonight?"

I nearly refuse, but the words Lisa forced me to repeat return: *"It's okay to enjoy the company of men. Within reason."* Still, I hesitate, and that's when I recall that I already have plans. "I'm sorry, but I can't."

His face clouds. "Stephano again?"

"No. Doo-Dah, my mother's other cat. My brother's going out of town for a few days and asked me to take Doo-Dah. He has an early morning flight, so he's dropping him off tonight."

"What time?"

"Around six."

"Then I'll pick you up at seven."

My imagination takes me for a spin on Maddox's 1298 cc, liquid-cooled, 16-valve, in-line four-cylinder bike. And we're both wearing leather. "No!" I pull my hand from beneath his. "What I mean is, I'm going to be busy helping to reintroduce Doo-Dah to Dumplin'. After all, it has been a while since the two were together."

Maddox arches an eyebrow and rises. "Seven o'clock, Harri."

Out of my mouth comes, "Okay. Seven o'clock."

He smiles.

"But, um, let's meet somewhere." Thankfully, it was only Elva who saw him kiss me last week, and other than ask me about it, she's kept it to herself. Next time I may not be so lucky.

He nods. "Far North Steakhouse in Cool Springs?"

Nice place, and not too far from Franklin. Unfortunately, it will mean immersing myself in the frenzied traffic characteristic of the affluent shopping area. "All right."

"I'll see you at the meeting." He heads toward Gloria, who waves him forward.

Okay, Lord, do You know what just happened? How I went from angst-ridden over dual services to accepting an invitation to enjoy Maddox's company? Not good. In fact, I should call him up and tell him I've changed my mind. Tell him it's a bad idea. Better yet—bad timing. Right. Er, any suggestions on what I should wear?

"Sure you're up to this, Harri?"

I look from my big brother's earnest face to the carrier in his hand to its barred door through which the placid Doo-Dah studies me.

Ready or not, Dumplin', here he comes. "Yeah. I can do this." I step back.

Tyler brushes past me as he enters. Lowering the carrier, he gazes around my living room. "Nice place."

I'm panged that he's never been inside. "I like it. It's comfortable and…"

"Safe."

"Yes, it's a very safe neighborhood."

"That way too, I'm sure. Keeps you on the straight and narrow, huh? Not much trouble you can get into running with the senior crowd."

That hurts. And I'm reminded of Maddox's hypothesis about my relationship with Tyler—that not only hasn't he forgiven me because I haven't forgiven myself, but he doesn't trust me because I don't trust myself.

I draw a deep breath. "True. The older folks are safe, but I am starting to branch out a little, so stay tuned for trouble." I laugh, but he doesn't respond in kind. In fact, his expression turns almost sheepish.

"Sorry, Harri." He lowers his chin. "That was uncalled for."

Staring at the top of his head, from which springs hair nearly the same shade of auburn as mine, I feel a flush of brotherly love. "No, like it or not, it *was* called for. I have been playing it too safe."

He lifts his head.

"But"—I smooth the skirt of my basic black dress—"as I said, I'm branching out. In fact, I have a dinner date tonight."

"Not with some tattooed, motorcycle-riding degenerate, I hope."

I bite back a smile. "Actually, Maddox does have a motorcycle."

Tyler's mouth tightens.

"And a tattoo."

Tighter.

"But as for being a degenerate, he lives in the park."

Not so tight. "You're dating someone who lives here in the park?" His nostrils flare, emphasizing the slight bend in his nose—a token reminder of the night it was broken when he came to my rescue. "*That's* branching out? It's not enough that you have to bury yourself among senior citizens; now you're dating them?"

Game called on account of rain. "He's not a senior citizen, Tyler. He's thirty-something, kind of good-looking, and has a real job."

"What?"

"Maddox is the consultant hired by First Grace. He's staying in the guest mobile home."

Tyler makes no attempt to hide his relief, short-lived though it is. "That's better than dating a man forty years your senior, but do you think it's wise to get involved with someone hired by the church?"

I sigh. "I'm taking a risk, but that's more than I've done in the last eight years." I narrow my lids. "And weren't you just giving me a hard time about playing it safe?"

He nods grudgingly. "Just be careful, Harri. I don't want to see you hurt."

Another flush of brotherly love, but as he turns to the door, all I can manage is "Thank you."

He hesitates, and for a moment I feel the unspoken words I long to be spoken between us. But then, without looking around, he waves a hand. "I'll call you when I get back." A moment later, he's heading down Red Sea Lane. And Dumplin' is heading toward me, eyes on the carrier, tail snapping.

"Bea didn't take it well."

Maddox pushes his plate forward, abandoning the remains of his steak and baked potato. "Can we talk about something other than First Grace?"

I know. I keep returning to today's meeting—not only because of Bea's reaction, which was to grab her purse and stomp out of the room, but because Maddox is bent on making *me* the topic of conversation.

He touches my hand. "I asked *you* to dinner, Harri, not First Grace." A smile draws a crooked path across his mouth, and he pulls his hand back. "And, yes, I felt that."

I am *so* embarrassed. Why did I have to alert him to my awareness of the electricity between us?

"So tell me what it was like growing up as a PK—" His cell phone rings. "Excuse me." He reaches into his jacket.

Though I don't care for cell phones, as they're always disrupting face-to-face conversation, in this instance, I'm grateful. However, Maddox doesn't so much as glance at the screen to identify the caller but presses a button to silence the ring. "Sorry about that. I forgot to turn it off."

"But shouldn't you at least see who it is?" Stephano does and answers nearly every call. "It might be important."

Maddox crosses his arms on the table. "Do you ever wonder how we survived without these contraptions? We must have been in a world of hurt."

I grin. "Amazing how much easier they've made our lives."

"Okay, so back to growing up in the shadow of your father."

Ugh. "I thought you didn't want to talk about First Grace."

"I don't, but as it has been the setting for most of your life, I suppose we can't avoid it entirely. So how was it?"

I push my own plate back. "Sometimes it was great—you know, being made to feel special and covered in prayer. Other times it was difficult, not only because of unrealistic expectations, but interrupted dinners and family time. And at other times, it was intolerable. But in hindsight, a lot of that was my own doing."

Maddox raises an eyebrow. "I've been told that First Grace nearly split, which would have been when you were about sixteen."

"Yeah, about that time." Now let's see if we can put this to bed. "There was a push for a contemporary form of worship, but the majority of our members, including my father, were against it. Thus, after months of consideration and squabbles that got closer and closer to home—my family's home—our board voted to remain traditional."

To my right, someone clears her throat. "Excuse me, sir… ma'am."

Feeling winded, I turn to the pretty server who has come alongside our table.

"Can I clear your plates and tell you about our desserts?"

Maddox smiles. "Certainly."

As she ticks off a list of delectable treats that range from Chocolate Paradise to Flaming Bananas Foster, I draw a calming breath.

Maddox looks at me. "What do you think?"

"They sound great, but I'm full."

"Then one Berries with Cream it is."

The server nods. "Coffee?"

We decline, but before she turns away, Maddox adds, "Two spoons, please."

Meaning he expects me to share his dessert? To dive into the same dish? To clink my spoon against his? Perhaps compete for the same berry? And what, exactly, does Motorcycle Man think he's doing eating Berries with Cream? Doesn't he know it's incompatible with leather?

"So what happened when it was decided to stay traditional— Harri-wise?"

"Most of those who supported the contemporary movement left quietly in search of another church home, but others made things difficult for my father, especially when they pulled me into it." The memories tumble in. "I felt betrayed by friends and their families who professed to care about me." Among them, Lisa's family. "I wanted my father to take us elsewhere, but he said that he was where God wanted him. So I rebelled in hopes he would realize how staying at First Grace was harming me."

Lord, I didn't mean to go into so much detail. Did You mean me to?

"I never meant it to go as far as it did, but it snowballed. I tried to stop, but then I'd get angry about something, and off I'd go again. I got into cigarettes, alcohol, stealing. Then there were the guys. By the time I hit eighteen, I was raring to go. And that's when it got really bad. Of course, I denied it every painful step of the way."

Is that enough, God?

"At least until you hit rock bottom."

He's letting me off the hook, telling me I don't need to reveal things for which I've been forgiven—even if I do still struggle with feelings of unworthiness. "Yeah. I imagine you landed in that place too, hmm?"

"I did some time there."

Before he can elaborate, the server returns with the Berries with Cream. "Anything else I can get you?" She sets the squat goblet between us.

Maddox smiles. "We're good, thank you." As she moves away, he lifts his spoon. "Join me?"

It looks good, and I'm not so full I couldn't enjoy a few spoonfuls, but there's the matter of competing over cream-drenched berries—silly, especially as we've done more with those kisses of ours, but why push it? "Maybe in a little while."

He digs in, and the expression that rises on his face is nothing short of bliss. "You have no idea what you're missing." So much for leather and Berries with Cream being incompatible. Where Maddox is concerned, they go well together.

He pauses, and only when that pause lengthens and his mouth curves do I realize I'm staring at a bit of cream on his upper lip. Avert! "You...uh...were saying you spent some time at rock bottom."

"I did."

I return my regard to his face, note the absence of cream on his upper lip, and am a little disappointed.

He finishes off another spoonful. "As you know, I got into trouble at seminary—had a hard time following the rules, though I was full of good intentions. You see, I grew up in a family that was active in church and I attended a Christian school, so my view of the world was limited." He grins. "Not that I didn't extend that view from time to time. The trouble came when I went away to college with the idea of becoming a preacher—an idea that was firmly implanted from years of being told that my ability to retain Scripture and my standing among my peers made me the perfect candidate." He slides more berries into his mouth and chews with such enjoyment that my fingers are drawn to my spoon.

Oh, why not? A moment later, I'm in the throes of a taste bud extravaganza.

"Good, huh?"

"Um-hmm." I return to the goblet, and as predicted, our spoons meet. *And* we're both chasing the same berry. Maddox overtakes it and, to my surprise, scoops it into my spoon.

I blush. "Thanks." I lift the spoon to my mouth. "Go on."

"Suddenly, there were so many possibilities. Everything I'd either heard about or glimpsed from the sidelines was available. So

I sampled them—parties, cigarettes, alcohol, women, motorcycles, tattoos…" He turns a hand up. "Hardly compatible with a seminary student. Still, I continued to pursue the life of a preacher—at least, until I was kicked out."

"Why were you kicked out?"

He fixes his gaze past me, but just as I conclude I've pushed into closets he's unwilling to open, he says, "A midnight venture into the seedy side of town, too much alcohol, a disagreement with a guy twice my weight, and a knife that I didn't see until it was too late."

I catch my breath, not only for what Maddox faced, but for the memory of Tyler taking on those two guys the night he came for me. No knife, thank God!

Maddox smiles grimly. "He got me in the stomach. I remember the sirens, the lights speeding past as I was rushed to surgery. Worst of all, I remember my mother's face when I awakened. And my father's ultimatum—get right or don't come home." He shakes his head. "I hated him for it, but it was what I needed. And so I made him a promise, one that got harder to keep when I was kicked out of seminary, but I kept it."

Just as I've kept the promise I made myself. The difference is that Maddox appears to have kept his without putting himself in lockdown. But then, maybe being a rebel wasn't in his blood…

Not surprisingly, that voice echoes through me as it did eight years ago. *"You can take 'em outta the bar, but you can't take the bar outta them. It's in their blood."*

"Have I shocked you?" Maddox's voice returns me to the present.

"No, I…I'm sorry about seminary."

"I didn't belong there, Harri. It takes a different kind of person to shepherd and love so many people. Someone like your father or Paul."

I nod, only to realize I've concurred with regard to Pastor Paul.

Maddox starts fishing around the goblet. "I only hope the members of First Grace know how blessed they are to be served by men like them."

"I think most know, but there will always be those who need something different in their journey toward God."

He looks up. "That almost sounds like forgiveness, Harri."

Do not be offended. "Though it's hard to forget, I have forgiven those who I felt betrayed me when I was young—"

"I'm talking about forgiving yourself—accepting that what happened is in your past, accepting that its only reflection on your life today is its proof that you needed something different on your journey toward God."

I nearly challenge him but am struck by memories. Despite what I did and who I hurt, I was forgiven. Not only by my father and mother, but by most of the congregation. Of course, that didn't extend to Tyler, who shrugged off my apologies as if they were little more than smoke.

"Bad memories, huh?"

I bring Maddox into focus and, before I can think better of it, nod. "Yeah."

"Of?"

You don't want to talk about this. So what if he shared the details of his personal rock bottom. That doesn't mean you have to share yours. True, but I want to. "I was thinking of my brother. I can't get right with him. But then, he did pay a pretty big price for my rebellion."

"What was that?"

"The girl he wanted to marry." Feeling my mouth tighten, a sure sign that tears could be in my future, I consider my miserable reflection in the silvery bowl of the spoon between my white-knuckled fingers. "She and I got along fine until I started getting into trouble."

Maddox's hand touches the back of mine, then eases my fingers open and sets the spoon aside. "Go on."

"Her parents were very conservative and so had stuck with First Grace through the mass exodus, but they started drawing the line at my behavior, which they believed reflected not only on my parents but on Tyler." I look up into Maddox's eyes that are poring over my face. "My brother pleaded with me to consider what I was doing to our family." I nod. "I did—for all of two seconds. A few nights later, I slipped out my window and was on my way to meet some friends when Tyler and his girlfriend drove past. He demanded that I get in the car. I refused. And that's when his girlfriend got out, stuck a finger in my face, and said that I was ruining not only my life but everyone's around me." I draw a breath. "I shouldn't have done what I did."

"What was that?"

"I slapped her."

He doesn't look shocked. Shouldn't he look shocked?

"Not just a tap on the cheek, Maddox. She nearly fell over."

His brow ripples. "I imagine that didn't go over well with Tyler."

"No, which is why I ran. And didn't come home for two days." My nose tingles, eyes water. "By the time I slunk back home, they'd broken up, her family had withdrawn their church membership, and Tyler wasn't talking to me."

"Then this has been hanging between the two of you for...ten years?"

"Yeah, but that's only the half of it." Over the next ten minutes, I tell him of the night that Harriet and Pam walked into the bar and found me dirty dancing with Contestant Number One.

At the end of the telling, Maddox clears his throat. "A broken nose and ribs. It's a good thing a knife wasn't involved."

"Yeah." I roll my eyes. "At least, not of the literal variety."

"What do you mean?"

"I was drunk and ashamed, and when Tyler got me to Harriet's home and started in on how my actions had endangered Harriet and Pam, I got defensive. I told him I hadn't asked for anyone's help so I was hardly responsible for what could have and did happen—including his injuries." Those tears that were in my future are now in my present, and I dash them away with the back of a hand. "Tyler looked at me with such loathing, then walked out. It took a month to get up the nerve to call him and apologize, but it was too late. He was so cold toward me."

Maddox lays a hand over mine on the table and smoothes my clenched fingers open. "You do know, Harri, that even if a person won't forgive you, once you repent, you're forgiven in God's eyes?"

"I know, but that hardly seems fair, especially to the people I've hurt. And then there's always the possibility—"

"That the old Harri is waiting for an opening to show her face again?"

I consider *his* face—the sympathy etched in the lines of his brow and the depths of his eyes. "You understand, don't you?"

"I do, though it certainly didn't take me eight years to stop playing it safe and start enjoying life again."

My shoulders sink. "I'm a fraud—taking as few chances as possible for fear of proving my supporters wrong, religiously reading God's promises but not trusting them to guide me."

Maddox chuckles. "You just need to apply what you know is the truth to how you live. And I have faith you can do it. After all, you're having dinner with me."

I am. And I even shared his Berries with Cream… As we stare into each other's eyes, my heart flutters. I'm falling for Maddox. Big time.

"Your check, sir." The server sets a little black book beside him. "I'll take that when you're ready."

"Miss?" Maddox says as she turns away. "What time does the dancing begin?"

Dancing?!

"In ten minutes, sir."

"Thank you."

Still very much aware of my hand beneath Maddox's, I narrow my lids. "Dancing?"

"Every Friday and Saturday night they bring a band into the bar."

Bar?!

He raises his eyebrows. "Nice way to end an evening, hmm?"

I pull my hand free of his. "I don't dance anymore, and certainly not in a bar."

He recaptures my hand. "No biker bar. No drinks. No dirty dancing. Just a dance, Harri. Then we'll call it a night. I'll get on my motorcycle, you'll get in your car, and we'll return to our respective homes. The end."

Feeling as if I'm standing on the edge of a precipice, I study his face. No leering, no suggestive smile, just his question marked by raised eyebrows. *Would one dance really hurt, you little fraud?* "All right, but not a slow dance."

Twenty minutes later, I jump up from the table in the bar where he steered me after settling our check. "This one." Then we can get out of here and I can put behind me the frisson of anticipation I felt while we watched the other couples move.

Maddox leads me onto the dance floor. As expected, I feel awkward and self-conscious as we move to the upbeat music. Why did I agree to this?

Catching my arm, he pulls me toward him. "It has been a while for you," he murmurs as I stumble against him. "Just hold on."

But I don't want to hold on. Well, actually I do. Which is why I don't want to.

"Let me lead, Harri."

The beat is fast, and it all comes back—how much I loved dancing. Add to that Maddox's hand moving from my back to my waist, and his encouraging smile, and I could almost forget what can happen—and did. But then it's over, and with the exception of Maddox's hand on my arm as he leads me to our table, he keeps to himself. Not at all like past experiences.

"How was that?" he asks as we near our chairs.

"It was…" *No, it was not "all right."* I peer sidelong at him. "I liked it."

"I'm pleased to hear it." Before I can sit, he picks up my purse and extends it.

I stare at it. "What?"

"Time to go."

I glance at the dance floor. "You don't want to stay awhile longer?"

"I do, but I wouldn't want to be accused of breaking you in too fast."

"Oh." Disappointed, though I shouldn't be, I let him guide me from the restaurant to my car.

"Thank you, Harri. I enjoyed it."

"Me too."

"Except…"

Oh no. Was I too enthusiastic? Did I cheapen myself? Show shades of bad Harri? Is this the real reason he didn't want to stay? "What?"

"Too much talk about First Grace."

Whew! "Sorry."

He steps nearer. "Next time, there will be no mention of work."

I shrug. "*If* there's a next time."

He leans in and lightly kisses me. "I'm counting on it."

And so am I, I realize as he follows me back to the park on his motorcycle and I'm caught up in imaginings of being on that bike with him.

Nineteen

Harri's Log:
- 2 days until Tyler returns for Doo-Dah (only a few bite marks—don't think Doo-Dah will attempt another coup of Dumplin's place on my bed)
- 5 days until the next *The Coroner* rerun (Lisa canceled—has a date)
- 9 days until Jelly Belly replenishment
- 162 days until the completion of Bible #8

Please mark your calendars for August 11, when we'll kick off our transition to dual services with a picnic." Blake shows off his big teeth and gums as a murmur of interest moves through the congregation. "First Grace will provide hot dogs and hamburgers and asks each family to bring a side dish or beverage. Additionally, we encourage you to invite friends and neighbors for what's sure to be a good time."

A good time? I'm shot through with uncertainty as I recall last summer's picnic. Friends and neighbors were invited, which was a blessing. Not such a blessing were the teenagers who showed up in baggy jeans, leather belts, and pocket chains. It was uncomfortable, and not just for the seniors. True, there had been no trouble, but a heightened sense of awareness hung over us, even if Pastor Paul didn't seem put out. He'd spoken with the teens, joked with a couple, and moved about as if nothing had changed. But it had.

"Relax, Harri," a warm voice fills my ear.

I look at Maddox, who slipped into the seat beside me as Blake began his announcements. "What?" But I know what. The man has no business reading me so well. And why did he have to sit by me? What if the others guess that we were out dancing last night?

"The picnic's a good thing, regardless of who shows up."

I return my gaze to Blake as he sets his fingers to the keys. "Now if you'll join in a song of worship…"

As Maddox and I stand, our hands at our sides touch, setting off memories of his kisses. Not until he nudges me do I realize I'm smiling like a lovesick pup. Flushing, I focus on the words on the projection screen. Thank goodness for that; otherwise I'd be fumbling through my hymnal—

Hold up! Thank goodness *for the projection screen?*

Scowling, I add my voice to those around me. The song is upbeat, and the band does it justice—evidence of their dedication. How nice that, after opening the service with two or three traditional hymns, Bea can sit back and—

What is wrong with you, Harri?

The next song is one I've heard, even if only in snippets as I sped through the radio dial. It's not as upbeat as the first, but it's moving.

I nod. Yes, God is amazing. My eyes mist. Yes, I'm awestruck. My palms tingle. Yes, there are no words to describe all that He is.

"Do it, Harri." Maddox smiles down that long nose of his. "You know you want to."

"What?"

"Raise your hands." He nods at Oona, who thrusts her hands heavenward. "That's what you want to do."

"I do not!"

"You're just too proud. Or afraid."

Even as I shoot a hand into the air, I realize I've taken the bait. Conservative Harriet Bisset has gone contemporary. But as much as I long to jerk my arm to my side, I once more join the others in praising our amazing God. And it's then that I notice the sway in my hips. *I'm turning into Oona! Or that other Harri…*

As another song starts, I remember that other Harri who had struck a bargain with her parents that were she allowed to attend contemporary services at a nearby church, she'd behave. My parents agreed, as my attitude was such that I was getting nothing out of attending First Grace. They had prayed it would be a good influence and that the experience would bring me back in line with God. It hadn't.

Because you didn't want it to. It was an excuse to get away from First Grace. Yes, you sang and raised your hands and swayed, but you never let the words touch you. It wasn't the music that led you astray, it was you and your hurt feelings.

"Are you all right, Harri?"

I blink at Maddox. "I was…" What? Acknowledging the unacknowledgeable? Accepting the unacceptable? It was *me* who was responsible for my rebellion. There were triggers, not the least of which was the disgruntled behavior of some church members, but I chose not to forgive as we're called to do. Though I'm tempted to share my realization with Maddox, this is hardly the place. So I decide to let him read between the lines. "I was just thinking how much I like this music."

His eyebrows rebound. "You're in good company."

True. It's not only the younger members who are enjoying the contemporary music but the older ones—at least, most of them. The profiles of some of them reveal neutral expressions, and only one appears displeased. That would be Bea. Of course, Jack isn't here, having gone fishing with his grandson.

The final selection is "Amazing Grace," but not the "Amazing Grace" I grew up with. The words are the same, but the beat is faster and the voice of the young lady who plays the keyboard rises above ours. But rather than sounding mournful, her voice is infused with joy.

I look at Bea. No hand in the air, but her displeasure is no longer evident. In fact, with her head bowed and eyes closed, I'd say she's a notch above neutral. Maybe this *will* work out. Maybe First Grace *will* be better for these changes.

"You know, it's probably not a good idea for you to sit beside me in service. As for walking me home, people might start to think—" I halt when it strikes me that Maddox is no longer at my side. He stands at the entrance to the park.

"Harri, they already think it and probably know we're seeing each other. You want to sneak around, rather than be honest about it?"

"No, I—" What *do* I want? I don't really know, only that I don't want anyone thinking he and I are sharing more than an occasional kiss. And even that bothers me. "Whatever happened to 'bad timing'?"

He closes the distance between us. "Maybe it isn't bad timing. Maybe it's God's timing, but we don't recognize it because either we're too caught up in the bad choices we made in the past or this isn't the ideal situation we envisioned. But what if the situation is ideal for God?"

As hope flickers in my breast, Maddox offers a hand. "If we're going to see each other, I won't sneak around as if I'm doing something wrong."

Does he really expect me to take his hand? To walk through the park looking like two people wrapped up in each other?

"There's no commandment against holding hands, Harri."

No, but there is a prayer that beseeches "lead us not into temptation."

He wiggles his fingers. "Only as far as the doorstep, and no kissing. I promise."

Though most residents usually head out for Sunday brunch following church, we're still bound to be seen by someone—

You're just holding hands, you big baby! I slide mine into Maddox's, and he gives a squeeze.

"That wasn't so bad, was it?"

Not at all. In fact, the *zzzzt!* was pretty nice.

"So, any plans for Friday?" Maddox asks as we resume our walk.

"No. Lisa and I were going to get together again, but she canceled because of a date, so I guess I'll be watching *The Coroner* alone—that's my favorite show, you know."

"I didn't know. I've never watched it, but I hear it's good."

"More than good. It's great!"

"Meaning that if I asked you out on Friday, you'd turn me down?"

Months ago, I would have, but now…I look up into dark eyes I once thought unremarkable. And just where did I get that notion? Long lashes aside, his eyes *are* remarkable. They're not just brown, but different shades of brown that range from golden to dark to almost black.

"Well?" His remarkable eyes sparkle. "Is it a date or not?"

Right or wrong, I'd much rather go out with Maddox. And not only because I mastered the VCR. "It's a date."

As I bask in the delicious tension between us, I hear the sound of voices approaching the park entrance and tug at my hand.

Maddox halts. "What's wrong?"

"Harriet's coming! And Pam."

"So?"

"They'll see us. And you're holding my hand!"

"I was under the impression you were holding my hand as well."

"*Was!*" Yank, yank.

The teasing in his eyes clears out. "I told you I'm not going to sneak around."

"I know, but you have no idea how Pam can talk up something as innocent as handholding." Slow, deep breath. "By the end of the day, it might very well be reported as kissing."

Maddox's teeth tighten. "We have kissed."

"Yes, but not in broad daylight for everyone to see."

His nostrils flare. "Is it Stephano you're worried about?"

"I—"

"Why, if it isn't Harri and Maddox. And they're holding hands, Harriet."

"They certainly are." The amusement in Harriet's voice makes the warble more pronounced.

"Great!" I grunt, looking over my shoulder at where they're staring at us from just inside the park entrance.

Pam smiles wide, drawing attention to red lipstick that clashes with the green and purple striped jacket and skirt she wore to church. "Are we interrupting something?"

"Only a difference of opinion," Maddox says.

"Oh?" Harriet glances from him to me.

"Perhaps you ladies can help."

Pam hastens forward with solid strides, while Harriet follows at a more sedate pace on her matchstick legs.

As Maddox turns me toward them, I rasp, "What do you think you're doing?"

"Prevention."

"So what's the difference of opinion?" Pam asks as she and Harriet halt before us.

Maddox gives my hand a squeeze. "After much ado, I convinced Harri that it's permissible for a man and woman who are courting—"

In concert with my gasp, Pam darts a knowing look at Harriet.

"—to hold hands. You see, she's afraid it could be viewed as inappropriate, and some might exaggerate the extent of our relationship. Thus, when she heard the two of you coming, she thought it best that we not be seen holding hands. Whereas I was certain that neither you nor Mrs. Evans would jump to unfounded conclusions."

As puzzlement flashes across Pam's face, I struggle to keep my jaw from crashing to the ground.

Harriet steps forward and pats Maddox's shoulder. "I believe I speak for Pam, as well as myself, when I say it's acceptable for two young people who are courting to hold hands."

"Uh...yes." Pam nods. "Nothing wrong with handholding. We are, however, protective of our little Harri, so we frown on anything more than that, especially at this stage in your relationship." She taps a finger to her lips. "Now should a ring be forthcoming—"

"Pam!" Harriet snaps. As heat floods my cheeks, she takes the other woman's arm. "Why don't we leave these two young people to their walk."

"I was just trying to lay the ground rules," Pam shrills as Harriet leads her friend away. "Don't want Harri going berserk again, do you?"

Harriet doesn't respond, at least not in any way audible. The two turn down their street, and I meet Maddox's gaze, but before I can apologize for Pam's "ring" comment, he says, "That went over well."

It did?

Neither of us speaks again until we reach my mobile home, and then out of my mouth pops, "Are you really courting me?"

He's smiling again, and in such a way that I'm tempted to press a smile of my own to his. "I thought that was obvious, Harri."

My heart flutters. "I've never been courted."

His thumb caresses mine. "I'm glad I'm your first."

Only where courting is concerned. Struck by regret, my face falls.

Maddox tips up my chin. "Accept forgiveness, and leave the past in the past."

I stare into his eyes and realize how much I want to do that— and with him. Before I can talk myself out of the impulse, I lean forward and kiss him. "All right." I draw back and am tickled by his surprised expression. *I* just kissed him, and in broad daylight. "Talk to you later." I loose my fingers, cross the lawn, and at the steps look around at where he stands alongside the road. "About Stephano..."

He raises an eyebrow. "Yes?"

"I won't be seeing him anymore."

"Why?"

Say it, Harri. Take a chance. Put it out there. See what flies back. "Because he isn't what I want." Ooh, that was bold.

Maddox's head tilts. "Are you offering an exclusive?"

I pull my bottom lip from between my teeth. "I am."

"Gladly accepted—and reciprocated. I'll pick you up Friday at six for dinner and a movie." He starts to turn away but pauses. "Should I rent a car, or is the pink helmet a possibility?"

Deep breath. "The pink helmet. Definitely."

"Harriet Josephine Bisset!"

The middle name—not good. I wince. Not only because it portends trouble when Harriet Evans lets it rip, but because it reminds me I've yet to receive a satisfactory answer as to why my parents didn't provide me with a parachute in choosing my middle name. Harriet—given to honor the woman who helped birth me, but Josephine? Merely a name my mother liked and which was to have been my first name. Both extremely old-fashioned, both unable to be shortened to anything rising above a male name. Thus, outside of "Harri," I had nowhere to go but "Jo."

Harriet blinks at me through the screen door. "Are you going to invite me in?"

"Of course!" I open the door.

She crosses to the sofa, plops her skinny bones down, and pats the cushion. "Come."

I glance at my recliner, from which Dumplin' lifts his head to meet my gaze. Oh well, he wouldn't have taken kindly to being evicted anyway, nor would Doo-Dah, from where he stretches on the kicked-out footrest. From the looks of it, you'd never know that the two were at a standoff when I entered the mobile home an hour ago. It was a disturbing sight, with Doo-Dah crouched on top of the refrigerator and Dumplin' pacing the linoleum below. Thankfully, I hadn't lost any Jelly Bellys to their tiff, as the lid held when the container hit the floor.

"I'm waiting." Harriet pats the cushion again.

I skirt the cat-infested recliner and lower beside the older woman.

"So"—she angles her body toward me—"you and Maddox McCray, hmm?"

"I guess."

"There's no guessing about it, Harriet Josephine Bisset."

The middle name again. I sink back into the cushions. "All right. Me and Maddox. But kissing is as far as it has gotten, and as far as it's going to—"

"Kissing?" Harriet draws back. "I thought you were at the handholding stage."

Oops. "That too." And here comes the lecture.

"Good for you." She beams. "Do you know how long your parents have been waiting for this?"

"What?"

"For you to date—or 'court,' as Maddox so nicely put it. They'll be thrilled. And I must say I'm pleased."

"You are?"

"Oh yes. For a while I couldn't decide who I'd rather see you with—Stephano or Maddox—but Maddox seems a good choice."

"Why?"

"Aside from being fairly good-looking…" She frowns. "Well, that nose of his is a bit long. And it's not exactly centered." She waves a warm brown hand. "But I suppose it adds to his character."

Struck with a longing to run a finger down that nose, I curl my fingers into my palm.

"Not to mention that curly hair," Harriet continues. "Now don't get me wrong. I like it, but it threw me at first. Makes him look a bit too mischievous, which is hardly what one expects from a church consultant."

Exactly how I felt—at least until I started wondering how well the curls would spring back into shape.

"Oh, and that motorcycle of his!" Harriet rolls her eyes. "Made me question Brother Paul's choice. I mean, how many men in Maddox's position would feel comfortable riding a motorcycle? Even if biking was their passion, they'd be discreet for fear of how it might reflect on them. Like it or not, they'd drive something respectable."

But not Maddox. He likes his motorcycle, and so do I. So much that I want to climb on again, batten down the pink helmet, and feel the wind on my face and my arms around him.

Harriet pats my hand. "Anyway, besides all that, I like the way he carries himself. Self-assured, but not to the point of arrogance. And the way he listens, and that when he says he'll do something, he does it. Nothing wishy-washy about him." She smiles. "The man knows what he's about and isn't afraid of what others think."

Simply Maddox. Well, maybe not "simply," but there's no trying to be something he isn't. Unlike Harriet Bisset, who does like biking and dancing and who, despite her fondness for older folks, enjoys spending time with others her age.

"So, what do *you* like about him, Harri—outside of kissin' and handholding?"

I'm so grateful for the distraction of Dumplin', who pounces into my lap that I gather the purring ball of fur close. But for all my attempts to reciprocate affection, I receive a nip on the knuckle.

"Ow!" I glare at Dumplin', who glares back, then walks over me to curl up in Harriet's lap.

Harriet shakes her head. "You can't move too fast with cats. It's up to them to set the scene, and up to you to fit yourself into it." She gives Dumplin' a rub between the ears, to which he thrusts his head up for more. "That's how it is with cats."

Dumplin' offers up his belly and begins to purr as Harriet scratches him.

I am *not* jealous. I do *not* care if that nasty nipper prefers Harriet over me. Even if I'm the one who feeds him, cleans his litter box, vacuums away the fur, wipes up the hairballs, and soothes his distraught nerves. Not jealous. In fact, he's not the only kitty in town.

I scoop Doo-Dah off the footrest and plop him down in my lap. Mistake number one. *How do you like them apples, Dumplin'?*

He doesn't, as evidenced by the cessation of his purring followed by a growl. But Doo-Dah likes it, purring loud enough for the two of them as I rub between his ears.

Gingerly, Harriet sets Dumplin' on the floor. "That's one of them scenes I was talking about." She shakes the fur off her hands. "So, Harri?"

Doo-Dah rolls, and I raise my eyebrows at Dumplin' as I rub the belly offered to me. Mistake number two. "So what?"

"What do you like about Maddox?"

"Oh." I take my eyes off Dumplin'. Mistake number three. "Actually, I think you covered it all. He's attractive and unpretentious."

"Yes, but what about this?" She thumps my breastbone. "Is there something going on in there that I should know about?"

My heart jumps at what I feel for Maddox. "Yes, and it frightens me. What if—?"

"No what-ifs. You know the difference between right and wrong. All you need to do is have faith in what you know to be true. Fortunately, I believe Maddox is honorable, so that's half the battle—or more."

True. Even if I do still have some of the hussy about me, Maddox wouldn't allow our relationship to progress beyond kissing. Would he?

"Aiyai!" The sharp teeth that nip my ankle make me come up off the sofa. Unfortunately, Doo-Dah reacts to the outburst by sinking his claws into my thighs to keep from tumbling to the floor where Dumplin' waits. Fortunately, Harriet pulls Doo-Dah off me and heads down the hall.

"Oh no, you don't!" she scolds as she slams the bathroom door. "You just leave him be, Mr. Dumplin'." A moment later, she reappears. Behind her slinks Dumplin', lowered ears and tail making him look like a kid returning to the classroom after a visit to the principal's office.

Harriet halts in the middle of the living room and puts her hands on her hips. "If you're gonna keep cats, you have to learn their boundaries."

As if keeping cats was *my* idea.

Harriet glances at her watch. "Speaking of which, you remember God's boundaries with regard to Maddox and you'll be fine." She steps forward, winds an arm around my waist, and bestows a bear hug that's at odds with her size. "Make me proud, girl."

Twenty

Harri's Log: • Day of church picnic
• 6 days until the next date with Maddox (Hopefully better than the last one—he was so distracted!)
• 6 days until another rerun of *The Coroner* (record again)
• 20 days until Jelly Belly replenishment (maybe more, as craving has decreased for some reason—Maddox?)
• 142 days until the completion of Bible #8
• 156 days until the café has a new owner!

I sniff the air. Juicy, seared hot dogs. *Sniff, sniff.* And charred all-beef patties that promise thick black streaks. *Crunch, crunch.* And is that…? Oooh! No one said anything about grilled corn on the cob. Fortunately, I'm only running half an hour late, so there should be plenty of pickin's left.

My contribution to the church picnic tucked beneath an arm, I pedal alongside the field between the café and the church parking lot that brims with vehicles. As I do so, I feel pride of ownership. Well, *pending* pride of ownership. Fueled by the meeting with Gloria about the upcoming jamboree that took an unexpected turn toward setting a date to pass the café into my hands, I shiver in anticipation. January. In less than five months I'll have the full down payment, and the loan for the remaining balance will be in place.

I look over my shoulder at the café that sits front and center on just over eight acres. My dream is about to come true. The only question that remains is, when should I give my notice to First Grace? If I'm right about Oona being receptive to returning to women's ministry, then the church won't be without a director for long. The problem would then be the volunteer children's ministry director position that Oona would vacate.

I draw a deep breath and am grateful to be distracted by the scent of barbecue. I'll worry about giving notice later. After all, the realization of my dream is five months out, so there's plenty of time to work through the logistics.

Several cars pull into the parking lot ahead of me, the last coming so close that I feel the heat rising off the black metal and correct my course to ensure I don't get thrown off my bicycle. As the car pulls past, a head appears in the back window, and from out of a pale face framed by dark hair, a teenage girl sticks out her tongue to reveal its pierced glory.

Great. Just the kind of people we want to attract. Rebellious youth who are here for anything but fellowship. Who'll have the older folks making tracks and the rest of us peering over our shoulders and moving about in packs, the better to watch our backs.

Calm down. They're just kids trying to find themselves as once you were trying to find yourself. They could be gathering at the mall, but they're at church, even if only for the free food. And somehow God will touch them, even if He hides His touch so deep inside they're unaware of it for a time.

I approach the bike rack next to the playground and smile at church members crossing the parking lot. From the sound of it— the conversation, bursts of laughter, and squeals of children—the picnic is in full swing. From the looks of it as I round the parking lot, it's a hit. Beyond the pavement, hundreds of people crowd the newly mown field that's checkered with picnic blankets and lightly hazed by the smoke from two enormous grills. I sigh. What could go wrong?

Five minutes later, I set down my chicken salad and peel off a corner of the plastic wrap to insert the spoon I tucked into my back pocket.

I turn, and heading toward me, plate loaded, is the darkly dressed girl who stuck her tongue out at me. Flanked by similarly dressed youths—a girl of stouter build and a lanky boy—she halts. "Look, it's the bike lady."

Look, it's the rebel.

"Nice bike." Rebel Girl throws a hip out. "Love the granny handlebars."

Do not take offense. This is all about her friends. Not you. I swallow. "Thank you. I'm rather fond of my mountain bike. So, are you enjoying the picnic?"

The boy picks up a hot dog, takes a bite, and around the mouthful says, "We're just here for the food."

Love them, Harri. Don't bite off their heads. "Well, we're glad to have you." I offer a hand to Rebel Girl. "My name's Harriet. I'm head of women's ministry."

She shrugs. "See ya around." She and the boy head off, but the stout girl hesitates. "Thanks for the eats," she says, then hurries to catch up with her friends.

I'm tracking their progress among our church members—some of whom give them a wide berth—when a shadow falls over me.

"Déjà vu?" Maddox asks.

Close enough for me to feel a thrill, but not so close as to appear inappropriate. I peer across my shoulder and am relieved to find his brow unlined, unlike this past week that's been rife with long hours as he and the vision team finalize First Grace's vision statement and plans for the future. "I was afraid you wouldn't make it."

He grins, then turns his attention to the youths. "So?"

"They remind me a lot of who I was ten years ago."

"And you're worried." As if trying to pull something from memory, he frowns. "A self-professed rebel in residence once said that just because people dress and behave in a rebellious manner doesn't mean they aren't open to God."

"I believe that rebel was speaking in hindsight, which isn't of much use at the moment." I pick out the youths, who now stand on the sidelines of a volleyball game. "Beyond the offer of a free meal, I mainly came to gatherings like this to get a rise out of people."

"And?"

"What?"

"You said 'mainly.' Why else did you attend?"

"I suppose on the chance that I might catch a glimpse of God. If He existed, even though I told myself He didn't, I was certain I'd be able to see Him in people like these."

"Did you see Him?"

No is on the tip of my tongue, but it would be a lie, as the memory surfaces of a fifteen-year-old girl who tried to sell me a T-shirt to raise funds for her church's youth program. Though I refused, she invited me to attend services with her and her family. I didn't. Then there was the old lady with the towering cotton-candy hair who, I'd realized, was half-blind, since she wasn't the least put off by my outfit or attitude. While my fellow party crashers were making mischief, she held me captive with stories of her youth. And then she started talking about Jesus and how much He loved me, and I was overwhelmed by the longing to burrow against her side.

I sigh. "Yes, sometimes I caught a glimpse of Him, other times an eyeful, but I told myself I was being manipulated and that those people didn't care about me."

"You were wrong."

"Yes, and most painfully with regard to my parents and church family. They—"

"Mr. Feterall, look! Harri brought Gloria's Hot Smoky Chicken Salad."

I pivot to face the older couple and am thrown by the sight of Mrs. Feterall without her head scarf. Wispy gray hairs curl all over her head, testament to the successful completion of her chemotherapy.

She ruffles the hair at her temple. "I thought it was time to show off these curls. What do you think, Harri? Maddox?"

I smile. "Absolutely."

"You look lovely."

Mr. Feterall slides an arm around her shoulders. "God's been good to us."

Thank You, Lord.

I prop a hand on my hip. "So I guess this means you'd like me to start adding a bit of spice to my chicken and dumplings?"

Mrs. Feterall shakes her head. "You keep making it the way you make it. I've come to appreciate the taste of food and have decided I'm not going back to the shakers. Better for my health too."

I make a face. "Well, you might want to think twice about Gloria's chicken salad, then."

She winks. "Everything in moderation."

They start to turn to the chicken salad, but Mrs. Feterall pauses and glances between Maddox and me. "You're a good-looking couple."

Maddox chuckles. "Enjoy the picnic, Mr. and Mrs. Feterall." He nods to where the line starts, and we set off. "So you got held up at the café again?"

He's not the only one putting in long hours. "Gloria and I had to finalize the details for the jamboree. It's less than a week away."

"My fault, then."

As we settle in line behind a family of five, I scowl. "That's right. If you hadn't suggested the jamboree, I wouldn't have been late."

"Sorry about that."

I'm not. Though I was against the idea, the older folks are buzzing with excitement. And even Bea signed up for dance lessons. Of course, I'm sure that was prompted by Jack, who was the first to sign up.

"Actually, I think it's going to be a good thing, not only for the café, but the older folks. If we pull it off, it'll be worth all the extra work."

Maddox studies me as we inch forward. "You put in a lot of time at the café."

Must tread carefully. "Well, Gloria *is* getting up there in years, and it's harder for her to keep things running, so I help out where I can."

Maddox hands me a plate. "I imagine she's starting to think about retirement."

Our fingers brush as I accept the plate, which I blame for what pops out of my mouth. "As a matter of fact, she…is."

"Really?"

The interest in his voice gives me another jolt. Of course, maybe this is the perfect opening to reveal my plans for the future. *And if your plans fall through?* They won't. After all, nearly everything's in place. Still…

"So what does she intend to do with the café?" Maddox lowers a hot dog bun to my plate. "Pass it on to family?"

"No. None of her immediate family are interested in running it."

He tongs a hot dog into my bun. "Meaning she'll probably sell it?"

"Yes." Desperate to change the subject, I follow the haze of smoke to its source. "Look! Stephano's working the grill." Ugh. Poor change of subject. Remembering Stephano's blank expression when I turned down his dinner invitation several days ago, I frown. Though it appeared he was putting on a brave face when I told him that Maddox and I had gone "exclusive," I don't think it had much to do with any real feelings he has for me.

"So he is." Maddox pauses in the middle of spooning slaw. "Nice apron."

I eye the lobster on the bib. Probably not the best choice to wear to a burger and weenie roast.

"Shade?" Maddox asks as we exit the line.

I peer at him past the strand of hair that's come free of my ponytail. "Definitely."

He takes my arm and guides me past a group of boys huddled around a collection of trading cards. As we pass the grills, a gathering beyond Stephano and his fellow burger flippers catches my eye. The rebel youths. And among their ranks are other teenagers, including Anna. Anna, who dropped by my mobile home several days ago. While Leah was off with Anna's brother, Pastor Paul "dragged" his daughter to church with him. Thus, with "nothing better to do," she appeared on my doorstep. And we talked. Well, mostly *I* talked, but she seemed interested and indicated that she didn't want to go down the path I'd gone down. So what is she doing with those rebels?

"Does it make you uncomfortable?" Maddox asks.

I snap my head around. "Yes!"

His face darkens. "Then you'd prefer that I don't hold your arm?"

That he didn't…? I shake my head. "Why do you say that?"

"You've gone all tense."

"Oh. It's not you." At least, not much. While it's now common knowledge that Maddox and I are dating, I'm still uncomfortable. "It's…" I look at the youths.

"Ah."

"Maybe I should go over and—"

"Leah's keeping an eye on her." Maddox nods at a group of ladies, and sure enough, Leah's watching her daughter.

He halts in the shade beneath an aged Bradford pear tree, and I look down. "Your blanket?"

He sets his plate on the woolen plaid. "I come prepared."

"I'm grateful." I steal another glance at Anna and the rebels as Maddox helps me sit, then settles beside me.

He sinks his fork into his slaw. "So dual services begin tomorrow. Heard any more rumblings—other than from Bea?"

*Every*one knows where Bea stands. Plain and simple, she doesn't like it. If Jack hadn't refused to join forces with her, I'm certain she would quit the church altogether.

"Though some of the older folks are a bit uneasy, mostly it's having a choice that's hard for them." I consider my charred, wrinkled hot dog. "One of our ladies won't go to the early service unless her friend will, but her friend won't because her husband is pushing for the late service because that's when their children will be attending."

"It'll work out, Harri."

"I know." I take a bite of the dog and am surprised at how juicy it is—so surprised that I'm aiming for another bite before I realize I'm being watched. "What?"

Maddox grins. "You said, 'I know.'"

I flush. "I did."

"Then you're starting to trust the direction First Grace is heading?"

I shrug. "I guess. Most of the older members seem to be adjusting, and the younger ones are in favor of the changes. As for drawing in the unchurched..." Another glance at the rebel youths. "We certainly are. I suppose the only questions we need to answer are, will this change make a difference in our members' relationship with God? and will it speak to those who don't know Him—do more than just draw them in for a free meal?"

Maddox lays a hand on my arm. "Give it time."

I consider his tanned fingers and realize I trust him. Despite our rocky start and the roller-coaster ride of the past few months, his intentions are good. First Grace is better for having known him. As am I. "Thank you."

"For?"

"Doing what's right for all of us. When you came, I thought you wouldn't care about our older members' needs. That you'd put numbers ahead of a bunch of old folks, especially those living out their last years in a mobile home park. I was wrong."

Maddox momentarily looks down. "You do know, Harri, that my work here isn't finished? That there will be more changes? More programs put in place?"

I nod. "Can't say I'm thrilled, but I suppose it's inevitable, and in the end it will be best for all."

He starts to say something but presses his lips together. When he speaks, it's with a rough edge. "I can't guarantee you'll be comfortable with what still needs to be done, but I assure you that it's necessary and that I'll do my best to watch out for the older folks."

My lids narrow. "So serious. As cooperative as I've been these past months—even if grudgingly so—are you expecting me to stir up trouble?"

I'm disappointed, and a little alarmed, when he doesn't immediately reject the possibility. "Let's just say that I have a special interest in avoiding your displeasure."

Curiosity roused, I poke at my Hot Smoky Chicken Salad. "So Maddox McCray is a little slippery after all."

He doesn't respond but begins to stack his burger with lettuce and tomato.

Over the next ten minutes, I mull over what he and his vision team have in store for First Grace. Three Sunday services? More musical instruments? Separate worship for youth? A recreation center—

No. Talk of enlarging the sanctuary is stretching it as it is. There isn't room for a recreation center.

I set aside my plate and venture another glance at the rebel youths. But they're gone. Heart ping-ponging, I snap my head around.

"What's wrong?"

"I don't see Anna."

"Look, Harri—"

"No. Really. I don't see her. Or the rebels." I scoot to my feet.

"There's Anna." As Maddox rises, he juts his chin toward the church. "Heading toward the playground."

She is, absent her church friends, but hardly lacking company. I scan the grounds. Though the progress of the pastor's daughter amid the darkly clad youths turns some heads, there's no sign of Leah. "Maddox, I have to—"

"I'll go with you."

Side by side, we stroll toward the playground. Halfway there, Leah intercepts us. "Have you seen—"

Maddox nods toward the playground. "Harri and I thought we'd take a walk in that direction."

Gratitude transforms her face. "I had to go to the car to get Lucas his football, and when I came back…"

I smile. "Don't worry, we'll keep an eye on her."

Shortly, we step to the sidewalk. Feigning interest in the little ones on the playground equipment, I keep Anna and the rebels in my peripheral vision. They haven't entered the fenced area, but their presence at the far end causes a stir among the supervising parents. Fortunately, not enough to make them grab their children and head for the safety of the pack.

Aware of the stares from the youths, I draw alongside Maddox at the fence. "We've been sighted."

He doesn't respond. Wondering at his curved mouth, I follow

his gaze to where a little girl is flying high on the swing her dad pushes. Eyes wide, round cheeks flushed little-girl pink, she calls, "Higher, Daddy, higher!"

That sweet voice grabs my heart. Those are the same words I cried out to my father when I was of a similar age. Years later, he'd found me on a swing in the park smoking a cigarette. Dad didn't rant or try to snatch it away. He gently lowered to the swing beside mine, and when he finally spoke, he recalled when I was little and he'd launched me in the air and I'd cried, "Higher, Daddy, higher!" That day, he looked past the smoke I blew out and said, "It's God you should be speaking those words to now, Harriet. All you have to do is ask, and He *will* take you higher."

The pain etched in his face caused my hard shell to soften, and for a moment I'd longed to crawl into his lap. But instead, I'd ground my cigarette beneath a boot and walked away. A month later, I graduated from high school—barely—and the day after, left home for good—

Make that *bad,* as the next two years saw me at my worst.

"Are you trying to bend steel, Harri?"

Realizing I'm gripping the top rail of the fence so hard that my knuckles are white, I lower my hands. "Just remembering a rebel moment."

"When was the last time you were on a swing?"

"Actually, that's the moment I was remembering."

"Then not a good one." He smiles. "We could replace it." He nods at the swing set. "I'll push."

"Are you kidding?"

He props an elbow on the fence's rail. "No."

"Well, thanks for the offer, but I'm twenty-eight years old and the director of women's ministry."

"So?"

I put a hand on my hip. "In the words of a man who once knew better—bad timing."

He laughs. "All right, but when the timing *is* right, count yourself in for a little swing time."

I smile, but only for a moment. Catching movement out of the corner of my eye, I step nearer to him. "We have company."

"Hey!" calls the darkly clad young man. "The preacher's daughter here says that's your bike."

Maddox follows his nod to the motorcycle where it stands to the left of the bicycle rack where I parked. "Would you like to take a look?"

The youth bobs his head, causing his bangs to obscure his eyes. "Yeah, man."

Maddox strides forward. "Name's Maddox. Yours?"

"Drew." The youth accepts Maddox's handshake, and soon the two stand over the motorcycle—and Anna and her rebel friends are advancing on me.

"Bike lady!"

Lord, may the words of my mouth and the meditation of my heart be acceptable to You. 'Cause what I'd really like to say wouldn't be acceptable at all.

They halt before me. "Uh, Miss Harri, this is Hannah." Anna touches the shoulder of the stout girl who earlier thanked me for the eats. "We have some classes together. And this is her sister, Becca. She's two years ahead of us."

The latter drops her chin to once more give me an eyeful of the interior of her mouth. "Remember me?"

I unclench my hands. "Of course. Nice tongue piercing."

She raises an eyebrow.

"Still…" I put my head to the side. "That one hurt."

"How would you know?"

Lord, I'm the last one who should be witnessing to rebellious teenagers, but I'll try.

"Believe me, I've had my share of piercings."

She snorts. "Ears don't count."

I glance at Hannah, then Anna, both of whom are following the exchange. "Do bellies count? Or is that now considered passé?"

Becca looks me up and down. "*You* have a belly piercing?"

"Not anymore."

She narrows her lids at me. "Belly piercing is all right, but tongue and labret piercings"—she jabs the as-yet-unpierced flesh beneath her bottom lip—"is where it's at."

"And tattoos." Anna takes a step forward. "Becca's thinking about getting one, Miss Harri."

In Anna's eyes is something like pleading. Does she want me to discourage her friend from handing herself over to the needle? I return my regard to the older girl. "A tattoo, hmm?"

"First I have to come up with the money. It's not cheap, you know."

Feeling caught up in a strange game of one-upmanship, I

nod. "I know, but wait until you have to come up with the money to have it removed. Now *that's* not cheap." I push up my three-quarter-length sleeve to reveal the crown of thorns. "See this? Beaucoup bucks to get rid of it. And it's only one of two that I have."

Eyes riveted on the thorns branded into my flesh, the girl sighs. "Cool."

Hardly a winning response. "When I was younger, it was cool. Now…"

Becca sneers. "Let me guess. They won't let you show it, you working here at the church and all."

"Actually, I choose not to show it."

"Why?"

"Because of what it reminds me of. But maybe you'll be different. Maybe ten…twenty years from now, you'll still like yours. Maybe your memories will be better than mine." With a glance at Anna, who's nibbling her lip, I lower the sleeve.

"I am never getting a tattoo," the stout Hannah declares.

Big sister throws her a look of exasperation. "As if Mom would let you."

"Well, she won't let you, either."

Becca sticks out her tongue. "I got this, didn't I?"

"Yeah, but wait till she finds out." Hannah folds her arms over her chest.

Becca swings away. "Drew! Let's get out of here."

The young man, hunkered beside Maddox near the chrome

muffler, turns, and there's no mistaking his disappointment. "Okay, Bec."

I consider Hannah as her sister scoots away. "Do you need a ride home?"

"No, my sister and her boyfriend were just dropping me off. I'm spending the night with Anna and"—she offers a sheepish smile—"going to church with her tomorrow."

Anna smiles. "Mom and Dad said she could."

"That's great. I look forward to seeing you tomorrow, Hannah."

She nods, then turns to Anna. "Let's check out the dessert table."

Anna catches my eye as she steps past and mouths, "Thanks."

A few moments later, Maddox returns to my side. "A bit lost, but Drew's a nice kid. How'd you do?"

Staring at him, I'm struck by a longing to be pulled into his arms—right here with the sun beating on our heads. But the timing is still wrong, so I slide my hand into his and savor the threading of our fingers. "Only God knows."

A quarter hour later, Maddox jogs off to join a game of touch football.

"Doing all right, Harri?"

I turn to Stephano, who once more looks his stylish self in the absence of the lobster apron. "Yes. You?"

"Could be better, but nothing a game of football can't cure." He juts his chin toward the field. "I'd better get out there." He takes a step away but looks over his shoulder. "I should warn you that there are more changes coming. Bigger than the move to contemporary worship and the transition to dual services."

Remembering my earlier talk with Maddox, I incline my head. "I know."

He searches my face. "No, I don't believe you do."

"What are you talking about?"

"I shouldn't have said anything." He raises a hand and sets off.

And I'm left to ponder his words. In the end, I remind myself of Maddox's assurance that what has yet to be done is necessary and he'll look out for the older folks. I trust him. He'll do what's right.

Twenty-One

Harri's Log:
- Day of jamboree
- 30 days until new season of *The Coroner* (should be more excited...)
- 16 days until Jelly Belly replenishment (binged over upcoming jamboree)
- 138 days until the completion of Bible #8 (considering joining the young women's Bible study that Oona agreed to help organize)
- 152 days until the café changes hands!

addox! What are you doing here?"

He halts with a hand on the door and gazes at me where I braked my bike in front of the café. "Harri."

"Don't tell me, another late lunch?" Actually, *very* late. It's approaching five, and his meetings with the vision team don't usually run *that* long.

"No." His gaze wavers, causing unease to brush the edge of my consciousness—at least until I clue in.

"Ah! Giving Gloria last-minute tips on tonight's jamboree. That's nice." I park my bike alongside his motorcycle and move toward the porch with its rustic timbers and handmade, slat-seat rocking chairs. "You are still planning on coming, aren't you?"

Helmet in hand, he meets me halfway. "I'll be here."

Just as it strikes me that his smile is forced, he lowers his head and touches his mouth to mine.

Rather fond of those smiles-turned-kisses, I step nearer to prolong the contact, and he deepens the kiss.

Still, it's over too soon. "Wow." I wrinkle my nose. "That wasn't standard fare."

"Couldn't resist."

I grin. "I do believe, Maddox McCray, that you like me more than a little."

"You know I do. What about you? Do you like me more than a little?"

Unlike my tone, his is far from light, with an intensity that once more rouses unease. *Is he considering taking our relationship to the next level?* I think back to the night of the Quilt Till You Wilt/Crop Till You Drop event, when he suggested he might be the man God intended for me. Then he kissed me.

Is he the one? As much as I long to believe it, I'm not ready. And yet… "Yes." I nod. "I like you more than a little."

He draws a hand down the curve of my face. "And you trust me?"

"You know I do. But why—"

"Don't stop." He kisses me again, then fits the helmet on his head. "I'll see you tonight." A few moments later, he accelerates out of the parking lot at a speed that would send excitement coursing through me were my arms around his waist.

Lord, no more cigarettes, tattoos, or wild nights, but surely You don't mind an occasional motorcycle ride?

Beginning to buzz with anticipation, I decide that, following the jamboree, I'll ask Maddox to take me for a short spin.

Upon entering the café, I hear voices in the kitchen and head for it; however, Gloria and Ruby's discussion ends the moment I enter, and both women turn around with wide eyes.

I frown. "What?"

Ruby bursts into a smile. "You don't look as nervous as we feel."

Averting her gaze, Gloria touches her brow. "This is all a bit much, isn't it?"

I don't know that I've ever seen her so frazzled. I cross to her and drop an arm across her shoulders. "I think it'll be great, but if it isn't a good fit, we go back to same-old, same-old. Just the way our customers like it."

"That's right." Gloria bestows a quick hug. "Lots to do!" She hastens from the kitchen.

I smile at Ruby. "What do you think?"

The big woman sighs. "I'm just praying that it all turns out okay."

Some kinks to be worked out, but the jamboree is a success. Though organized with the older folks in mind, several young and middle-aged couples are in attendance, including Chip and Vi Gairdt, and Pastor Paul and Leah. Provided the novelty doesn't wear off, I'd be a fool not to continue what Gloria put in place at Maddox's urging.

I sigh. He really does know what he's all about. Now the only question is, where is he? I look over the heads of Lum and Elva, Bea and Jack, Pam and Ross, and a dozen other couples who are availing themselves of the expertise offered by the dance instructor. No Maddox, even though we're nearly two hours into the three-hour event.

Lisa sidles alongside. "Wonder what's keeping him?"

I shrug. "Maybe he got stuck in a vision team meeting."

"Yeah." She glances over her shoulder. "Do you know what's up with Gloria? I know this is new for her, but she seems off."

I zero in on the older woman as she heads for the kitchen. "I've tried to talk to her, but I can't get her to stand still long enough."

"Well, now's your chance." Lisa nudges me.

I look around the dining room. With the exception of desserts and coffee, the buffet tables have been cleared. "All right."

But Gloria and Ruby aren't in the kitchen. However, before I can turn back, their voices drift through the open doorway that leads out back.

"But if you're wanting to retire, Gloria," Harriet says, "why not sell the café to First Grace?"

I halt in the middle of the kitchen and stare at the shadows that the porch light throws across the patio. Three of them.

"Because…"

"Go on, tell her," Ruby prompts.

Gloria sighs. "This stays between us, Harriet."

"All right."

"I can't sell the café to First Grace because I've agreed to sell it to Harri."

A long silence descends that I feel like a cold wind.

Harriet's shadow shakes its head. "Sell the café to Harri? Since when?"

"We've been talking about it for years, and she's been saving her money. She didn't want anyone to know. Afraid it wouldn't happen, I suppose—that she'd fail. But she didn't, and so at the beginning of the year, the café is hers."

Harriet's shadow drops its head into a hand. "Lord, what are we to do? First Grace needs this land or…"

Or what? And what does First Grace need the land for? But that's a foolish question. They want it for expansion.

"But surely they won't do away with the mobile home park," Gloria implores.

I grasp the nearest counter. Gloria's wrong. If not the café's land, then the park's, which was originally purchased with expansion in mind. Were it not for the near split years ago, which caused membership to fall off, the eyesore would have been mowed down. Instead, it was transformed into a senior community that has not only been the home of many of our older folks, but also generated a decent income for the church. But if Pastor Paul has his way—and Maddox—that's about to change.

My breath catches at the realization that this is the reason Maddox was interested in Gloria's retirement. And it explains his strange behavior this afternoon when he asked that I not stop trusting him, as well as Gloria and Ruby's behavior.

Voice warbling, Harriet says, "I don't see that they have any choice, Gloria. If you have an agreement with Harri, there's nowhere else to go but the park."

"Oh dear." Gloria's voice is tense. "Harri's going to take this hard."

Yes, she is. Or, more accurately, she isn't going to take it. This time, they've gone too far. The cutback from weekly communion to monthly. Very well. The shift from traditional to contemporary service. If they must. The addition of a second service. All right. The expansion into the mobile home park. Not all right.

"Yes, she is." Harriet's shadow is still. "Especially under the circumstances."

I hear someone enter the kitchen. Guessing it's Lisa, I don't move. Not that I could if I wanted to.

Ruby's hulking shadow presses its shoulders back. "How soon before they close down the park, Harriet?"

The smaller shadow turns its palms up. "A year, perhaps longer. Before they can break ground, they'll want to have the building campaign up and running."

"What about the residents?" Gloria asks. "Where will you all go?"

Harriet clears her throat. "First Grace will make arrangements."

"Harri?"

I don't jump when Maddox's soft, rumbly voice invades my personal space. I'm perfectly still—at least until his hand touches my shoulder. I spin around. "Trust? You?!"

He lowers his arm. "I was going to tell you."

"Harri!" Gloria shrills. "What are you doing in here? And Maddox?"

I look over my shoulder at where she stands with a hand on the door frame, her face pale beneath the fringe of silver hair. Behind her are Harriet and Ruby, eyes wide.

"What am I doing here? Witnessing the beginning of the end of First Grace as we know it." I swing back to Maddox, whose nose is longer than I remember, eyes so dark as to appear sinister, and that hair… It would be forgivable to mistake the two curls on his brow for horns.

"Harri—"

"No, Maddox. I don't need you to explain. I know what's going on."

"You don't." He lays a hand on my arm, but I pull free.

"Oh dear." The Katharine Hepburn warble is even more pronounced.

I remove my apron, drop it to the counter, and sidestep Maddox. I long for him to allow me to escape someplace where I can think this through, but he follows.

As I walk from the kitchen into the dining room, I feel the interest stirred by my appearance and Maddox's. I don't stop, even though I know I should attempt a smile for the older folks. But then I might cry and make things worse. If that's possible.

I slap a hand to the front door and march out into the warm night that lingers over the last weeks of August. As I step from the porch, Maddox's hand closes around my arm.

"We need to talk, Harri."

Think Scripture! What does the Bible say about anger? "Be slow to—"

No. Too late.

How about, "A fool is hotheaded and reckless. A quick-tempered man...woman...whatever!...does foolish things."

Maddox moves in front of me.

I snap my chin up. "Do you mind? I happen to be in the middle of searching for the right Scripture to deal with all this."

He studies my face until the door at my back whispers open. "Let's go someplace where we can talk."

"I don't want to talk, and certainly not to you." I look over my shoulder to find Pastor Paul standing behind me. "Or you."

He pushes his hands into his pockets, obviously deferring to Maddox's powers of persuasion.

"Harri, I need you to understand what we're trying to do—for everyone."

"Everyone?"

He releases my arm. "You have no idea how much time has gone into finding a way around the problem of future expansion, a way to keep the park."

I stamp my foot. "What about dual services?"

"It's good for a year, perhaps two if we move to three services, but eventually a new sanctuary will have to be built."

"What happened to plans to enlarge the existing sanctuary?"

"Initially, that seemed the best solution, and it may still be. But were we simply to enlarge the sanctuary, that would not only eat up a large portion of the existing parking, but First Grace's greater capacity would require more parking. So it was proposed that we offer on Gloria's property and expand in this direction. Unfortunately, though you mentioned she's talking retirement, when I approached her this afternoon, she told me she isn't interested in selling to us. I asked her to take some time to think it over, but she said she has no intention of changing her mind."

Confirmation that she didn't tell him the reason—me.

"That leaves us with the mobile home park. Despite it being a less costly option, since the land was purchased when it was inexpensive, First Grace was willing to pay a premium for Gloria's property to keep the senior citizens in their homes."

A premium. More than what Gloria and I agreed upon? Likely, as her price to me was set years ago. And still she said no, even though it must have thrown her into turmoil knowing that, by honoring our agreement, she'd be displacing those who frequent her café.

"I'm sorry, Harri, but if our projections hold—"

"*If* they hold? Then you could be wrong. Maybe First Grace is fine just the way it is. Maybe dual services is enough."

"No."

"Then three services."

"Not likely. Development in this area is booming, with hundreds of new families moving in every month, and a good number are looking for a church home."

I press my shoulders back. "We're not the only church in town. There are plenty of others."

"Yes, but despite First Grace being at the outer fringe of the development, it's getting more than its share of new families."

"That could change."

Maddox draws a sharp breath. "You're splitting hairs, Harriet."

I cross my arms over my chest. "At least I'm not the one splitting up the church."

If I'd thought Maddox's eyes couldn't darken further, I was wrong. "There isn't going to be a split. Sometime in the next two years, the mobile home park will be closed and arrangements made to assure that, regardless of where the residents relocate, they continue to have easy access to First Grace."

And that's that. I grasp at Scripture to douse my resentment.

"Be slow to become angry, for man's anger does not bring about the righteous life that God desires."

Slow? I'm *way* past slow.

"A gentle answer turns away wrath, but a harsh word stirs up anger."

Gentle? Yeah. Right.

"A fool gives full vent to his anger, but a wise man keeps himself under control."

I never claimed to be wise.

"Harri?"

I narrow my eyes. "You can't do this. The park is their home. It's where they've chosen to live out the rest of their lives. Now you're going to snatch it away?"

His hands clench at his sides. "We'll help them relocate—"

"That is *not* acceptable." I whip my head around to meet Pastor Paul's weary gaze. "Whatever it takes, I will not abandon my family as First Grace is so willing to abandon them."

"Whatever it takes?" Maddox's voice is rock hard.

I look back at him. "Whatever…it…takes."

"No, Bea." The creaky voice that drifts across the porch has us peering into the far shadows where two figures rise from rocking chairs.

Above my groan, I catch Maddox's borderline expletive. It couldn't have gotten worse, but it did. Within the next hour, every resident will hear of the plans to erase the park. Had I allowed Maddox to take me elsewhere, this could have been avoided. Or at least delayed.

Told you that a fool gives full vent to his anger. Fool!

"So that's the way it is, hmm?" Bea approaches Pastor Paul with Jack on her heels. "Gonna give us old folks the boot."

"Now, Bea…" Jack lays a hand on her arm.

"Don't 'Now, Bea' me, Jack Butterby. They're gonna take our homes, and all so they can turn our First Grace into a mega monstrosity."

"Bea…" Pastor Paul touches her rounded shoulder. Brave man. "When the time comes, we'll do our best to make the transition easy for the residents and will bear the expense to move the mobile homes to other parks."

She jerks her shoulder free. "My last years with Edward were spent in that park."

Pastor Paul momentarily closes his eyes. "I know you're upset. All I ask is that you and Jack and Harri not go sounding alarms before we talk some more with Gloria. She might still be convinced to sell."

No, she won't. Because of Harri's dream…

"Let me drive you home, Bea," Jack entreats.

Face brightly splotched in the light from the porch, Bea pulls shallow breaths as if about to explode. Thus, I'm surprised when her shoulders sink and chin drops. A few moments later, Jack leads her from the porch.

As they draw alongside me, she clutches my arm. "Don't let them do it, Harri." Her voice is hoarse, eyes large and pleading.

I fumble a hand atop hers. "I won't." How shallow is that? There's only one way to stop them, and that means sacrifice. A sacrifice I can't possibly make.

Bea releases me, and Jack urges her toward his car.

I stare at the ground. I need to be alone. Sidestepping Maddox, I cross to my bike.

"Harri?" As I throw a leg over, Maddox takes hold of the handlebars. "I know you're upset, and I understand. However, this is not insurmountable. It's…"

"Bad timing?" If my smile looks as bitter as it feels, he won't be kissing me anytime soon. Which is the way I want it. And from his hardening expression, the way *he* wants it. But to be certain there's no misunderstanding, I add, "It was never bad timing, Maddox. It was…" I draw a breath. "…a bad idea all around."

And that's all it takes. He releases the handlebars, steps back, and lets me pedal away. Just. Like. That.

- ? days until the next *The Coroner* rerun? Don't care.
- ? days until Jelly Belly replenishment? Don't care.
- ? days until completion of Bible #8—Simply don't care.
- 151 days until the café changes hands...

A hangover. And not just any hangover. A Jelly Belly/crying-fit hangover. Of course, the lack of oxygen is probably contributing to the throb behind my eyes. I really ought to come up for air. But I like it under here. It's warm and dark, and the stuffing does a fairly decent job of muffling the phone's ring. Not to mention the doorbell. Speaking of which…

I clamp the pillow tighter against my head to drown out the cheery *ding-dong*. After giving it a few minutes to assure that whoever's at the door goes away, I lift the pillow to peer at the clock. Seven thirty, meaning I'm a half hour late for work, meaning even if I drag myself out of bed, I'd be an hour late, meaning I probably should stay put. But I'm conflicted. Though Thursdays are slow at the café, in typical *old* Harri fashion, I'm letting people down—Gloria, Lisa, and the others. Not to mention the older folks who have been calling and knocking since fifteen minutes after I got home last night.

I groan. Must find a way to get through the day. Shoving the pillow aside, I do the army-man crawl—much to Dumplin's dismay—to the mattress edge and slide to the floor onto my knees.

I clasp my hands against my forehead. "Lord, You know what the old folks need. You know what First Grace needs. You know what I need. And we can't all have what *we* think we need. Help us." Then I'm stumbling upright to survey last night's damage. There's the empty tissue box, crumpled tissues, and Jelly Belly container. Notably absent are the highlighter, sticky tabs, Bible, and a *God's Promises* book. I just couldn't.

Fifteen minutes later, having dressed and applied excessive makeup to conceal puffy eyes and ruddy cheeks, I check to confirm that no one's lurking outside my mobile home. All clear. Rather than risk being spotted on Red Sea Lane, I put my mountain bike to good use and bounce across the field that backs up to the park. As I pass behind the church, heat begins to seep through my clothing. It may still be morning, but by mid-August it's hot 24/7.

On my approach to the café, I'm taken aback by the abundance of cars in the parking lot, the majority of which belong to park residents. Not good.

I enter the kitchen to find it deserted, the sound of excited voices coming from the dining room. Doubtless, Bea has stirred everyone into a panic.

"Get it over with," I mutter, but as I start for the dining room, Lisa enters.

"Everyone's looking for you!" She rushes forward. "They're going on about how First Grace has turned its back on them, talking about leaving the church, and pushing poor Gloria to sell the café to save the park."

Oh, Bea, why couldn't you have exercised some self-control? "I know."

Lisa gives me a push. "So get out there and calm them down before Ruby starts bouncing those old folks out the doors—walkers and all."

I could almost smile. As imposing and outspoken as Ruby is, the closest she'd come to bouncing the older folks would be to offer piggyback rides. "All right." I start to step past her.

"Did you hear how much First Grace offered for the café?"

"No."

"Neither did I, but Ruby and Gloria were discussing it this morning. Apparently, it was very generous, because Gloria was agonizing over turning it down. She said it was enough to assure her a very comfortable retirement."

I swallow. "Then she is considering First Grace's offer?"

"Nope. That's why she was agonizing. Said her word was nothing if she couldn't keep it—as if she's already made an agreement with someone else."

I consider the tiled floor; the grout could use a scrub. And that's not all that could use a scrub. As for the best place to start, that would be the truth. "Gloria does have an agreement with someone else. Me."

Lisa's eyes widen. "This is your dream? To own the café?"

"It is."

"Wow. Talk about being caught between a rock and a hard place."

"Is that what this is? I was thinking more along the lines of rolls of barbed wire."

She gives a sympathetic nod. "So what are you going to do?"

Tears blur my vision. "I don't know. Maybe what I don't want to do. What I'm screaming inside not to do."

Lisa closes the distance between us. "Harri, you don't have to give up your dream. No one would blame you if—"

"If I let the old Harri out? Thought only of myself? Didn't care who got hurt?"

She does a double take. "You really think that whatever you do today will be judged by your past?" She shakes her head. "I'm disappointed."

"Why?"

"Because I thought you believed in God's promises."

"I do!"

"Then why haven't you accepted His forgiveness? You asked for it, didn't you?"

I draw a sharp breath. "Yes."

"Then it was given, and yet here you stand stinking of unforgiveness, considering throwing away your dream in hopes it will absolve you of things you've already been absolved of."

Is that what I'm doing? Maybe a little. But, really, after all I put everyone through, I got off way too easy.

"The old Harri doesn't exist anymore, so do us all a favor and come to terms with who you are now—a forgiven woman. Then, and only then, decide what to do. If you don't, you'll end up bitter. And nobody wants that, especially God."

Is she right? Am I setting myself up for martyrdom?

"Okay, Harri?"

Not really, but… "Okay."

Her arms come around me, and I sink against her and drink in her friendship for all it's worth—until a commotion in the dining room pulls us apart.

"They're getting worked up." I glance past Lisa. "I should talk to them."

"Just don't make any promises, hmm?"

When I step into the room, it looks more like a town meeting than a dining experience. Immediately, all eyes turn to me. As a murmur goes around, I survey the faces. Of the forty or so occupants, all but a dozen are park residents. And Bea isn't among them.

Jack offers me a reassuring smile, which I do my best to return as I cross to where Gloria stands before those gathered.

"Harri!" Pam jumps up from the Daisy table. "You have to do something. You can't let them tear down our park."

A small, squat gentleman who's rarely seen outside his mobile home, rises. "You have to convince Gloria to sell the café."

As I position myself alongside Gloria, a ratchety voice calls, "You have to take a stand."

Lum and Elva help each other up. "You have to help us, Harri."

"Yeah," pipes up an old-timer who, though he's attended First Grace since its inception and is inching toward eighty years old, still lives on his hundred-acre ranch. "You have to get your father back here. He'll put a stop to all this nonsense."

Mrs. Feterall raises a hand. "You have to talk to Brother Paul about this."

You have to this...have to that...

Harriet jumps up. "Harri doesn't have to do anything. What *we* have to do is pray." She looks around. "We have to ask God to make a way—to provide for us whatever the outcome. Isn't that right, Harri?"

It certainly is. "I'll do what I can, but Harriet's right. Prayer is what we need."

Gloria heaves a sigh. And I ache for her, knowing it can't be easy to look like a solution that refuses to cooperate. And all because she gave me her word.

"Now settle up your bills," Harriet calls, "and let Gloria get back to business."

Reluctantly, the older folks stir from their flower-bedecked tables.

"Our agreement stands," Gloria says to me, leaning near. "You hear?"

I am touched that she knows me well enough to sense what's going through my mind. "We'll see."

"Oh!" I halt before the porch, where my perspiring brother sits with Doo-Dah on his lap—Doo-Dah, whom I agreed to watch again. "I forgot!"

"Obviously." Though Tyler's mouth is tight, his eyes are beyond fluent, as in "That's the Harri I know. Good *old* unreliable Harri."

I try not to take offense, because he has no idea what kind of day I've had—trudging through my waitressing job and hiding out in my office at First Grace to avoid Maddox. "I'm sorry. You're not going to miss your plane, are you?"

"It'll be close, but I should make it." He straightens and hands Doo-Dah to me as I mount the steps. "I would have left him, but I never got the carrier back from you."

My fault—surprise, surprise. I tuck Doo-Dah against my chest. "I really am sorry. It's just that…" I blink away tears.

"Are you all right?"

Why does he have to sound concerned? Frustration, even anger, I can handle, but not this. "Yeah." I fumble for the keys in my handbag. "It's just been a long day."

"Liar."

I startle in remembrance of the last time he called me that—when it was true in a very bad sense. Fortunately, he doesn't seem to notice my reaction. He's too intent on brushing my hand aside and rooting out my keys.

I don't protest, and a few moments later he lets me into my mobile home.

"Thanks." I lower Doo-Dah, and Dumplin' comes bounding down the hall. "Be nice!" I call as he zips past.

"Better you than me," Tyler mutters. Hand on the doorknob, he sighs. "I really don't have time for this, Harri, but what's up?"

How strange is that? My big brother is taking the time to find out why my insides are such a mess. I have every intention of brushing off his question, but a sob escapes.

"Harri?"

I wave a hand. "You'd better—*hic!*—go or you'll miss your—*hic!*—plane."

He takes my arm. "You're going to owe me for this, so you might as well get your money's worth and tell me."

I long to send him away, but more, I long for someone to talk to. And so, sitting beside him on the sofa, I spill the beans. "So what do you think?" I draw the back of a hand across my moist eyes.

"It's not up to me to tell you what to do."

My laugh is bitter. "Why not? You used to be pretty good at it."

He raises an eyebrow. "Is that how you got yourself into so much trouble—by listening to me?"

He has a point. "I'm talking about before I…went 'prodigal.'"

"Well, times have changed. You're an adult now, and I'm no longer the know-it-all big brother. Whatever you decide about the café, it has to be from you. And prayer."

"You're right." I draw a deep breath. "Thank you for missing your plane for me." For *me*.

He rises. "If I'm going to catch the next flight, I'd better get going."

"Sure."

"See ya, Doo-Dah…Dumplin'." He heads for the door.

It's then I realize I haven't heard a peep from the kitchen. Shouldn't I have heard something—something low and threatening? After all, Dumplin' was visibly pleased when Doo-Dah left the last time. As I cross to the door, I glance into the kitchen. And there they are—Dumplin' under the table, keeping an eye on Doo-Dah, where he sits on the refrigerator between the Jelly Belly container and the pink helmet.

At the door, Tyler turns and, after some hesitation, says, "I'm proud of you for the hard work you put into buying the café."

Proud. "Really?"

"The only thing is, even if you hold Gloria to her word, your expectations are unrealistic."

"What do you mean?"

"This idea that everything will be perfect, that you'll live happily ever after with the regular café crowd." He sweeps a hand up. "They're old, Harri. Near the end of their lives. And you aren't even close to the middle of yours. You need to stop playing it safe and just be you: Harri, who has been forgiven."

Why does he have to sound so much like Maddox? And Lisa? And Harriet? And did he really say "forgiven"?

I don't want to cry again, but the tears and the hiccupping return. And, to my surprise, Tyler's arms come around me. It's a forced hug. An awkward hug. A not-sure-I'm-ready-for-this hug. But a hug.

"Tyler?" I say into his shoulder.

"Yeah?"

"I'm going to say this one last time, okay?"

I feel him stiffen. "What?"

I pull back. "I'm sorry. Sorry I slapped Gina, sorry for breaking up the two of you, sorry she and her family left the church, sorry about your broken nose and ribs." I replenish my air. "Sorry that I messed up your life."

He stares at me, jaw convulsing, then nods. "I know. But what you need to know is that you didn't mess up my life."

"But you're not married."

His eyes widen a moment before he chuckles. "That's because I haven't found the woman I want to spend my life with, not because Gina was the love of my life."

"But you wanted to marry her."

"We were nineteen, Harri."

Rushed with relief, I'm tempted to hug him again and hold on tight, but I know he's in danger of missing the next plane out.

He pushes the hair out of my eyes. "All better?"

"Oh yeah. Lots." I lean forward and kiss his cheek.

He startles, but when I draw back, it isn't distaste on his face, but a smile. "You have my cell number. Call me when you decide what you're going to do."

Clearly he means it. I watch him all the way to his car, and five minutes later, I'm on my knees thanking God for what just happened between us. Fifteen minutes later, I'm on my stomach flipping through my Bible and coming back time and again to 1 Corinthians 1:10: "Brothers and sisters, I encourage all of you in the name of our Lord Jesus Christ to agree with each other and not to split into opposing groups. I want you to be united in your understanding and opinions."

No division—in its most extreme form, a "split." Would it really come to that? Probably not, but there would be discontent among the displaced senior citizens. And it's within my power to prevent it...

But what about my dream?

- ? days until the next *The Coroner* rerun? Still don't care.
- ? days until Jelly Belly replenishment? Still don't care.
- ? days until completion of Bible #8—Should I care?
- ? days until Harriet Bisset owns her own café—God knows.

I called her last night."

After a long silence on the other end of the line, Tyler prompts, "And?"

"She invited me over, and we talked until midnight."

"You're letting the café go, I assume."

I stare out my office window at the mobile home park visible through the trees. "I had to do it. I can't let their homes be taken when it's in my power to help them."

"That sounds a lot like regret."

"I do regret it. It's one of the hardest things I've ever done." Dropping my head back, I shift my gaze to the ceiling. How strange it is to feel numb after all the wracking emotions of yesterday. "But it's for the best."

"You did pray through it, didn't you?"

Did I? "I…some."

"Well, I'm sure you made the right decision. So when will Gloria give them the good news?"

My laugh is dry. "Everyone will know soon enough." Though not of my role in it. Gloria objected to keeping quiet about our agreement, but I insisted. I know these old folks, and I won't burden them with a feeling of indebtedness when *I'm* the one who's indebted to them for the love they showed me when I returned broken and needy all those years ago.

"You did good, Harri."

Tyler's praise causes a smile to flow to the corners of my mouth. "Yeah, the old folks won't be going anywhere anytime soon."

"Unless First Grace goes megachurch and ends up needing the mobile home park after all."

My breath catches.

"Now, Harri, *if* that happens, it will be years from now, and by then…"

By then, most of the old folks will be gone. But what about those who come after? whose fixed incomes necessitate affordable housing? who long for fellowship among Christian peers? who need easy access to their church home?

"Forget I said anything. Okay?"

Impossible.

"Remember, don't worry about tomorrow. Tomorrow will worry about itself."

Tyler leaves the Scripture for me to finish, and I do so grudgingly. "Each day has enough trouble of its own." To my surprise, the dark clouds that were descending lift, and not just because of the words I spoke, but because Tyler and I shared them.

I lower my gaze from the ceiling and catch sight of something. Or someone. Maddox, who stands in my doorway wearing a face so unmoving a chill goes through me. "Uh, can I call you back? I've got someone in my office."

"Sure."

"'Bye." I lower the handset.

"What have you done, Harri?"

His eyes are cold and distant. Miles away from me. Perhaps continents. Scrabbling back through my exchange with Tyler, I try to recall what I said. It's sketchy, but the one-sided conversation to which Maddox was privy made it sound as if I were up to no good. Unfortunately, I can't correct him—at least, until Gloria makes the final decision about the café, and that largely depends on a meeting she's trying to set up with her accountant.

I press my shoulders back. "Hasn't anyone ever told you it's impolite to eavesdrop?"

He strides forward and presses his palms to my desk. "Don't get in the middle of this. Whatever you've done, you have to pull back."

He thinks the worst of me. That hurts.

He leans forward. "I give you my word. First Grace will not abandon the park residents."

I believe him, but considering what this is costing me, I'm too human not to resent him and his vision team. Eventually, I'll let it go, but right now it's too raw. And to make matters worse, I still have feelings for this human wrecking ball. "I want what's best for the older folks."

"What's best for them has to be what's best for First Grace, its other members, and the community."

"I know that."

He searches my face, then lays a hand over mine. "Talk to me, Harri. Tell me what's going on."

All of me leaps, and I'm tempted to tell him everything. However, not only isn't it my place to tell, but I'm still angry with him. Though he's unaware of the decision I made, I can't help but blame him for putting me in this position. I pull my hand from beneath his. "I can't. Not yet."

A shadow falls across his face, and he straightens. "All right." He turns and strides from my office.

Aching, I look at the phone and silently beseech Gloria to call. But the call I'm longing for probably won't come until the beginning of next week, as it's not likely she'll be able to arrange a meeting with her accountant on such short notice.

I clasp my hands in my lap. *I'm trying, Lord. Trying hard.*

Twenty-Four

Harri's Log: • Nothing worth counting down...

I'd rather cat-sit a dozen Dumplin's and Doo-Dahs than attend today's pre-Sunday meeting. Rather read my Bible out of order. Rather miss the first episode of the new season of *The Coroner.* Rather gobble down a half-chewed mass of mango Jelly Bellys—

No, that would be pushing it. With a shake of my shoulders, I traverse the hall and step into the meeting room, only to draw up short at the sight of the two people sitting at the table. Only two, and yet I'm ten minutes late.

Pastor Paul looks up, the lines of his face etched so deeply that he appears ten years older.

As for Maddox's face, it's a study in controlled anger. "Come in, Harri."

I glance behind. "But where are the others? They—"

"The meeting has been cancelled."

"Oh." Then I've finally done it. This is the "Good-bye, Harri" I've feared. Ironically, it's worse than expected, and all because my loss is no longer limited to First Grace. I glance between the two men. Yep, my life has officially fallen apart. Again.

Lord, help me accept this with dignity. Strengthen me so I can be Christlike.

Maddox rises from beside Pastor Paul. "Join us, Harri." He nods at the chair opposite them, but I can't move, so he comes around the table and takes my arm. *Big* mistake. Or nearly so, because the moment before I say words I'll regret, a kind of peace— apathy?—washes over me, and the lamb is led to the slaughter.

I settle in the chair Maddox pulls out and track him as he resumes his seat. He settles in, then reaches for the paper in front of Pastor Paul and pushes it toward me.

Guessing it's a letter of termination, I lower my gaze. But the typewritten letter isn't addressed to me. It's addressed to Pastor Paul. At the bottom, the letter is signed, "A <u>VERY</u> concerned member of First Grace."

As I read through it, my stomach rises. It's a letter of complaint. Worse, it's a letter of threat. In short, if First Grace proceeds with its plans to dismantle the park, the truth about Pastor Paul's exit from his last church will be exposed. As for the reason for his exit, it was an act of indiscretion—sexual harassment of a church employee.

Hands trembling, I drop them to my lap and look from Pastor Paul, who regards me with pressed lips, to Maddox, who isn't as versed at tempering his emotions. Only then do I understand what this is about—not that it isn't tied to my termination. "You think I did this."

Maddox's eyes bore into mine. "Are you involved?"

"What do you mean 'involved'?"

He retrieves the letter. "Composed on an old typewriter, complete with strikeouts. I'm guessing Bea Dawson."

As am I. "And you believe I had a hand in it."

Maddox shoves back in his chair. "Harri, the night of the jamboree, you said you would do whatever it took to stop First Grace from closing down the park. Then yesterday, when you were on the phone, you said you weren't going to stand by and allow the older folks' homes to be taken from them when it was in your power to help them. And that you regretted what you'd had to do."

Realizing how that sounded in light of the letter, my anger begins to drain off. I force my gaze to Pastor Paul. "It's true that, during the conversation Maddox eavesdropped on"—yes, *eavesdropped!*—"I voiced regret over something I'd done, but I didn't write that letter."

"Or conspire with anyone?" Maddox presses.

The tide once more turns toward anger. "Or conspire!"

"You're saying that your phone conversation had nothing to do with the mobile home park?"

There goes the tide again, and all I can do is work my mouth in search of words that not only won't betray Gloria's confidence but won't make me a liar. Unfortunately, a half truth is the best I can do. "All right. My conversation *was* about the park—and saving it—but not like this. I know nothing about the accusation in that letter."

"Then Anna didn't tell you what happened at the last church I pastored?" Pastor Paul asks quietly.

Realization opens its fingers to offer up an explanation for Anna's angst and rebellion. She must have seen her father forced out, as some had tried to force out my father. Must have experienced how deeply Christians can hurt one another.

"No, Anna didn't say anything to me. But if she had, I wouldn't have broken her confidence." Does he believe me?

"I did make a mistake at my last church," he finally says, "but not what I was accused of. I had to fire one of our staff. Thinking it could be done amicably, I met with the woman without a witness present. She became angry and stormed out of my office. The next day, she accused me of sexual harassment and threatened to go public if the board didn't demand my resignation. I defended myself, and the board sided with me; however, in the end it was determined that it would be best if I left, especially since I'd only been at the church for two years and my attempts to grow and update it were constantly challenged by the predominantly elderly congregation." He draws a deep breath. "It was hard on our family."

And I'd thought it fortunate that neither Leah nor Anna had ever had to deal with anything like I'd had to deal with...

"Did my father know?"

"Yes, as did those on the board who approved me."

Among them, Bea's departed husband. *Oh, Bea.*

"I won't be blackmailed, Harri."

I nearly protest, but it *is* blackmail—driven by fear and self-preservation, but blackmail nonetheless. And it sounds as if he believes I'm the one doing the blackmailing. Here comes that tide of anger, but before it reaches my shores, I tell myself I will not be angry. I will accept this as God's plan and do what I should have done years ago.

"If I have to," Pastor Paul continues, "I'll address this accusation with the congregation, even if it means putting my family through more turmoil." He glances at Maddox. "I won't be forced out again. I'm seeing First Grace through."

Feeling Maddox's gaze, I rise. "I hope you will. And I won't stand in your way. I'll finish out this month, then…" Then, what? After all, the café is pretty much spoken for.

Pastor Paul's brow furrows. "What are you saying?"

I try to smile, and surprisingly, it isn't all that hard. "I'm resigning."

Maddox stands. "Harri—"

I throw a hand up as Pastor Paul also rises. "This isn't where I'm supposed to be. It was just a stopover that I allowed to become permanent." I jut my chin at the letter. "As for that, I'll take care of it." I blow out a breath. "There. That wasn't so hard." Actually, it was, but not as hard as I expected. Of course, there's always "delayed reaction." I step toward the door. "I know you have lots to do in preparation for tomorrow's service, so I'll let you get to it."

"Harri, we have to talk about this." Maddox comes around the table—Maddox who believed me capable of blackmail.

"No, we don't. It's for the best." I walk into the hallway. Part of me wishes he would come after me and apologize for what he believed me capable of, but the other part is relieved when I enter the park alone.

Shortly, Bea opens her door to my rapping and peers at me through puffy, bloodshot eyes.

"What's wrong, Bea?"

She frowns, but just when I'm certain she's going to close the door in my face, her countenance crumples. "Oh, Harri, I did something bad. And I don't think Jack will ever forgive me."

Ten minutes later, between sobs and nose blowing, the story of the letter to Pastor Paul and how Jack found out about it is laid at my feet. This morning, when Jack came to check on Bea, who'd holed herself up for the past few days, she invited him in. As she set coffee to brewing, he entered the kitchen holding a draft of the letter she'd inadvertently left out. He told her it was wrong, and that though he understood her fear of being uprooted, he wanted nothing to do with such un-Christlike behavior.

Bea blows again and adds another tissue to the pile on her sofa table. "I knew it was wrong, but every time I looked around and remembered Edward and our years together here—even that last year when he was so sick—I got madder until I was certain that he would want me to do whatever it took to save the homes of our friends."

Whatever it took… "And so you used what he told you about Pastor Paul and put it in a letter."

Indignation leaps into her eyes. "What kind of man do you think my husband was, Harriet Bisset?"

I blink. "I just—"

"Just nothing, missy! Edward was a model of Christian manhood. He would never have told me what went on behind closed doors."

"Then…?"

A flush creeps up her cheeks. "I didn't mean to listen in on a discussion between him and your father, but when I returned home from shopping, the kitchen window was open, and they were sitting out back discussing Pastor Paul's qualifications. I couldn't help but overhear."

"Did you also hear that the accusation was false?"

She startles. "False? How do you know that?"

"I just came from a meeting with Pastor Paul and Maddox McCray."

Her face starts to crumple again. "Then he received the letter."

"Yes."

Crumple, crumple. "I was praying that a postal machine would chew it up—you know, bite it into greasy little pieces like the ones you sometimes get in a baggy from the post office with a note of apology." Her mouth trembles. "What did Pastor Paul say?"

"That he's staying put and won't be..." No, not *blackmailed.* "Won't be pushed out. He's going to do what's best for First Grace and its members, Bea."

She nods wearily. "I just wanted to stop him from taking my home like he decided to take my organ. But I wouldn't have done it—gone public about that woman's accusations."

"The accusation was false."

She lowers her head. "Oh, Harri, Edward would have been so disappointed in me—just like Jack. And if either of them knew about the projector bulbs..."

Case of the missing bulbs solved.

She reaches for another tissue. "It's hard being old, and alone, and unwanted, and...afraid."

Despite what she did and the suspicion cast on me, I scoot nearer and slide an arm around her. She stiffens slightly but allows me to draw her close. "I know, Bea. Well, not the old part."

She tries to laugh, but the sound ends on a sob.

"Don't worry. Everything will work out—First Grace, the park, even Jack."

"You promise?"

"Better yet, why don't we pray about it?"

An hour later, Jack sees me to the door of his mobile home. "I'll take it from here, Harri." He glances at Bea, who's seated at his kitchen table where she and I settled a while ago to ask for Jack's help in sorting out the mess. "I'll call Pastor Paul and see if he'll come talk with us."

"Thank you, Jack."

"No." He gives a nicely wrinkled smile. "Thank *you*, Harri."

Praying that Bea hasn't caused irreparable damage to their budding relationship, I wave as I descend the steps.

Neither Dumplin' nor Doo-Dah greets me when I unlock my door, which is disappointing. I've become partial to having a reason to come home—someone...er, some*thing* that's happy to see me. Even if it is only for the food. However, in the next instant, the reason for their absence becomes evident. They have trashed my bookshelf. My perfectly ordered Bibles are everywhere, as are my *God's Promises* books and collection of inspirational fiction.

"Dumplin'," I growl as I close the door. "Doo-Dah!"

Neither one owns up, wisely digging in wherever they are.

I cross to the shelf. Most of the books fell onto their front or back, but several flew open during Dumplin' and Doo-Dah's Wild Ride and are sprawled with their pages bent and edges crimped. I pick up my King James Bible that I read through in 2001. The pages of Nehemiah and Esther are folded in on themselves, and the lower edge of Lamentations shows evidence of sharp teeth.

Gnashing my own teeth, I collect the books, but as I begin to order them for their return to the bookshelf, I realize what a waste of time it is. As I've given my notice to First Grace, I'll have to find another place to live. I might as well box them up.

I'm okay, at least until I set the last Bible into the cardboard box. Then I start to bawl.

Water is amazingly restorative, especially when delivered over a long period of time in a very toasty state. Unfortunately, though my taut muscles find relief in the heat and spray, it does little for the pounding at the back of my head. Strangely, when I drain the water heater of its last hot drop and turn off the taps, the pounding grows louder.

Someone's at the door. With a congested snort, courtesy of my crying jag, I wrap myself in a towel. "Go away," I mutter as the pounding continues. But whoever it is, doesn't. In jeans and an oversized sweatshirt, I open the door. Be still, my wretched heart.

Maddox sizes me up, from my towel-dried hair to my bare toes. "I was beginning to think I might have to break down the door."

I glower at him through the screen. "How did you know I was here?"

"Plumbing."

"What?"

"I could hear the water running through your pipes, so I guessed you were showering."

"Well, aren't you a regular Sherlock Holmes." I step nearer and peer left and right. Sure enough, curtains are moving as my neighbors keep tabs on me—no doubt curious over the ruckus Maddox caused.

I cross my arms over my chest. "What can I do for you?"

"Invite me in."

"That would hardly be appropriate."

"There's still plenty of daylight, and you can leave the door open. Besides, I'm not afraid of false accusations."

"After what happened to Pastor Paul? You should be, because, until today, you probably didn't believe me capable of blackmail either."

Regret shifts across his face. "That's why I'm here. Or one of the reasons."

Then he knows Bea owned up. Though relieved to have my name cleared, I'm angered by the necessity.

Maddox glances at Elva, who has popped her head out the door. "May I come in, Harri?"

I want to say no, but that's petty. All fingers pointed to me being involved in the writing of that letter—especially my own— and it's not as if my relationship with Maddox is longstanding and he ought to know I'm incapable of such behavior. Or so I tell myself past the ache.

I push the screen door open. "Come in."

Elva is still watching, and I raise a hand as Maddox steps inside. "Everything's fine."

She nods and heads back inside her mobile home.

When I turn, Maddox's back is to me where he stares at my boxed books. He looks around. "You said you would finish out the month at First Grace."

"I will. I just thought I'd get a jump on packing." No need to tell him that Dumplin' and Doo-Dah gave me the idea.

"You may want to rethink your move."

"Why?"

"That's the other thing I need to talk to you about, but first, I owe you an apology."

Not until I feel my nails sink into my upper arms do I realize I'm gripping them. "Pastor Paul's letter."

"Yes. As I was on my way here, Paul called and told me he'd met with Bea and Jack." He spreads his hands. "I didn't want to believe you'd had anything to do with that letter, Harri, but what you said and what I overheard…" Beneath his white button-down shirt, his shoulders rise with a large breath. "I smelled a 'split,' so I did what I was hired to do. Assess the problem. Find a solution. Unfortunately, it appeared that you were part of the problem. I'm sorry."

I don't doubt his sincerity, but today's meeting sits with me like an overdose of Jelly Bellys. "All right."

His gaze flickers, evidence he was looking for more than acknowledgment.

I lower my arms to my sides, but a moment later clasp my hands, desperate to hold on to something, even if it is only me.

"Your right hand will hold me fast." I grasp at Scripture—the assurance that God will hold on to me—but I can't quite feel His hand. And it's all because the old Harri is breathing down my neck.

"Can we sit down?"

I step past him, and as I perch on the edge of my recliner, he lowers to the sofa. "The other thing I need to talk to you about is Gloria's property. While Paul was meeting with Bea and Jack, I met with Gloria and her accountant."

They had a meeting? I glance at the answering machine. Sure enough, the light is blinking—was probably blinking when I came home. I experience a spurt of regret at not picking up the message that's surely from Gloria, though it's not as if it would make any difference. It is what it is.

"I believe we've reached an agreement with her to sell the café to First Grace." Maddox begins to smile. "The mobile home park will stay, Harri."

That's that, then. Good-bye, dream. Not that it isn't what I wanted, but it *isn't* what I wanted—the selfish side of Harri, that is. "Good. It's for the best."

His smile reverses. "I have to say that I was expecting a more enthusiastic response. Though the church's finances will be strained, Gloria has been offered a generous sum that will not only assure her a comfortable retirement but allow the elderly folks to remain in their homes."

"For how long?"

"You're worried that, if First Grace outgrows Gloria's property, the park will once more be threatened."

"Yes."

"I don't see that happening, and certainly not in the near future, but I suppose it's possible down the road. Regardless, I assure you that the current residents have nothing to worry about."

"Well, I am happy about that."

He seems doubtful, and he should be. I *am* happy that Gloria's retirement will be more comfortable and the residents won't be forced to move, but there's still the matter of my loss. I'll just get over it.

Maddox gives a throaty sigh. "Now all that remains is to decide what to do with the café."

I scoff. "Mow it down. That's what you're buying it for."

"Ultimately, but it would be foolish not to take advantage of its ability to generate income until First Grace is ready to expand. Which is where you come in."

"Me?"

"Gloria says she'll retire at the beginning of the year, and since you're leaving women's ministry, I thought you might want to run the place."

Would that fall under the heading of adding insult to injury?

"She says you're indispensable, that she couldn't have made the café a success without you."

He has no idea how much that hurts.

"Interested?"

"No." The word bursts from me. Best to cut the ties and see if I can knit some new ones together elsewhere.

"Why?" His question is sharp, as is the look in his eyes. "Let me guess—now you're not happy about the café closing down."

"Of course not."

His jaw shifts. "Look, it's just a waitressing job."

I shoot to my feet. "It is *not* just a waitressing job! It's my—"

What are you doing?! You are going to accept this with grace. So calm down and—sheesh!—stop with the heaving chest.

Maddox rises. "It's your what?"

"The café is…an important part of this community, especially for our older folks."

Is that suspicion sweeping his face? "And obviously important for you."

Does he know?

He takes a step toward me. "Are you sure you aren't thinking only of yourself, Harri?"

That doesn't sit well. "Thinking only of myself?" *Stop it—now!* "Myself!" *I mean it!* "I am *not* that Harri anymore. You have no idea what I—"

"You're wrong." Maddox closes his eyes, and when he opens them, they're shot with regret. "Tell me about the café."

Oh no. That *was* suspicion.

He starts to lift a hand toward me, but drops it to his side. "Tell me."

I cross my arms over my chest. "You were baiting me."

"I was."

"Well, there isn't much to tell beyond what you've already guessed."

"Yes, there is. You're the reason Gloria wouldn't sell to First Grace."

That wasn't a question. I swallow a painful lump. "Yes, we made an agreement years ago."

"And now she's backing out."

He's baiting me again—the raunch! "No."

"You were going to allow me to believe the worst about you."

My eyes sting. My nose prickles. My throat constricts. "No more than what you already believed regarding my involvement in writing that letter to Pastor Paul."

Even before regret deepens across his face, I'm awash in my own regret over such a juvenile response. "I'm sorry. The hurt just…came out."

"I'm sorry about that." He broadens his shoulders, appearing to make room for a great weight. "Why didn't you tell me about your plans to buy the café?" The question has shades of accusation, as if I kept something from him. As if he had a right to know.

"Why didn't you tell me about First Grace's plans to acquire the café? The day of the picnic, you knew, and yet you said nothing."

Maddox's face hardens. "I could say that, as a consultant to First Grace, there are certain things that I'm not at liberty to discuss, and it would be true. However, the reason I didn't tell you was that I didn't want to alarm you or the residents, especially when the possibility existed to acquire Gloria's property." His lids narrow. "So what's your excuse for not being up front, Harri?"

Fear of failure should I lose control of the new Harri, who still struggles against foul words, occasionally longs for nicotine, falls prey to ugly thoughts, could be persuaded to trade in her bike, car, and mobile home for a motorcycle, and isn't certain she wouldn't yield to temptation given the right—er, *wrong*—circumstances. Circumstances that have everything to do with Maddox.

"Admit it, you're afraid that you'll find yourself on the back of a motorcycle, spewing foul words, tattoos proudly displayed, and virtue up for grabs."

Lord, why are You letting him in my head?

"Yes, you said you aren't *that* Harri anymore, but now you have to believe it, not just live like it. You have to allow that you're going to stumble like the rest of us and trust God to give you a hand up."

I can't stop myself, can't tamp down the defensiveness that jumps through me like a frog on steroids. "Don't preach at me, Maddox McCray."

"I'm simply telling you that *this* Harri"—he lays a hand on my shoulder—"is different from the old one, as further evidenced by what *this* Harri gave up for her friends."

I shrug out from beneath his hand. "Unfortunately, for all *this* Harri gave up, it's only a temporary fix." There. Focus off of me, even if I have brought us full circle. "Though you say that if further expansion happens it will be years from now and the current residents aren't likely to be affected, what about those who move into the park in the meantime—who make it the home of their last years?"

"Then you don't trust me or First Grace to do right by them?"

"No, I don't."

You know, Harri, if you thought before you spoke, you could avoid that stone of regret that just dropped through your stomach. I cannot believe I said that, especially as it isn't true. Well, not exactly…

The shifting in Maddox's eyes tells me he can't believe it either—that he took the words the way I said them. But not really the way I meant them. That was mostly hurt talking. And fear.

He lowers his head, and one of those curls that I have yet to test the springiness of—and probably never will—shifts off his brow. "I should probably go."

No, I won't be testing it. "Yes, you should." I cross the room and push open the screen door.

As he steps past me, he pauses. "One of these days, you're going to have to accept that you're forgiven, Harri."

I stand straighter. "I know I'm forgiven."

"Then start living like it." He descends the stairs, leaving me with a sudden craving for a cigarette that causes my fingers to twitch. And to top it off, I'm tempted to curse. See! I am still warped.

As much as I long to close the door on Maddox's retreating back, I watch him cross to the other side of Red Sea Lane. And that's when I'm struck by the irony that he's on one side and I'm on the other. And it's doubtful there will be any parting of the Red Sea that lies between us. After all, I said I didn't trust him.

Jelly Bellys.

I told him to go.

Jelly Bellys.

I held the door for him to walk out of my life even though I…I…

Jelly Bellys.

I let my shoulders slump. Even though I've fallen for him.

Jelly Bellys—a couple coconuts, a few cherries, maybe a piña colada…

That'll do it. Still, I don't turn back until Maddox disappears inside his home, then I declare, "That's that."

My chin drops a notch, lips quiver, lids flicker. *Oh Lord, that's… that!*

I rip into the kitchen, grab the Jelly Belly container from beside a startled Doo-Dah, and race to my bedroom. But the Jelly Bellys don't taste all that good. After a dozen attempts to jump-start my taste buds with the most potent flavors, I set the container aside. Now what?

Oooh! I can almost taste a cigarette—gross, but satisfying. To make matters worse, my nose is running, and my eyes sting. As I reach to the tissue box, my gaze falls on the *God's Promise* book atop my Bible. I open to the contents page, and the subject that catches my attention is *Fear.* I skim the related scriptures, several of which I've highlighted.

"Do not be anxious about anything, but in everything, by prayer and petition, with thanksgiving, present your requests to God."

Stroking Dumplin's head, I vaguely wonder when he crawled into my lap. I scan the contents again. *Forgiveness.* I tell myself that I'm good with God, but I don't really believe it. Just like Lisa and Maddox don't believe I believe it.

The little book lists seven scriptures, the first being, *"If we confess our sins, he is faithful and just and will forgive us our sins and purify us from all unrighteousness."*

I know that, but it's too easy. I mean, how valuable can forgiveness be if it doesn't require something approaching a pound of flesh? Or a dream…

"Praise the LORD, O my soul, and forget not all his benefits—who forgives all your sins and heals all your diseases, who redeems your life from the pit—"

I *was* in the pit.

"—and crowns you with love and compassion, who satisfies your desires with good things so that your youth is renewed like the eagle's."

But how can my youth be renewed? It was so dirty…so dark. And just like that it's renewed? Not that I don't believe God's Word, but there's always fine print, isn't there?

Note: This offer does not apply to Harriet Josephine Bisset who broke practically every commandment, hurt her family deeply, nearly ruined her father, and disappointed the entire congregation. Should said sinner wish forgiveness, nothing short of a sacrifice will be accepted (i.e., the café), and only then with the stipulation that she suffer deeply over her loss.

Suffer deeply so First Grace can grow and flourish without regard for those that growth hurts—

Stop it, Harri! Do what God would have you do. If you don't stamp out this resentment, it's going to suffocate you.

I trudge into the kitchen for a glass of water and, on the return, stop at the answering machine.

"Harri, it's Gloria."

I stare at the machine as her message of hours earlier plays out, informing me that she's decided to sell to First Grace. She thanks me for thinking of her and for my "sacrifice" for our friends.

No, not a sacrifice. The right thing—for everyone. I have to believe it.

Gloria ends with the suggestion that I open my own café with the money I've saved. Not that I haven't already considered that. It's just not a sure thing. Still, it's past time that I step out of my comfort zone. As for Maddox's suggestion that I run Gloria's café until it's closed, even though it would allow me to save more money and make a better start, I should leave. Sadly, I don't want to. Not only will I miss the older folks but also the mobile home park, and—yes—First Grace. To make matters worse, I'm scared.

Twenty-Five

Harri's Log: Don't want to think about it...

I don't know how I made it to church after everything that happened yesterday, but I'm here. Bleary-eyed and drained, but here. The music is good—

Well, the words. As for the instruments, they're screechier than usual. Or is that my nerves? Regardless, it's a nice song. In fact, if I weren't so down and out, I might raise a hand to shoulder height.

The next selection is slower and unfamiliar, but the words pluck my emotions—"By grace I am forgiven." Was this planned? I glance left and right, but no one is looking at me. Okay, coincidence. But then up on the screen pops, "I stumble and fall, and always You lift me." I blink as the words Maddox spoke yesterday haunt their way back to me. *You have to allow that you're going to stumble like the rest of us and trust God to give you a hand up.*

Oh dear. I really want to raise my hand but mustn't. I'm too down. However, an older woman on the front row has no such qualms, as evidenced by an arm that slowly rises. Hardly able to believe my eyes, I squint. It's Bea, all right, and beside her is Jack. Jack, who has forgiven her. More important, God has forgiven her.

"By grace I am forgiven" pops up on the screen again, this time against the backdrop of a desert sunrise. My right hand quivers, and I have a feeling it's going to rise on its own, especially when joyful voices repeat, "By grace I am forgiven."

I know. I just have to accept it. Completely. Without question or worry over fine print.

My hand quivers more forcefully, and I have a vision of it shooting up and everyone staring at me. So I give an inch, then a few more. When my hand reaches chest level, I press it to my heart and feel the steady *thump, thump* through my clothing. Jesus has forgiven me for everything. By *grace* I am forgiven. And will be again if I stumble.

Oh. I feel it. I really do. Closing my eyes, I splay my hand across my chest to keep the certainty of those words from escaping. "By grace I am forgiven," I whisper. He loves me regardless. Has provided a clean slate. Didn't require me to offer up my dream like a sacrificial animal to forgive me for my sins. Repentance was all He asked, and it was given years ago.

Eyes moist, I lift my lids to find that I'm the only one standing. And the music has stopped.

Sucking a breath, I shoot back down. How long was I standing there? I peek at Blake who meets my gaze and smiles a toothy smile before pulling the microphone toward him and welcoming everyone. "Now if you'll open your bulletins, I'd like to draw your attention to the insert."

Papers rustle around the sanctuary, and belatedly, I open to an insert titled: First Grace Vision Statement Proposal.

"As you can see," Blake says, "our vision team has drawn up a vision statement, the purpose of which is to guide First Grace on its journey to growing in a direction that honors God. Please follow along as I read." He clears his throat.

"We seek to know fully the Lord God Almighty, to experience His incredible goodness and grace—"

By grace I am forgiven.

"—and to be totally amazed that He would choose to live within us."

I am amazed.

"Our desire is to know Him so intimately and trust Him so completely that His will for us becomes the dominant desire of our lives."

Is it really possible to surrender so completely?

"We seek to use the gifts that God has placed within us to serve others, seeking to meet every physical and spiritual need."

Young and old alike.

"Therefore, we welcome everyone—"

Including those with a penchant for black clothing, chains, and tattoos. Even rebels like Harriet Josephine Bisset.

"—so that we may point each to Him and to our Savior and Lord Jesus Christ, who alone redeems and transforms us into His image."

A God-moment chill goes through me. Absolutely beautiful. And from the murmurs on all sides of me, I'm not the only one who thinks so.

"Over the next week," Blake says, "please take time to reflect on the statement, and let us know if you have any questions or comments. Next Sunday we'll vote for adoption." His smile widens.

"And now we have a special announcement. As you know, First Grace is growing. Our vision committee has been hard at work solving the problem of expansion. While the adjoining mobile home park was purchased years ago with expansion in mind, First Grace was faced with the dilemma of what to do with those who make the park their home. Thus, the church looked elsewhere to expand, and I'm pleased to announce that an agreement has been reached with the owner of Gloria's Morning Café."

Gasps of relief arise from the park residents, and to my right, Elva grips Lum's arm and turns a smiling face up to him.

I did the right thing, even if not entirely for the right reason.

"But there's more," Blake continues, "and I'll let Gloria tell you about it."

Gloria's here? Lowering the bulletin to my lap, I crane my neck and watch her rise from a front pew. Upon reaching the podium, she taps the microphone. "Good news, but it gets better. During a late-night meeting with your vision team, a new proposal was put on the table that I find very satisfying and believe First Grace's members will as well."

A *new* proposal?

"Though I agreed to sell my property to First Grace, it was proposed that a trade be made instead—my café and property for the mobile home park."

Her…for…First Grace's…?

"This arrangement will prevent First Grace from straining its finances and yet still allow them to acquire my café property. As for my ownership of the mobile home park, not only will I be provided with a steady income for a while longer, but it will give the park residents peace of mind with regard to future expansion." She grins. "And me something to do."

Maddox did this.

Gloria meets my gaze. "I'm very pleased with the arrangement and am sure everyone else will be."

Slack-jawed, I watch as Gloria steps from the stage amid murmurs of approval. As she nears, she gives me a smile.

I smile tremulously back. A trade. It's perfect. Or as near to perfect as one can get. Yes, the cafe may eventually be razed if expansion reaches its doors. Yes, one day First Grace may come knocking to buy back the mobile home park for further expansion. But that would be years from now, and if I know Gloria—and I'm pretty sure I do—mama bear won't let anything happen to her cubs.

I stare unseeingly at the bulletin in my lap, but slowly the Scripture on the front comes to focus. *"Therefore, if anyone is in Christ, he is a new creation; the old has gone, the new has come."*

Old Harri—gone. New Harri—here. Another God-moment.

As Pastor Paul takes to the podium, I feel a sudden need to search out Maddox. Though I scanned for him when I entered the sanctuary, I didn't see him. I scan again, but he's not here. And he's always here.

I startle. What if he's left First Grace? Stuck the pink flamingos and artificial shrubs back in the lawn and up and gone?

I consider the teenager who slipped in beside me a few minutes into the worship. He's slouched with his knees against the back of the pew in front of him. As I consider the feasibility of stepping over him, he looks at me.

"Um, I need to get out."

"Sure." He swings his legs aside to let me past.

Feeling self-conscious, I walk down the aisle as Pastor Paul begins his sermon on…forgiveness.

The gathering area is empty. No sign of Maddox. Maybe he *has* gone.

"Seems like Maddox McCray saves the day."

I swing around. "Stephano."

"So what do you think about the news, Harri?"

"It's…great."

He shoves his hands into his pockets. "Yeah. It worked out well for all concerned." He frowns. "Seems like Maddox knows what he's doing after all."

And Stephano is admitting it? "I'm surprised to hear you say that."

"So am I. Still, I'll be glad when he moves on and we get back to a semblance of normalcy."

Considering all the changes ahead, normalcy hardly seems likely, but who am I to burst his bubble? "Speaking of Maddox, have you seen him?"

"Not recently, but I'm sure he's around."

I offer a half-baked smile. "I think I'll try to find him."

Fifteen minutes later, Maddox is nowhere to be found. I step outside, dejected. Though August is on its way out, it's going to be an intensely hot day, as evidenced by the toasty breath of air that awakens my sweat glands. I start walking and shortly halt before the children's playground. It's deserted. Quiet. Not even a breeze to stir the swings.

Hooking my fingers in the chain-link fence, I stare at the swings that wait for children to jump on them...grip their chains...take to the air...fly...laugh...squeal...and yell, "Higher, Daddy."

"Higher," I breathe, remembering my father's words to his rebellious teenage daughter: *It's God you should be speaking those words to now, Harriet. All you have to do is ask, and He will take you higher.*

Throat tightening, I nod. I *was* meant to go higher, meant to try new things, meant to take chances. And it's not too late. Unhooking my fingers, I push open the gate and cross the wood chips to the swings.

It starts off innocently enough, just a little back and forth, progresses to a lot of back and forth, and eventually goes full tilt. Face buffeted by the wind I create, hair flying back, I swing forward and up...up. Hair sweeping into my face and catching in my mouth and lashes, I swing back. And again, going higher with each pass. Practically flying. In fact, were I twenty years younger, I'd see how far I could launch myself. But that might hurt. Besides, it feels wonderful just the way it is. As does my heart that is alternately chanting, "By grace I am forgiven" and "I am a new creation."

Forgiven. A new creation. Free of my past and all the wrong turns I took. Simply forgiven. And ready to go higher.

I smile, I shout, "I'm a new creation!" I laugh, I yell, "Higher, Daddy! Higher!" Then I do the stupidest thing I've done in a long time. I launch myself out of the swing. A moment before impact, I attempt to get my landing gear down—that would be my feet—but I'm no longer eight years old. As I rake up a mouthful of wood chips and register the sting of scratches across my chin and palms, someone shouts my name. Then that someone's turning me over.

"Are you all right?"

Maddox.

"What were you doing?!"

I push my tongue forward to expel a wood chip.

"What do you think you are? A bird?"

I smile weakly and spit out another wood chip. "Felt like it for about a second."

He raises an eyebrow, then looks me up and down. "Anything broken?"

I shake my head. My hair is going to be full of wood chips! But so what? "Not anymore."

His face lightens. "Yeah?"

I push onto my elbows. "Thank you, Maddox."

"For?"

"You know what for—the trade. It will put a lot of people's minds at ease."

His mouth jerks, foretelling the smile that appears. "I hoped you'd be pleased."

"You have no idea—"

"Yes, I do."

I nod. "Just like you know how much it means to me. I should have trusted you."

His face slips back into seriousness. "*Do* you trust me?"

"Yes." No hesitation. "And I'm sorry that I didn't tell you about the café. I was just so afraid of messing up and everyone finding out and thinking I hadn't changed at all." I replenish my air supply. "And about the old Harri… After you left yesterday, I did a lot of thinking and praying and searching through my Bible. Then this morning, that song about being forgiven by grace…and the Scripture about being a new creation—the old has gone, the new has come—I knew the old Harri really was forgiven and that I need to get on with the new Harri's life."

The poor man couldn't look more taken aback had you smacked him across the face. I swallow. "Are you following?"

His wide eyes ease and his mouth tilts. "Trying to. So what you're saying is…"

"That *this* Harri is going to start living like she's forgiven— because she is—that she's going to"—I throw a hand up—"*I'm* going to start believing in myself, hanging out with others my age, having fun, taking chances."

"Oh."

Just "oh"? And why does he look doubtful? I finally get it, and he doesn't appear the least inclined to give me a high-five.

Maddox cocks his head to the side. "Just like that, hmm?"

I open my mouth to protest, but after a quick replay of my running at the mouth, I nod sheepishly. "I guess not 'just like that.' After all, old habits are hard to break. I'll just…take it a step at a time."

"Sounds like a good plan." He glances away momentarily. "What about us, Harri? Do you think we could start over?"

Oh dear. "What about what I said yesterday?"

He regards me with such intensity that I can hardly breathe. But then he takes my hand and pulls me to standing. "Though we've both made mistakes about each other's character, that's far from a relationship breaker. In fact, it's normal. It's how people figure each other out."

"Then you still like me?"

The start of a smile. "I do."

My heart lurches.

"In fact…" He skims a finger down my cheek. "…I more than like you."

Double lurch. "I more than like you too."

He looks at my mouth, and I know he's thinking about kissing me, so I close my eyes and lift my face. He nearly kisses me, right here on the playground. His warm breath fans my lips, but then he steps back. "How about a ride?"

"A motorcycle ride?"

"What other kind of ride is there?"

Uh…it sounds so…and very…and extremely…and it is broad daylight…ultravisible. I mean, what would people think if they saw me—?

Calling this *Harri, not* that *Harri! And correct me if I'm wrong, but you were going to allow him to kiss you a moment ago!*

As Maddox's smile starts to fade, I nod. "I'd like that, but I have to go home and get my helmet."

His smile returns to its former glory, and an ultracurly curl shifts on his brow. "You didn't throw it out?"

"Of course not. Pink helmets are hard to come by, you know."

He chuckles. "Let's go."

"Wait." I reach up and pull the curl between thumb and forefinger. To my twisted delight, it springs right back. "I've wanted to do that for a long time."

"Are you telling me that you, who told me I should cut my 'boyish curls,' have a curl fetish?"

I nod. "You don't mind, do you?"

"Not at all."

Hand in hand, we walk back to the mobile home park, and while I'm retrieving the helmet, Maddox retrieves his motorcycle.

"So," I say when he pulls up to my little mobile home, "is the offer for me to run the café still good?"

"If that's what you want."

"It is. It will allow me to save more money, and then…"

"Then?"

I tighten my chin strap, throw a leg over the seat, and meet his gaze as he looks back at me. "Then I'm going to open my own café. I don't know where or when or exactly how, but I'm going to do it. Even if, in the end, I fail. I'm not going to be afraid anymore."

Maddox grins. "That's my Harri."

His Harri… If that doesn't warrant a heavy sigh, I don't know what does.

And so, with my arm around his waist, we ride off into the sunset. Well, not exactly the sunset. The present. And the future— whatever that may be.

Discussion Questions

1. Harri was a rebellious preacher's kid who crossed over to the "prodigal" side. What are your experiences with PKs? Do you think expectations are too high for them?

2. *Splitting Harriet* is set during a time of tremendous change at First Grace Church—change that makes Harri and some of the older members feel threatened. What changes have you experienced in your church that made you feel threatened or uncomfortable?

3. What are your feelings about the trend toward contemporary forms of worship? Does it keep members engaged and present a greater opportunity to reach the unsaved? Or does it shift the focus away from God and toward entertainment?

4. Fearful of being hurt as she was when a teenager, Harri avoids meaningful friendships with women her own age. How are your relationships with women affected by your early experiences?

5. At the height of Harri's rebellion, her brother suffered fallout from "guilt by association" when his girlfriend

broke off their engagement. Have you ever been found guilty by association? How did it affect you?

6. Harri tends to "play it safe." When have you played it safe? How do you think your life would be different had you taken a risk instead?

7. Harri reads the Bible daily, translation after translation. However, her actions and fears contradict the depth of her knowledge of God's Word. What do you do to guard against a "surface" reading of the Bible? What helps you to internalize and apply Scripture to your life?

8. Though attracted to Maddox, Harri is put off by his appearance for fear he will be a bad influence. Do you tend to stereotype people? Have you ever been stereotyped?

9. Harri has a difficult time accepting the fullness of God's forgiveness. What struggles have you faced in accepting God's forgiveness?

10. Though Harri longs for the safe, predictable future she envisions she'll have once she buys the café, she sacrifices her dream for her friends. What dreams have you had to sacrifice? Any regrets?

KATE'S CREED:
Thou shalt embrace singledom and be unbelievably, inconceivably happy.

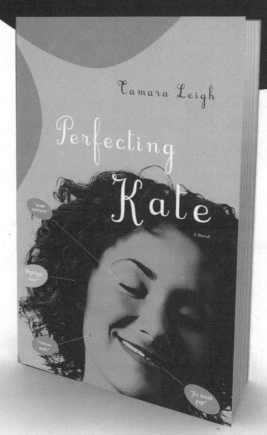

Enter into Kate's world - As a successful San Francisco artist looking for a nice, solid Christian man, she is stunned when not one but *two* enter her orbit in rapid succession. The question now is, what kind of work will Kate do on herself…and who exactly is she trying to please?